I0702574

# LESSON LEARNED

KATIE CAWOOD

# Author's Note
## & content warnings

Dear reader,

What began as a (mostly incoherent) note on my phone in the middle of the night has turned into this—my debut novel. I'm ecstatic to bring the characters that have long resided in my mind to life within these pages. They're in your hands now!

Please be advised, this book involves a flirty workplace romance—and at times, the chemistry and interactions between Owen and Sarah may escalate to an intensity level that blurs the boundaries into an emotional affair, a topic I'm aware can spark a little controversy.

You'll also find some explicit language, alcohol & cannabis use, and sexually explicit scenes in *Lesson Learned*. If any of the things I've mentioned aren't your cup of tea, that's perfectly fine—but this novel may not be your ideal choice.

Lastly, I hope the Swifties out there enjoy the many TS references sprinkled throughout this book. Can you find them all?

Thank you for coming along on this journey with me!

Much love,
Katie

# LESSON LEARNED
## *official playlist*

1. "Somebody's Baby" by Phantom Planet
2. "When You're Ready" by Shawn Mendes
3. "Bad Habit" by Steve Lacy
4. "Add It Up" by Violent Femmes
5. "Why Can't I?" by Liz Phair
6. "Sometime Around Midnight" by The Airborne Toxic Event
7. "Question...?" by Taylor Swift
8. "Jealous" by Ingrid Michaelson
9. "The Writing's On The Wall" by OK Go
10. "Say Yes to Heaven" by Lana Del Rey
11. "Just Like Honey" by The Jesus and Mary Chain
12. "Sweet" by Cigarettes After Sex
13. "Understand" by Hippo Campus
14. "August" by Taylor Swift

# chapter one
## *sarah*

I never paid much attention to the phases of the moon until I started teaching fifth grade.

My first year, when a veteran teacher warned me about the full moon's effect on the students' temperaments, I was skeptical. Surely it was just a coincidence my students behaved like they'd washed their cereal down with Red Bull that morning, breaking both of my pencil sharpeners and engaging in a full-on slap fight in the middle of their grammar lesson.

But it happened month after month—the kids were always completely feral when there was a full moon. Maybe it was just confirmation bias, but after six years of teaching, I was a firm believer. I tracked the moon cycle religiously, so I was always prepared.

The only thing more challenging than teaching during a full moon? Making it through the day after Halloween unscathed.

And as I readied my classroom for the day on the first of November, I braced myself for a trifecta of chaotic events: not only did this month's full moon overlap with the day after Halloween, it was also a Monday. After a weekend of trick-or-treating, eating candy for every meal, and toilet-papering Principal Cates' house, these kids weren't going to sit still for a lesson on conjunctions.

However, I was armed with a full night's rest and twenty ounces of coffee. So when it was time to stand at the door and greet arriving students, I was in such a good mood I was whistling. I wasn't going to let this full moon scare me. *Bring it on*, I thought.

Standing just across the hall in his usual spot outside his own classroom was my best friend and the other half of the fifth-grade dream team, Owen Gardner. He raised one eyebrow at me as he sipped his own coffee, assessing my overly cheery demeanor. "Lavely, please tell me you're not whistling a Christmas song already."

"I don't know, am I?" I whistled the tune again. "Oh, that's 'Deck the Halls', isn't it?"

"There's something fundamentally wrong with you," Owen said, leaning against his doorframe. As much as he wanted to pretend to be annoyed with me, an amused smirk spread across his face. "I mean, at least wait until the Halloween decorations are down."

I turned to look at the Halloween bulletin board next to my classroom door, clutching my insulated coffee mug in one hand and flipping my long, brown curls off my shoulder with the other. I was having a good hair day, which only further elevated my mood. "I don't know if I'm ready to say good-bye to Hilda," I said, eyeing the witchy display Owen had reluctantly helped me with a few weeks ago.

"Hilda is begging to be put out of her misery," Owen said, nodding at the way our witch was missing one eye and her black tulle skirt was now dangling, ready to fall to the floor at any second. I loved the way Owen went along with my ceaseless naming and characterization of every googly-eyed creature who appeared on our shared bulletin board. He must have decided, after years of working with me, it was better to be a willing participant in the craziness rather than waste his time trying to resist it. "She's had a good run."

I giggled. "I guess it's time for Trevor the Turkey to make his return."

Owen just shook his head as he looked down at his watch. We still had a couple of minutes before the kids would fill the hallway, probably finishing Hilda off as they passed.

Every morning, Owen and I started our day exactly like this. We stood at our classroom doors and talked about anything and everything as we both sipped our coffee. The students had an arrival window of fifteen minutes, and we chatted the entire time, only stopping to greet kids as they walked past.

After years of this morning ritual, I wasn't sure I could function without it.

"Did you see Cates' house?" Owen asked, running his fingers through his floppy dark hair. "They got him good this year."

Cates lived in a big brick house just down the road from Grissom Elementary School, making him an easy target for egging and toilet papering. I sort of felt bad, because of all the administrators I'd worked with, Cates was probably the least-deserving of getting TP'ed. I guess it just came with the territory when you're a principal, though. "I saw that. There's not any toilet paper left on the shelves at the store, from the looks of it."

"And it rained last night, too," Owen said. "You know that soggy toilet paper is going to be impossible to clean up."

"I'm surprised you didn't hop out of your car and clean it up for him first thing this morning." I peered over my mug at him as I brought it to my lips and winked. I loved teasing Owen about his tendency to suck up to Cates. He denied it, but the whole school bore witness to his brown-nosing ways. It was rumored Cates would be retiring within the next couple of years, and everyone assumed Owen was after his job.

And they were right. I'd spent the last few years witnessing Owen complete his master's degree and quietly work through the required licensure program. Though he never admitted it out loud, he had his eye on that job.

After my jab, he rolled his eyes with a grin. "That's above my pay grade." He ran his fingers down the length of his tie to straighten it. His navy button-up shirt was tucked into camel-colored dress pants, and his atom tattoo just barely poked out from the edge of his sleeve. The district clung to its outdated rule against visible tattoos, preventing me from ever getting a good look at Owen's muscular forearms. Not that I needed to, or anything. But the curiosity was there.

I brought my eyes up to Owen's face. "So, what'd you do for Halloween, anyway?"

He yawned. "Nothing. I spent the whole weekend recording and editing new episodes for *STEM for the Win*." In his spare time, Owen hosted a podcast for science and math teachers. As he neared his hundredth episode, the show was gaining in popularity—turning it into more of a side hustle than a hobby for him. "But I did steal some Reese's pumpkins from my nephews."

"You didn't go out? No Halloween parties or anything?"

He winced. "That doesn't even sound remotely appealing. I'm getting too old for that." Owen was just shy of thirty, which I would hardly call "old." But then again, he had two years on me, so what did I know?

After checking to make sure there weren't any kids around yet, I said, "Shame. You missed your opportunity to hook up with a sexy nurse."

Owen laughed. "Come on. I could do that any day of the year."

"Then how come you haven't been on a date in, like, six weeks?" I asked him, accidentally revealing I'd been keeping track.

He cleared his throat. "So, Lavely, what did *you* do for Halloween?"

"I dressed up like a black cat and passed out candy to trick-or-treaters," I told him, pausing to take a sip, "and then I fell asleep watching *Scream*. Barely made it past Drew Barrymore getting slaughtered."

I omitted any mention of Eli from my story, as I often did when talking to Owen. While his aversion to hearing my boyfriend's name was usually subtle, I always noticed the slight unease in his eyes. The men were polar opposites. Eli was the varsity football coach down at the high school and didn't care or talk about much else. While Owen was a casual Cubs fan, he rarely mentioned sports. Science was more his realm, his eyes lighting up whenever he had the opportunity to horrify me with the most revolting fact—like how much bacteria was living on my face at any given moment.

Owen likely thought guys like Eli were the ones who beat up guys like him back in high school. And, well, he probably wasn't wrong. But I knew there was a lot more beneath the surface of the man who kicked over a cooler of Gatorade at the last Friday night football game—there was a soft side there, too, that only I witnessed. I didn't know how to begin explaining the complexities of Eli's personality to Owen, so I didn't try.

"No parties for you, either?" Owen asked me as the hallway filled up with students' voices around the corner. I just shook my head, greeting the first group of students to make their way to us. Their elevated energy level was almost palpable, and the sheer volume of their voices that morning made me want to cover my ears with my hands. Hilda's tulle skirt was ripped to the floor so quickly, I hadn't even seen the culprit.

"Full moon on the day after Halloween," Owen said, high-fiving one of his students as she made her way past him. "We're in for it, Ms. Lavely."

"You know what, Mr. Gardner?" I asked, tucking my hair behind my ears. He and I always addressed each other formally in front of the students. "I actually have a good feeling about it this time. It's going to be a good day."

He threw his head back with a groan. "No! You just jinxed us."

"Nope, the day is what you make it—right, Jordyn?" Jordyn Ellis just raised one eyebrow at me as they walked past—a typical response from them. "And I'm manifesting the best Monday ever."

"Oh, is that so?" Owen asked, pulling his sleeve down to better cover his tattoo. He was distracted by something happening at the end of the hallway. "Well, one of your kids has someone in a headlock down there—you gonna 'manifest' yourself out of that one?"

I knew it was Bentley Brooks before I even turned my head.

Bentley, Bentley, Bentley. I'd probably said his name a thousand times already that school year at varying levels of volume and irritation. It was one incident after the next, no matter who I sat beside him or how hard I tried to redirect his violent tendencies. The kid was carrying an enormous chip on his shoulder, and he made it everyone else's problem.

The thing about Bentley that not everyone noticed, though, was how desperately he just wanted to feel included. I could see it in his eyes during independent work time, when he stared longingly at the other kids, who sat close and chatted about whatever video game they were currently obsessing over. He'd try to chime in with an awkward comment, but one of the popular kids would say something really cruel, and Bentley would retaliate by saying or doing something ten times worse. I'd seen this exact scenario play out more times than I could count.

He wanted to be liked, but he didn't know how.

Owen and I reached Bentley at the same time, pulling him off Noah Simon, who crumpled to the floor. "You're such a freak!" Noah shouted before scurrying away into my classroom. With an aggressive jerk, Bentley slid free from my grasp. Owen let go, too, careful not to break any rules about restraining students.

"I guess I'll just go to the office," Bentley said, running his fingers through his unkempt blonde hair. "And nothing will happen to Noah. Again."

"What did he do?" I asked. "Because it looked to me like you had him in a headlock."

"He called me a pussy-ass bitch and flicked my ear."

My mouth fell open. Owen turned his back to us, probably for the same reason. He could never keep a straight face when one of these ten-year-olds cussed. I drew in a deep breath, trying to keep my composure. "Well, you didn't have to repeat it like that," I muttered. I grabbed Owen's wrist and pulled it close to my face to look at his watch. "It's almost time for class to start, so I'm going to have to call Mr. Cates to come retrieve you."

"That's what I thought."

"*And* Noah," I added. "You guys need to talk this out."

Bentley rolled his eyes again. I put my hand on his back, nudging him down the hall. I motioned for him to sit on the floor and asked Owen to keep an eye on him while I stepped in the classroom to call the front office. When I returned to the hallway, Bentley was wrapping the black tulle from the bulletin board around his hand like a bandage. I let it slide, deciding to choose my battles.

"I told you," Owen said from across the hall. He raised his eyebrows at me as he sipped his coffee, begging me to tell him he was right.

Instead, after making sure there weren't any students looking my direction, I grinned and scratched my eye with my middle finger.

# chapter two



While I hadn't thumbed through the district handbook in a while, I was pretty certain there were rules against using contracted time to work on a side hustle. However, that didn't stop me from answering podcast-related emails while my students were busy with online math work on their school-provided laptops.

*STEM for the Win* had grown into something bigger than I'd ever imagined when I initially sat down to record the first episode. Now, I found myself scheduling interviews with podcast guests, selling workbooks to other teachers, and struggling to keep up with all of my social media accounts. It had reached a point in which I either needed to hire someone to help me run the business, or accept it was time to give up certain aspects of it.

The increasing chatter amongst my afternoon students pulled me out of my email trance. My class swapped with Sarah's for an hour and fifteen minutes each day—her students came to my room for math and science instruction while she taught my students reading and grammar. The two other fifth-grade rooms did the same. Not only did it help prepare our students for middle school, it allowed us to teach to our strengths.

I'd taught English Language Arts before. I didn't like it. I was still processing the traumatic ending of *Bridge to Terabithia* years after the fact. That kind of stuff was better left to Sarah, anyway.

I looked up from my computer and watched Bentley Brooks fold his science study guide into a paper airplane. I was fine with this until I saw him pick it up and pull it back over his shoulder, aiming it toward Noah Simon's head. "Whatcha got there, Bentley?" I asked.

Every head in the classroom turned from me to Bentley as he lowered the paper airplane and dropped it on his desk. He didn't respond. So I stood up and strolled over to him with my hands in my pockets. A few kids "oohed" like I was going to pick up the kid and throw him out to the hall or something. Instead, I bent down and picked up the paper airplane, turning it over in my hands to assess its construction.

"Just how far do you expect this to fly?"

Bentley just gave me an apathetic shrug. I flattened the paper out on his desk, letting him assume for a second I was trying to return the study guide to its original form. But instead, I refolded the paper airplane the way my brother, Jake, taught me to make them when I was around Bentley's age.

"See, here's how you have to fold it if you want to make it more aerodynamic," I said, running my finger along one of the folds. "You want the wings to push the air backwards and downward—thrust and lift. Think about what it feels like when you stick your hand out the car window—have you ever done that before?"

Bentley was too stubborn to answer, but he and all of the kids within earshot were listening and watching intently, so I continued.

"You probably notice a difference between when you hold your hand flat and when you stick it upright like this, right?" I asked, bending my wrist to demonstrate. "Think of paper airplanes the same way. If you want them to glide through the air for a long time, you have to fold the wings in a way that won't drag it back."

I lifted the paper airplane and angled it toward the smartboard at the front of the room before drawing it back and releasing it. The plane soared over the students' heads, picking up speed until it crashed into the smartboard and dropped to the floor.

Considering it was made out of Bentley's study guide, I retrieved it from the front of the room and brought it back to him, sitting it on the keyboard of his laptop. "So now you know the science behind it." I bent down to get closer to his face, forcing him to look me in the eyes. "And if you're going to make a paper airplane in my class, I better not see you aiming it at anyone's head. All right?"

He nodded and I returned to my desk.

I hadn't really expected to teach an impromptu physics lesson today, but I could tell from the way Bentley was studying every fold of the paper airplane that it was worth it. He was no longer interested in what Noah Simon was doing. Potential crisis averted.

I smacked my spacebar to bring my computer back to life and settled into my desk chair, absentmindedly chewing on the end of a pen. At the very top of my inbox, there was a new email. It was from one of the companies I'd reached out to recently in hopes of getting more sponsors for the podcast. Expecting a rejection to my bold proposal, I clicked on the email and quickly skimmed it.

This was no rejection.

The big-name science toy company I'd reached out to was interested in a long-term contract with *STEM for the Win*. They wanted to secure six months of ads, which would bring me close to an extra $3000 in revenue.

I pulled the pen out of my mouth. This couldn't be real. SFTW had never pulled in that kind of money all at once. And if one company was willing to fork out that much for my show, chances were I could find other sponsors willing to do the same.

This was huge.

I was so caught up in my excitement, I almost missed the kids' transition time. Some of Sarah's students started closing their laptops and talking amongst themselves even louder, indicating they knew it was almost time to go. "If any of you are behind on your online math work, please make sure you're caught up by Friday," I said, standing up from my chair. "And maybe we can play math-sketball to review for the quiz."

The kids erupted into cheers. I'd invented math-sketball years ago, and it had become so popular now that kids would ask about it on the first day of school, having learned about it from their older siblings. Truth be told, I enjoyed it as much as they did. Tossing paper balls in a trash can to review for a quiz really broke up the monotony of the day.

"What was all that cheering about?" Sarah asked me in the hallway as our students switched rooms.

"Math-sketball."

She just nodded, needing no further explanation. "And was everyone on their best behavior?"

I knew whose behavior she was specifically concerned about. "No issues today," I said, looking over Bentley's shoulder as he sauntered past. I was eager to tell Sarah about the ad deal, so I lingered in the hallway once all the kids had cleared out. Just as I turned to say something about it, she opened up her mouth and started to speak instead.

"If he would just make a friend—just one friend—I know things could be different for him."

I stuck my hands in my pockets and gazed down at her. A while back, we'd worked out that she was seven inches shorter than me—sometimes less on the rare occasion she opted for heels instead of flats. "Right. But you can't force these things. As much as you may want to try." I was probably right to assume Sarah was already plotting some kind of scheme to help Bentley make a friend. "Sometimes natural consequences aren't such a bad thing, Lavely. He'll learn."

She sighed and crossed her arms against her chest. "I know. I just want to give him a little nudge in the right direction. Get the other kids to like him a little better. I don't know why they're so mean to him."

I took a step forward to get a little closer to her, bringing my mouth to her ear. "Because the kid's a little shit," I said low enough that I wouldn't be overheard by any eavesdropping students.

Sarah gasped and gave my waist a hard shove. "Owen!" I laughed, and she eventually grinned, too. Knowing I'd get to see her smile like that was the entire reason I'd made the risky comment in the first place. She shook her head at me, locking her emerald eyes on my face. "You're awful."

"I didn't mean it," I said, wanting to make sure she knew I wasn't a complete asshole.

"I know." After a moment, her smile started to fade, and I could tell she was back to worrying about Bentley. Every single year, Sarah inevitably took it upon herself to choose one student to "fix." She never set out to do it, but she often got so wrapped up in reversing a bully's behavior pattern or helping a shy kid come out of their shell that it became an obsession. "If I could just help him find something he's good at...."

I decided I'd tell her about my news at a time when she was less distracted. Walking backwards toward my classroom door, I said, "Don't spiral, Lavely." She just nodded. It was too late.

I kind of loved that about her, though. Nobody at this school cared more about the students than Sarah Lavely. Her insistence on building a positive relationship with every student, even the ones who were hard to like, was admirable. Sometimes I just had to step back and look at her in awe, knowing I could never match her level of passion.

When I returned to the classroom, the email about the $3k sponsorship deal was the farthest thing from my mind. All I could think about was the way Sarah's eyes twinkled when she looked up in mine and how good it felt when she shoved my side. Every time she touched me, it ignited something within me, spreading a warmth through my entire body. I wanted more than anything to grab Sarah and hold her in my arms; to know what it felt like to be the person she came home to at the end of a challenging day.

But she was my best friend, and I'd never do anything to jeopardize that. Even if she were single. Our relationship was strictly platonic, and I was okay with that. Just to know her like this was enough. Of all the teachers I could work across the hallway from, I'd ended up with the woman who gave inanimate objects personalities and cried when she watched videos about ducklings looking for their mom.

I was already so lucky.

# chapter three
## sarah

My students' sudden and inexplicable obsession with paper airplanes was driving me insane. After one of them soared past my head in the middle of a read-aloud lesson on Wednesday morning, I banned paper planes from the classroom altogether. "Save them for recess, please. But make sure you bring them inside—nobody likes a litterbug."

Once the kids were preoccupied with their independent reading time, I walked up and down the aisles between the desks, picking up abandoned paper airplanes from the floor. I paused when I reached Bentley's desk. He was hunched over a drawing with a fistful of colored pencils in one of his hands. I couldn't help but notice the top of his paper said: WHEN THERE'S A REAL EARTHQUAKE.

"What's this?" I asked, sliding the drawing to the edge of his desk to get a better look. Bentley sat up a little straighter, awaiting my reaction. Upon closer inspection, I could see his drawing was actually a comic strip. In the first panel, there was a cartoonish drawing of a man who looked an awful lot like Principal Cates, with brown skin, a navy-blue suit, and glasses, speaking into the intercom. The text bubble coming from his mouth said, "Students! This is an earthquake! But don't worry, your desks will protect you!"

The next panel depicted Grissom Elementary School reduced to a pile of rubble with Mr. Cates standing off to the side saying, "Oops."

I laughed out loud, feeling a little relieved I hadn't stumbled upon something far more inappropriate. "This is really funny, Bentley. Where'd you get that idea?"

He shrugged. "I don't know… I just thought about it during the earthquake drill last week."

I studied the comic strip, noting all the little details he'd thought to include—like Cates' snazzy bowtie he always wore for special events and the dilapidated statue of astronaut Gus Grissom, which currently stood in our school's main vestibule. The entire thing was cleverly executed. "Have you drawn comics like this before?"

Bentley nodded, shifting uncomfortably in his seat when he noticed Noah was watching him.

"It's a shame we don't have a school newspaper, isn't it?" I asked him, leaning over to pick up another paper airplane from the floor. "Something like this could be a regular feature."

"Wouldn't I get in trouble?"

"With whom, Mr. Cates?" I scoffed. Bentley nodded, like it was obvious. "No way! Mr. Cates would love this as much as I do." Another student's hand shot up on the other side of the room, so I left Bentley alone with this thought.

As the day went on, his comic was all I could think about. Bentley had been hiding a secret talent all along. Chances were, he could come up with other comic strips just as clever as this one—he just needed an outlet to share them. I considered creating a comics corner on one of the bulletin boards or scanning them to put on the back of our fifth-grade monthly calendars, but the idea of a school newspaper kept coming back to me.

I already sponsored the Creative Writing Club after school once a week, so the last thing I needed to do now was add something else to my plate. But if I didn't initiate it, who would?

Maybe if I hosted the newspaper club in my classroom during last recess once or twice a week, that would give the students plenty of time to put together a simple monthly or bi-weekly paper. I could make up for the loss of prep time somehow.

Besides, it was worth it. I knew it would give Bentley a little extra incentive to behave. Students weren't allowed to participate in any extra-curricular clubs after three disciplinary strikes. And maybe, if he could tone his violent tendencies down a notch, it would even help him make a new friend or two.

I skipped eating lunch in the teachers' lounge that day so I could formulate a plan for this new undertaking. I'd have to run this whole idea past Cates, of course—and more importantly, it would be smart to double-check Bentley was interested in the first place. But the gears in my mind were already turning with no sign of slowing down.

Halfway through lunch, there was a knock at my classroom door, and Owen wandered in munching on a Granny Smith apple. "Not feeling social today, huh, Lavely?"

I was almost afraid to tell him about my new project, knowing he'd give me a hard time about it. He always said I did too much. "I may or may not be in the process of forming a new student club."

He chuckled and took a bite of his apple. After wiping his mouth with his thumb, he said, "Of course you are."

I explained where the idea sprouted from, and how I hoped it would give Bentley a sense of belonging. As I spoke, Owen pulled himself up onto a student's desk in the second row, resting his feet on the chair in front of him. He listened to my entire explanation without a single interruption or even a judgmental smirk. When I finished, he looked down at his apple and nodded. "So the sole purpose of this club is to help one kid make friends?"

I blinked. "Not its sole purpose, no. Don't you think this school should have a student-led newspaper?"

"They're kids. What are they going to report on, the new teeter-totters on the playground?"

I stared across my desk at him and answered with a firm and unironic, "Precisely."

Owen stayed right where he was as I finished typing up a quick proposal for Cates. It wasn't uncommon for him to hang around in my classroom like this while I worked on something, or vice versa. Sometimes we'd sit together and grade worksheets or work on IEPs, keeping each other company to make it less grueling.

Without getting up, Owen chucked his apple core into the trashcan that was a good twelve feet away from him. All those days playing math-sketball with the kids were really paying off, I guess. "So," he said, leaning back onto his hands. "Guess what?"

I immediately perked up, noting the excitement in his voice. Whatever he was about to divulge, I knew it was the reason he'd strolled into my room in the first place. "What is it?"

"I had a toy company sign a three-thousand-dollar ad contract for *STEM for the Win*."

My jaw dropped. "Shut up."

"I just sent their invoice. It's legit."

"Owen!" I slid my desk chair back and leapt up to run over to him. This kind of news was hug-worthy. As I wrapped my arms around him, he let out a muffled laugh into my shoulder and awkwardly hugged me back with one arm. "Oh my God, this is huge! I'm so excited for you!"

The man was smiling from ear to ear as I pulled away from him, keeping one of my hands on his upper arm in a sort of congratulatory hold. "Thanks," he said. "I hope they're the first of many."

"They will be. Gosh, that's incredible. I feel like we should celebrate your big win."

"How?"

"I don't know—maybe we should go out Friday night?"

He paused a moment to study my face. And then, fixing his eyes on the desk in front of him, he asked, "Who, me and you?"

I tucked my hair behind my ears, reconsidering. We'd socialized outside of work plenty of times before, but it was always in a group setting. Celebratory dinner and drinks alone with him would cross the line into more-than-just-friends territory, something I tried to avoid. I'm sure all of our colleagues would have a lot to say about that if they caught wind of it. "Maybe a double date."

Owen lifted his eyes to my face again. "A double date?"

"Yeah."

"Okay. Great. Sounds perfect. Just one tiny, minuscule problem there, pal."

"What's that?"

"I don't have a date."

I laughed. "And you can't find one by Friday? Come on, I thought Owen Gardner had game." Though he shook his head in protest, I knew I was right. Other women were crazy for him—I'd seen it with my own eyes. Up until a few weeks ago, Owen had been going on Tinder dates pretty regularly and breaking hearts left and right. Always finding something wrong with them. And it was often something insignificant, some minor flaw that didn't matter much in the grand scheme of things.

He was looking for perfection when that didn't exist.

"Just message one of your Tinder matches."

"No," he answered without hesitation. "I gave up on that whole scene, remember?"

I looked up at the clock on the wall. Our students were probably done with their lunch and heading outside for recess right now. I had fifteen minutes to convince Owen to come out Friday night. That was plenty of time to get him to change his mind—something I knew from experience. "I've been thinking for some time that it would be great for you to get to know Eli better, too. This will be the perfect opportunity. It's his first free Friday night of the season."

The high school football team had just squandered their last game, which meant they weren't going to state that weekend. Eli had been brooding about it for days, doing his best to avoid the judgmental commentary from the whole community about his coaching skills.

Owen shook his head, still leaning back onto his hands. "It's already Wednesday, and you're really asking me to find a date for Friday night?"

"I know you can. Ooh—you could ask that cute redhead you had a good night with back in August—the one with all the cats?"

He scrunched his nose.

"Okay, maybe not her. But you can ask *someone*."

He sighed. "What if I don't want to?"

I dropped my hands to the desk and leaned forward, the sudden proximity causing him to draw in a shaky breath. With wide, pleading eyes, I unleashed my most irresistible puppy-dog expression. I only said one more word, knowing that was all it would take to crack him: "Please?"

It was a little much. But when his entire body softened before me and he reached for his phone in his back pocket, I started to clap, knowing I'd won.

So. Easy.

I returned to my desk while Owen focused on the assignment I'd just given him. As I worked on a list of newspaper column ideas, I could see him swiping and tapping away. He was messaging someone. Maybe multiple someones. After a few minutes, he looked up from his phone and said, "Okay. Let's do it."

"Really? That fast? Well, who is she?"

"Myra. 28. Loves reading, yoga, and her orange cat. And she's free Friday night." He flipped his phone around so I could see the photo on his screen. I was straining to see, so he rose to his feet and walked up to my desk to give me a closer look.

The woman in the photo, clutching a wine glass to her chest, was drop-dead gorgeous. She had jet black hair, beautiful dark eyes, and prominent cheek bones. Her complexion was flawless.

"Aw, Owen," I said, looking into his eyes as he stared down at his phone screen. "She's perfect."

"Meh. I'm really more of a dog person."

I crumpled a piece of paper into a ball and lobbed it at him. Owen turned just in time, making it bounce off his back. Laughing, he bent down and picked it up before tossing it toward the trash can, but it hit the rim and fell to the floor. When he walked over to the bin to pick it up, he raised one eyebrow at me.

"Okay, there are a *lot* of paper planes in there."

"Yeah, my kids won't stop making the damn things. And they're all experts at them, for some reason? I don't know where this obsession came from."

"Hmm, weird," he said, shoving his hands in his pockets and whistling on his way to the door. The jerk—I should have known he had something to do with it. I tore out another sheet of paper from my notebook and crumpled it up, but Owen escaped into the hallway just in time.

# chapter four

*owen*

Poppy's Bar & Grill wouldn't have been my first choice for a double-date on a Friday night in Woodvale, Indiana. It wasn't exactly my type of crowd, and it was usually so noisy you had to strain to hear what the person right beside you was saying.

The six or seven TVs up on the wall were in a constant duel with the jukebox, which played the worst watered-down, pseudo-alternative rock from the past decade. It was fine for a night with the guys, but it wasn't ideal for making conversation.

But it was the place Sarah and Eli picked. And Myra was okay with it, too, so that's where I found myself on Friday night at 5:55. I had offered to pick Myra up, but she suggested we meet there instead—which was probably smart. I'd listened to Sarah retell enough stories from true crime podcasts not to question my date for being cautious.

I waited just inside the restaurant, hoping Myra would arrive before the others. I was suddenly feeling nervous. I'd been on plenty of first dates this year, but it was just beginning to sink in that Sarah was about to witness one. I looked at my watch. Still just 5:56. I thought about how I could probably dart out of here before any of them arrived and say I had car trouble or something. But I'd be cutting it close, and they were probably already in the parking lot anyway. I'd be spotted. And I was better than that.

I could do this.

Much to my relief, Myra arrived first. That meant I'd at least get a couple of minutes to get to know her before the awkwardness started. She stepped in the door and squinted as her eyes adjusted to the darkness inside. And then she saw me. "Owen?"

"Hey," I said, giving her a little wave. She was pretty, just like Sarah said. She had shiny jet-black hair that she flipped over her shoulder as she reached out to shake my hand. Very formal. "The others aren't here yet," I told her.

"Oh, okay," she said, pressing her dark red lips together. We stood against the half-wall across from the hostess stand to wait for Eli and Sarah out of everyone's way. Myra clutched her purse under her armpit and crossed her arms tightly against her chest, eyeing the group of people who came in after her.

Immediately, something felt off. She didn't seem overly happy to be there, or maybe she'd decided I wasn't as good-looking in person as I seemed on the app. After all, I had been using one of the professional headshots I had taken for my podcast promos—maybe it was time I replaced it with something more natural.

Or maybe she was just nervous, like me. Since it didn't seem like she was going to initiate some kind of conversation, I tried to think of something to say. "So, have you been here before?"

"Oh, yeah." She tucked her hair behind her ears and went back to crossing her arms. "My ex used to bartend here."

I didn't know how to respond to that, so I just nodded. And before I could think of another question to ask, the door opened and in walked Eli and Sarah. At least I'd learned one new thing about Myra before the night got started, I guess: her ex was a bartender.

After rushed introductions, we followed the host to a booth. "I hope you haven't been waiting long," Sarah said breathlessly as she sat down. She was wearing a black dress I'd never seen before, probably because it was so low-cut it went against Grissom's dress code. "We had a little mix-up about what time we needed to leave the house."

"Oh, no worries—we just got here, too," I said, sliding into the booth after Myra. Eli took the seat across from me, absentmindedly scratching his bearded chin. Our eyes met briefly before he diverted his gaze to Myra, his lingering glance undoubtedly fixated on her chest.

It's not like I wasn't guilty of the same thing with Sarah a mere ten seconds ago, but Eli's lack of subtlety was almost comical.

The host passed out our menus, and a moment of silence settled over the table as we all decided what to order. I was dying on the inside, trying to come up with something—anything—to spark a conversation with Myra. But my mind drew a blank, offering up nothing even remotely interesting to say.

Once our server took everyone's order, I could no longer safely hide behind the menu. I turned to Myra, fully aware of Sarah's eyes on me from across the table. "So, your bio said you're a yoga instructor, right?" She nodded as she took a sip of her water. "Do you have your own studio, or—?"

"No, right now I'm sharing a space with a friend."

I nodded, resting my elbows on the table. I knew nothing about yoga beyond the fact there was a position called the downward dog and some people did it with goats. "Oh, that sounds neat," I replied, hoping to spark a livelier exchange. As I waited for her to steer the conversation, she simply sipped her water in silence. At this rate, she'd need a refill before our food arrived.

Across the table, Eli was focused on one of the television screens behind the bar, and Sarah's gaze was fixated on Myra.

Her smile had a mischievous quality to it, like she was plotting something. "Myra, did Owen tell you he has his own podcast?"

"No, he didn't mention that," Myra answered, turning to me. "What's it about?"

Oh boy. My nerdy podcast was a topic I normally saved for second dates, but I supposed Sarah had no way of knowing that. "It's a STEM podcast for educators," I said. "Basically, I help elementary and middle grade teachers get their students excited about math and science."

"And he just landed a *huge* sponsorship deal," Sarah said, looking at Myra. "Which is part of the reason we're out tonight. To celebrate." Her eyes shifted back in my direction.

"Wow, that's awesome," Myra said, smiling over at me. "Congratulations."

"Thank you," I said, desperate to take the attention off of me as soon as humanly possible. Just then, the server returned with our drinks from the bar—domestic beers for Myra and Eli, and cocktails for Sarah and me—and let us know our food would be out soon.

"Should we toast?" Sarah asked, lifting her glass. "I feel like we should toast." Myra and I glanced at each other before lifting our drinks, too. Eli emitted an exasperated groan, like participating in this act would absolutely pain him. But he rolled his eyes and lifted his bottle anyway, frowning the entire time. "To *STEM for the Win*," Sarah said, "and its continued success."

"And to the birth of a school newspaper," I added.

"Right!" Sarah smiled, turning to Eli. "And to the Woodvale Panthers, who played their hearts out this season."

"Don't remind me," Eli said, shaking his head. A recent newspaper headline came to mind—if I remembered correctly, the words "CRUSHING LOSS" were emblazoned across the entirety of the front page. The whole community had been talking about Eli's coaching abilities, questioning if he was the right choice for the team.

Come to think of it, this probably had a lot to do with his mood tonight.

I couldn't help but notice the way Sarah's smile faltered for a millisecond as she shifted her gaze from Eli to Myra. Just a flicker of hesitation before she regained her composure, facing Myra with an eager grin. "Do you want to toast to anything?"

"Um," Myra said, giggling as she thought of something to contribute. "Tinder?"

"Cheers to that," I said, and we all clinked our drinks together. I sank half my Jack & Coke in one swig, praying it would help ease my nerves a little more.

When our food arrived, Sarah continued attempting to keep the conversation alive, searching for anything Myra and I might have in common, which amounted to very little. As for Eli, he may as well have not been there at all, because he'd made zero contributions to the conversation so far. Half the reason for this night out was for the two of us to get to know each other better, too. I waited until he tore his eyes away from the TV to cut his steak to ask him a question.

"So, how do you think the Colts are going to do against the Raiders on Sunday?"

I knew he was a Colts fan because Sarah mentioned they went to Indy for a game at least once per season, and I only knew the Colts were playing the Raiders because I looked it up earlier that day in preparation for this very question. Eli made a face, letting out a single, "ha!" before swallowing a bite of his steak. I gathered from this reaction he didn't think the Raiders had much of a chance. And then his focus returned to the game on TV.

I looked at Sarah and shrugged, as if to say, *I tried.*

Beside me, Myra was spending a lot of time texting someone. Her phone was never far from her reach. This night was hopeless. I sighed, barely able to enjoy my cheeseburger. Across the table, Sarah was muttering something to Eli through gritted teeth.

"What are you saying?" he asked her.

"I *said* you're not even making an effort to participate in the conversation," she repeated, barely loud enough for me to hear.

"What conversation?!" Eli boomed, motioning across the table toward us. I didn't dare look at Myra's reaction—I was too embarrassed. Even Eli, who hadn't been listening to a word we'd said all night, could tell this date was doomed. "I'm sorry," he continued, "but this whole thing was your idea. I'm here, like you wanted."

"I didn't think you'd just sit there and watch the game the entire time," Sarah said.

"You specifically let me choose this place for that very reason."

Sarah's body tensed as she took a deep breath. "Let's talk outside. Now." She was using her teacher voice on him. With a dismissive eyeroll, Eli threw his crumpled-up napkin down on the table before sliding out of the booth before her. The two of them stepped outside to argue, leaving me alone with Myra.

The noise level inside the bar was steadily rising as the space filled up with more and more people, all of them laughing and having a drunken good time. And there we were, sitting in silence with our hands in our laps. The server approached to clear our plates and asked if Eli and Sarah were done with theirs.

"Um, I don't know," I said, straining to see them through the window. I could only make out one of Sarah's flailing arms.

"I'll just come back," the server said.

I finished my Jack & Coke and turned to Myra, who was texting someone again. When she noticed me looking at her, she said, "This has been really awkward."

"I'm sorry. A double-date probably wasn't the best idea."

"No, it wasn't," she said, reaching for her purse. "And actually, I think I'm going to go."

Ouch. "Oh, okay. I'm really sorry, again." She started to pull some cash out of her wallet, but I motioned for her to put it away. "Please, let me take care of it."

"Are you sure?"

I nodded, standing up so she could get out of the booth. "It's the least I can do."

"Well, okay," she said, standing in front of me. She tucked her purse under her arm. "Um, it was great to meet you."

"Yeah, you too," I said, scratching the back of my neck as she practically bolted for the door. I'd been on some pretty bad Tinder dates before, but this one really took the cake. I slumped back down in the booth, awaiting Sarah and Eli's return so I could sheepishly tell them my date ditched me.

At least we'd have something to talk about.

But when the door opened again, it was only Sarah who returned to the table. As soon as she sat down, she ate one last French fry off her plate before pushing it away with so much aggression it slammed into Myra's glass. The sound of the two dishes clinking together was loud enough to catch the attention of the people at the table next to us. They all turned and stared at me, like I was the one who'd pissed Sarah off.

"Everything okay?" I asked warily.

"No. I told Eli to fuck off and I'd get a ride home with someone else." She looked over her shoulder toward the bathroom. "What happened to Myra?"

"Same," I joked, trying to make her laugh. She didn't even crack a smile.

"This whole terrible fucking night was my fault," she said, dropping a rare Sarah Lavely f-bomb. She normally reserved those for when she was three tequila shots deep at the staff Christmas party. "I feel so fucking stupid right now." Ah, another one already.

I stared at her for a moment before reaching for the tiny dessert menu from the condiment basket. "You know, I really want to try a slice of their pumpkin cheesecake, but it looks huge. I could never finish it myself. Do you want to split one?"

"Abso-fucking-lutely."

# chapter five
sarah

Pumpkin cheesecake was exactly what I needed to lift my spirits.

"I'm sorry Eli wasn't very talkative," I found myself saying, reaching for one of the two forks our server had brought along with our dessert. I was desperately trying to hide my humiliation. "He just hasn't been in the greatest mood the past week—I should have guessed he wouldn't be up for a night out. Not this soon after the big loss."

Owen nodded, his gaze fixed on the piece of pumpkin cheesecake between us as he reached for his own fork. We both took a bite, and though he was silent, I could sense the weight of all the thoughts he was keeping to himself. He didn't have to say he disapproved of the way I was excusing Eli's behavior—it was written all over his face. Whatever he was thinking, he'd never say it out loud.

Instead, his lips curled up in a gentle smile. "His 'what conversation' comment is actually kind of funny to me now."

I giggled. "Oh, God. I tried to help you two—I really did." I scooted forward in my seat so I could be closer to him. The volume inside Poppy's was increasing by the minute as the football game was entering its fourth quarter. The men standing around the bar all hooted and hollered simultaneously, their cheers almost drowning out the Imagine Dragons song blaring from the speakers nearby. "So Myra wasn't a match, huh?"

Owen shook his head, sinking his fork into the cheesecake for another bite. "I guess I literally repel women now," he said. "I'm really letting Ava Greentree down." I laughed. Ava was a student in Owen's class, and she was always asking him if he had a girlfriend yet—usually followed up by a "why not?" Once, she even asked me if *I* was Owen's girlfriend, only to be disappointed by my response. I couldn't remember being that obsessed with my teachers' love lives when I was her age, but it was kind of adorable.

"You do not repel women," I told him. "There's clearly something wrong with Myra if she couldn't see how great you are."

"Nah," he groaned. "She was smart to run away."

"Come on," I said, rolling my eyes. "Don't act like you're not a catch. You've got a secure job, plus your own business. You dress well. Good hygiene. You're a good-lookin' guy. You respect women. And on top of all that, you're funny. What's not to love?"

I held myself back from mentioning the dimples on his cheeks—my favorite physical feature of his—which became more pronounced as he tried to suppress a smile. Owen was never great at accepting compliments, usually deflecting them with some self-deprecating comment. Sure enough, as he looked down at our dessert, he muttered, "Yeah, every woman around here is dying to get with a guy who sponsors a robotics club."

"Oh, shut up. The right girl is out there for you."

Finally, his eyes flitted upward, and his fork hovered over the plate. I waited for him to counter my last words, but he had nothing to say. So, sensing his discomfort, I took this as my cue to change the subject.

"Oh—did I tell you I'm going to be an aunt?"

My sister, Samantha, hadn't officially announced her pregnancy yet, but I knew it was safe to tell Owen. "Wow, really?" he said, clearing his throat. "You'll love it. Being an uncle is just the best. I get to spoil the hell out of them, get 'em all riled up, and then… leave."

I laughed. "Right? I'm so excited. But I just feel so behind in life."

"How so?"

"Samantha's three years younger than me, yet she's married with a baby on the way. I'm oh-for-two."

"You act like you're running out of time or something. I'm the one turning thirty next month."

I took another bite. "I'm just starting to doubt Eli will ever propose."

Owen sat his fork down and took a sip of his water. Then, leaning comfortably against the corner of the booth and the wall, he asked, "Is that what you want?"

"Marriage? Of course."

"That's not what I meant." He stirred his drink with his straw, keeping his eyes locked on mine. I knew exactly what he was implying—did I want to marry *Eli?* Unable to answer, I quickly took another bite to buy me some time. Marrying Eli had been part of the blueprint for my life since the first time we dated, back when we were just teenagers. Practically babies. We'd been dating longer than all of our friends—even when you counted our three-year hiatus during college.

Who would I be without him?

I couldn't say any of that to Owen, however. Fortunately, our server returned to check on us, allowing me to evade his question altogether. "I think I'd explode if I ate another bite," I told the server, and she laid our bills on the table.

"All right, then," she said, picking up our dessert plate. "Just pay me when you're ready."

Owen leaned forward to get his wallet out of his back pocket. "Hey, since I'm, like, *super* loaded now, will you let me take care of the bill?"

"Absolutely not," I said, reaching for my purse. "I'm not let—"

"Shh." The man actually shushed me, leaving me momentarily speechless. With a dismissive wave of the hand, he said, "Come on. It'll give me a much-needed ego-boost if you let me take care of it. So you're actually doing me a major disservice if you refuse." I let my hand hover above my purse. Before I could say anything else, Owen reached across the table to grab my bill, placing it on top of his.

"Thank you," I said. I bit my bottom lip as I watched him sign both of the tickets with a generous tip and hand the server his debit card. Considering part of the reason we were out was to celebrate his podcast, it felt unjust to let him foot the entire bill. At the same time, I could tell it made him happy—like I was the one doing *him* a favor right now.

When the server returned, neither of us made a move to grab our jackets and go. Instead, we remained there in that booth and talked for almost another hour. I even slipped off my shoes and pulled one foot up underneath my butt to get more comfortable.

It was the best Friday night I'd had in ages.

Owen listened to me ramble on about the newspaper club and how I hoped it would pay off for Bentley's sake. We both celebrated the fact Bentley had miraculously kept himself out of trouble since the headlock incident on Monday morning.

He told me what his robotics club was up to, excitedly describing the cranes they were building. And I shared my wild idea for starting a garden on the school lawn, which he pointed out I'd already mentioned to him three or four times.

"I told you about that already?"

He playfully rolled his eyes as he sipped the last of his water. "Yes. You also told me you want to plant a patch of pollinating wildflowers for the bees, and how you'd have fresh cherry tomatoes for your salads because you can just go outside and pick them during lunch."

"Oops," I giggled, surprised he'd remembered those details—which I was only just now remembering myself. "At least I know you're paying attention."

We meandered from one topic to the next, never returning to his question about the prospect of marriage with Eli. I had seven unopened messages from him on my phone, but I didn't want to look at them. I was having fun now, and I didn't want him to bring my mood back down.

Eventually, our server stopped refilling our drinks, and it was getting late. Now that the game was over and everyone was celebrating an apparent win, we were the only sober guests left in the entire establishment. "We should probably head out," I said. "I'm sorry you're stuck having to drive me home."

"It's no problem at all." We grabbed our jackets and Owen stepped out of my way, letting me lead us out. Just as I turned the corner by the bar, one of the men who'd been seated at a barstool on the end spun around and stood up, bumping into me so hard he knocked me backward into Owen. The beer he was holding sloshed onto my shoes.

"Oh fuck, I am so sorry," the guy said, grabbing me by the arm. He was standing so close I could smell the alcohol on his breath. Staring me up and down, he said, "Let me buy you a drink to make it up to you."

I tried to lean away from him, but his grip remained firm. Owen, whose hands were still resting securely on my lower back after stopping my fall, cleared his throat and interjected, "No, I think she's good." He raised one arm between me and the drunk idiot, who held up both hands to show he was backing off.

Funny how some men can't respect your personal space until they think you belong to someone else.

With one hand remaining on my lower back, Owen gently guided me through the throng of people to the door. He reached forward to open it with his other hand, ushering me out.

Once outside, he shoved both hands inside the pockets of his leather jacket as we walked toward his car. Was he blushing? It was too dark to be certain. He seemed embarrassed about putting his hands on me, but it's not like he hadn't done it for a good reason.  "Thanks," I told him as we walked around the side of the restaurant toward the parking lot. I needed him to know it was okay.

Owen simply shrugged. "I just didn't like the way he was looking at you."

It was my turn to blush. I liked Protective Owen.

Once we reached his car and buckled our seatbelts, I couldn't tear my eyes off Owen's face. It didn't make any sense that this man had been single for so long. Any woman would be lucky to have him. "You know," I said, hugging my purse on my lap, "even though the double-date didn't work out, this night wasn't a total bust, was it?"

"Nope," he said, shifting the car into reverse. "It sure wasn't."

# chapter six

## owen

It was night. I was working late in my classroom, grading a stack of math assignments. All of a sudden, a knock echoed through the room, and I looked up to see Sarah wearing the same cleavage-baring dress she'd worn to Poppy's Bar & Grill. I put down my red pen. "What are you doing here so late?"

"You, I hope," she said, lifting up her dress to reveal she wasn't wearing any panties. Without hesitation, I leapt up to grab her and set her down on my desk. She threw her head back in laughter, wrapping her legs around my waist. Just before I lowered my mouth to hers, the fire alarm started going off above our heads.

My eyes shot open, and I realized it was my Monday morning alarm on my phone I'd heard, not the school fire alarm. And I was in bed with a raging boner, not in my classroom.

Sex dreams about Sarah were a pretty regular occurrence. They almost always took place in the classroom—sometimes mine, sometimes hers—and I often woke up just before the action started. Not every time.

And I always felt this incredible amount of shame upon waking up, like I was betraying her somehow. If Sarah knew I dreamt about her like this, she'd be just as disgusted as I was with myself. I took a cold shower before heading to the gym for my morning workout, trying to get her off my mind.

When I got to school, I was already disgruntled when I remembered we had a morning assembly. Ten minutes after the first bell, the entire school packed into the gymnasium to watch a speaker use magic tricks to teach about bullying. I knew that as soon as this was over, at least half of my students would hop on their laptops to research beginner magic kits, wanting to get started on their newly-discovered dream of becoming a magician. It was inevitable.

As we got our kids to sit in rows along the gym floor, I couldn't shake my bad mood. Assemblies were the worst. You'd think a break in the monotony would be good for everyone, but all they did was cut down on important instruction time and make the kids hyper for the rest of the day. "Let's try to show the younger grades how to behave, all right? Set a good example," I warned, eyeing Jayden Niehaus, who couldn't seem to sit still.

As the presentation began, I positioned myself at the back corner of the gym next to Sarah and one of the fourth-grade teachers, Vicki Santiago. She was a good friend of Sarah's. "Hey, Gardner," Vicki said in a low voice, peering around Sarah to see me better. "I heard your Tinder date walked out on you Friday night."

I looked at Sarah. "You've been spilling the tea about me, huh?"

"I'm sorry," she said, giggling. "But if it makes you feel any better, I told her how Eli abandoned me, too."

She hadn't brought up Eli's name that morning while we chatted over coffee, so neither did I. But I wanted to be a good friend, so I felt obligated to ask, "How'd that go, by the way? Did you guys, you know, work things out?"

"Yeah," she said. "We made up when I got home."

Vicki leaned forward to butt in. "Yeah, twice!" she blurted with a wink. And at that, Sarah elbowed her in the ribs, her cheeks turning red as she muttered for Vicki to shut up. She stared straight ahead, refusing to look at me. I was suddenly very thankful for Jayden Niehaus for putting acorns in the hood of the person in front of him, because it gave me an excuse to walk away from this conversation.

I confiscated every last one of Jayden's acorns and reprimanded him, sounding a little more hostile than I intended. It wasn't his fault. I couldn't shake the image of Sarah going home to Eli and "making up" with him after he'd embarrassed her. We'd had this wonderful time together, engaging in deep conversation over a shared slice of cheesecake, and she went home and crawled right into bed with him.

I loathed the way that made me feel. I never wanted to be this guy—the guy who lamented about being "friendzoned" by a woman who owed him absolutely nothing. Sarah was a terrific friend. My best friend, even. I never expected anything more from her. But that didn't take away all the occasional pangs of jealousy when she mentioned his name, or, God forbid, someone else brought up their sex life. I hated myself for it.

As I made my way back over to the wall where Sarah and Vicki stood, I tried to focus my attention on the magician up on the stage. He was putting one of the kindergarten teachers, Ms. Devin, in a box, promising to make her disappear. The entire gym erupted into shocked laughter as he revealed the now-empty box, somehow relating this stunt to bullying.

I glanced at my watch. Because I'd completely forgotten to work this assembly into my schedule, I was going to have to push the morning class's test review back one day, which messed up my lesson plans for the entire week. And suddenly, this thought entered my mind—a thought I'd been battling with since at least the start of this school year:

*I can't do this anymore.*

As that singular thought replayed over and over in my head, I went into a sensory overload. Everything in the room was suddenly more bothersome than before. Beside me, Sarah brushed against my arm, giggling at something Vicki was telling her, and I instinctively pulled away. A few feet from us, Jayden was back to terrorizing the kids around him every way he could. On stage, Ms. Devin emerged from the magician's box again and the gym exploded into cheers.

And a second thought emerged: *I would rather be working on my podcast right now.*

When the assembly was over, I led my class out of the gym past Principal Cates, who was giving students high fives by the double doors. "Hey," I said, forcing myself to spit the next words out before I had a chance to lose the courage. "I need to talk to you at lunch."

"You know where to find me," he said.

Back in the classroom, the kids were too amped up to focus on anything math-related, so I gave them some free time while I collected my thoughts. I pulled out a yellow notepad and began making a pro and con list, the word "RESIGN?" written at the top.

The pro column was easy. I'd have more time to work on my business. I could significantly increase my income, too, if I made all the right moves. I wouldn't have to get out of bed before 7:00 a.m. ever again, and my days wouldn't be spent grading sloppy math homework or fielding questions from nosey ten-year-olds about my lackluster love life.

The con column took a little more time. Of course, there was the Robotics Club. I wished I could meet with those kids every afternoon, not just once a week. I had as much fun as they did—truly. If I were to resign, I'd have to come up with a new way to teach coding and engineering to local youth. Maybe at the library? After giving that some thought, I crossed Robotics Club off the con list, realizing it could carry on outside of school and I'd have even more control.

Then I wrote "no benefits." Entrepreneurship didn't come with benefits like health insurance and a 401(k) plan. I'd have to figure all of that out on my own, somehow. Yet millions of other entrepreneurs managed it, didn't they?

I spent the next twenty minutes researching retirement options for business owners, only breaking focus when my class started loudly arguing about how the magician had made Ms. Devin disappear. "Take it down a notch, guys," I warned, crossing "no benefits" off of the con column. It would take some more research, for sure, but at least I had a couple of ideas for where to start.

When the lunch bell rang and it was time for my students to head to the cafeteria, there was only one word in the con column. One name. She was my entire reason for showing up here every day, and that was no longer enough.

**

In Cates' office, I cut right to the chase. He attempted to make small talk, but I scooted to the edge of my chair and said, "I need to be upfront with you about something that's been weighing heavily on my mind." He just nodded, pressing his fingertips together. I continued, my right leg shaking up and down uncontrollably. "I'm not quite sure my heart's fully in this job anymore. I've been suffering from burnout for a while. I think I'm finally ready to admit to myself—and to you—that it's time for a change."

Mr. Cates held up one hand. "I'm going to stop you right there. Before you continue, I want to share something with you that can't leave this room. Understand?"

"Yes, sir," I said, giving him a confused look.

"At the end of this school year, I will be officially retiring."

"Oh, wow," I said. "That's—that's great. Congratulations."

"Thank you. John and I are really looking forward to taking the RV out and seeing the country. It's been a long time coming, let me tell you." He paused, touching the edge of a picture frame on his desk. In the photo, he and his husband were standing in front of their RV with a mountainous landscape behind them. "But anyway, the reason I'm sharing this with you now, Owen, is because there's obviously going to be an opening for my position."

My leg stopped shaking. "Right."

"And now, while there will be a thorough interview process for all candidates with a full panel and all that rigamarole, I just want to say—your name has already come up more than once in my conversations with the superintendent."

"It has?"

"Yes. And I strongly urge you to consider applying when the time comes. If I could hand-pick my successor myself, well...." He casually waved his hand my direction, leaning back in his desk chair. "I couldn't imagine a better person for the job."

I swallowed. This was a lot for me to process, and not at all how I expected the conversation to go. "Thank you," I said, staring down at his desk. "I'm not even sure what to say."

"I won't be making a formal announcement to the rest of the staff for a few weeks, so sit tight with this information for a bit," Mr. Cates said. "And of course, you're not guaranteed the position by any means. But it would be wise of you to hold off on… whatever it was you were about to tell me." He looked at me over the top of his glasses.

Becoming principal of this school was something I used to fantasize about when I was a little younger, before I had the podcast to distract me. It would certainly be a sizable salary increase for me. However, it would also mean I'd have to let my business go, because not only would I no longer have time for it, it might even be considered a conflict of interest. The school district had weird rules about that kind of thing. But would it even matter? I wouldn't need to hustle to earn extra income if I got this promotion.

Mr. Cates could probably see the gears turning in my head. "I know it's a lot. In the meantime, I want to warn you about something."

I looked up. "What's that?"

"Well," he said, picking up a pen and tapping it on the desk. "It's been brought to my attention that there may have been some… inappropriate interactions between you and Ms. Lavely."

"Inappropriate interactions?" I blinked. "Who said that?"

"Actually, I've been hearing these rumors for a couple of years now from numerous people. Lori is the eyes and ears of this building, you know—nothing flies under her radar." Lori was the school secretary, and while most people needed food and oxygen to survive, she required gossip.

"But there hasn't—" I stopped myself mid-sentence because Cates was giving me this "don't try and fool me" stare with one eyebrow raised. Like Sarah, he knew me too well. I hung my head in shame. "Sarah's a good friend. People are just misinterpreting what they're seeing."

"I would advise you to be mindful of the way you interact with her in the future. Something like that could definitely hinder your chances of becoming principal."

I just nodded. "It won't be an issue."

# chapter seven



Thanksgiving break was fast-approaching, meaning I had a limited amount of time to recruit fourth and fifth-graders for the Newspaper Club and help them complete the very first issue of the Grissom Gazette. A lot of the interested kids overlapped with my Creative Writing Club, which wasn't a surprise. While Owen's Robotics Club attracted all the nerds, the creative kids flocked to me.

And then there was Bentley.

"You want me to give up two recesses a week for this?"

Coaxing him to join the club was no easy feat. At first, I tried to subtly point out that he never seemed to be an active participant in any games played at recess, anyway, but he wouldn't budge. It wasn't until I casually wondered aloud if Noah might be interested in giving the comic strip a shot that he finally said he would go to the first meeting just to check it out.

Dirty tactic, but it worked.

By mid-November, I had a total of eleven students diligently working on the first issue. It was going to be more of a newsletter than a full paper—just one sheet, front and back—but I was proud of the work they were doing, nonetheless. Bentley's earthquake comic was going to take up a third of the back page, which seemed to satisfy him. He spent our meetings redrawing it, perfecting every detail.

Jordyn Ellis wrote a scathing review of the school pizza, which they gave a 4/10. The lunch ladies wouldn't know what hit them the day this issue dropped. One of the fourth graders polled kids at recess on the best video games, ultimately deciding that Minecraft was Grissom Elementary's favorite. I gave one of the kids the assignment of photographing the girls' basketball game, and showed another student how to make a Thanksgiving crossword puzzle using an online generator.

Ava Greentree insisted on interviewing Owen as our Teacher of the Month for the inaugural issue. The idea was purely hers, and I let her run with it—after all, it wasn't a bad idea. When she handed me her completed article, I couldn't help but smile—especially after reading the very last line.

"'Mr. Gardner is single and looking'?" I raised one eyebrow at Ava, who was giving me a wary smile. "Ava, did Mr. Gardner say that?"

She slumped in her chair. "Well, not the second part. But he did say he doesn't have a wife yet or even a girlfriend."

I held in a laugh. "Okay, since he didn't say that he was 'looking,' let's leave that detail out. In fact, we probably don't need to mention his love life at all, do we?"

"I guess not," she conceded.

I couldn't wait to tell Owen about this little exchange with her. I didn't see him for the rest of the day, though. Perhaps I was imagining it, but he seemed a little distant lately. He'd been eating his lunch in his classroom more often, which wasn't all that unusual, but that combined with the fact that he hadn't ventured into my classroom for a quick chat during any of his prep periods lately had me worried I'd said or done something wrong. Yet his demeanor in the mornings was unchanged—he was still the same old Owen.

Maybe he was just busy with *STEM for the Win*. I knew he worked on his business during contracted hours sometimes—a secret he only shared with me—so it was likely that's all this was. However, as I sat in my classroom after school, putting the newspaper layout together and printing enough copies for every student and staff member, I couldn't get him off my mind. To be truthful, I was missing him. Our morning conversations or brief encounters while swapping students weren't enough.

That's why, as I was locking my classroom around six o'clock and noticed he was across the hall, I decided to pop in for a visit. We were probably the only two people remaining in the building—his Robotics Club let out just a little while ago.

I knocked on his open door and poked my head inside, startling him. He was wheeling a cart carrying a partially-assembled crane back to his storage room, stopping so suddenly when he heard me knock that the crane almost toppled over. "What are… what are you doing here so late?" he asked, holding the robot steady so it wouldn't teeter off the cart.

"Newspaper stuff," I said, holding up the completed issue in my hand. "I'm sorry, I didn't mean to scare you."

"No it's fine," he said, clearing his throat. He wheeled the cart so that it was in front of his body. "I thought I was alone in the building. Just glad you're not a ghost."

"Speaking of ghosts," I said as he continued to wheel the cart into the storage room. I waited for him to come back out before I continued. "I feel like I haven't seen much of you lately."

He walked over to the counter at the back of the classroom where I stood and leaned against it with his hands casually tucked into his pockets. "I'm sorry. I've been working on my business every free moment I get these days."

"That's good. One of these days, you're going to leave us all behind and make *STEM for the Win* full-time, aren't you?" I asked, swapping my heavy tote bag to the other shoulder.

Owen took a deep breath, running a hand through his hair. "I have something to tell you."

As soon as he spoke the words, my skin prickled with dread. I couldn't even put my finger on why—what did I think he was about to say? Whatever it was, it meant a lot to him, and it probably had something to do with why he'd been acting a little off lately.

"What is it?"

"This can't leave this room." I pretended to zip my lips, and he continued. "Cates is retiring at the end of this year, and he thinks I have a good chance at taking his place."

I gasped. "Are you serious?" First, I reacted to the thought of Cates leaving, and then the second part of his announcement began to sink in. Owen would be my *boss*. "Oh, Owen. That's… huge. Is this still what you want?"

Another sigh. "I honestly have no idea what I want," he said, pulling his hands from his pockets to cross his arms. "I thought I knew, but then Cates approached me with this, and now I'm not so sure. I mean, I used to want nothing more than moving up to admin—I did the damn licensure program. Finished my master's. But… all of that was before the podcast blew up."

I could hear the uncertainty in his voice—it was clear this decision-making process was stressing him out. "Did you make one of your foolproof pro and con lists?"

"You know it," he said with a chuckle. "But that didn't help. I kept finding things to add to both sides."

"Well," I said, hoisting myself up onto the counter to sit on it. If the kids could see me breaking one of their most-hated rules, they'd revolt. "The salary increase would be... substantial." That was an understatement.

"Right," he said, placing one hand on the counter beside me. "And that's obviously a huge factor."

"But when you're principal, you won't have any time for your podcast."

"Hence the dilemma. And, actually, I've decided that if I don't take this position," he started, pausing for a moment to glance at the floor. "I'm going to resign at the end of the year."

I froze. "What?"

"I just... I can't teach forever. I don't want to," he quickly added. "So I'm leaving it up to fate. I figure if I get this job, then it's meant to be. And if not, then, well, I'll take it as a sign I'm meant to move on to bigger things."

"Wow." I crossed my ankles against the cabinet below. "So the choice is really between principal or podcast, then? You're leaving the classroom, no matter what?" He nodded in confirmation, and I could do nothing but sit there and blink at him. Whether he took this position or not, I was going to lose my "teacher bestie" across the hall. As happy as I was for him to break free from the classroom, I couldn't help but think about what that meant for me. Us. Our friendship.

"Hey," he said, making me look up. His expression was solemn all of a sudden. "We're always going to be friends, Lavely."

Could he read my mind? "I know," I replied at a volume just above a whisper. Perched on that counter, I found myself at eye level with him for once—no longer having to tilt my head to meet his gaze. And now, standing before me, his eyes were locked on mine like there was something more he wanted to say. With anyone else, such a prolonged stare would make me uncomfortable, but Owen tended to say more with his eyes than he ever did with his words.

And at that moment, he was saying a lot. So much, in fact, that I swallowed and looked over at the clock behind his desk just to break the tension. "Gosh, it's late."

Owen cleared his throat and stepped away from the counter, glancing at his watch. "Yeah—let me finish up, and I'll walk you out."


As we made our way out of the building a few moments later, the late autumn sun was on the verge of disappearing below the horizon. I silently cursed myself for choosing such a flimsy jacket that morning as the chilly breeze cut right through me. Owen and I made our way to the last two cars in the parking lot, sitting one space apart. We stopped right in the middle of them, turning to face each other.

He started to say good-bye, but I blurted out, "Do you want to go grab a coffee?" I don't know what made me say it—I think, perhaps, I wanted him to prove we'd remain friends even if we weren't working across the hall from one another. If we'd no longer be able to chat over coffee every single morning, maybe we could make up for it another way.

Like having coffee at six in the evening, for example.

Owen stared at me, zipping his coat up just a little more so it covered his neck. "Uhh…." He looked over his shoulder at his car, aiming his remote starter at it. After the engine started, he turned back to me, his arms dangling at his sides. "I can't. I have to go rerecord an entire podcast episode. My stupid mic's starting to cut out on me, and… yeah, I've gotta go do that."

"Oh, okay," I responded, trying not to let my disappointment show. "Is that why you haven't uploaded a new episode in two weeks?"

"That's part of it, yeah. Wait, you knew that?"

"Well, of course," I said, letting out a little laugh. I hadn't missed a single episode since he began this whole journey almost two years ago. "You think I'm not an avid listener of *STEM for the Win?*"

"You don't even like STEM."

"But I like the host."

He glanced down at the dead brown and yellow leaves on the ground between our feet, trying not to smile. If it weren't for the single light pole above illuminating his face, I might not have noticed his cheeks turning the slightest shade of pink. It could have just been from the chilly air, but it was cute, nonetheless.

"See you tomorrow, Owen," I said, confused by the sudden pang of sadness in my chest.

"Night, Lavely."

# chapter eight



On the morning of December 3rd, I awoke to a call from my mother at exactly 5:52 a.m. I groaned as I reached for my phone. Before I could even utter the word "hello," she launched into the birthday song just like she had every single December 3rd at the exact time of my birth for as long as I could remember.

"Thank you, Mom," I said when she finished. "You really don't have to do this, you know."

"Owen Andrew. There's going to be a day you'll miss these calls."

"Mmmmph."

"Before I forget, I wanted to tell you that Jake and Stacy can't make it for your birthday dinner until seven tonight because Caleb has practice. And your sister is bringing that guy she's been seeing. That'll be interesting, won't it?"

That was far too much information to process at this ungodly hour. "Yep."

"Will you be bringing anyone, by the way?"

"Nope."

I could hear the disappointment in her voice when she said, "All right, then. Maybe one day." Oh, brother. She was always probing me about the women in my life, or lack thereof. Maybe she and Ava Greentree could get together and talk about me. I laughed at the thought of the two of them sitting in a coffee shop, scrutinizing every detail of my dating history. "What's so funny?"

"I'll see you tonight, Mom," I said, hanging up. And I rolled back over, deciding I wouldn't be going to the gym today, giving myself an extra half hour to sleep as a birthday present. But when I closed my eyes, I could only think about how much I wished Sarah could be the woman I brought home to meet my family. I fantasized about doing things like that with her just as much as I dreamt about seeing her naked. My mom and siblings would adore her, especially after Rachel—nobody in the family was all that fond of the woman from my last serious relationship. Rachel was shy, which everyone misinterpreted as rudeness. After our break-up, however, I think they may have been right about her all along.

That relationship ended two years ago, and I hadn't been past a third date with anyone since.

Jeez, no wonder my mom was acting like I was completely hopeless. I was now thirty years old and nowhere close to giving her more grandchildren. Well, now that my younger sister had a boyfriend, maybe that would take the attention off of me for a while.

I sighed and rolled over onto my back. Knowing sleep was unattainable at the moment, I stuck my hand down my boxers and gave myself permission to masturbate to the image of Sarah in my mind, guilt-free. It was my birthday, after all.

**

My students weren't supposed to know it was my birthday. I avoided telling them about it on purpose, because things like that tended to become a big distraction. However, the very first two students who arrived called out, "Happy birthday, Mr. Gardner!" as soon as they rounded the corner. Someone told them.

After the sixth or seventh kid said it, I looked across the hallway at Sarah, whose cunning smile looked rather suspicious. "You told them, didn't you?"

"I don't know what you're talking about," she said, taking a sip of her coffee and staring at me over the top of the mug. The green sweater she was wearing that day really made her eyes pop. When I remembered that I'd thought about her that morning while my hand was around my dick, I stared down at the floor, feeling ashamed. "How does it feel to be in your thirties?".

"My neck hurts."

She laughed. "I guess I have something to look forward to in a couple of years, then." We greeted the next few kids who came in, every last one of them telling me to have a happy birthday. Ava showed up with a handmade card and ran off into the classroom before I could even open it, too embarrassed to wait for my reaction. "You can't tell me that doesn't brighten your morning," Sarah said when I showed her how Ava had glued multi-colored paper hearts all over the card.

"Meh," I said, but Sarah could see right through my fake apathy. I smiled as I folded the card and put it in my back pocket. This was the kind of thing I'd miss when I was no longer teaching. I'd kept every single drawing and handmade card a student had ever given me in one of my desk drawers. It didn't feel right to throw any of them away.

When the first bell rang, Sarah asked, "What is your class usually doing at 9:15?"

"Uh, working on their online math assignments. Why?"

"No reason. Have a good day!" She quickly shut her classroom door behind her before I could ask any questions. Interesting. I wasn't sure, but I thought 9:15 was normally the time her class went to one of their specials—music, art, etc. She was scheming something.

We started giving each other gifts for our birthdays a couple years ago. Last year, she gave me an insulated coffee mug—the very one I used every morning. For her birthday in August, I gave her a book about Ted Bundy, her favorite serial killer.

You wouldn't expect a bubbly schoolteacher to have a favorite serial killer, but Sarah had a Top 5. I made sure to never piss her off, because she knew all the best ways to kill someone.

Better stay on her good side, just to be safe.

At 9:18, there was a knock on my classroom door. All of my students were peeking over their laptop screens at me, giggling and covering their mouths. "You guys are acting pretty suspicious," I told them, making my way over to the door. I opened it to see Sarah standing there holding something behind her back. "Oh look, it's Ms. Lavely," I said, feigning surprise.

She walked right past me, counting to three, and suddenly my entire class was singing "Happy Birthday" to me. When they finished the song, Sarah handed me a canvas painting of a tree— all of its leaves made from their thumbprints.

"Wow," I said, taking it from her. "This is what you guys did over in reading class yesterday, huh?" I asked, looking at the kids. They were all still giggling goofily as I carried the painting over to the whiteboard at the front of the room, propping it up on the little ledge. I felt a little guilty, knowing I never would have thought to do something this creative for Sarah. "Thank you, guys" I said, taking a step back to get a better look at it. There were more than just one class's worth of fingerprints here, which told me her class was in on it too.

There was a chorus of you're-welcomes, and when I turned around, I noticed Sarah was still holding something. It was a large, blue gift bag, bigger than a shoebox. "And this is just from me," she said, extending it toward me. "You can open it now, or wait, or… whatever you want to do."

"Hmm," I said, taking it from her hands. I looked at my watch and turned back to the class. "You guys can go ahead and return to what you were doing. Don't forget, you have to have two math lessons completed by the end of the day." I sat the gift bag down on my desk chair. "I'm scared."

"Just open it, silly."

"So impatient," I teased, removing some of the tissue paper. And I froze once I saw what was inside. It was a microphone for recording podcasts. And not just any microphone—it was one of the higher-end ones, which I had been researching but couldn't justify purchasing just yet. "Sarah…." We never addressed each other by our first names in front of students like that, but it sort of slipped out.

"Is it a good one?" she asked. "It had a ton of five-star reviews."

"It's…." I was actually speechless. I removed more tissue paper to get a better look at the box. I'd looked at this exact microphone on Amazon not too long ago.

The kids at the front of the room, who'd witnessed this whole thing, were demanding to see what was in the bag. So I pulled the microphone all the way out and sat it on the desk, still too stunned to react. The kids oohed and ahhed, and the murmuring quickly spread to the back of the room. I heard someone mention my podcast, quickly followed by a, "He has a *podcast*?!"

Sarah was waiting for me to say something. "Is it the right kind of mic?" she asked, folding her hands under her chin.

"Yes," I said, flipping over the box to read the specifications. "It's perfect. And—hey, can we talk out in the hallway for a minute?" I put the box and all the tissue paper back in the bag and left it on my desk chair before leading Sarah out the classroom door.

"I already know what you're going to say," she said as I eased the door shut behind us, leaving it slightly ajar so I could still hear my students. "It's—"

"You shouldn't have spent that much money on me."

"I know," she said, "but when you mentioned your broken microphone last week, I couldn't help myself. You know me. When an idea pops into my head, I just can't let it go."

"I know," I said, widening my eyes at her. "But the painting would have been enough. I can't accept it, Sarah. You have to return it."

"Stop it," she said, giving my shoulder a shove. "You deserve it, okay? And it's really more than a birthday gift. Think of it as my way of congratulating you on your hundredth episode. Which premieres this week, right?"

I nodded slowly, realizing this was probably the kind of thing Cates was referring to when he mentioned "inappropriate interactions." And the whole class knew about the gift—by the end of the day, it would be the talk of the school. And if Lori caught wind of it? I was toast. "But I only gave you a book for your birthday."

"And I loved it," Sarah said, clutching my wrist. "Just accept the gift and say thank you, or I'm going to make the whole school sing 'Happy Birthday' to you in the lunchroom."

Glancing behind her to make sure we were alone in this hallway, I leaned in for a friendly hug. "Thank you."

I closed my eyes for a moment, taking in the intoxicating scent of her coconut shampoo and the satisfying way her small frame fit just right in my arms. Oh, I could get used to that. But when I felt her starting to tighten her grip around my waist, my eyes shot open, and I quickly pulled away before this hug had a chance to be perceived as anything other than platonic. And then I asked the question that had been lingering in the back of my mind since the second I opened the gift.

"So, what did Eli say about the microphone?"

Her face went a little pale, and her eyes darted back and forth. "Well, I haven't mentioned it to him yet," she said, taking a deep breath before adding, "He just doesn't really understand our friendship."

I glanced downward, our proximity evident in the small gap between our feet. My brown dress shoes, her black flats. With a subtle shift, I lifted my eyes to meet her gaze, intense and searching. I couldn't bring myself to say the words on the tip of my tongue: *neither do I.*

Instead, I thanked her again, and we went our separate ways.

# chapter nine
## sarah

Owen was being ridiculous. I'd only wanted to get him something nice. I'd been thinking about his upcoming birthday for a couple of weeks, struggling to come up with the perfect gift, so when he mentioned needing a new microphone, I knew what I had to do. I'd ordered the thing after our conversation that night while I was still sitting in my car in the parking lot.

I hoped he knew I didn't expect him to do anything remotely similar when my birthday rolled around next year. This was a "no strings attached" gift. I simply wanted to do something nice for a friend, my best friend, who had been under a lot of pressure lately. I could see how much having to make a major life decision was stressing him out.

In a sense, giving him the microphone was my subtle way of telling him to go after his dream—a gesture meant to convey that I believed in him wholeheartedly. Because as much as I'd miss him if he resigned, I had no doubt in my mind it was the best choice for him. I could hear the passion in his voice in every single podcast episode. He hadn't brought that same energy with him to school in a long time.

Which is why I didn't think he was really all that suitable for the principal position. Would he do a great job? Sure. He possessed all the qualities of a capable leader, and people at this school adored him. But I knew in my heart he wouldn't be happy. I tried to imagine him sitting in Cates' tall desk chair, having to oversee the daily operations of the school, and I just didn't see it.

But as his friend, I would support whatever decision he made.

There was one thing Owen said I couldn't forget about: *"So, what did Eli say?"* His accusatory tone suggested he already knew the answer. I felt a twinge of embarrassment when I had to admit I hadn't mentioned the gift to Eli. Yet.

Considering we had separate bank accounts, Eli was often unaware of how I spent my money. Since we'd started renting our house together, though, we'd sort of developed this unspoken rule in which we'd at least consult each other before making any major purchases. At the time, I hadn't considered the microphone to be a very big deal, but Owen's reaction was making me second-guess why I hid this from Eli in the first place.

He deserved to know about it.

I decided to tell him the next morning while we both got ready for work. I was seated cross-legged before our floor-length mirror, straightening my hair, as he stood behind me getting dressed. "Hey," I began, making sure I had his attention before I proceeded. He looked up at my reflection in the mirror as he zipped his jeans. "You know how Owen has that podcast?"

"You've mentioned it, yeah."

"His microphone broke, and he was struggling to put out new episodes because of it."

Eli shrugged as he put on his deodorant. "Okay, why are you telling me this?"

"Well," I said, sliding my straightener down the length of my hair. "I just felt so bad for him, so I got him a new mic for his birthday." I looked up at his face in the mirror.

His eyes widened. "Aren't those expensive?"

"It was around a hundred bucks."

"Seriously?!" He sat his deodorant on his chest of drawers and grabbed his polo shirt from the bed. "I hope he fucking appreciated that."

"He did. I just, you know, I hated that he wasn't able to record anything new for a while. and that podcast is his life, you know? I only wanted to do a nice thing for a friend." I cringed at the way I'd said "you know" too much in an attempt to sound super casual. Whoops.

"You're always doing this." Eli grabbed his belt from a hook on the wall and started sticking it through his belt loops. "You spend way too much on people for birthdays, baby showers, whatever—and people never do the same for you in return. You care too much."

I exhaled. "I know. I can't help it." He was right. I was always going a little over-the-top with gifts. It wasn't just Owen. When my college friend, Jenny, and her husband closed on their new house, I bought them an air fryer as a housewarming gift, despite the fact they both made six figures and could easily afford their own. And when Vicki was pregnant with her first son after having three girls, I couldn't walk into Target without picking up something for the little guy.

Gift-giving was my love language.

"When are you going to let people treat *you*, huh?" he asked, flashing a smile at me in the mirror—the same smile that captured my heart all those years ago in high school. "I doubt he'd do the same for you."

A sense of relief washed over me as Eli shifted his attention from Owen to my extravagant gift-giving habits. All that worrying seemed to have been in vain.

But then Eli added, "On second thought, I'm pretty sure that guy wants to fuck you."

I almost dropped the straightener on my lap. "What?"

"You're talking about Owen, the dude we went on that stupid double-date with, right?" He sat on the bed to put his socks on, and I nodded. "Yeah, he wants you."

I put the straightener down on the floor in front of me. "No he doesn't."

"Please. That poor guy has been in the friendzone with you for years. I promise you, no guy is friends with a girl for that long without wanting something more. But hey, at least he got a new microphone out of it." He was cracking himself up now.

"Stop it," I said, rolling my eyes. I picked up the straightener and went back to fixing my hair. "It's not like that. He's just a co-worker. A friend."

"Whatever you say." Eli came up behind me and bent over, lowering his chin to my shoulder as he wrapped his arms around my chest. "I mean, look at you," he said, eyeing my reflection. "You're probably fighting guys off left and right. Lucky for me, I got to you first. Back when you had those braces and walked the halls with your nose stuck in the fattest books I'd ever seen."

I smiled, elbowing him away. "You're going to make me burn myself." A decade ago, we were everyone's favorite love story at Woodvale High School—the jock fell in love with the wallflower. College separated us when he got a football scholarship at Notre Dame, only for us to find our way back to each other when we were hired by the same school district in our hometown.

Eli picked up his phone and looked at the screen, shaking his head.

"What?" I asked him.

"Nothin'. Just picturing what you'd say if I spent a hundred bucks on one of my female co-workers." He paused to laugh. "This conversation would be going a lot differently."

A knot formed in my stomach. Eli was right—if he bought a gift like that for another woman, especially without discussing it with me first, I'd probably be livid. Now, his reaction almost seemed too forgiving, too understanding. As I continued getting ready for work that morning, I felt a twinge of guilt in the back of my mind. And if Eli's accusation was true, that Owen "wanted" me, that made this situation even worse. It would certainly explain Owen's flustered reaction upon opening the gift.

No. It wasn't like that. I shook my head, dismissing Eli's words as I slung my tote bag over my shoulder on the way out the door that morning. While it was true our friendliness with one another crossed into flirting territory from time to time, it was just harmless fun. Even if there was a slight attraction there, it didn't mean anything.

Probably.

Following that conversation with Eli, I became hyperaware of every lingering glance or touch of the hand between Owen and me. I couldn't shake what Eli had said. *That guy wants to fuck you.* I didn't want to believe it, but every time Owen grinned at me over the top of his coffee cup in the mornings or took a deep breath when my hand barely grazed his arm, it seemed like less and less of a falsehood.

Memories of our past interactions flooded my mind, like the way he blushed after touching my lower back on the way out of Poppy's not so long ago, and how he sided with me at every staff meeting, no matter how unconventional my ideas might have seemed. I swallowed when I remembered how he scraped the snow off my car in the parking lot last winter—he hadn't done it for anyone else.

I decided to put Owen to the test. I sought out to prove Eli wrong, while at the same time, satisfying my own curiosity. I had to know how Owen felt about me. I could say something flirty enough that it couldn't be misread as friendly banter—maybe something a little suggestive, even—and his reaction would tell me everything I needed to know. Right?

My other option was to ask him outright, but that would be too uncomfortable. It would force us to have a conversation neither one of us wanted to have. So I chose a more subtle approach—something that wouldn't put our friendship on the line.

I waited for the perfect opportunity to come along naturally, but it's difficult be flirty when you're surrounded by ten-year-olds. Especially when one of them is chomping at the bit for any sign her two teachers could be in love. Poor Ava Greentree.

The moment finally came the night of the fifth-grade Christmas program. It was easily the most chaotic day of the school year for us, so trying to flirt with Owen was actually the farthest thing from my mind as we ushered the kids onto the stage. It was like herding cats. Half of them were too distracted by finding their parents in the crowd to pay attention to where they were supposed to stand, and the other half were shaking the jingle bells they'd been given despite being instructed to wait for the right moment. I was relieved when they all found their place on the risers, and Owen and I stepped to the side of the stage—they were the music teacher's problem now.

"I don't know how Mrs. Shearer does this every year," I whispered to Owen backstage. We were standing behind the burgundy curtains, just out of view from all the families in the gym.

"I don't know how *I* do this every year," he said as we listened to Mr. Cates welcome the audience. Cates was wearing a red sequined bowtie, looking snazzier than ever. When I realized this would be his last Christmas program as principal, my heart sank a little. Owen must have had the very same thought, because he said, "That could be me up there next year."

I turned to look at him. Snazzy, sequined bowties weren't his thing, but he was wearing a comical tie featuring Santa in swim trunks on the beach. He was holding a Santa hat in his hands, having removed it while we were lining the kids up on the stage. I watched him pull the hat back onto his head and began to grin—knowing the opportunity was right in front of me.

"What?" he asked.

I bit my bottom lip. "If I sit on your lap, can I tell you what I want for Christmas?"

Owen's mouth dropped open. As he studied my face to assess whether I was joking or not, the sound of the kids' goofy rendition of "The 12 Days of Christmas" were drowned out by my own panicked thoughts. Immediately, I knew. I could see Owen's true feelings in the depths of his brown eyes, which were darting back and forth from one of mine to the other, like he couldn't decide which one to focus on.

I forced out a giggle, preparing to say something to indicate it was merely a joke and I'd really appreciate it if we never brought up this awkwardness again.

But then Owen said, "You're getting coal this year."

"Why's that?"

He crossed his arms against his chest, looking me up and down in a way he never had before. "Because what you just said was pretty naughty, Lavely," he said with a low, husky chuckle that made me tingle all the way down to my toes. He was staring

65

at me with this hungry look in his eyes, and it was my turn to drop my mouth open in bewilderment.

This was Owen, my best friend in the entire world. Yet right now, he had me feeling like there was nothing else I'd rather do than sit on his lap and tell him what I want.

What the hell was this feeling?

The kids transitioned into "Jingle Bells," singing and jingling their little hearts out. I eyed Bentley, who was getting a little out of control with his jingle bells, before turning back to Owen. I reached for the curtain beside us, running my fingers down the length of one of the supple folds of fabric. With Owen distracted by my hand, I shifted all my weight to the foot closest to him, saying, "But I've been a good girl all year."

That was pushing it. I knew it was. But Owen's reaction made the risky comment entirely worth it. I watched him squirm before me, unsure of how to respond or where to look. Finally, his eyes settled on my chest, just inches from his. I was wearing a tight-fitted Grinch t-shirt tucked into a long, red skirt, and this ensemble really accentuated my chest. If any other man ogled me the way Owen was at that moment, I'd probably say "my eyes are up here, asshole," but instead, it was turning me on a little.

Owen shoved his hands in his pockets and leaned closer to me, saying, "Guess I need to check my list twice." The words were innocent enough, but his flirtatious tone combined with the way his hot breath felt on my neck made me weak in the knees. Good God.

Just as I opened my mouth to gasp out a reply, a commotion erupted on stage. I whipped around to see what was going on just in time to observe Bentley give Noah a forceful shove, knocking him into another kid, who proceeded to fall to their knees. The kids' voices faded out and Mrs. Shearer's piano-playing came to an abrupt stop.

Oh, Bentley.

Though it was after school hours, the disciplinary rules were the same. This was strike one.

Cates, who'd witnessed the entire thing from the other side of the stage, scooped Bentley up from the back of the risers and carried him over to us. "Why did you do that?" I asked Bentley.

"He hit me with his jingle bells!"

Owen tried to shush him. Just a few feet away, Mrs. Shearer was desperately trying to get the attention back on her so the concert could continue. They picked up with the second verse of "Jingle Bells," singing a little less enthusiastically this time. "I'm sure it was an accident," Owen said.

"No it wasn't!" Bentley proclaimed. "He did it like eight times! And nobody stopped him!" Whoops. Owen and I exchanged glances, knowing why we hadn't exactly been paying attention to the kids. "I hate Noah, I *hate* him!"

Cates, with his hand firmly resting on Bentley's shoulder, said, "Bentley, I'm sensing a pattern with you—you always claim it's Noah's fault, yet nobody ever witnesses his supposed aggression. Are you sure you didn't instigate it this time?"

"Nobody ever witnesses it because Ms. Lavely and Mr. Gardner never notice *anything* except each other," Bentley spit out. My heart dropped to my stomach as Cates looked from me to Owen, his eyes widening. "They were probably back here making out."

"All right, that's enough," Cates said, eyeing Owen, who looked absolutely mortified. He shook his head at Cates, who just adjusted his bowtie with a heavy sigh. "Let's go find your parents, Bentley." Bentley jerked out of Cates' grasp, but he still followed him down the stairs at the side of the stage.

Owen and I turned back around to face the rest of the kids, leaving a full foot of space between us now. I stared straight ahead, nodding along to "Jolly Old St. Nicholas," but I couldn't focus. Three thoughts were circling around my mind: one, Owen had some more-than-platonic feelings for me. That was made clear by his reaction to my flirting. Two, the only thing my little test accomplished was making me aware there was at least some small part of me that wanted him, too.

And three, our attraction to one another was so obvious even our students were picking up on it.

# chapter ten

*owen*

It's not like we hadn't flirted before.

There'd been plenty of sexual innuendos in the past, always playful in their nature and often in front of a crowd. There would always be the occasional "that's a big package you got there" comment sprinkled with a few "oh you're 'coming', huh?" remarks. We kept the interactions friendly enough that they never gave me any kind of mixed signals—it was always clear as crystal Sarah was only joking and I shouldn't read into any hint at attraction.

However, our exchange behind the curtain during the Christmas program completely threw me for a loop. I knew she was just toying with me—that was pretty evident from the way she talked like we were filming the opening scene of a cheesy Christmas porn video. She hadn't meant it. At least, not at first.

When I dished it right back, I noticed something shift in her. I'd caught her off guard, too. Maybe she'd expected me to laugh it off or change the subject, but I was enjoying it entirely too much. And so was she, if her pointy nipples were any indication of her arousal.

The next morning, it appeared things were back to normal between us. Sarah was so excited about the upcoming holiday issue of the Grissom Gazette she wouldn't talk about anything else. I enthusiastically went along with it, hyping her up to the best of my ability, despite my three and a half hours of sleep.

But in the teacher's lounge that day, when I was in the middle of a pre-Christmas meltdown with my head down on the table, Sarah did something else she'd never done before—she absentmindedly scratched my back while I was slumped over the table, giggling at my melodrama. I froze. "You okay there, Gardner?" she asked, flipping through a catalog of classroom furniture with her other hand.

She must not have been able to see the goosebumps on the back of my neck.

We weren't alone in this room, which is why I found her behavior especially odd. It was a good thing Cates wasn't in there, considering I'd just sent him an email assuring him he had nothing to worry about regarding Sarah and me, and Bentley's comments were just due to his vivid imagination.

I lifted my head and sat back, seeing stars. Another downside of being thirty—you can't sit up too fast without getting dizzy. I tapped my watch to reveal my Christmas break countdown. "Eight days. Three hours. Twenty-four minutes. Aaaand… ten seconds."

"Are you going to make it?"

"It's not looking very promising." My vision started to return to normal, and I looked around the room to see if anyone was paying attention to us. Everyone seemed pretty preoccupied with their lunch or their own conversations. "My kids are literally climbing the walls."

Sarah turned a page in the catalog. "Okay, and what are you doing for behavior management?" she asked, ignoring my improper use of the word "literally"—a struggle I was sure posed a challenge for someone with a master's degree in English.

I pinched the bridge of my nose. "I told them if they didn't chill out, Krampus would come snatch them up."

She glared at me like I was an idiot, but across from us, Ms. Devin let out a giggle. Okay, maybe someone was paying attention to us. "How's that working?" she asked.

"I expect the phone calls from concerned parents to start rolling in by 4:00."

Ignoring Ms. Devin, Sarah turned to me. "Did I tell you about my desk elves? They're just like the desk monsters I did at Halloween." Back in October, Sarah had glued googly eyes to some black and orange craft pom poms and turned them into a reward system for her class. "I'm doing the same thing now, but for Christmas. Everyone got a tissue box to decorate and turn into a little house for their elves. And they get to have the desk elves out if they're quiet and getting their work done. If the noise level is too high, they have to put them away. It's a whole-class reward system. You should try something like that, Owen."

"Desk elves?" Ms. Devin asked.

"Yeah," Sarah answered, tucking her hair behind her ears. "I just, um, hot glued googly eyes on some big red and green pom poms."

"For all of your students?" Ms. Devin raised her eyebrows. "That sounds like too much work."

I took a sip of my Dr. Pepper and grinned. "You're talking to the woman who founded a club just to help one troubled kid gain a sense of belonging," I interjected. "She doesn't know the definition of 'too much work.'"

Ms. Devin shook her head in disbelief. "We don't get paid enough for that, girl." At first, I chuckled, wanting to agree, but then I saw Sarah's face. She wasn't amused. I was only trying to praise her, not throw her under the bus.

"That's not why I did it," she said in a monotone voice, flipping a page of the catalog so fast the page ripped. It was starting to feel like Ms. Devin and I were ganging up on her classroom management strategies, so I decided to change the subject.

I reached for a copy of last month's Grissom Gazette in the middle of the table and flipped it over with a sigh. "Anyone got a pen? I can't resist a crossword puzzle."

Sarah was ignoring me. Ms. Devin, on the other hand, reached into the pocket of her dress and slid a pen across the table to me. "You'd think the Grissom Teacher of the Month would have his own pen," she said, clicking her tongue. I just smiled as I wrote the word GRAVY in the crossword puzzle. Ms. Devin looked over her own copy of the Grissom Gazette at me. "Today I learned this school has a Robotics Club."

"Yep," I said, eyeing Sarah again. She hadn't turned a page in her catalog for a while. "We finished our crane robots this week," I continued. "We had them lifting all kinds of stuff—books, water bottles, you name it—it took me forever to get my room back in order afterwards."

"That's amazing. Now you've got me wishing I could join your club," Ms. Devin said, flipping her blonde hair over her shoulder and leaning onto her elbows on the table.

"You'll have to fight one of the fourth or fifth-graders for their slot."

"I can take 'em," she said with a laugh. "I wish I could see those cranes. My students would love them."

"Well," I said, trying to come up with a plan. "I could load one up on a cart and come do a demonstration for your class, if you want." Ms. Devin loved this idea, so we arranged for a time for me to visit her class during my prep period the following day.

"Thank you so much, Owen. They're going to love it," she said, getting up from the table.

"Anytime."

She and all of the lower-grade teachers started filtering out of the room since their students would be returning from lunch recess soon. After a few minutes, only Sarah and I remained. And she was giving me a long, hard stare.

"What?"

She sat the catalog down in front of her. "What the hell was that?"

"What was what?"

"You and Kendall."

I blinked. "Who's Kendall?"

Sarah brought her hand to her forehead in frustration. "Oh my god—Teacher Barbie? She's worked here since August. How do you not know her first name?"

"Okay, my bad," I said, chuckling at her Teacher Barbie comparison. "But what are you talking about?"

"The flirting," she said, like I should have known. "I've never even seen you talk to her before until today. I half-expected her to crawl across the table and rip your clothes off right here in the teacher's lounge." I couldn't be sure, but I thought I was picking up on a little bit of jealousy from Sarah. Or, at the very least, strong disapproval.

"I just offered to do a demo for her class. I'd hardly call that flirting," I said with a shrug, reaching for my empty Dr. Pepper can. I glanced at my watch before looking back up at Sarah, whose lips were pressed tightly together in a straight line. Could it be she wanted to be the only teacher at Grissom allowed to flirt with me? It made me grin.

"Well," she said in a huff, pushing the catalog away from her on the table. "I know flirting when I see it."

She did, huh?

I got up from my chair and walked over to the trash to throw away my empty soda can. And then, after glancing around to ensure we were still completely alone in this room, I approached Sarah from behind and leaned over her, putting my hand on the table beside hers. Lowering my mouth to her ear, I whispered, "You sure about that?" I waited for her to turn her head, knowing it would bring our faces dangerously close together. Her breath hitched, giving me the exact reaction I'd wanted. I hovered there for just a second or two before I tore my hand off the table, turned away, and walked out of the teacher's lounge.

She started it.

# chapter eleven



The last week of school before Christmas break was always a little crazy, but the children were especially feral this year for some reason. Maybe it was the weather? Temperatures had been hovering around freezing all week, and they were stuck inside for recess every day. These kids were desperate for some fresh air and physical activity, but they weren't getting either.

They'd been putting all of this pent-up energy into desecrating the desk elves I'd made for them. By now, most of them had lost at least one of their googly eyes, and some of my more creative and destructive students had found ways to turn them into something else entirely—giving them eye patches, diapers, and swords made out of construction paper. I'd be upset if their creations weren't so impressive.

As I set up the classroom on the final day of school before break, passing out the remaining un-mutilated desk elves, I took a deep breath. I only had to make it through one more day. And these kids would be loaded up on sugar cookies and fruit punch, so it was going to be nearly impossible to get them to focus on their final test of the semester. It was also pajama day, which for some reason was always an added distraction.

I was wearing a cozy reindeer onesie complete with antlers attached to its hood. It's funny, the things you can get away with wearing when you're an elementary school teacher.

The only downside was the staring from strangers when I had to pump gas on my way to work that morning. "I'm a teacher," I told the curious middle-aged man at the pump next to mine. He just laughed at me.

It was worth it for the kids' reactions as they poured into the school. Most of them laughed, and some of them called me Rudolph. "I'm not Rudolph, silly," I said, touching my nose. "See? No red nose. I'm Dasher."

Across the hall, Owen took a sip of his coffee and muttered, "I would've guessed you were Vixen." I might not have had a red nose, but my cheeks were certainly turning a bright shade of pink. I smiled and shook my head at him but otherwise ignored his comment as I greeted the next student to walk in.

As for Owen, he was wearing a navy bathrobe over his regular clothes. Minimal effort. "Really, Mr. Gardner? Just a bathrobe?"

"I'm sorry, my reindeer onesie is out for dry cleaning."

"You're just jealous of my butt-flap," I said, turning around to show him how this onesie had a flap over my butt, with three buttons securing it at the top. Of course, I was wearing some shorts beneath this thing to prevent any wardrobe malfunctions—two years ago, I wore a cow onesie for Halloween, and one of the butt-flap buttons popped right off when I bent over to help a student with his test. Thankfully, Vicki had come to my rescue with a safety pin, but I wasn't going to chance it again.

"Wow, Ms. Lavely," Owen said, smiling over his mug as I finished wiggling my butt. "How very, um… convenient."

I grinned back at him from across the hall over the kids' heads. Our Santa conversation backstage at the Christmas program seemed to ignite something between us. And maybe the flame had always been there, but it was like we were finally giving ourselves permission to acknowledge it, allow it to burn.

We were careful to never cross the line, though it seemed that line was constantly being erased and redrawn farther away.

Over the past few days, Owen had been finding every excuse to touch me, like picking a speck of glitter off of my cheekbone after I'd spent the morning doing a Christmas craft, or not bothering to move his leg when our knees touched beneath the table in the teacher's lounge. Then again, I didn't pull my leg away, either.

And on Wednesday, when he wore his glasses to school because his contacts were irritating his eyes, I told him he looked handsome in them. On Thursday, he wore them again. When I asked him if his contacts were still bothering him, his answer was merely, "No."

He'd worn them for me.

"You going to wear that to the party tonight?" Owen asked, raising his eyebrows at the reindeer onesie in amusement.

"It's so comfy, I just might."

The annual staff Christmas party was an event I'd been looking forward to all month. It was always held in the party room in the basement of La Cocina, Woodvale's most popular Mexican restaurant. Our meals were covered by the district, along with one beer or cocktail. This was considered our Christmas bonus. They always set up a bar for us downstairs, and everyone got pretty toasted and sang karaoke. Even Mr. Cates.

It was always fun seeing everyone outside the walls of Grissom Elementary, semi-dressed up and just letting loose. Not thinking about lesson plans, IEP meetings, or submitting grades. Just tacos and tequila.

"Is, um… is Eli coming tonight?" Owen asked just as the 8:05 bell rang. The question caught me a little off guard.

"Yeah," I said, tucking my hair behind my ears. "Why wouldn't he?"

Owen put his free hand in the pocket of his bathrobe. "I was just wondering. I mean, he didn't come with you last year." I was surprised Owen remembered. But it was true, Eli didn't accompany me to the party last Christmas. He said he'd had a rough semester and didn't want to spend the first night of winter break at some stupid party.

However, Eli didn't complain at all about having to go to the party this year. He was even willing to wear the outfit I'd hung on the closet door for him this morning without making a single "I don't need you to dress me" comment. His uncharacteristic enthusiasm for attending this event was a little strange, but I decided it was best not to question it.

He would be by my side all night, which meant Owen was going to have to tone himself down. Way down. "Don't look so disappointed, Gardner," I said, noticing the way his smile had faded as he went to close his classroom door.

"I'm not. He should be there with you." He stopped and picked at some of the peeling paint around his doorframe. "But you *are* different when he's around."

"You mean you and I can't flirt," I blurted.

He didn't say anything right away. He just kept picking at the chipped paint, causing a few flakes to fall to the ground. I'd heard him chastising his students for doing that very thing before. Nervous habit, I guess. Finally, he looked up and said, "I just want you to be able to have a good time. And, I don't know, it seems like he prevents you from doing that sometimes."

This had been stewing in his head for a while. It was clear he didn't like Eli, and he never had. At least now I understood why.

Behind me, my class was starting to get noisy. "I need to get in there," I said, glancing over my shoulder. And, turning back to him, I said, "I'm not going to let anything prevent me from enjoying myself tonight."

"Good."

We both had our hands on our doorknobs now, neither of us making a move to leave the hallway. Like so many times before, Owen's eyes expressed more than his mouth ever would. If he someday found the courage to say the words on the tip of his tongue, there'd be no looking back—which I knew was exactly the reason he kept them to himself.

Just before he pulled his door closed, he turned to face me, saying, "It's going to be a good night, Lavely."

# chapter twelve

## owen

*Tonight's the night.*

I walked down the dimly lit stairwell into the party room at La Cocina knowing this would be the final day Sarah wouldn't know my true feelings for her. She probably had an inkling. But after tonight, there would be no room left for uncertainty.

It was time to put it all on the line.

I had no idea how I would do it or what I'd even say, but I was determined to find some way to pull her aside and let her know. My confidence she reciprocated my feelings had only grown over the last week. She was giving me every indication she had no intention of moving forward with Eli, or so I hoped.

And if I were wrong? Well, at least she'd know how I felt, and vice versa. We'd have all of Christmas break to put it behind us and, hopefully, return to school in January with some sense of normalcy.

Either I'd get the woman of my dreams or I'd get the closure I needed to move on, once and for all.

Sarah wasn't at the restaurant yet when I arrived. The tables were arranged into four long rows and covered in alternating red and green tablecloths. Each one was decorated with miniature foil Christmas trees and a scattering of candy canes and jingle bells. There were baskets of chips with salsa sitting out, which everybody was already diving into. At one end of the room, there was a small dancefloor in the corner with a TV and karaoke machine. There was a makeshift bar set up at the other side of the room, which was just two folding tables positioned in an L-shape with a limited selection of beer and liquor. The poor bartender had no idea how completely unhinged some of these teachers were about to get after just a little booze.

With it still being so early, most of the other teachers hadn't found their seats yet. There was a small group gathered by the bar, and others were crowding around a table of giveaway prizes. Lori, Cates, and their spouses were standing near the karaoke machine, chatting away.

I approached Heath Lawson, one of the few other male teachers, who was standing next to the bar. He'd been teaching third grade at GES for three or four years. I didn't have much in common with the guy, but we always ended up chatting at these types of things. "Hey man," he said, speaking up over the loud Christmas jazz music playing over the speakers. "Some of us are getting the night started with tequila shots. You in?"

It was a little early for that, but I was feeling a sense of spontaneity. "Yeah, why the hell not?" And before I knew it, I was taking shots with him, Kendall Devin, and a couple of other teachers. As I sucked on my lime slice, Heath leaned over to me and said, "We've established a 'singles' table over there."

He nodded toward the end of one of the middle tables, where there were already a few coats draped over chairs. He was implying I should join them. Before I could say I would likely sit with Sarah and Eli when they arrived, he was waving for me to follow them all back to their table. I sat at the end of their group, though, hoping Sarah would see me when she arrived. I considered hanging my coat on the back of the chair beside me to save her a seat, but that seemed ridiculous.

"Owen showed me his robots the other day," Kendall was saying to Heath. They were both seated across from me. Kendall reached for a tortilla chip. "And now all my kids want to be engineers when they grow up."

"You got a robot demo, huh?" Heath asked her, looking at me. "What kind of strings do I gotta pull around here to get something like that for my third graders?"

I took a chip from the basket and dipped it in salsa. "We could arrange something after…" Sarah had just walked in the room, and I completely lost my train of thought. Everything else faded into the background. She was wearing a dark green dress that hung off her shoulders, exposing her collarbone, and there was something different about her hair—some of it was pulled back, with a couple of curls framing her face. Her lips were bright red, which was far different from her everyday school look.

Goddamn it. Could I really look this beautiful woman in the eyes and tell her I was in love with her?

I looked down, realizing I was still hovering over the salsa bowl with my tortilla chip, and I'd completely forgotten what I was about to say. But that didn't matter, because Cates got on the microphone and asked everyone to find their seats because he had an announcement he wanted to make. Before I could catch Sarah's attention, Vicki Santiago whisked her and Eli off to a different table at the other end of the room to sit with her and her husband. Sarah didn't even notice me before she took her seat.

This was merely a minor setback. So we wouldn't be sitting together—no big deal. I'd have to come up with an excuse to get her alone, somehow. Before Cates began his announcement, the server came to our table for everyone's drink order. I asked for a beer—I might be needing the extra liquid encouragement.

Cates waited another moment or two for everyone to find their seats and get quiet. "Hello, folks," he said. "I wanted to say a few words before we got started. First of all, I want to thank Lori for putting these decorations together for us tonight. Didn't she do a nice job?"

Everyone sat their drinks down to give Lori a round of applause.

"Also," Cates continued, "I want to remind everyone to drink responsibly tonight. The second you walk up those stairs, you're representing GES. Please, I implore you, get a ride home with a colleague if you've had too much to drink. Everyone look out for one another."

"As if any of us are going to be sober at the end of the night," I heard Kendall mutter to Heath. He smiled as he took a drink of the cocktail in his hand.

"Lastly, I have a big announcement I've been wanting to make, and I thought tonight was the perfect time." He paused to glance at his husband, who gave him a thumbs up. "After twenty-two years as principal, and thirty-six years at Grissom Elementary altogether, it's time for me to finally hang up my hat. I am officially retiring at the end of May."

There were audible gasps all around. Across from me, I heard Heath say, "Holy shit, I wasn't expecting that." Cates went on to say how it had been a pleasure working with us all, and Lori started a standing ovation. All around me, some teachers started tearing up as we applauded. I felt a lump forming in my own throat. It was going to be the end of an era— Cates would be leaving behind a legacy, that's for sure.

I swallowed, imagining myself filling his shoes. Trying to picture all of these same people giving me a standing ovation when I would one day retire. Would it be just like this?

Once things quieted down, Cates said, "Now, let's make tonight the best Christmas party yet." The room erupted into cheers. And just before we all sat back down, I caught Sarah's eye from across the room. First, we exchanged smiles, and then she scrunched her face up in an overdramatic frown—which I assumed was in reference to us being seated at different tables. I just shrugged, and then I pointed at my watch. She looked confused. So I held up my pointer finger to indicate "wait," and she nodded.

We'd just had an entire conversation while standing 30 feet apart.

I was still grinning to myself as we all looked over our menus. The server was already approaching our end of the table, so I didn't have a lot of time to decide. Eventually, I settled on ordering nachos and a second Modelo. "Damn, Gardner's gonna get wasted tonight," Heath said once the server picked up our menus and moved onto the next table.

Kendall peered over at me, laughing as she ate another tortilla chip. "So, who do you think is going to replace Cates?"

Heath shook his head. "Probably some outside person we're all going to hate."

"You don't think it'll be someone in this room?" Kendall asked.

He looked around. "Watch it be Eli Meeks. He's got that charisma."

"The football coach?" Kendall scoffed. "God, I hope not."

At this point, I had to butt into their conversation. "Please, it's not going to be Eli Meeks," I said, thanking the server for the beer he handed me.

"Why, do you know something?" Heath asked.

"Oh, no," I said, pausing to take a swig. I shifted in my seat. "I just know Eli's charm isn't going to work on someone like Cates. Or the superintendent."

"It sure worked on Sarah," Kendall muttered.

"Oh yeah," Heath said, looking their direction. "I didn't even think about that. If he were principal, she wouldn't be able to date him. Pretty sure that's against the rules."

I looked over my shoulder at Sarah, who was laughing at something Vicki had just said. Of course I'd thought about that. If Sarah and I were to ever acknowledge we were more than just friends, I wouldn't be able to become principal of this school. Entering into a relationship with her would give me no choice but to pursue making *STEM for the Win* my full-time focus.

I'd have my dream woman *and* my dream job.

The longer I sat there and thought about it, the more I realized it was all entirely up to me. *"Manifest it,"* I imagined Sarah telling me. As I ate and listened to Heath and Kendall gossip about everybody in the room, I repeated two sentences over and over in my mind:

*I'm going to get the girl.*

*I'm going to get the job of my dreams.*

By the end of the meal, I was starting to believe both of those statements. Or it might have just been the alcohol starting to do its job. Either way, I had all the confidence of a fifth-grader who thought they could plagiarize from Wikipedia and get away with it.

When Sarah walked up to the bar alone, I saw my opportunity. I looked over at Eli, who was busy talking to Vicki's husband. Perfect. I made my way to the bar area and sidled up behind her in line. "Gonna ignore me all night, Lavely?" I asked.

"Owen!" She turned around and threw her arms around my neck for a sloppy hug. Apparently I wasn't the only one who'd been indulging in a little too much alcohol. "I'm so sad we aren't sitting together this time," she said, moving closer to the bar as the people in line in front of us scooted forward.

"I'm at the 'singles' table," I said, nodding toward Heath, Kendall, and the other hopelessly single teachers. "And I'm getting all the hottest goss' about the school."

Sarah laughed. "Sounds like you need to take a tequila shot with me."

"Actually," I said, sticking my hands in the front pockets of my dress pants. I glanced over at Eli, who was still in the middle of some story with Vicki's husband. And then I looked back at Sarah, who was staring up at me, waiting for me to continue. Even with the added height of her heels, she was at eye level with my chin. "Can we talk outside for a sec?"

"Outside?" she asked, pushing one of her curls out of her face with a smile. "It's freezing out there."

"Upstairs, then?" I asked.

When she saw the look on my face, her own expression gradually became more serious. "Sure," she said, glancing over her shoulder at Eli. And she followed me up the stairs to the hallway at the back of the main restaurant. Without hesitating, I took her by the hand and led her toward the farthest end of that dark hallway, away from the kitchen and the bathrooms. I couldn't risk being interrupted. This was too important.

"Sorry," I said, letting go. "I had to get away from all the noise."

"It's okay." Sarah bit her bottom lip. My hand—the one that just held hers—was tingling. "But you're making me a little nervous right now."

"I'm sorry," I said again. She stared up into my eyes in anticipation, probably somewhat aware of what I might be about to say. I hoped she couldn't notice how much I was already sweating. "I've just been thinking tonight, and…" I cleared my throat. "If I go after this principal position, it would mean I could never date anyone at Grissom. That would be completely off the table. Forever."

Sarah didn't say anything. She didn't even move or blink—she was frozen before me, all the color draining from her usually warm complexion. She knew.

So I continued. "And I just want to know what you think I should do. Should I go after this job, Sarah?"

Her lips parted and she finally broke eye contact, staring down at my chest. "I mean, I don't—you just—don't you want to do the podcast, anyway? Isn't that the reason you've been having second thoughts this whole time?"

"Yeah, but…." I said, tilting my head to the side. "That's not the only reason."

Sarah put her hand up to her forehead, pushing one of her loose curls out of her eyes. "I don't know why you're telling me this."

"Come on," I urged, taking a step closer to her. "Are you really going to make me say the words out loud?" It was starting to feel like this hallway was spinning around us as I waited for some kind of reaction from her. She brought her eyes up to mine, still silent, and lifted her hand to reach for my tie. My heart raced as she gingerly straightened my tie with one hand, preparing a response. Maybe I could coax it out of her.

I reached toward her, putting my fingers under her chin to tilt her face upward. Forcing her to look at me. "Sarah," I whispered.

But before I could get the next words out, there was a noise behind me—loud, running footsteps coming up the stairwell. I dropped my hand just as Vicki appeared in the hallway, all wide-eyed and frazzled. "Sarah!" she yelled. "I thought I saw you come up here. Eli's looking for you." Her eyes darted back and forth from me to Sarah, indicating she was picking up on the intensity of the moment.

"Can you tell him to wait a sec?" Sarah asked, widening her eyes at Vicki.

"Um, no—he really needs you to come downstairs. Now."

Sarah muttered something under her breath as she slid past me. She avoided my gaze, following Vicki into the stairwell. I remained in that dark hallway for a moment, my fingertips grazing the rough surface of the wall, trying to make sense of what had just happened. Or almost happened. I hadn't gotten the words completely out, though it seemed she understood exactly what I meant to say.

And I got the feeling that if we hadn't been interrupted, she might have even reciprocated.

I followed the wall with my hand, starting to feel the effects of the tequila shot and two beers. I really should've eaten more today—I was already buzzed. I made it to the top of the stairwell, smiling as I remembered how it felt to have her hand touching my chest when she straightened my tie. Downstairs, a voice boomed over the karaoke speakers. "Can I get everyone's attention for a minute?"

I walked down the first few steps, gripping the railing tight. It sounded like Eli.

"Sarah, from the moment I very first laid eyes on you in fourth period Algebra II all those years ago, I knew deep in my heart that you were the one for me. And although we spent some years apart—I'm so glad fate brought us back together."

Oh no. I took three more steps and listened.

"We've had plenty of ups and downs, but through all that, one thing has remained clear: you and me? We're soulmates. And now, I can't think of anything I'd rather do than spend the rest of my life with you by my side. Sarah Jane Lavely, will you marry me?"

I couldn't get down the remaining stairs fast enough. It felt like I floated down them, like my legs weren't even my own. Somehow, they managed to get me to the bottom step, where I stopped and looked over at the karaoke area. There Eli was, down on one knee with a ring in his hand in front of Sarah, whose mouth was slightly agape. My heart pounded in my chest, drowning out the cheers that were already erupting in this room. Couldn't they all see she was hesitating? Or was I the only one who noticed the way she leaned ever-so-slightly away from him, trying to process what was happening to her right now?

As she looked down at Eli, a smile slowly began to form on her face, but her eyes lacked their usual sparkle. "Yes," she choked out with a laugh. And Eli slipped the diamond ring on her finger before scooping her up, twirling her around, and kissing her in front of the cheering crowd.

It felt like the room was getting smaller. The walls were closing in all around me and the floor beneath my feet seemed to undulate. I touched the wall by the stairs with one hand, trying to steady myself. As everyone else crowded around the newly engaged couple to congratulate them, I suddenly felt like there wasn't enough oxygen in this room. I grabbed my coat while everyone was preoccupied and made my way up the stairs and out of the restaurant.

She said yes.

Sarah was going to marry Eli.

I shook my head, trying to plan what to do next. It didn't seem right to leave—I could be an adult about this. If I left now, everyone would speculate why and many of them would probably come to the proper conclusion. I just needed to collect my thoughts for a few minutes. And then I'd go back in there and pretend to be happy. Sarah was my best friend, after all, and she just got engaged—I'd have to congratulate her at some point tonight.

So instead of bolting, I made my way over to a bench in front of the restaurant, where I sat and buried my head in my hands. There was frost forming on the grass between the sidewalk and the parking lot, but I hardly noticed the cold. I thought about Sarah, replaying every interaction from the last few weeks in my head, trying to figure out how I'd ended up here. I'd been misinterpreting her this entire time. Moments ago, I had thought she was on the verge of telling me she wanted to be with me, too, but reality quickly shattered that delusion. Because no matter how much we flirted and joked around, Eli was the man for her.

I was such an idiot.

A crowd of people approached the restaurant from the parking lot, and I pulled my feet out of their way so they could pass. I probably looked pathetic sitting there—I thought I caught a glimpse of one of them giving me a sympathetic smile as they walked past. I sat up a little straighter, trying to work out how I would act when I went back down there. As the crowd of people entered La Cocina, Kendall stepped out, her phone pressed to her ear.

"Sorry, I couldn't hear anything you said in there," she was saying. "One of my co-workers just got engaged and everyone's freaking out." Her back was turned to me. I sat still on the bench, trying to be as quiet as possible, as she continued her conversation. "Anyway, just tell Mom we can exchange gifts on Christmas Eve this year. It'll be fine."

I hadn't wanted Kendall to notice me sitting there, but she looked my direction just before she turned to go back inside. She said good-bye and hung up, sticking her phone in the pocket of her black skirt. "Owen?" She took a few steps in my direction. "Aren't you freezing out here?"

"I don't really mind the cold," I said, crossing my arms against my chest.

"Okay, Elsa," she said with a giggle as she walked over to me. She sat beside me on the bench, tucking her hands beneath her legs. "Are you okay right now?"

"I just needed some fresh air. I was feeling claustrophobic in there."

Kendall stared at me for a moment. I could have been mistaken, but she looked like she knew exactly what I was upset about. It was probably obvious. However, she didn't mention it. I watched as she reached into the pocket of her skirt and pulled out a pink flask. "God, I love skirts with pockets," she said, unscrewing the lid of the flask and handing it to me.

I took it from her hand. "What's in this?"

"Take a sip and find out," she said, crossing her legs. I looked from the flask to her face and back to the flask, shaking my head at her before taking a swig. Whatever it was, it burned going down my esophagus. I coughed, handing it back to her. "Wow," I said. "Kindergarten teachers—who knew?"

She laughed. "It's Jim Beam," she said, taking a sip herself. She handled it better than I had. "I knew the drinks were going to be overpriced tonight and I wasn't about to sit through this stupid thing sober."

"Smart."

"So," she said, settling back into the bench some more. "Are you going to apply for the principal position?"

I slowly nodded. "I think so."

"Good," she said. "I think you'd make a great one."

We sat in silence for a moment, and she passed me the flask again. The whiskey went down easier this time, suffusing me with a comforting warmth. Beside me, Kendall was shivering and rubbing her bare upper arms. As we sat there passing that flask back and forth, I wondered why she didn't just go back inside. However, when I noticed her gradually and deliberately inching closer, I began to understand her choice to remain here with me. I could have moved away, but I didn't. "Do you sneak this flask into work?" I asked, passing it back to her.

"No," she said, giggling. "And if I did, do you think I'd admit it to my future boss?"

"Don't jinx me." I watched her screw the lid back on the flask, which was almost empty now. She put it back in her skirt pocket, moving even closer to me as she straightened back up. "Hey, tell me something," I said, struggling to focus on her caramel-colored eyes. My head was feeling fuzzy now. "How did that magician make you disappear?"

She threw her head back in laughter. "It's a secret."

"I need to know," I said, my words beginning to slur as I put my arm on the back of the bench behind her.

"I'll never tell," she said, batting her eyelashes at me over her shoulder.

This woman wanted me. There was no guessing about it— all the signs were there. The way her knee was pressing into my thigh. How she couldn't stop giggling. Her insistence to remain here with me in thirty-degree weather with her exposed arms now covered in goosebumps. Everything about her behavior gave me a clear invitation to make a move. So, now that any chance I thought I had with Sarah had dissipated into thin air, I leaned closer to Kendall and asked her, "Can you keep another secret?"

Her eyes brimmed with desire. "Absolutely."

And then, after a quick glance around to make sure none of our co-workers were outside, I pressed my lips against hers in a fervent kiss. She kissed back, slipping her hands under my jacket to pull me in closer. I rubbed her ice-cold arms before dropping one hand between her knees, inching up her skirt.

This felt nice. Not perfect. But nice.

# chapter thirteen

sarah

By 9:00, the drunken karaoke phase of the party had officially commenced. Eli bought a round of tequila shots for everyone to celebrate our engagement, and even Mr. Cates was pretty toasted. His infectious, deep belly laugh echoed through the basement, only making the people around him laugh even harder. His husband kept shaking his head, but even he couldn't resist the urge to crack a smile.

In the midst of all the revelry, my head was spinning in bewilderment. The night had been a blur, starting from the moment Owen whisked me upstairs to talk alone. And when Eli knelt before me, it was like I was dreaming or watching someone else's marriage proposal unfold. It couldn't be real. And as Eli's question hung in the air and everyone's eyes were fixed on me, I couldn't dare look up. I didn't even know if Owen was in the room when I choked out the word "yes," my heart heavy with uncertainty.

His interrupted confession lingered in my mind, entangling with my mixed emotions about the proposal. I so desperately wanted to hear the words he was about to say when he held my chin in his hand, but the night had taken quite a turn. The moment slipped away—and evidently, so did he.

I scanned the room for his face. After the proposal, I was immediately swept up in a frenzy of congratulatory remarks and endless fawning over my engagement ring. When I finally got a moment to breathe and look around, Owen was nowhere to be seen. Maybe he missed the entire thing?

"So, did you suspect he was going to ask you tonight?" Vicki asked as she slumped into her chair beside me, having just finished her karaoke performance of "Hit Me With Your Best Shot." This was her first night out without children in six months, a fact she'd mentioned at least three times, and she'd had more tequila than any of us, I think. In contrast, I had sobered up pretty quickly after that surprise proposal.

"Um, no," I said, twisting the ring around my finger. It was a half-size too big, and the enormous princess-cut diamond felt heavy on my finger. Had Eli's behavior lately shown any indication at all he planned to propose, besides his willingness to accompany me to this party? I guess I'd been too wrapped up in the newspaper club and this sudden weirdness with Owen to notice any conspiring on Eli's part. But there I was, engaged. To Eli Meeks. Little sixteen-year-old Sarah, with SL + EM written inside all her notebooks, would be so thrilled to know this was her fate.

Eager to change the subject, I opened my mouth to ask Vicki if she wanted me to get her a water when I noticed Owen returning to his table. His cheeks and ears were as red as the tablecloth in front of him as he unzipped his leather coat. Had he really been outside this entire time? I watched him drape the coat on the back of the chair beside Heath and immediately jump into the conversation at his table. As he spoke to the people around him, he used his hands to tell some story in this lively, animated way, making every single one of them laugh. Especially Kendall Devin, who looked up at him with a wide-eyed smile.

I wished I could hear the story he was telling them. Was it the one about how he wore two different brown shoes and didn't notice until after lunch, when one of his students pointed it out? Or could it be about the student who used his school-provided laptop to order a pizza, which Owen and Mr. Cates ended up eating in his office?

Maybe it was about the racoons who lived in the dumpster behind his house—he had a lot of great stories about them. When I saw him mimicking an animal climbing something, I knew exactly what he was saying—it was about the ramp he made out of cardboard for the raccoons to help them escape the dumpster when they were trapped two weeks ago. As much as he liked to call those little guys the bane of his existence, he felt compelled to save their lives.

"You can't stop looking at your ring, can you?" Vicki asked, elbowing me in the ribs. I hadn't realized I'd been staring down at my hands. "Don't gaze at it too long, you might go blind."

"I'll try not to," I said with a little laugh.

Owen didn't leave that table for the rest of the night. Others were coming and going, but he was glued to his chair, never so much as glancing in my direction. I practically begged him with my eyes—*look at me. Talk to me.* I was telepathically screaming at him from across the room.

Unsurprisingly, it didn't work.

I don't know what I expected. After what almost transpired between us upstairs, it's not like I was counting on him to pretend to be happy for me, congratulating the two of us and fawning over my ring like everyone else. In actuality, I thought he might bail on this party altogether the second Eli slid the ring onto my finger. I wouldn't blame him if he had.

But there he was, laughing and having a good time. If he was feeling jealous, he wasn't letting it show. I was just starting to think I'd misinterpreted our conversation in the hallway when I caught a brief flutter of sadness on his face during a lull in conversation at his table. He stared at his glass, stirring the ice with his straw, seemingly lost in thought. There was a crinkle in between his brows, and I knew all too well that was a telltale sign he was feeling distressed.

Seconds later, he leaned in to listen to something Kendall was whispering, and the lines in his face smoothed out, replaced with a gentle smile. I swallowed as Owen turned and replied to her, saying something that made her rake her fingers through her long, blonde hair with a giggle. She never took her eyes off of him.

That made two of us.

By the end of the night, when the party was wrapping up and all the giveaway prizes had been awarded, I finally accepted that Owen was intentionally avoiding me. There was no other way to explain his behavior. We'd been to so many staff parties together, and he was never distant like this, even when Eli was glued to my side. Owen still found a way to talk to me and make sure I was having a good time. Always. Until tonight.

And that's why I cornered him as he was putting on his coat. Eli was preoccupied, deep in conversation about the Colts with Vicki's husband. "Hey, Owen," I said. He looked up at me with wide eyes, adjusting his coat collar. It didn't dawn on me until that moment that I hadn't prepared anything to say. But he was waiting. "I just, um—wanted to say I'm sorry we didn't get to talk more tonight."

"It's okay," he said. "You were caught up in all the excitement. Oh, congratulations, by the way."

"Thanks."

As I spun the loose ring around my finger, Owen fiddled with the zipper on his coat and looked over his shoulder at Heath and Kendall, who were making their way up the stairs. It was clear he was desperate to get away from me.

Eli approached me from behind, throwing his arm around my shoulder. "You ready to get out of here, babe?"

Owen extended his hand toward Eli. "Hey man," he said as they shook hands. "Congratulations on the engagement."

"Thanks. Say, are you going to go after that principal position?" Eli's drunkenness amplified the volume of his voice to a level just short of yelling.

Owen zipped his coat all the way up and stuck his hands in his pockets. "Yeah, I think I probably will." And, with a subtle glance in my direction, he added, "I don't see any reason not to."

"Hell yeah, man," Eli said. "You ought to shake things up at that school. Give my girl a raise. She's got a wedding to plan."

Owen let out a hollow laugh, and I could only stare at the ground. I pulled on Eli's arm, indicating I was ready to go. Now. Thankfully, he caught on, and we all said good-bye and headed upstairs. When we reached the parking lot, Owen muttered "Merry Christmas" and jogged toward his car. But I watched him make his way past it and quickly hop into the passenger seat of a black Nissan Altima I'd seen in the parking lot at school before. Maybe Heath's?

"Are you going to tell your mom?" Eli asked as I started his truck. I hated driving this monstrous thing, but he'd had a few too many to drink, and I had no choice.

"Tell her what?"

"Babe." He slapped his thigh. "I thought I was the drunk one."

"Oh," I said, laughing at my own idiocy. "Let's tell her on Christmas."

As I waited to pull out onto the street, the Nissan pulled up behind us. Traffic was backed up on Fourth Street like always, especially this time of year, so I sat there for a couple of minutes waiting for my chance to pull out.

But when an opening came along, I missed my opportunity. Because the light of a passing car perfectly illuminated the face of the driver of the car behind me for a solid three seconds.

It was just long enough for me to recognize Kendall Devin in the driver's seat, throwing her head back in laughter at whatever funny thing Owen just said.

# chapter fourteen



As I lay on my back in a strange bed, the warm body next to mine just as unfamiliar, I felt empty. Kendall's breathing slowed, indicating she was about to fall asleep. But I was fully awake, mesmerized by the shadows of the falling snowflakes on her bedroom wall cast by the streetlamp outside her apartment. The scene was quiet and serene, but my mind was far from tranquil.

Every time I closed my eyes, I thought of Sarah's fingers gracefully trailing down the length of my tie—an image that was quickly replaced with the more recent memory of Kendall yanking my tie to pull me through her door.

It started with an impulsive, alcohol-fueled kiss—which turned into an even sloppier embrace in the hallway, the same hallway in which I'd almost confessed my feelings to Sarah. And when Kendall whispered that she was going to take me back to her place, I surprised myself when I didn't even hesitate before saying, "Okay." I needed to feel wanted. And with Kendall, there was no guessing, no mystery. She exuded desire, a stark contrast to the uncertainty I felt with Sarah.

At least now I had my answer. I almost thought I had her, only to have the rug yanked out from beneath my feet. She never had any intention of turning our flirty banter into something more—she was always going to stay with Eli. I felt like such a fool for allowing myself to believe otherwise.

Nestled in the crook of my arm, Kendall stirred, and the faintest gasp escaped from her mouth. "Are you still awake?" she whispered.

"Yeah."

"Look, it's snowing."

I twisted my body around to get a better view of the falling snow through Kendall's open blinds. There was an awkward pause as I searched for a place to rest my free hand, finally settling on her hip. I thought about my car getting covered with a blanket of snow back in the parking lot at La Cocina and wondered how or when I'd return to it.

"It's kind of perfect, isn't it?" Kendall asked, clutching her pale blue sheet to her chest. I was glad she couldn't see my face, because she might get a sense of the panic and regret surging through me. I probably should have been upfront with her about my intentions before our clothes came off—but we didn't exactly engage in much conversation.

I inhaled, deciding it was better I tell her now than wait to say it in a text. "Hey," I started. She rolled over in my arms so she was facing me directly. "I need you to know... I'm not looking for a relationship."

Kendall blinked. "Didn't think you were."

"I mean—I just—I didn't want to give you any false hope or lead you on. I'm not in a good place to start dating anyone."

"Good," she said, keeping her eyes locked on mine. "I'm not either."

"Good," I echoed.

"I just got out of a seven-month relationship, so you don't need to worry about me, like, getting attached, if that's your concern. It's just sex, Owen." She giggled, alleviating some of the tension within me. I didn't feel as exploitative now that I knew she was using me, too. This was purely physical. Nothing more, nothing less.

"I would also appreciate a little discretion," I added, "since I'm applying for the principal position. I think what we just did goes against district policy." The last thing I needed was for anyone at work to catch wind of this encounter. Sarah's accusation Kendall had been flirting with me in the teacher's lounge came to mind. I imagined what she might have to say about this now, quickly deciding she could never find out.

"I get it. You want me to be your dirty little secret," Kendall said, a playful smile tugging at the corners of her lips. "That just makes it a hell of a lot more fun." She rolled over again, assuming the position of the little spoon. Now that we'd established some boundaries, I found it easier to shut off my brain and fall asleep.

* *

"You look like you need this," my brother, Jake, said to me on our parents' deck on Christmas Day. He pulled a joint from his shirt pocket and offered it to me.

I held my hand up to decline. "Nah," I said, "I can't risk that right now."

Shrugging, he lit up beside me, glancing at the sliding glass door behind us. His kids were on the other side of it in the living room, sitting in the middle of a pile of freshly-opened toys. "Suit yourself," he said, taking a long drag before exhaling into the crisp winter air.

We'd been coming out to the deck for a smoke on Christmas Day since we were teens, once the festivities were over and our dad had fallen asleep in his recliner. It had become just as much of a tradition as the Christmas ham Mom cooked every year.

"What's going on with you?" Jake asked, narrowing his eyes at me. I hadn't realized I'd been giving off the impression anything was wrong, but my brother was pretty intuitive when it came to my moods. He was barely a year older than me, and we shared a bedroom for most of our childhood. I had no secrets. Now, in our thirties, I still couldn't hide anything from him.

I sighed. "Just school stuff. My boss is retiring, and I think I'm going to apply for the principal position."

"No shit?"

I nodded. "It looks like I have a pretty good chance of getting it, too. If I want it, that is."

"Why the hell wouldn't you want it?"

If I tried to explain it, Jake wouldn't get it. I hated talking about my business with my family. Excluding my mom, none of them ever listened to my podcast, and they didn't understand how it could possibly earn any revenue. I think they saw it as a fun little hobby. A distraction. "I don't know," I said, turning away from his puff of smoke. "I'm not sure it's right for me."

"Why not? Wasn't that the whole point of your master's?"

"Not the whole point," I said, running my fingers through my hair. "It gives me some credibility with *STEM*—"

"*STEM For the Win*, I know," he interrupted. "And I'm guessing that's the reason you're hesitant to take this job."

I didn't say anything.

"Look, let me give you some brotherly advice." With one hand on my shoulder, the other holding the joint up to his lips, he said, "If you're offered this promotion, take it. Don't be stupid about it. I know you love that podcast, but you have to think about the long-term, right? How long can that last?"

Staring down at the railing, I pondered his words. I knew he had a point, but Jake didn't know the first thing about the intricacies of podcasting or online business. He'd been running his own landscaping company for the last six years, which he believed gave him the authority to offer unsolicited business advice every time the topic of my podcast came up. He meant well, but I knew to take his words with a grain of salt. "It's more than the podcast, you know. I—"

Just then, I felt my phone buzz in my pocket. I pulled it out and glanced at the screen. It was a text from Kendall. The second I tapped on the notification, a sultry photo filled my entire screen—it was hard to make out what I was looking at because I closed out of it so quickly, but there had been a lot of skin.

And a whole lot of nothing else.

"Whoa, what the fuck?" Jake asked with a hearty laugh. The photo was on my screen for mere seconds, but apparently that had been enough for Jake to take it all in. "Who was *that*?"

I shook my head. "Nobody. Just a girl from work."

"A *teacher*?" He coughed, choking on smoke. "You're kidding. Let me see."

"Don't be a perv," I said, slipping my phone back into my pocket. I turned toward the sliding door. "Shouldn't you go see if Stacy needs help?"

"You're just trying to get rid of me." He tapped the end of his joint on the railing before returning it to his shirt pocket. I wondered what Stacy thought about him coming out here to smoke while she dealt with the kids and helped our mom with the dishes. He nodded toward the phone in my back pocket. "Was that Sarah?"

I swung around to face him directly. "What? Sarah Lavely? How—?"

Jake rolled his eyes. "Come on. The teacher you talk about every single time we're together? The one who teaches across the hall from you, right? Please tell me that was her in the pic."

"No," I said, clearing my throat. I hadn't realized I'd mentioned her so many times. "It wasn't her. She's engaged."

"Engaged? How the fuck did you let that happen?" We both put our backs against the railing now to face the living room, where our father was walking around with a trash bag, picking up all the wrapping paper and shredded cardboard boxes. The kids' raucous playing probably woke him up from his nap.

I blew on my hands to warm them and crossed my arms against my chest. "She's just a friend."

"Don't lie." Jake looked me in the eyes. "I know I'm wrong about a lot of things. But I know you. And you've got it bad for that woman."

I shook my head, but I didn't argue. "Well, like I said. She's engaged."

"Let me see a picture of her."

"What? No."

"Come on. Bet you've got one on your phone."

I had plenty of them—mostly selfies she'd sent me during professional development meetings to show me how bored she was. And because I wouldn't mind looking at a picture of Sarah myself, I pulled my phone back out of my pocket and, quickly closing out of the text from Kendall. navigated to my most recent photo from Sarah. It was from the day before Christmas break, when she'd had on the reindeer pajamas. She had the hood pulled up over her head with a few wispy curls sticking out here and there, an overexaggerated horrified look on her face. The accompanying caption read: *I just remembered I have to go to the post office during lunch looking like this.*

Jake insisted on holding my phone himself to get a better look, smacking my hand away when I tried to grab it back. The longer he ogled the picture of her, the more uncomfortable I felt. Then, he began scrolling through our past texts and exchanged selfies, his smile growing wider by the second. All I could do was stand there and shake my head.

Finally, he shoved the phone at my chest, almost dropping it. And then, fixing his eyes on mine, he gripped my shoulder tight with one hand. "Please, for the love of all that is holy, fuck that woman and get it over with already." And with that, he pulled the sliding door open, hollering at the kids to start picking up all their new toys.

I stared down at my phone screen and started to scroll through my messages with Sarah. It seemed like I scrolled for an eternity, but I had only gotten as far back as August, when she texted me a picture of her empty classroom and complained about having to wait for the floors to be waxed before she could set everything up. I sighed as I swiped left, making the decision to delete our entire conversation. All the photos, all the messages—they were all gone now. There was no need to continue like this with her, now that she was engaged and I was doing my best to move on. And moving on meant the flirting— every bit of it—had to stop. I decided that when winter break was over, everything would be different.

My phone buzzed in my hand just before I turned to walk inside. Another message from Kendall. I took a step back, knowing opening this in front of my nieces and nephews was too risky.

**Kendall:** holiday family drama gives me so much anxiety. I need something to help me de-stress 😊

Going back for seconds with Kendall wouldn't be very smart, would it? I held my phone against my chin, trying to come up with an excuse. Something that wouldn't sound completely heartless.

However, the thought of going home to an empty bed on Christmas infiltrated my mind. I knew this thing with Kendall was nothing more than a band-aid, barely holding together a gaping wound. But sleeping with her the first time had done a decent job of distracting me and numbing the pain, so the allure of temporary relief outweighed every rational thought I had.

**Owen:** hmm, I have the perfect solution for that

# chapter fifteen

*sarah*

The Christmas tree in my mom's foyer was bursting with so many oversized ornaments, it was a wonder the thing didn't buckle beneath all the weight. My mother worked for a real estate agency, staging homes for showings, so she had an uncanny knack for transforming any space into an absolute spectacle. "Guess how many gnomes there are?" she urged, ushering Eli and me through the front door on Christmas evening.

"I don't know, Mom—why don't you tell us."

"Oh, it's more fun when you guess," she whimpered, taking my coat.

I sighed, eyeing all the gnomes perched perfectly on the tree. Before I could say anything, Eli enveloped my mom in a bear hug. "You've really outdone yourself this year, Nicole," he said with the usual charm that accompanied him when we visited my parents. My mom's eyes twinkled as Eli scanned the tree, twisting his mouth in concentration before he made a guess. "Fourteen?"

My mom laughed. "Try twenty-six!"

The gifts in my arms were getting heavy, and we hadn't even made it past the foyer. Thankfully, my sister, Samantha, appeared at my side, taking one of the gift bags from my white-knuckled hands. "Is she making you count the gnomes?"

"You guessed it," I replied as we followed her into the living room to the other Christmas tree—the one with all the mismatched ornaments that held some sentimental value—where I added the presents we'd brought to the growing pile. My little brother, Steven, home from college for the holidays, briefly acknowledged our arrival with a nod before returning to his X-box. Samantha's husband Zach, seated at the other end of the couch, raised his beer bottle in the air as a way of saying hello. It was only a matter of time before Eli would tease him about his Purdue hoodie—which I was certain Zach had worn for precisely that reason.

Turning back to Sam, I eyed the way her hands rested on her protruding belly, which had grown significantly since the last time I saw her. "Look at you," I said with a smile, reaching out to give her belly a pat. "How far al—"

"Aren't you going to show everyone the shiny new accessory you got for Christmas?" Eli interrupted, wrapping his arms around me from behind.

My mom froze on her way out of the room, our coats draped over her arm. Her eyes widened as she whipped her head around to face us. "Is it what I think it is?"

"Looks like it," Sam answered, eyeing my ring-adorned hand, which still dangled at my side. My mom's mouth dropped open as she looked from me to Eli, and it was mere seconds before she made it across the room to see the ring for herself. She shoved our coats into the arms of my sister, who mumbled, "Finally, something to take the attention off of me."

"When did this happen?" my mom demanded to know, her eyes widening with excitement. "Tell me every detail." I could practically see the wheels turning in her head as she mentally prepared a Facebook status that would undoubtedly garner a flurry of likes and comments.

I told her about Eli's proposal at the staff Christmas party. She clapped her hands together and shrieked in response, catching my dad's attention from the kitchen. So I recounted the story again—not that there was much to it. Eli interjected to boast about buying a round of celebratory tequila shots for everyone, a detail that made my dad chuckle as he shook his hand in congratulations. "Well done," my dad said. "I know you'll take good care of my girl."

I swallowed. My parents adored Eli like he was already family—like he was their son. Like me, they'd been waiting for this proposal to happen for years. Their enthusiasm only made me feel worse about the nagging uncertainty lingering in the back of my mind.

When we finally got around to opening gifts, I was relieved to be out of the spotlight for a while. Steven managed to convince our dad to try out his new VR headset, which provided a much-needed distraction. My mother, sitting beside Samantha on the couch, touched her belly and said, "Next Christmas, we'll have a little one crawling around, won't we?" And then she turned to Eli and winked. "Maybe two."

"Mom!" I grunted, tucking my hair behind my ears. "Let us get through the wedding first."

She laughed, and then her face lit up as an idea crossed her mind. "Oh! You know what? We should get out my wedding tote. There's probably something in there you can use as your 'something old' or 'something borrowed.' Will you go down there and get it?"

My first instinct was to protest this suggestion, to say it was far too early to even begin thinking about such things, but I was eager for an excuse to get away for a couple of minutes. I knew precisely which tote she was referring to—it was the same one she had brought up from the basement a couple of years ago for Samantha. It held a treasure trove of mementos from our parents' wedding day. When we were kids, my mom would retrieve that tote from the basement just to reminisce, getting all misty-eyed over her dried wedding flowers or the cloth napkin she stole from the venue.

I found it right away, in its usual spot between a box of our old baby clothes and the wooden play kitchen Samantha and I fought over when we were little girls. But because I wasn't ready to return to the conversation upstairs, I sat on a dusty stool and took a deep breath, crinkling my nose at the musty smell. Above my head, the sound of my mom's laughter reverberated through the floorboards.

My mind involuntarily wandered to Owen, much like it had countless times since the staff Christmas party. I couldn't help but wonder what he was doing at that very moment, and if he, too, had been consumed by thoughts of me. Instinctively, I pulled out my phone to reread our last few text exchanges. I'd typed and deleted so many messages to him since the party, often hesitating at the word "hey" followed by a comma before hitting the backspace.

What could I possibly say to him now? The weight of his unfinished confession sat heavy on my chest, suffocating any possibility of casual conversation. In years past, we'd send each other a quick "Merry Christmas" text accompanied by a Santa emoji or some ridiculous meme. That didn't feel appropriate now—but then again, neither did, *"Hey, can we pretend that you weren't about to tell me you have feelings for me?"*

The urge to address the awkwardness and smooth it over kept tugging at me, but ultimately, I chose silence. Instead, I navigated to Instagram and looked up Kendall Devin's name. She wasn't difficult to track down since we had a lot of mutuals. Unfortunately, her account was set to private. "Damn it," I muttered under my breath.

I didn't know what I was looking for, anyway. It's not like she'd have anything on her profile indicating some connection to Owen. There would be nothing there to answer the burning questions in my mind: did he go home with her Friday night? Did they… sleep together?

As the realization of my unwarranted interest sank in, I closed the app, reminding myself that I had no right to care.

Just then, I heard the creaking of the basement steps, and I looked up to see Samantha making her way down, one hand on her belly and the other gripping the rail. "Mom sent me to see what's taking you so long," she said, shuffling toward me.

"I couldn't watch Dad climb an invisible ladder with the VR goggles on for another second," I said, and we shared a laugh.

Samantha made her way over to a lidless box on one of the deep wooden shelves next to me, and began absentmindedly flipping through its contents. The sounds of our family's boisterous conversation drifted down from upstairs. "I'm glad Eli and Zach get on so well," she said.

"Me too."

Samantha's eyes settled on an old Statue of Liberty snow globe, a souvenir our parents brought back from their trip to NYC when we were younger. As she flipped it over in her hands, watching the snow fall, she said, "So, he finally sealed the deal, huh?"

"Finally," I repeated.

Samantha put the snow globe back and rested her hands on the edge of the box, looking over the rest of its contents. "You're not really good at hiding it when you're annoyed, by the way."

"Annoyed by whom, Mom?"

"Not this time. I'm actually talking about Eli," she said. I stared at her, confused, waiting for an explanation. She thumbed through a stack of Disney World maps from our childhood. "You rolled your eyes when you had to repeat the proposal story the second time."

Oh. "I'm just a little irritated that he proposed to me in front of all my co-workers," I confessed. "All those eyes on me. What if I had wanted to say no?"

"But you didn't want to say no," Samantha said—and though it was a statement, there was a question in her eyes.

"Of course not. I just—" I paused, attempting to gather my jumbled-up thoughts. "I know I'm incredibly fortunate to have what I have with Eli. Marrying my high school sweetheart—it's a love story for the books."

"I feel a 'but' coming on…"

I grinned from one corner of my mouth. "But, I think—even though I'm happy and can't wait to marry him," I said, my smile fading as I hugged my knees to my chest, "there's always going to be this part of me that regrets not experiencing… more."

More what, I wasn't sure. But my sister not-so-eloquently put my thoughts into words. "More penises?"

I burst into laughter, feeling my cheeks burn. "Jesus, Sam. That's not what I was trying to say."

"How many have you had anyway?" Samantha crossed her arms. "You've never told me about that. Besides Eli, who have you done the deed with?"

My number—or my "body count," as some people like to call it—was lower than most. While I had friends who lied about their number for being what they felt was too high, I was always the one embarrassed to admit that I'd only slept with two men in my entire life.

First, there was Eli, when we were both sixteen. The sex we had was messy and awkward, but we figured everything out together. And then, during our break in college, there was Justin, who couldn't find the clitoris if there was an arrow pointing to it.

After Justin, there was Eli again, and that was the extent of my sexual history. So maybe Samantha was correct in her assessment that I hadn't had very many… penises.

"Three?" she guessed.

"Lower."

She gave me a horrified look. "One?"

I shook my head.

"Okay, so—two. Eli and what's-his-name? Justin?"

I didn't want to be having this conversation with my little sister anymore. "Stop, I wasn't talking about sex when I said I regretted not experiencing *more*. It's just—" My mind flashed to Owen. Every "what if?" thought in my mind circled around him, and I struggled to put my feelings into words without mentioning his name. "I've always believed Eli to be my soulmate, but what if that's just because I have next-to-nobody to compare him to? What if there's someone out there who would be a better fit for me? How would I know?"

Samantha dropped the stack of theme park maps back in the box and brought her hands to her belly. "Well, I suppose there's no way of ever knowing. I mean—look at Zach. He has his shortcomings. Could there be a guy out there who maybe, possibly, could be a better partner for me than him? Sure. But it doesn't make me feel like I'm settling for less. Zach is the one who's *here*. Loving me, every single day. Just like Eli loves you." She paused for emphasis, and I could feel her studying my face. "I don't actually believe 'soulmates' exist, and searching for one will only lead to disappointment."

I nodded. Above our heads, there was another burst of laughter, and someone started clapping. I rose to my feet, starting to feel a little sore after sitting on that tiny stool for so long. Twisting my body to stretch my back, I said, "I guess life's not a Disney movie, is it?"

"Nope." I picked up the wedding tote, and Samantha turned away from the box of old vacation mementos. As we made our way over to the stairs, she grasped my arm just as my foot touched the bottom step. "Are you satisfied with Eli?"

My brows furrowed. "Yes." Was I, though?

Samantha lowered her chin, raising one eyebrow at me. "You know what I mean. Is he *satisfying* you?"

"Sam!" I elbowed her away from me and continued up the stairs, eager to get away from this conversation. Behind me, my sister laughed, muttering something about "his penis" under her breath as I made my way through the basement door into the kitchen.

We used to talk about Barbies. What happened to us?

I was grinning when I walked back into the living room, clutching the wedding tote in my hands. My eyes caught Eli's gaze. There was a subtle softening of his features when I entered the room, like he was relieved I'd returned—it could have just been because I'd left him alone with his future in-laws for too long, but the smile on his lips was comforting. Familiar.

Keeping my eyes on him as I handed the tote to my mom, I decided at that moment Samantha was wrong. Soulmates did exist, and I had found mine.

And I wasn't going to let a silly workplace crush get in the way of that. So that's why, on January 3rd, I intended to show up and pretend like everything was normal. When we stood in the hallway with our coffee, I'd ask Owen if he had a good Christmas, just as I had for the last several years. And we'd carry on as usual, forgetting about what happened—or almost happened—between us.

Except on January 3rd, Owen wasn't there.

Well, he was *there*. But when 7:50 came, he did not join me in the hallway. All the lights were on and his door was open, indicating he—or someone—was in the classroom. But there was an empty space where he usually stood across from me. I greeted both my students and his as they skipped down the hallway, rambling about what they got for Christmas.

Maybe he called out sick? Owen didn't miss work often, but it was possible he had called in a substitute that day—and it was highly unlikely "engage in flirty banter with the teacher across the hall" was written into the sub plans, which would explain why I was standing alone in the hallway that morning.

I needed that to be true.

After a couple of minutes, however, I heard his voice. "Are those new Jordans?" he was saying. "Guess you weren't on the naughty list after all."

That voice—and that warm chuckle of his—felt like home to me. Yet my heart began to ache when I heard it, because it only confirmed the one thing I feared most: he was avoiding me.

Bentley greeted me with a side hug when he arrived, which gave me a much-needed distraction and a total mood boost. I hadn't imagined him as much of a hugger, so the affection was a welcome surprise. "Did you have a good Christmas vacation, Bentley?"

"It was okay," he said, pushing his hair away from his eyes. "This probably sounds stupid, but I sort of got homesick over break. But, like, homesick for school."

"School-sick?" I suggested.

He stuck his thumbs behind the straps of his backpack. "Exactly. Is that weird?"

I glanced across the hall. "No, that's not weird at all. I was school-sick, too. And guess what? We have a newspaper meeting today." This made him smile again. I grinned back as he walked past me into the room, noticing he was holding his head a little higher now.

It was almost time for the first bell, and Owen still hadn't made an appearance in the hallway. I tried to make more excuses for his aloofness in my mind. Maybe he just had a lot of prep work to catch up on—he wasn't a planner, like me. It was entirely possible he'd shown up to school and realized he had nothing prepared for his morning lessons. He could have been in there scrambling to get ready for the day. But when the 8:05 bell rang and he sent one of his students to close his door, I knew he was intentionally avoiding me. Why else wouldn't he at least take a second to say good morning? I sighed, staring at the "LEARN, YOU MUST" Yoda sign on the back of his door.

He was shutting me out.

I pulled my door shut and walked over to my desk to set my coffee mug down and turned around to face my students, all of them chattering about what they got for Christmas. They weren't ready to start learning yet, and I wasn't ready to teach.

This was the first time the entire school year Owen had missed our daily morning chat, and it wasn't until that moment I realized I needed it as much as I needed the heavy dose of caffeine in my cup. As I mustered up my best teacher voice to ask my students to find their seats, something inside of me felt a little off. All morning, I fought the urge to grab my phone to text him and ask if everything was okay between us.

But I already knew the answer.

# chapter sixteen

*owen*

I had thought I could handle seeing her. Really, I did.

I was going to stroll right out there, coffee in hand, and just act like everything between us was the same as it ever was. I even picked up my mug and started walking that way, but the second I heard her voice, I froze.

"I've missed you so much!" she was saying to one of our students. My heart leapt to my throat and my legs immediately turned to Jell-O. I'd always heard that expression, but never really experienced it—it felt like my own legs couldn't hold me up anymore. I turned right back around and sat at my desk, which is where I remained until the very last kid walked in.

Like a coward.

It wasn't just the fact that it hurt to see her, knowing she'd never be mine. I'd had plenty of time over the last couple of weeks to accept that reality. Even more, I wanted to avoid having to lie to her. Because she was going to ask me what I did over Christmas break, and she would instantly detect I was hiding something from her. She always knew.

Talking to her about Kendall was not an option. I had sort of hoped the thing with Kendall would fizzle out before our return to school, but considering she woke up beside me that very morning, it appeared this was going to continue a little while longer. Our one-night stand had turned into something else entirely.

I'd spent more nights with Kendall over Christmas break than without her, confined within the four walls of my house—or, sometimes, her apartment. We ordered an ungodly amount of take-out, binged our favorite shows, and took care of each other's loneliness. It wasn't an ideal situation, something both of us acknowledged, but it served as a temporary distraction from the sting of Sarah's rejection.

I knew I couldn't avoid her forever. I briefly considered eating my lunch in my classroom, which wasn't particularly unusual for me to do, but I knew I would have to stop hiding, eventually.. So I headed to the teacher's lounge with my lunch, surprised to find the room mostly empty. Only Mrs. Hawley, the librarian, was in the room, eating a burrito and watching a loud video on her phone. Everybody must have been busy trying to catch up on lesson plans after the break. I found a seat at the long table and popped my earbuds in so I could listen to a podcast while I ate my sandwich.

Sometimes I put my earbuds in without listening to anything at all—it was my way of indicating to everyone else I wasn't in the mood for conversation. This strategy had a 50/50 success rate, depending on who happened to walk into the lounge. My older colleagues were usually the ones who failed to notice the headphones, or didn't care. Some of them would even ask, "Whatcha listening to?" and spend the entirety of our lunch period asking me questions about it.

I was just four minutes into a podcast about climate change—just barely past the introductory, off-topic banter between the two hosts—when Sarah walked into the teacher's lounge. She noticed me right away, fixing her eyes on the floor as she made her way to the microwave carrying a plastic container. Instinctively, I took my earbuds out and dropped them into my shirt pocket while she tapped a few buttons on the microwave.

She hit the start button but remained in front of the appliance with her back to me. I tilted my head back and looked up at the ceiling as if to ask "why me?"

I was going to have to be the one to initiate this, wasn't I?

"Hey," I said, and she slowly turned around. I watched the efforted way she lifted her eyes to meet mine, like it pained her to have to even look at me. I swallowed, trying not to read too much into the way she had sadness etched all over her face. "Did you have a good break?"

She stared at me for a moment, the corners of her eyebrows pointing downward. "Yeah," she said, scratching her elbow. "Um. I visited my family. Ate a lot of cheese. Drank a lot of wine. You?"

I stretched and folded my hands behind my head, trying to appear calmer than I felt. "I basically stayed in bed and binge-watched *Schitt's Creek* the entire two weeks." I glanced down at my half-eaten sandwich, unable to look her in the eye. Would she be able to tell I was omitting a certain key detail? "I got too used to not setting my alarm," I continued. "I feel like I deserve some sort of reward just for getting out of bed before seven today."

A smile slowly crept onto Sarah's face, and she reached into the pocket of her gray slacks and pulled out a large green pompom with one dangling googly eye and a tiny underwear-shaped piece of cardboard glued to the front. She walked over to the table and sat it down directly in front of me, extending a metaphorical olive branch. "This is the last remaining desk elf," she said. "I found him under my desk."

"Wow," I said, picking it up to get a closer look. "This little guy has been through it."

"He looks how I feel," she joked.

We exchanged smiles as I sat the desk elf back down on the table. Maybe this was going to be okay, after all. We could just go on pretending like nothing awkward happened between us and everything was perfectly normal. If she wasn't going to bring it up, neither would I. All of that panic and worry for nothing.

I was just starting to relax, taking a bite of my sandwich as Sarah stirred her hot food at the counter, when Kendall walked into the room carrying a coffee mug.

I almost choked.

Kendall gave me a coy smile as she passed, making her way over to the coffeepot. "Hey guys," she said, filling up her mug. I looked up at Sarah, who had her back to us as she returned her food to the microwave for another minute. Kendall tore open a packet of sugar and poured it in her cup before turning around. "Did you guys have a good break?" She blew on her coffee before taking a sip.

"Uh, yeah," I said, picking up my phone and pretending to be really interested in something on the screen. I just refreshed my Facebook feed over and over, not processing a single thing I saw. "How about you?"

"It was great," she said. "I pretty much just laid around watching *Schitt's Creek* the whole time."

Damn it. "That's funny," I said, shifting in my seat. "We were just talking about that, weren't we, Sarah?"

Sarah finally turned around. "Yep," she said, staring right at me. "Weird."

Kendall, peering over her coffee mug, looked down at Sarah's feet. "Are those flowers on your shoes?"

Sarah glanced downward. "Oh, yeah. Daisies."

"They're so cute."

"Thank you." Sarah's eyes traveled up Kendall's body, finally settling on her charm bracelet, which she probably decided was the only thing about Kendall's entire ensemble she liked. "I love your bracelet."

I wanted to sink through my chair and melt right through the floor. Hell is being in the same room as the woman you're in love with and the one you've been sleeping with while they exchange pleasantries. I cleared my throat, fully aware of the building tension in the room. I had to do something about it. Sitting up a little straighter, I smoothed out my tie, saying, "Well, jeez. Is nobody going to compliment me on my new tie?"

"That is one spectacular tie, Owen," Kendall said with a giggle.

"Yes, we're all accessorizing really well today," Sarah said, her tone dripping in sarcasm. The microwave behind her beeped, but she didn't move. This was torture. Thankfully, Kendall glanced up at the clock and announced she needed to return to her classroom. But as she pushed the door open with her hip, she turned to give me a not-so-subtle wink.

Sarah carried her leftover pasta to the table and sat across from me. But she didn't take a bite. Instead, she stared at me with her arms crossed on the table.

"Kendall looked really cute today, didn't she?" she asked. I swallowed. I knew I couldn't answer this. It felt like a trap. So I just raised one eyebrow and shrugged like I hadn't noticed Kendall at all. Sarah continued, saying, "I'm surprised she gets by with wearing dresses that short. Did you notice that?"

I blinked at her a couple of times. "No, I did not." Not taking that bait.

"Is she seeing someone?"

"Why, are you interested?" I asked, unable to hide my frustration. I took a deep breath. "You're being really weird, Lavely."

"No. *You* are," she said. She still hadn't taken a single bite of her lunch. "You've been weird ever since the Christmas party, and I don't like it."

"What do you mean? This is the first time we've even spoken since the Christmas party. How would I—"

"Exactly," she said. She glanced down at the other end of the table, where Mrs. Hawley was still watching videos on her phone. And then she leaned closer to me so she wouldn't be overheard. "You didn't even come out and talk to me this morning."

"I had to set up my classroom," I said, glancing down at my lap. I hope she couldn't tell I was lying. "Nothing's changed. Oh, but—that reminds me." I looked back up at her face. "How's the wedding planning going?" I shouldn't have said it like that, in this "gotcha" way, but I was desperate for anything to take the focus off of me.

A faint blush tinged her cheeks. "I've been engaged for two weeks. I've hardly had any time for wedding planning."

"Ah." I nodded and picked my phone back up. This conversation felt too strange and awkward, like we were entering some new phase of our friendship. Or, as much as I hated for it to be a possibility, a phasing out. This was starting to feel like… a fight. We'd had little arguments before, mostly over school-related matters, but this was worse. A lot worse.

Sarah took a couple of bites, and I thought the Kendall interrogation might be over. But when Mrs. Hawley finished her burrito and left the room, Sarah wasted no time at all before leaning across the table to ask, "Did you sleep with Kendall?"

I could feel the blood draining from my face. How could she figure that out just from our two-minute interaction? Was it really just the *Schitt's Creek* comment that gave it away? Or did she catch Kendall winking at me? Seconds ticked by, and I thought of nothing to say, but the look of shock on my face likely confirmed her accusation.

Before I could conjure up some kind of lie, the door to the teacher's lounge opened and Heath walked in. He and I exchanged friendly head nods as he made his way over to the fridge. As he bent over to grab his protein shake, he began making small talk about the holidays, unaware of the tension in the room. I was in the middle of telling him how difficult it was to get out of bed that morning when Sarah snapped the lid back on her lunch and sprang up out of her chair, bolting out of the room without so much as a glance in my direction.

Heath shook the protein shake he'd just removed from the fridge. "Sheesh. What's wrong with her?"

"Who knows? I think she's just having a bad day."

# chapter seventeen



"Bentley, while I enjoy your sense of humor, is there any way you can draw Mrs. Shearer in a way that's less, um… mean?" I was staring down at his first comic strip of the semester. In the first panel, labeled "WHAT THE AUDIENCE SEES," Mrs. Shearer had her back to the crowd, and there were hearts and music notes floating around her head. In the second one, captioned "WHAT WE SEE", it showed her yelling through gritted teeth: "Smile!" "Stand up straight!" "ENUNCIATE!"

Although I was impressed he'd spelled 'enunciate' correctly, I had some reservations about the way he'd drawn Mrs. Shearer in the comic. He had emphasized the size of her rear end in the first panel—it was three times wider than her head. Mrs. Shearer carried a little extra junk in the trunk, but I wasn't sure this exaggerated detail was necessary.

"But you said you liked it when I included lots of realistic details," Bentley said. He and the other newspaper club members were seated around the long table at the back of my classroom. Beside him, Jordyn was trying to stifle a giggle. This didn't go unnoticed by Bentley, who began to smile when he realized he had their attention. "And Mrs. Shearer has a big butt."

Jordyn couldn't hold it in anymore, and before long, both of them were laughing uncontrollably.

"Bentley," I said, scowling. "I can't publish this unless you change that… particular detail. Okay?" I held eye contact with him until he sighed, flipped his pencil over, and started erasing. With that problem out of the way, I turned to Ava, who was hand-writing her rough draft about Mrs. Tucker's therapy dog, Wally, who had practically become a Grissom mascot over the past couple of years. "How's it coming, Ava?

"Good. When I'm done with this, I'm going to write the Teacher of the Month feature and then get started on my math bowl article."

I nodded. I hadn't assigned all of these articles to Ava—she was an ambitious little thing. She'd write this entire paper herself if we let her. "Good deal," I said. While the kids worked on their various features, I sat at the head of the table, clutching my planner against my chest. I don't know how long I spaced out— it could have been twenty seconds or five minutes—but the newspaper club was the farthest thing from my mind.

Owen couldn't even give me an honest answer. Just a simple "yes" or "no" would have sufficed. I knew I wasn't owed a response from him—I could have just respected his privacy and kept my mouth shut. But the question was dying to be asked, and my curiosity got the better of me.

The answer was an obvious "yes," based on his squirmy reaction. In just one night, he'd gone from implying he wanted more than friendship with me to jumping into bed with Kendall Devin. I supposed he was feeling pretty rejected after the whole proposal thing, but his feelings for me couldn't have been very strong to begin with if he was able to move on that fast.

I hated everything about our conversation in the teacher's lounge—the accusatory way he asked me how wedding planning was going, and how it seemed like we were on the verge of a full-blown fight with every word we spoke.

This wasn't us.

"Ms. Lavely." I snapped out of my daydream to focus on Bentley, who was trying to show me his revised comic strip. "Is this better?"

I looked down at his sketchbook. He'd redrawn Mrs. Shearer's bottom half, and while it still seemed like he was exaggerating certain features, it was no longer bordering on offensive. "That's fine, Bentley. I'll scan it tomorrow."

By the end of the day, I wanted nothing more than to hurry home and crawl back into bed. However, the four-foot Christmas tree still on display in the corner of my classroom was irking me, and I knew I wouldn't be able to stop thinking about it until it was taken down. The Virgo in me was ashamed I hadn't already taken care of it over break.

So I was carefully placing ornaments in a plastic tote when there was a gentle knock on the door around 3:30. I glanced up to see Owen hovering in the doorway with his messenger bag over his shoulder and his hands in his pockets. "Hey," he said.

"Hi."

"Can we talk for a sec?"

I finished wrapping a student-made reindeer ornament with bubble wrap and placed it in the box. "Of course." Owen strolled across the room and looked over some of the ornaments left on the tree. Most of them were gifts from students over the years, but his eyes stopped on the Alice in Wonderland ornament he'd given me three years ago when my entire classroom was Wonderland-themed.

With his hands still in his pockets, he turned to me and took a breath before asking, "How did you know about Kendall?"

I reached up to take down the Alice ornament, carefully covering it with a piece of bubble wrap. Without looking up, I said, "I saw you in her car after the Christmas party."

He nodded like it finally made sense. "Oh." He was quiet for a moment, and then he dropped his messenger bag on the rug and began helping me take down ornaments. He was just as careful as I was, wrapping them in the same way I had been.

"Why didn't you just tell me?" I asked. "You always share this kind of thing with me."

Owen scratched the back of his neck. "It just felt a little awkward. Not just because she's a teacher here, which makes it different, but after the Christmas party…."

"I get it," I said when his voice started to trail off. I didn't want to make him revisit his botched confession at the Christmas party. He seemed a little relieved, and together we continued taking ornaments down.

"Also," Owen began, stopping to inhale. "She and I have to be discreet since I'm putting my application in for the principal job, you know. Not that I think you'll tell anyone I'm seeing her—I trust you."

All of a sudden, I felt like I'd just been punched in the gut. I had thought his night with Kendall was only a one-time thing they'd soon forget about, but he was talking about her in the present tense. He was *seeing* her. What did that even mean? I hoped he couldn't tell my hands were shaking as I put the lid on the plastic tote, now that all the ornaments were put away. "Of course," I said. "I won't tell anyone."

"Thanks."

I started jerking the Christmas lights off the tree. "She's a little young, isn't she?"

Owen's brows furrowed. "She's twenty-five."

"Ah," I said. That still seemed young to me. "Not that I was judging or anything."

"Right. Of course not." For a moment, I thought my comment might have angered him, but when he jumped in to help me remove the lights from the tree, I thought I caught a little glimmer of a smile on his face. Like he was amused by my apparent jealousy.

When the lights and the tree itself were packed into their respective totes, Owen helped me put all the boxes away in the storage room. Then he picked his messenger bag up off the floor. "I'll walk you out if you're leaving now."

I tucked my hair behind my ears. "Um, I have something else I have to do."

"Oh, all right." He draped the strap of his bag over his head and started toward the door. Just before he got to the doorway, he turned back around to say, "Sarah, I just want you to know, I'm really happy for you and Eli." Even if he didn't mean it, he wanted me to believe he did.

I gave him a half-hearted smile. "Thank you." He said good-bye and disappeared into the hallway, leaving me standing there with my hands on my hips.

So Owen Gardner finally had a girlfriend. Well, good for him.

I walked over to my desk and collapsed into my chair, desperate to shake the image of Owen and Kendall together from my mind. I sunk even lower in my chair, wondering if this was how Owen had felt all this time, whenever he saw me and Eli together.

Swallowing hard, I fought back tears as I stared down at the diamond on my finger. My jealousy made me feel so ashamed— I had no right, no right at all to feel this way. The window of opportunity, our chance to explore what it might be like to turn our workplace flirtation into something more, had long closed.

I laid my head down on my desk and let the tears flow, reminding myself I was the one who had closed that window.

# chapter eighteen



The job opening for Cates' replacement was officially posted on the school website by the second week of January. Cates stopped me in the hallway the day it went up, urging me to get my application in as soon as possible. "The panel is going to start reviewing candidates in just a few weeks," he told me. "Let's get you at the top of the stack."

I couldn't get my brother's voice out of my head. Thanks to him, I was starting to doubt the longevity of *STEM for the Win*. What if I ran out of episode ideas in a year? In two years? Then what would I do, go back to teaching? The principal job would be filled, and I'd have to start over at a new school.

It would be incredibly stupid of me to let this job opportunity slip through my fingers.

So I found myself poring over my resumé for the first time in several years, adding my achievements at Grissom to the list. Besides forming the Robotics Club and completing some admin training, there wasn't much to add.

If things weren't so weird with Sarah, I'd ask her to look over my resumé for me. She was really good about that kind of thing. It wasn't uncommon for me to ask her to proofread some of my blog posts for the *STEM for the Win* website—I think she got some kind of odd pleasure out of finding and fixing others' mistakes. I knew she wouldn't hesitate to rewrite my cover letter, which was embarrassingly short. She'd be able to pad it out in a way that made me look good on paper.

But it didn't feel right to ask her for a favor right now. There was still too much tension between us, and not the good kind. Every time we spoke to each other in the morning, it was obvious we were both sidestepping certain subjects. Kendall. Her engagement to Eli. Our awkward conversation at the Christmas party.

Our usual banter was replaced with talk of her newspaper club, grading essays, and even the weather.

"Hope we get some more snow this winter."

"Me too."

"It snowed a lot last winter."

"Yeah, it really did."

She wasn't the same Sarah, and I wasn't the same Owen.

By the third week of the semester, I'd stopped eating lunch in the teacher's lounge. I couldn't handle being in the room with Kendall and Sarah at the same time. I could feel Sarah's eyes on me, carefully analyzing every interaction between Kendall and me. She'd look down at her planner or scroll on her phone, but I became acutely aware of the way she glanced up at us every minute or so.

And Kendall wasn't the best at being subtle. She often made a point to sit next to me at the long table in the lounge, which was something she never would have done before. Surely our colleagues noticed the way she leaned in close when we spoke? Sarah certainly noticed. And not once, but twice, Kendall slid her hand up my leg beneath the table, testing how close she could get to my groin before she made me squirm. The second time was the last day I ate lunch in the lounge.

It was like she was trying to get us caught.

One day, she came up behind me at the mailboxes in the main office and pinched my butt, well within Lori's peripheral vision. It was a subtle, quick movement, but if Lori hadn't been distracted by a phone call with a parent, she surely would have noticed. "I cannot believe you just did that," I whispered, keeping my eyes locked on the postcard in my hand so as not to arouse suspicion.

"Relax, nobody saw."

"This time," I said, flipping over the postcard. I looked up at Cates' slightly ajar office door. "You need to work on your subtlety."

She pulled a flyer out of her mailbox and, with a glance over at Lori, she whispered, "Where's the fun in that?" And without warning, she reached for the front of my pants this time, giggling at the way I dodged her hand.

I had to do something about this. She was going to cause me to risk everything, and she wasn't even worth it. Walking away from the mailboxes, I nodded for her to follow me to the hallway. I led her down to her empty classroom, the door closest to the office. Her students were in one of their special classes— mine, recess.

The second Kendall's door closed, she wrapped her arms around my midsection, pulling me in for a kiss. For a minute— and only a minute—I forgot the reason I was there and kissed her back, pushing her against the classroom door. She giggled against my mouth, sliding one of her hands into my back pocket. It felt good to be kissing someone like this, someone so eager to touch and be touched. The front of my pants began to tighten.

When my eyes shot open, my attention shifted to the googly-eyed penguins on the door, all of them staring at me with their judging, lopsided eyes. I wasn't about to make out in a kindergarten classroom, for Christ's sake. I yanked away from her grasp, taking a step back. "Sorry, I can't. Not at school."

"It's just a kiss, Owen. Don't be such a square," she teased. She grabbed the collar of my shirt and pulled my face toward hers, kissing me again. And when I felt her rubbing me through the front of my pants, I peeled myself off of her and pushed her hands away.

"Stop! We're not going to do that here—ever! Okay?" I lifted my hand to my forehead in frustration. Her shoulders sunk and she stared up at me, all doe-eyed and blinking. I hadn't meant to raise my voice. I sighed. "Sorry."

"It's okay."

"God. I'm really sorry," I said again. I pinched the bridge of my nose, feeling a stress headache coming on. "I didn't mean to yell at you. I feel like such an asshole."

A smile slowly crept onto Kendall's face, though, and she bit her bottom lip.

"What?"

"I've never seen you mad before, and it's kind of hot."

Jesus. "I need to get back to my room," I said, reaching past her for the door handle. When she stepped out of my way, one of the googly-eyed penguins fell to the floor. I bent over to pick it up for her, half-afraid I'd be violated somehow on the way down. Thankfully, she kept her hands behind her back, grinning innocently as I attempted to re-tape the penguin to the door. "I'm sorry again, for yelling. But please… try to keep your hands to yourself when you're around me. I can't risk it."

"I'll do my best," she said with a wink. That didn't sound very promising. I shook my head at her as I left, closing her classroom door behind me. I looked down at my watch—I had just a couple of minutes to get back to my room in time for the kids to return from recess. When I looked up, I saw Sarah stepping out of the office. She'd seen me, too, and she could tell I was coming from the direction of the kindergarten classrooms.

I cleared my throat when I caught up with her. "Hey," I said, stealing a quick glance over my shoulder at Kendall's door. "I was just… talking to Kendall."

Sarah shrugged with one shoulder. "Okay." We started walking toward our classrooms together. She was carrying her mail, which made me realize I'd left all of mine in the office. Oh well. "How is she today?" she asked. There was something about her tone that bothered me—like she didn't really want to know the answer and was only asking to be polite.

"She's fine," I said, walking with my hands in my pockets. "You know, we were just talking. I don't want you to think that I—that we—"

"It's not really any of my business, Owen," she said, looking straight ahead as we walked. "I don't care what you do with her. Or where you do it."

"I know," I said. "But I care. I wouldn't want you thinking I'd do something, you know, inappropriate. Here."

"'The gentleman doth protest too much, methinks,'" she said as we turned the corner at the fifth-grade wing. Leave it to her to quote Shakespeare at a time like this. Knowing I had no way of defending myself without sounding like a broken record, I decided to drop the subject.

When we reached our classroom doors, we paused in the middle of the hallway, an uncomfortable silence settling between us. Every moment with Sarah was now punctuated by all the thoughts left unsaid, a mutual avoidance of those forbidden topics. I put my hands in my pockets and stared down at her, watching her fingers as she fiddled with her lanyard. Twice, I opened my mouth to make small talk, but everything I could think of to say felt wrong. So instead, I pressed my lips together tight, willing myself to keep quiet.

As the bell rang over our heads, Sarah turned to me and pointed at her chin, saying, "Might want to wipe the lipstick off your face before the kids get in here."

Shit.

# chapter nineteen



It was time for a new distraction.

The dreary, gray January skies were really doing a number on my mood. After two weeks of rain that should have been snow, I'd forgotten what the sun looked like. And with Owen becoming more and more distant with each passing day, it was getting harder to drag myself out of bed on the dark mornings. I needed something to light me up again.

Of course, I had a wedding to plan. Samantha had given me some of her now-outdated bridal magazines, which I'd thumbed through already, and I'd been looking at a few ideas on Pinterest. I even pinned ideas on a board called "Our Wedding," formerly titled "One Day." I hadn't decided on any details yet. Not a theme, not a color scheme, or even a season. Settling on any one thing would make this wedding a reality, and I was still in the "is this real?" stage of processing my engagement.

So, while waiting for the wedding enthusiasm to kick in, I felt the urge to start a new project at school. Something to make me feel like I had a purpose. I had a backlog of project ideas—everything from new clubs I didn't have time to sponsor to schoolwide fundraisers everyone else would hate me for—but there was one that always made its way to the forefront of my mind.

The school garden idea.

One of my teacher friends from another district, Mallory, was instrumental in creating her school's student-led garden. It was a peaceful area nestled in a sunny spot between the building and their fenced-in playground, with raised garden beds full of fruits and vegetables the students had planted themselves. The paths were lined with flowers, and there were ivy-covered trellises on both ends. Every class, she explained, took turns maintaining the garden throughout the school year.

I ate lunch in my classroom one day and sent her an email when I couldn't get the idea out of my head—just asking her how the project came to be and where I'd need to get started if I wanted to follow in her footsteps. She replied just as I was packing up my things at the end of the day.

*Hey Sarah!*

*I'm so excited for you! Our school garden has been such a rewarding experience for students and staff. As far as planning goes, you would need a committee of teachers and perhaps some parent volunteers who are knowledgeable about gardening to put together the plans. And then of course you'll need to decide who's responsible for garden upkeep. We now have a Gardening Club at our school with a handful of students who help us with weeding, watering, and harvesting.*

*It was all made possible due to a grant we received. I also suggest reaching out to the community for donors. Especially parents of your students who might be local business owners.*

*Our garden is my most favorite thing I've ever done since I began teaching. If you get started now, you can probably have your school's garden up and running before the summer! Let me know if you have any more questions!*

*Mallory J.*

Okay, so this was going to be an enormous project to take on. There's no way I could do it alone. I knew enough about gardening—Eli and I had a small one in our backyard by the garage, and lately I'd been growing herbs in pots inside. And I was no stranger to grant writing, either. Last year at the Innovative Educators Summit, I'd taken a half-day workshop about school grants and subsequently applied for one to get some more flexible seating in my classroom.

I printed the email from Mallory and immediately headed toward Cates' office with the idea, eager to get started. If we wanted to break ground on the garden by springtime, I'd have to get funding in place as soon as possible. And in order to do that, I needed the go-ahead from Cates.

He was just getting ready to head out for the day when I caught him in his office buttoning his coat. "Oh brother," he said when I walked toward him with a paper. "You've got that crazed look in your eyes, Ms. Lavely. Do I even want to know?" He smiled as he took the paper from my extended hand.

"I've been sitting on this idea for a while," I said as he read the email. "We've got the perfect space for a garden, and I know the students would really benefit from this. And if we—"

"Say no more," he said, handing the paper back. "This is great."

I tucked my hair behind my ear. "Really?"

"Getting the funding is going to be the hardest part, but I'm sure you know that," he said, adjusting his glasses. "Tell you what. Get Owen to oversee this, and then come back to me once you've done some more research."

My mouth fell slightly agape. "You want me to have Owen… 'oversee' this?"

He pulled a pair of gloves from his pockets and started putting them on. The man was in such a hurry to leave, he didn't notice my scowl. "With the two of you on a project like this, I know it'll be solid."

"Oh," I said. "Um, thank you. Will do."

And then he offered me a piece of peppermint candy from his pocket, which I accepted, and the conversation was over. While I was thrilled to have been given the green light on this dream project, I was disheartened that he'd suggest someone else oversee it. Let alone the fact it was Owen.

As far as Cates knew, Owen and I were each other's ride or die at this school. He had no reason to believe I'd hesitate at all to ask for his help. But he didn't just want me to just ask for Owen's assistance. My mind kept circling around that word— "oversee." Leading a project like this was sure to help pave the way for Owen to become Cates' successor, wouldn't it?

The peppermint did nothing to get the bitter taste out of my mouth.

* *

I didn't have a chance to talk to Owen about the project until the following day after school. I'd mentioned it in the morning, letting him know I had something I wanted to discuss at the end of the day. As much as I hate to admit it, I got a little bit of pleasure from making him wonder all day about what I might want to talk about. I hadn't given him so much as a hint. Watching him squirm might have been the highlight of my entire day.

When I entered his classroom after the last bell, he was working on his laptop at the long table at the back of the room, his leg bouncing up and down as he watched me approach him. I pulled up a chair beside him and plopped my laptop and a handful of printed articles onto the table. "Wow," he said, eyeing the stack of papers. "What's all this?"

"My new project," I said. "Actually, *our* new project."

140

He tilted his head to the side, his eyes widening. "Is that so?" He picked up the top sheet of paper, an article that gave an overview of starting a school garden, and scratched his chin as he read. The corners of his mouth turned up a little, and I knew without him saying a word that he was going to help me. "So on top of sponsoring two clubs, you're finally going to do this whole garden thing, huh?"

"Yep." I scooted my chair a little closer to his. "And when I brought up the idea to Cates, he suggested I ask you to 'oversee' it," I said, making air quotes with my fingers. "So here we are."

His brows furrowed. "Why would he say that? Because I'm the science teacher?" I shrugged in response, and he turned back to the paper in his hands, flipping it over to read the next page. "I've never even applied for a grant before, but you have. He knows that, doesn't he?" And then, with a wince, he added, "Or maybe I'm just a kiss-ass."

"I wasn't going to say it."

He lifted his eyes to meet mine, and I smiled so he would know I was joking. He grinned back, shaking his head. "Well, I'm not overseeing this. You are. But I'm happy to be your right-hand man, if that's what you want. Just tell me what you need me to do, Lavely, and I'll do it."

Neither of us had anywhere we needed to be that afternoon, so we pored over every article we could find about planning and funding a school garden. Owen suggested building a small greenhouse so we'd be able to grow plants year-round, and he kept himself busy looking up plans for that while I researched local and federal grants. Unfortunately, it seemed we'd just missed the cut-off date for the most relevant grants, and unless we wanted to wait until next school year, we'd have to come up with a new idea. "What about Hagan Acres?" Owen asked, slouching back in his chair, tapping a pen on his knee.

Hagan Acres Farm was practically a household name around Woodvale—and all of central Indiana, really. The Hagan family owned a decent sized chunk of the county, farming watermelons in the summer and pumpkins in the fall. They were known philanthropists, and thanks to them, Woodvale had acquired a covered pavilion downtown for hosting farmers' markets. There was also a scholarship in their name, as well as countless other charitable efforts. Why hadn't I thought of them to begin with? "You think they'd be willing to donate something?"

"Their grandson goes here," Owen said. "He's a second grader, I think. I only know that because I interviewed Jerry Hagan for the podcast about modern irrigation systems. Fascinating stuff."

"Oh my god, that's right! I forgot about it. Don't hate me, but I didn't listen to the full episode."

Owen laughed. "No worries. But anyway, Jerry's a pretty nice guy. I could give you his contact info. And if you drop my name in the email, that can't hurt. He really likes me." He searched through his emails for Jerry's contact information, and I scooted close to copy it down on the back of one of my papers.

"Thank you so much," I said, slowly closing my laptop with my free hand as I continued jotting down Jerry's email address. "I feel like we're already off to a good start." I started gathering up the papers, tapping them against the table to straighten them. Beside me, Owen yawned and stretched, lifting his arms high above his head. His untucked shirt rose up his abdomen, and it was all I could do not to fixate on the waistband of his green boxers sticking out ever-so-slightly from his khaki pants.

"Before you go," he said, dropping his hands down by his side, "I have a favor to ask you."

"Sure, what is it?"

Owen crossed his arms against his chest, resting his knees on the edge of the table. "I need to get my resumé turned in for this principal position, and I'm having a hard time with my cover letter. I just can't get it to sound right."

I mirrored the casual way he was sitting, folding my hands on my stomach and slouching back in my chair. Pointing my knees toward him. "You're really going to do it, huh?"

He nodded, staring down at the table. "Yeah," he said. "I just feel like it'd be really stupid if I didn't go for this. I can't guarantee *STEM for the Win* will continue to grow the way it has been, and then what, you know?" He took a deep breath and started picking at one of the buttons on his shirt. "I can't let an opportunity like this slip through my fingers. This is what I want."

I narrowed my eyes, knowing Owen hadn't meant a single word he'd just said. He was trying to convince himself just as much as he was trying to explain it to me. I could hear the wavering in his voice. Becoming principal of this school would never light him up the way his podcast did.

He was simply making the safe choice.

And there was something else. "You wouldn't be able to date Kendall," I said, my voice low, as though someone in the hallway could overhear. His eyes flitted upward toward mine, and I knew we both had to be thinking about the same thing. I pictured him cornering me in that hallway at La Cocina to tell me he wouldn't take the principal position if it meant he had a chance with me. Those weren't his exact words, of course, but we both knew it's what he meant.

"I know," he said, looking away.

"So that's not a dealbreaker, then?" What I really wanted was a confirmation of whether he was still seeing her or not.

Owen shook his head and scratched the back of his neck, staring down at his lap. "We don't have to talk about her," he said. I hadn't meant to make him so uncomfortable. So to help ease the tension, I asked to see his resumé, and he opened up the document on his laptop, sliding it toward me on the table.

I regretted bringing up her name.

I pulled his laptop closer to me and got started. Owen was no idiot, but writing wasn't one of his strengths. After reading over his cover letter, I made a couple of changes. Cutting down some of the wordier sentences. Swapping some of his adjectives for something better. And then, I added a few sentences to punch it up a little, telling him, "This is one of the few times it's perfectly acceptable to brag about yourself. Don't be too humble."

He leaned in close to read what I was typing, nodding in approval as he rolled up his shirt sleeves to button them just below his elbows. I glanced at the atom tattoo on his forearm, a part of him I'd laid eyes on so infrequently I'd forgotten it was there, and suddenly I couldn't concentrate anymore. As he put one hand on the back of my chair, I realized we'd been gradually scooting closer and closer together so much that our legs were touching now. His knee and thigh rested against mine beneath the table, and I couldn't remember how long it had been that way. Had I initiated this, or was it him? Or was it a mutual effort?

Regardless, I didn't pull away, and neither did he. I could feel the warmth of his body beside mine, and before long I was so distracted by the sound of his breathing next to me that I read and reread the same sentence five times before I remembered what I was doing. Forcing myself to take a few slow, deliberate breaths, I prayed he couldn't somehow hear how fast my heart was beating.

When I was finally satisfied with his cover letter, I turned toward him, unaware of how close his face was to mine now. "All done," I said, getting lost in his chestnut eyes. He was staring back at me with the same level of intensity. His gaze briefly flickered down to my cleavage, making me aware of my shirt's gaping neckline. I resisted the urge to adjust it, knowing that would only draw attention to the fact I'd caught him looking. I swallowed and wiped my palms on my jeggings.

He must have been able to tell how nervous his closeness was making me, because he cleared his throat and yanked his hand from the back of my chair to reach for his laptop. "Thank you for doing this. Now I might actually have a chance."

"You're welcome," I said, gathering up my things. I knew my armpits were sweaty, so I held my arms close to my side. "And thank you for everything you're doing to help me with, um, you know. The thing. The garden."

"Of course," he said as we both stood up and pushed in our chairs. He put his hands on his hips. "Let me know when you hear back from the Hagans."

"Yep."

When I got back to my classroom, I sunk into my desk chair and laid my head on the desk for a few minutes. This project was meant to serve as a distraction. From *him*. That was a little hard to do when he was brushing up against me, rolling up his sleeves beside me, and staring into my eyes like he could pounce on me at any second.

And it was all I could think about.

# chapter twenty

*owen*

Nothing says Friday night like hot tea with honey and a marathon podcast recording session.

The tea helped soothe my vocal cords, and I'd sort of become addicted to earl grey while living with Rachel years ago. She went through this whole British television phase, insisting we drink tea the proper way like they did on all her favorite shows. Somehow, I'd ended up with the tea kettle after we split. Now, I struggled to get through multiple podcast recordings without some kind of hot beverage within my reach. Coffee kept me up all night, so tea it was.

I flipped through my handwritten notes for each episode, which I'd jotted down on one of my trusty yellow notepads. I always gave myself a basic script to follow, but kept it pretty open and informal. My intention was to never sound like I was reading from a script.

I was about to begin recording an episode about collaborative STEM projects for middle schoolers when my phone lit up with a text from Kendall.

**Kendall:** it's killing me not to tell her all about you

She was having dinner with her sister, making this my first Kendall-free night in a while. When I thought about it, I realized she'd been at my house every night for at least the past week, often bringing take-out from the Chinese restaurant a few blocks down the street. Sometimes I cooked for us, finally getting around to using the panini press my mom insisted on getting for each of my siblings and me two Christmases ago.

Without really meaning to, Kendall and I had fallen into a routine, a semblance of what could almost be considered… a relationship.

I was in over my head with her. With every passing day, it was growing increasingly evident she was catching feelings. The more time we spent together, the harder she fell. I'd narrowly avoided the "what are we?" conversation two or three times now, but my luck would soon run out. It was well past time to rip off the band-aid—I just didn't know how to do it.

And having someone to hold onto during those cold January nights, even if she wasn't who I wanted her to be, wasn't all that bad.

That's why, every time I nearly built up the courage to end this, I kept coming up with reasons to justify postponing the inevitable. A never-ending, perfectly-balanced mental pro and con list.

My worst nightmare.

I didn't have time to respond before she followed up with another text, this one with a sultry selfie attached. She was in the restaurant bathroom with her skirt hiked up to reveal the infamous pink flask secured to her thigh with a garter. Her favorite accessory.

**Kendall:** come over tonight? Please? My roommate's gone and I'll be home by 10

I leaned back in my chair to prop my feet up on the desk, glancing at my watch with a yawn. I'd been at this for three hours. If I didn't quit now, my tiredness would be obvious in my next recording. To be honest, though, a nap sounded more appealing to me now than driving all the way to her house. I didn't respond right away, trying to come up with a good excuse.

To pass the time, I switched over to Instagram and was immediately assaulted by Sarah's engagement announcement—a close-up of her shiny diamond ring, with dozens of congratulatory comments. "About time!" many of them said. "He finally put a ring on it!" I joined the hundreds of people who liked the photo and added my name to the list.

After all, it's what a supportive friend would do.

I clicked on her name and scrolled through her profile. Just two rows down, there was a selfie she'd taken with me at a professional development meeting back in August, both of us with overexaggerated serious expressions. The caption read, "Can't get through PD without my teacher bestie."

And then there was the photo from the last day of school back in May. I'd just received a pie in the face in front of the entire school because my students had collected the most canned goods for the year-long food drive Sarah had organized. For some reason, part of their reward was watching the class clown shove a pie plate full of whipped cream in their teacher's face. And of course Sarah was there to document this momentous occasion, laughing her ass off.

Seconds after that photo was taken, I'd scooped up a handful of whipped cream and slapped it against Sarah's cheek. Before long, we were engaged in a whipped cream fight in front of a chorus of cheering and hollering students. It didn't end until Sarah slipped on some of the whipped cream on the gym floor and I had to help her up, laughing so hard I wasn't sure I could stand, either.

The smile on my face faded when I remembered Cates' "inappropriate interactions" conversation. That was probably one of them. Oops.

A third text from Kendall popped up. Another selfie, this one a little dirtier than the last. I stared at it for a moment, trying to guess where she'd propped her phone to get such a high-quality photo of her entire ass. She was certainly keeping herself entertained in that restaurant bathroom, that's for sure—putting in the work to tempt me to come over. I leaned my head back and sighed, ashamed that it was working.

**Owen:** see you at 10. try to keep your clothes on until then

Just after I hit send, my phone rang. Sarah's name flashed on the screen, and for a second, my skin crawled with dread. Had I accidentally liked one of her old photos? Was she going to question why I was stalking her online? I answered with a panicked "…hello?" and she immediately launched into some eager, incoherent rambling.

I took my foot off the desk and sat up straighter, as though that would somehow help me hear her better. "English, please?"

"Sorry." She took a deep breath and restarted. "We've secured a donation from Hagan Acres."

"No shit?"

"Jerry Hagan says they'll contribute $2500, and they want to be involved as much as they can to help us with everything. He even mentioned the possibility of supplying us with a bunch of materials. Greenhouse plastic and garden tools and I don't even know what else. I'm so freaking pumped, Owen. I just had to tell you!"

I hadn't heard her ramble this excitedly since the morning after the *Supernatural* finale. "Wow. $2500? That's not a small chunk of change."

"Right? And they want you and me to come pick up the check after school on Monday. They even suggested contacting someone from the paper to come and write up a little story on it. Probably because they want some clout, but who cares? We're getting our garden funded!"

"Wow. Do you think it'll be one of those comically huge checks, like people get when they win the lottery?" I relaxed into my chair again, spinning it back and forth. "Because that'd be pretty dope."

"I don't know, maybe?" She giggled. "I hope you weren't in the middle of something, by the way. I just now saw the email, and I didn't want to wait to share the news."

"It's okay. I've just been recording a couple of episodes, and I needed a break."

"Is that new microphone still working out?"

"Oh, absolutely. Total game-changer."

"Good," Sarah said. "I noticed you've been uploading new episodes more consistently lately." I grinned to myself, pleased to hear she still listened to every episode. It was a little embarrassing, though, because it wasn't uncommon for me to completely nerd out about some new scientific discovery. I also regularly made self-deprecating jokes on the show, which I think might have been a huge factor in its popularity. And to think that Sarah sat at home or in her car and listened to that week after week made me hyperaware of just how dorky I probably sounded.

"I think you and my mom might be the show's two biggest fans," I said, grabbing a pen and drumming it on the desk. "But at least you don't call me every time a new episode drops to make me explain what everything means."

"Your mom sounds adorable."

"Adorably oblivious, maybe," I said, and she laughed. We kept talking about the podcast, and the conversation eventually steered back to the garden. I listened to her talk about all her plans for the space and how she wanted to get every class involved in some way. As she talked, I thought about how this might make a good podcast episode once the garden was finished. She'd probably be delighted to be a guest on the show.

"We likely won't be able to break ground on this until after IES," she said. She was referring to the Innovative Educators Summit, a weekend-long conference in Indianapolis in March. A handful of teachers from Grissom went every year, along with Cates. Though it was usually a rotating group of teachers in attendance, Sarah and I hadn't missed one for the past few years. "Don't you think?" she asked.

"Sounds good to me. I almost forgot we were coming up on the conference again."

"We should probably go over the workshop schedule and coordinate soon." Each year, Sarah and I made sure we attended separate workshops during the conference so we could copy each other's notes afterwards. Cates encouraged it. "Vicki's going this year," Sarah continued.

"Nice,' I said, looking down at my watch. It was almost 10:00. I shuffled across the bedroom and started putting my shoes on as Sarah continued to talk about the conference. She'd found a schedule online and was reading some of the available workshops to me. I grabbed my keys and coat from the living room and continued listening as I headed outside to my car.

I couldn't help but wonder if Eli was there with her. Could he hear my end of the conversation, too? Did it bother him that she was spending this much time talking to me?

"Did I just hear your car start?" she asked. "Where the heck are you going this late?"

"Umm…."

I took a deep breath, feeling uncomfortable answering this question. Thankfully, she was able to come to the conclusion herself. "Oh," she said with a little laugh. There was an awkward silence as I sat there on my cold leather seat, not wanting to start driving yet. I didn't want this conversation to end. "Well," she said, clearing her throat. "Have fun."

"Yeah. See you Monday." We hung up and I tossed my phone into the passenger seat, suddenly feeling less enthusiastic about what I was about to go do. My phone had connected to Bluetooth and a text from Kendall popped up on the dash. It was just an emoji, so it was safe to assume there was another nude photo attached. I didn't pick up my phone to look—I was about to see it in person, after all.

I would have rather stayed on the phone with Sarah all night.

# chapter twenty-one
## sarah

Hagan Acres Farm was situated just a few miles north of Woodvale on Hagan Road. On Monday afternoon, I drove us down the winding backroads past a cow pasture and a little white country church until we reached the farm. Near the front of their expansive property, there stood an enormous red pole barn with truck ramps for loading produce. On one side of the barn, there was a row of empty, wooden wagons parked for the winter. Just behind the barn on the other end sat the Hagans' home, an old yellow farmhouse that had probably been in the family for over a century.

When we got to Jerry Hagan's office, which was located at the end of the barn closest to the house, he was already mid-conversation with the reporter from the Woodvale Times. "Look at that," he was saying, handing her the biggest arrowhead I've ever seen. "Found that while tilling the potato garden back in 1997. Feel how heavy that is."

"Wow," the young reporter said, looking up at Owen and me as we walked in. "Oh good, you're here." When I got closer, I recognized her as Meghan Dobson, a girl I'd gone to high school with. Though we were on the English Academic Team together, she was a grade or two below me, and we were never very close. To be honest, she sort of intimidated me—back then, she had dyed black hair, thick eyeliner, and more piercings than I could count. She exuded this "I'm cooler than you could ever dream of being" energy, and I just tried to stay out of her way.

Now, her dark hair was pulled into a professional-looking bun, and her make-up was flawless. She still had a stud in her nose, but it was the only piercing that I could see. The socks peeking out from the bottom of her dark pants had skulls all over them, giving just a hint of her old emo self. "Hi Sarah," she said, reaching out to shake my hand. "You probably don't remember me, but we—"

"Of course I do, Meghan," I said, looking over at Owen, who was shaking hands with Jerry Hagan. And then we swapped, laughing at the way our arms crisscrossed. "I'm Sarah Lavely," I said, looking at Jerry. "And I guess you already know Owen."

"Yes," the old man said, putting his thumbs underneath the straps of his overalls. "The science guy."

"Oh, I wouldn't steal that title from Bill Nye," Owen joked. Jerry's eyes paused on Owen's face for a moment, trying to make sense of what he'd just said—he was too old to have watched Bill Nye. Thankfully, Meghan stepped in to speed things along, asking Jerry if she could go ahead and photograph us with the check before doing a quick interview.

"Sure thing," he said, waving for us to follow him out of his office into the main section of the pole barn, where there was a fleet of green tractors, a monstrous combine, and all kinds of other farm equipment stored for the winter. "It's right over here."

Much to Owen's delight, it *was* one of those comically oversized checks. Unfortunately, we couldn't keep it since it was actually a dry erase board designed to look like a check, with their farm logo in the corner. Jerry explained they reused this for all of their charitable contributions, and it was just for press purposes. Meghan pulled a Nikon camera out of her bag as she ushered Owen and me over to a blank wall with the giant check.

We stood shoulder-to-shoulder behind it, holding it by opposite corners. "Make sure to get my good side," Owen teased as he straightened his tie, causing Meghan to erupt into giggles as she fiddled with her camera settings.

"Oh, I don't think you've got a bad side," she said, blushing as she lifted the camera to her face. Owen placed his free hand on my lower back, blissfully unaware of the effect he had on people.

Jerry pulled out his phone to get a picture, too. "My daughter would shoot me if I didn't get a picture for our website," he explained, squinting at his phone screen. It took him a moment to figure out his camera settings, and Meghan had to step in to help. I was sort of glad, because it meant Owen's hand would be on my back that much longer. His touch felt warm, and it made me want to just melt into him.

After the photo op, Meghan pulled out a pen and a small notebook and jumped right into the interview. She explained she would do a lengthier write-up once the plans for the garden were put into action. This article, she said, would just be a little blurb. We made sure to mention how grateful we were for the Hagans' donation.

Once we wrapped up the interview, Owen and I followed Jerry back into his office for the actual, normal-sized check. "I can't thank you enough," I said, clutching the envelope close to my chest. "This is going to make so many kids happy."

"And that's what it's all about, isn't it?" he asked, scratching the side of his head. He started showing off his arrowhead collection when Meghan caught my attention from outside, nodding for me to come over and talk to her. I left Owen with Jerry and joined her just outside the door. "Awkward question," Meghan started, "but I'd hate myself if I got out of here without asking. Is he seeing anyone?"

I looked over my shoulder at Owen, who was nodding along as Mr. Hagan spoke. "Uh, I'm pretty sure there's a Mrs. Hagan," I joked, "but I can ask, if you want me to." I grinned, fully aware this was the kind of thing Owen would have said if the situation were reversed. His sense of humor was rubbing off on me.

Meghan shoved my arm. "Shut up. You know what I mean. Is Owen single? Because…." Her voice trailed off and she tilted her chin down, giving me this *look*. I knew exactly what that look meant, and I fully concurred.

"He has a girlfriend," I told her, looking over at Owen, who was getting a complete tour of Jerry's expansive arrowhead collection. He glanced our direction at the exact same time, raising both eyebrows as if to say *rescue me from this conversation, please.*

"Well, that's unfortunate," Meghan said. "He's adorable. Those dimples?" She placed her hand on her heart.

"I know." My eyes widened, realizing what I'd just admitted out loud. "I mean, he's—he's—" I tried to say something to make up for my blunder, but it was too late. Meghan was already laughing. There was no way I could save myself from this, so I chuckled at myself, deciding to just go with it. "I mean, I'm not blind."

She pulled a tube of Chapstick out of her pants pocket and applied it to her lips, giving Owen another glance. "I wouldn't be able to keep myself together if I had to work in the same building as him day after day." She shook her head as she put the lid back on her Chapstick, rubbing her lips together. "Anyway, I'm going to head out—but get in touch with me when you break ground on the garden, okay?"

"I sure will."

I rejoined Owen inside the office, where we shook hands with Jerry, thanking him again. He told us to stay in touch and lean on him for support for this garden project. "It's a wonderful thing that you all are doing. Kids need this kind of thing."

* *

As I pulled out of the gravel lot onto the country road, I glanced over at Owen, who looked like an absolute giant in my passenger seat. His six-foot-four frame occupied every inch of the available space, with his knees pressing into my dashboard. I had to bite my lip to suppress a grin. He was just so comically and adorably… large.

Just as I opened my mouth to make a comment about this, my phone rang over the car speakers and Eli's name flashed upon the screen on the dash. Not wanting Owen to hear anything Eli had to say, I quickly disconnected my phone from Bluetooth and held it up to my ear. "Hello?"

"Hey, where are you at, babe?"

"Just leaving the Hagans—I told you about it, remember?" I'd been rambling about the garden to Eli all weekend, forcing him to look at my sketches and plans of all the things I could accomplish now with the Hagans' donation. He barely attempted to hide his disinterest, so it was no surprise he'd forgotten about this.

"Oh, right," he said. "So you're going to get the ball rolling with that whole thing now, huh?"

"Yup," I answered, knowing where this conversation might be heading. Not only was Eli disinterested, when he did have something to say about the project, it was typically negative or dismissive. He was convinced it was a waste of time—because elementary school kids couldn't possibly care about gardening. *"And that Bentley kid will probably destroy it or something,"* he had said.

I was prepared with a rebuttal for every problem he raised. But now, I didn't even want to hear it.

"And keep your negativity to yourself today, please," I said, pulling up to a four-way stop. I mouthed "sorry" to Owen and kept my foot on the brake—wanting to end this conversation before we got closer to town.

Eli sighed. "I just worry that you're sinking a lot of time, money, and energy into something that will be forgotten about by next school year. Nobody's going to match your level of excitement about your project—and I hate seeing you disappointed."

I glanced at Owen, who had pulled out his own phone to text someone, probably sensing this was about to get awkward. "It's not just my project. I already have other people on board. We—"

"For now," Eli cut in. "And I'm not trying to be negative, babe. I'm just being realistic and preparing you for the inevitable disappointment when you struggle to bring in volunteers. And this is just going to distract you from wedding plans. Which you're welcome to start anytime, by the way."

I closed my eyes for a second, bringing my free hand up to my forehead, annoyed that he'd managed to bring my mood down in a matter of minutes. I worried Owen could hear Eli's half of the conversation, so I switched my phone to my left ear. "Look, I'm just sitting here at a stop sign, so I need to hang up. I'll see you at home."

I ended the call and dropped my phone into the cupholder between Owen and me. With an abrupt push on the gas pedal, the car jolted forward through the intersection. Beside me, Owen adjusted in his seat, leaning forward to slip his own phone in his back pocket before turning to me with a look of concern. "Everything good?"

I rolled my eyes. "Eli's just not totally on board with this idea. He thinks it's going to be a waste of time and I'm only setting myself up for failure. Like I'm going to be the only one who gives a shit about this garden and it's just going to be covered in weeds by this time next year." I paused to blow a loose strand of hair away from my face. My heart was racing. "I'm going to be really pissed if he's right."

Owen drew his hands together in a prayer-like gesture beneath his chin, sucking in his bottom lip. I could tell he was carefully considering his next words. I hadn't meant to rant just then—he was probably afraid of what I might say next. Or perhaps he was praying my anger wouldn't cause me to steer us off the road into a ditch.

He released a breath and dropped his hands to his lap. "The newspaper club—you started it just to help one kid belong, to have a place to utilize his talents."

I turned to him, my brows furrowed with confusion. "Yeah?"

"And it was worth it, right?"

I blinked, understanding where this was going. I turned back to the road, gripping the steering wheel with both hands as we approached the edge of Woodvale. "It was."

Owen slowly began to nod, reaching up to wrap his long fingers around the handle above his head. "Okay. So if this school garden impacts just a handful of kids in a positive way—which it will—it's going to be completely worth our efforts then, isn't it?"

My heartbeat began to slow to a normal pace. *"Our efforts,"* he had said. Not *"your."* The significance of his choice of words—to let me know I wasn't alone in this—sent a warmth throughout my body, and all of my doubt, the sliver of fear that Eli could be right, melted away in an instant. Owen had the

uncanny ability of bringing a sense of calm to every situation—
something I would surely miss when he would become too busy
with his principal duties next year. "Thank you," I told him,
because I didn't know what else to say.

He shrugged with a sideways grin, like it was nothing.
Effortless. "Welcome," he said. I felt his eyes on me as I drove
into town. My phone buzzed twice in the cupholder, but I
ignored it, thankful I'd disconnected from Bluetooth. I didn't
need Owen reading whatever Eli was spewing at me.

A couple of minutes passed and Owen crossed his arms
against his chest, his lips curling into a playful smile. "So. What
were you and that reporter laughing about?"

I grinned. "If I told you, I'd have to kill you."

He shifted in his seat. "Okay, that all but confirms it was
about me."

"Relax," I said, reaching to adjust the heat. "She wanted to
know if you were seeing anybody."

He shook his head like he didn't believe me, but the man
couldn't help but smile. "Guess I'm missing the joke."

"Well," I said, deciding to say something I might regret,
depending on his reaction. "The topic of your attractiveness also
came up."

"Ah," he said, adjusting his arms against his chest. Was he
blushing? I could barely manage to keep my eyes on the road,
glancing his way every couple of seconds instead. And then he
continued, saying, "Must have decided I'm pretty ugly, judging
from the laughter."

"You guessed it. We came to the conclusion you're rather
grotesque, actually."

"I knew it."

"The words 'adorable' and 'cute' and 'dimples' definitely
didn't come up. At all."

My goodness, he was blushing even harder now. I was having entirely too much fun with this. "Uh huh," he said, pressing his lips together in an attempt to suppress his smile. "And Meghan was the one making all of these observations?"

I bit my bottom lip. "Stop fishing for compliments, Gardner," I said, trying to keep the tone casual. "It's not very attractive."

It was those dimples, those long fingers of his, and that tattooed forearm I seldom got to lay eyes upon that I thought of that night when my detachable showerhead found its way between my legs.

# chapter twenty-two

*owen*

Sometime after that outing with Sarah, the daily text messaging began.

You could say it was because we were working on a project together. At least, that's how it began. She'd get an idea and run it past me, or we'd send each other links or pictures from our research. But the conversation always veered to something else. And before long, we weren't talking about the garden anymore at all.

> **Sarah:** I don't think I trust people who can go about their day without drinking copious amounts of coffee.

Kendall questioned the onslaught of notifications. I was halfway honest with her, saying things like, "It's Sarah fretting about something again," leading her to believe I was annoyed by Sarah's constant project updates. And of course, I wondered who Eli thought she was conversating with this whole time. Truth be told, if either of our partners snooped on our phones, what they would find there would be completely innocuous. We talked about work, coffee, podcasts, and serial killers—it was just friendly, innocent banter. Sometimes, it didn't even make sense.

The only incriminating part about it was the frequency of the messages.

It became an ongoing conversation with no end in sight. If I picked up my phone, I was texting Sarah. If I had a notification, nine times out of ten, it was from Sarah. We were in communication with each other morning, noon, and night.

**Owen:** Do you trust them more or less than people who drink their coffee black?

**Sarah:** Oh, those people are all serial killers.

We continued this conversation at school. "How do you think Ted Bundy took his coffee?" I asked her in the hallway, sipping my own coffee, which was about as beige as my khaki pants. Students hadn't begun to arrive yet, but we were both ready early.

"Two sugars. No creamer."

"Why do I get the feeling you've thought about this before?"

She just raised her eyebrows at me in this playful way, lifting her mug to her lips as the first group of students arrived for the day. After we took a break from our talk to greet the kids, she turned back to me and said, "Oh yeah—I wanted to run something past you."

"What's that?"

"I'd like to ask Kendall to join the garden committee."

My eyes widened. For the past few weeks, I'd done everything within my power to avoid being in the same room with Kendall and Sarah at the same time. Eating my lunch in my classroom, checking my mail when I knew Kendall was busy teaching, etc. So far, I'd skillfully evaded any awkward interaction between the three of us.

But now, Sarah was insisting on torturing me by suggesting Kendall join the garden committee? This was the worst idea she'd ever had. "My Kendall?" I asked, forgetting there were students nearby. "I mean—are you talking about Ms. Devin?"

Sarah nodded. "Well, yeah," she said, holding her mug with two hands. "Don't you want her to be included?"

Earlier that week, she'd told me about her plan to ask one teacher from each grade to join. She wanted all of the grades to be represented, and this was the best way to ensure the whole school could be involved with the project. There were the obvious choices like Vicki Santiago, who was eager to get involved, and Mrs. Nichols, a second-grade teacher who was a self-proclaimed gardening expert. Asking them for their help made sense.

But Kendall?

I stared back at Sarah, unsure of how to answer this question in a way that didn't make me sound like a total asshole. "Gardening's not really her thing," I said, although I had no idea whether she cared for it or not.

"I thought she could come up with some fun ways to get the younger kids involved," Sarah said. "She doesn't necessarily have to be good at gardening. It was just a thought."

"Well…." What was I supposed to say? The first bell rang, and I stretched, reaching for the top of the doorframe. "I mean, it's your committee."

"*Our* committee," she corrected, her eyes darting upward to my wrist against the doorframe.

"Go ahead and ask her, then," I said, resting my head on my extended arm. "It doesn't matter." It did matter. It mattered a lot. But how could I explain that to Sarah? *No, I don't want to spend time with my girlfriend in front of you?* It was settled, and there was nothing more I could say about it.

I had thought Kendall would instantly turn down the offer to join, because it didn't seem like her idea of a good time, but she was 100% on board. And now that I would be working closely with her on this project for the rest of the semester, breaking things off with her now or anytime soon would make these garden committee meetings unbearable. So I'd be holding off on that, at least for now.

By the end of the week, Sarah had assembled a committee of seven teachers to begin planning the garden. The morning of our initial meeting, my nerves were through the roof as I made my way into Sarah's classroom a few minutes early. Much to my horror, Kendall was already there, and the two of them were fully engaged in a conversation about Sarah's classroom decór. "I just love all the neutral colors in here," Kendall was saying. "It's so calming compared to my room, which looks like a rainbow threw up on it."

"Well," Sarah said. "Neutrals are less stimulating, so, you know—anything to keep them focused on me." She stopped when she saw me walk into the room. They both turned toward me and then glanced back at each other, neither of them entirely sure of how to greet me. As far as Kendall knew, Sarah had no idea we were seeing each other.

"Ladies," I said, lifting my coffee cup as a greeting. I wasn't sure where to look, so I just took a seat at the table where Sarah had placed a lime green folder in front of every chair. I opened the folder in front of me, not surprised at all to see it contained the names of everyone in the committee and their contact information, along with details about everything she and I had researched together thus far. "Wow, Lavely," I said, staring down at a copy of a hand-drawn map of the projected garden area. "You've really outdone yourself."

"Is that a compliment or an insult?" she asked, and she and Kendall laughed together.

I peered up at them over photo-copied pages from a seed catalog. "I'll get back to you on that."

"You wish you were half as organized as me," Sarah said, making her way over to the table as a couple other teachers—Heath and Mrs. Nichols—walked in together. Sarah took the seat beside me at the head of the table. Kendall sat across from me, on Sarah's other side. I could feel her eyes on me, so I pretended to be really interested in Sarah's list of local plant nurseries.

The rest of the teachers continued to file in, and Sarah officially started the meeting at five after.

(She'd complain to me later about the ones who had arrived late. I could almost count on it.)

"As you can see, Owen and I have already conducted a lot of research and have come up with a pretty basic plan as far as the garden layout goes." At the mention of my name, she absentmindedly rested her hand on my arm on the table, keeping her eyes on the packet of paper in her hand. I looked across the table at Kendall, who definitely noticed this friendly display of affection. If her eyes could shoot lasers, Sarah's hand would be a goner.

"But today, I thought we could discuss everyone's role in this committee," Sarah continued, pulling her hand away to flip over a page in her packet, "as well as make decisions on exactly what to plant—and when. Judy, I'm counting on your expertise for that."

Mrs. Nichols nodded. "That's what I'm here for."

For the next forty-five minutes, Sarah went over everything that was included in our folders, and she gave everyone assignments to complete before our next meeting. It turned out we were going to need a little more funding for the project, so some of us would be focused on finding more donors. Mrs.

Nichols liked the idea of forming a student Garden Club to maintain the garden throughout the year, and Sarah put her in charge of recruiting kids for that.

I was happy to see her delegating something for once, instead of trying to do it all herself.

Any time the conversation veered from the topic at hand, Sarah quickly got everyone back on track. She would have kept talking if it weren't for us all needing to get to our own classrooms before students arrived. "Does everyone have a clear understanding of their role and expectations? Any questions?"

Mrs. Nichols was notorious for asking unnecessary questions at staff meetings, so everyone naturally glanced at her in anticipation. However, Sarah had been so thorough with her explanations, maps, and lists, that even Mrs. Nichols understood exactly what needed to be done next.

Sarah Lavely for president.

Once the meeting was officially wrapped up, I picked up my folder and coffee and gave Kendall and Sarah a quick nod, thankful to get away. Forty-five minutes of having to act like I wasn't in a relationship with one of them while also pretending I wasn't pining for the other was enough for me.

Before I even reached my desk, I heard footsteps behind me. I turned around expecting Sarah to unload all of her thoughts about the meeting on me, but instead I was face-to-face with a sulking Kendall. I almost didn't want to know what was wrong. Before I could ask, she blurted, "So, is Sarah into you, or what?"

I froze. "What?"

"Did you not feel her touching your arm? You didn't think that was a bit much?"

I grabbed a stack of math worksheets from my desk and removed the paperclip from them, sticking it in my pocket. "No.

She's just like that. We've been friends for ages. She's like a… sister." I forced myself not to wince as the last word came out.

Kendall put one hand on her hip, holding the green folder in the other. "So there's nothing weird going on there with all the texting and the touching? Nothing I should be concerned about?"

"Of course not. Trust me, she doesn't have any feelings for me whatsoever," I said, my eyes widening. "You don't have to worry about that."

I could tell from Kendall's face these weren't the right words to say. "Why'd you say it like that, like you're so certain?"

"Because," I said, blinking. Looking over Kendall's shoulder, I could see Sarah standing out in the hallway, waiting for me. "Because she knows I'm with you. I accidentally let it slip one day."

Kendall dropped her arm by her side, relaxing her eyebrows. "Oh, she knows?" I nodded at her. "I'm kind of relieved."

"You are?"

"Yeah," she said, clutching her folder against her chest. "Because that makes her less of a threat. Not that she was a threat, I mean. Just, you know. Now I don't have to worry about her. Because she knows you're taken."

"Right." I licked my lips as I started passing out papers. Students would be arriving any minute now, and Kendall would need to hurry to get to her own classroom in time. She appeared to be lost in thought, however, as I made my way up and down the rows with the worksheets.

"Gosh," she said dreamily. "It's going to be so nice to have someone I can actually talk to about you."

No.

No, no, no.

# chapter twenty-three
## *sarah*

Every February, all the fifth-graders at Grissom Elementary went on a field trip to the art museum in Indianapolis. The city was over an hour away, so it was a full-day excursion. Though the museum had a café, the students were required to bring a sack lunch—because I couldn't imagine anything more hellish than ordering food for 60 picky and indecisive fifth-graders. Mr. Woods, the art teacher, always led the students through each exhibit, asking them to stop and sketch what they observed. Between the sack lunches, sketchbooks, and everyone's gift shop money, it was a lot to manage.

Owen loathed this particular field trip, dreading it every year. And that morning wasn't any different. I awoke to a text from him trying to convince me he'd come down with strep throat. I would have believed him, too, if he hadn't followed it up with a text about also having a sudden bout of explosive diarrhea.

**Sarah:** That's what cough drops and diapers
are for. Suck it up, buttercup. I'm not doing this
alone.

"I just realized I left my coffee on the bus," Owen groaned as we made our way through the first exhibit in the museum. The students were scattered throughout the room, crouched over their sketchbooks while Mr. Woods rambled on about shadows and shading.

"Do you want to run and get it?" I asked. "I can watch your group." Between Mr. Woods, the parent chaperones, and the two of us, we each had a group of eight students to keep track of that day. I was already in charge of some of the rowdiest kids myself, so tacking Owen's group onto mine for a few minutes wouldn't make much of a difference.

"No, I'll just suffer," he answered, yawning. I couldn't help but notice the dark circles beneath his eyes or the stubble on his chin. And though he hated all field trips, he seemed a little crankier than usual today. He'd already raised his voice at Jayden Niehaus twice, and he didn't even crack a smile when one of the kids asked Mr. Woods if he was wearing a toupee.

"What's with you today?" I asked him. We were standing in the center of the room between two encased pieces of pottery, which some of the kids lying on the floor by our feet were sketching as they half-listened to Mr. Woods.

"I was up all night," Owen answered.

"Do I even want to know?" I was hoping he wasn't about to share any details about his sex life with Kendall, because I didn't think I could bear to hear them. I'd seen him come from her classroom during his prep time on more than one occasion, and that was enough for me.

"I was working," he asserted, dipping his chin. He took a step closer to me so we could speak more quietly. "Writing."

I stuck my thumbs behind the straps of the backpack I was wearing, which contained a first-aid kit and emergency contact information for every student. "Wait, what? You were writing? Voluntarily?"

He nodded, glancing over at some of the kids across the room who couldn't seem to sit still. "Yeah," he said, crossing his arms. "I had this idea last night to repurpose some of the info from my podcast into a book, and I spent hours outlining the entire thing."

My mouth dropped open. "A book? Are you serious?"

"Yeah," he said with a shrug, like it wasn't a big deal. "Sort of a collection of all the STEM projects I've come up with over the years. I don't know why I didn't think of this sooner."

"Wow! That's going to be incredible," I said, reaching out to touch him on the arm. I would have hugged him if we didn't have an audience. "I am so proud of you."

"Thanks," he said, finally smiling for the first time that day. "I want to get it finished this summer because I won't have the time or energy for this kind of thing if I get the principal job."

I nodded, but what I wanted to do was grab him by the shoulders and shake him for still considering this whole principal thing. Why wasn't it as obvious to him as it was to me that *STEM for the Win* should be his primary focus? Couldn't he see his own potential?

When he switched topics from his so-called side hustle to his possible promotion, all the sparkle left his eyes and the passion in his voice diminished, like he didn't really believe in what he was saying. Did he really not feel the difference himself?

He already had his mind made up about this, though, so I kept my opinion to myself as Mr. Woods wrapped up this segment of the field trip, leading us all into the next exhibition room. The kids scattered with their sketchbooks again as Mr. Woods droned on, asking them to notice the artists' use of leading lines in the paintings around the wall. Owen and I separated for a few moments, walking around the room to observe the artwork ourselves. We found each other near the center of the room again, where I told him, "I would love to help you with your book, if you'll let me."

"Good," he said, standing with his hands folded behind his back. Sunlight poured in through the domed skylight above us, brightening his features. Suddenly, he didn't look so tired, and that twinkle in his eye had returned. He playfully bumped his shoulder against mine, adding, "Because I need you."

* *

As the students eagerly scattered around the gift shop at the end of the day, picking out souvenirs to take home, I let out a sigh of relief. We'd made it through the day without any behavioral issues or major snafus. I almost rejoiced in our good fortune out loud to Owen, but I didn't want to jinx us. For all I knew, the bus could blow out a tire on the way home or something.

I watched as the kids excitedly counted their money and examined the various trinkets, toys, and art supplies on display. Some kids huddled in groups, deliberating over what to buy, while others had already made up their minds and were proudly showing off their new possessions to their classmates outside the gift shop.

My wandering eyes stopped on Bentley, who was standing in front of a display of art supplies with his hands in his pockets, eyeing a set of manga brush pens. I felt a pang of sadness as he watched his classmates carrying their selections up to the counter. If I had to guess, Bentley probably hadn't brought any money with him. He circled the display, looking it up and down, before coming back to the pen set.

Owen approached me with a Vincent Van Gogh finger puppet, wagging it in my face. "You want to hear a Van Gogh joke? Well, ear goes…."

I was too distracted to laugh. I nodded at Bentley. "Look, he didn't bring any money," I whispered. "It's everything I can do not to go over there and buy those pens for him."

Owen removed the puppet from his finger, widening his eyes at me. "Um, please don't."

"I'm not stupid." I didn't need him to remind me how inappropriate it would be for a teacher to buy a gift for a student. "It just breaks my heart a little, that's all."

"I'm sure he's not the only one who didn't bring money. He'll be okay." Owen put the puppet back on the display shelf just as Ava approached him, wanting his opinion on which magnet she should buy.

After a few minutes, I made an announcement that everyone would need to make their final selections because it was almost time to head back to school. I felt sorry for the gift shop clerk for having to deal with a slew of ten-year-olds who had yet to grasp the concept of sales tax, many of them changing their minds about their purchases at the last second. All of the parent chaperones, having to count money and do math on the spot, looked like they regretted their decision to join us that day.

After most of the kids had filtered out of the gift shop to join the others waiting in the corridor outside, I wandered over to the rack of art supplies. Bentley was no longer around. I picked up one of the pen sets he'd been eyeing and flipped the package over to read more. These pens would be perfect for his comics—much better than the colored pencils he'd been using.

And that's why I decided to buy them. Not for Bentley, but for the newspaper club as a whole. They would remain in the classroom, and could be used by anyone who happened to be interested in drawing comics. I hurried over to the counter before I could change my mind.

Out in the corridor, I found Bentley sulking alone on a bench, far away from the other kids. I sat at the other end of the bench clutching the sack from the gift shop against my chest. "Do you want to see what I bought for the newspaper club?"

He gave me a sideways glance and shrugged.

I pulled the pen set from the sack, expecting Bentley's face to light up when he saw it. However, his eyes momentarily widened before he scrunched up his face like he wanted to cry. Not exactly the reaction I was hoping for. "I saw you looking at these," I said, looking down at the pens in my hand to ensure I hadn't accidentally picked up the wrong thing. "Won't they be perfect for your newspaper comics?"

Bentley scowled down at the floor, his shoulders rising and falling as he took a few deep breaths. I couldn't figure out if he was feeling overwhelmed by my kind gesture or possibly embarrassed, knowing I had been watching him long after the pens in the gift shop. He brought one hand to his face and began to cry.

"What's wrong?"

He sniffled and leaned forward, reaching behind him for something. And I watched in horror as he pulled an identical pen set out of the back of his pants. "I stole them," he cried out. His shoulders shook as he dropped the package to the floor, sobbing. "And now I don't deserve them at all."

My blood went hot with disappointment. At the same time, it was all I could do not to grab the boy and hug him. After all, he'd just confessed to his literal crime. I froze for a moment, too stunned to even speak. The kids closest to us were watching in curiosity, whispering and pointing. Fighting back my own tears, I said, "Bentley, I am so disappointed."

Owen approached us carrying the first aid backpack, which I'd pawned off on him sometime after lunch. "Hey, I'm going to have everyone round up their—what's going on?" He noticed Bentley's red, blotchy face and the two packages of pens and looked at me for an explanation.

"I bought this set of brush pens for the newspaper club," I said, looking up at Owen's face. "But Bentley has apparently already given himself the five-finger-discount."

Owen's mouth dropped open. "Oh sh… oh no." I nodded, turning back to Bentley, who had his elbows on his knees and his head in his hands. I bent over to pick up the package he'd dropped on the floor. Owen looped his thumbs around the backpack straps. "What… what do we do?"

"He's going to have to take them back to the gift shop and apologize, for starters," I said. I put the pens I had bought back in the sack, and held the other set out toward Bentley. He didn't take them right away. "Come on. You have to make this right." He accepted them, wiping his nose on his shirt collar.

"Do you need my help?" Owen asked.

"Just help corral the others while I take care of this," I said, standing up and motioning for Bentley to follow me.

We meandered through the crowd of his classmates, all of whom were watching him with curious eyes. I led Bentley to the nearest gift shop clerk, a middle-aged woman with short, brown hair who was rearranging the stuffed animal display after the fifth-graders annihilated it. "Oh hello," she said with a smile. "Did we change our mind about something?"

I put my hand on Bentley's back. "Tell her."

He stared down at his feet and extended his arm out for the woman to take the pens. "I took these."

She looked at me in confusion. "Without paying," I clarified.

"Oh dear," the clerk said, taking the pens from Bentley's hand. "That's not good, is it?" She glanced over her shoulder at the man behind the counter—her manager, I presumed. He was ringing up Mr. Woods, the last of our group to check out. "Well," the clerk said, turning back to Bentley. "Thank you for bringing them back."

Bentley nodded. "I'm sorry I stole them."

"I can tell from the look on your face you'll never do this again," she said, shaking her head. "You know, when a grown-up steals, they have to go to jail."

"That's right," I agreed, a little wary of where this conversation might lead if I didn't step in. "Thank you for doing the right thing, Bentley. Now let's go."

I smiled at the clerk before motioning for Bentley to follow me out of the shop. As we exited, he turned and said, "What's going to happen when I get to school?"

I took a deep breath. Having never dealt with this type of behavior on a field trip before, this was all new territory for me. "That's probably up to Mr. Cates," I said, "but I know your parents will be getting a phone call about this." His shoulders sunk. Had he really thought he could shoplift without his parents finding out? "And you have only one strike left if you want to stay in the newspaper club."

"I know."

"Bentley." I waited for him to look up at me. "You're a good kid. I know you can do this."

He wiped his nose on his shirt again, and I wished Owen was nearby with the backpack so I could grab the poor kid a tissue. His crusty shirt was getting the job done, though.

Owen, Mr. Woods, and I each did a separate head count to make sure we weren't leaving any kids behind at the museum before loading them up on the bus. Once everyone was settled, Owen and I sat in the seat behind the bus driver. He propped the backpack up on his knees as I unzipped it to shove the pens inside, my enthusiasm about them having completely dissipated.

"Well, it was almost a perfect day," Owen said, watching me struggle to re-zip the backpack. After my fifth or sixth attempt to yank it shut, each pull getting more aggressive than the last, he gently pushed my wrist away to do it himself. Of course the zipper effortlessly glided shut for him.

I slid the hair-tie off my wrist and pulled my hair back into a messy bun. "I need a drink of the alcoholic variety," I said, settling back into the seat. I crossed my arms, sliding my butt forward to sink down further. I didn't like the way the back of the bus seat was smashing my bun, though, so I took my hair down again, sighing in frustration as I ran my fingers through it. Giving up on my hair, I looked out the window. "How are we not even out of the parking lot yet? What's taking so long?"

Owen was looking at me like I was a wild animal who might attack at any moment. "Uhh, I hope you get that drink soon."

I managed a little grin, suddenly remembering I was due to start my period any day now. That might have had something to do with the added irritability on top of my frustration with the Bentley situation. "You and me both," I said, putting my hands on my knees. "I can't believe this happened today. You should've seen the look of shame on his face when he had to tell me what he did."

"I could see it."

"It almost makes me wish I didn't have to discipline him any further, you know?" I looked into Owen's eyes. "He's had to deal with me and the gift shop clerk and now Cates and his parents. It's a lot."

"The kid shoplifted, Sarah," Owen said before yawning and slumping over the backpack to use it like a pillow. "Hopefully this will teach him to never do it again."

"I know. I just hate this. He had to stand there and watch everyone else buy what they wanted, knowing he didn't have any money to spend. It's really not fair, when you think about it. I wish we had allocated funds for things like this. Give every kid the exact same amount to spend on a field trip instead of putting that burden on the parents." I shook my head, knowing this idea was next to impossible. And then I gave him a side glance. "Maybe next year's principal can work on something like that."

Owen smiled, still resting his head on the backpack. "Yeah, schoolwide communism will be first on my agenda."

"I'm just giving you a little taste of what your life is going to be like next year," I teased. Maybe that would scare him into withdrawing his application and putting this whole principal thing to rest. "I'm going to be in your office every single day with new ideas, each one of them more insane and controversial than the last."

He turned his head and pressed his face into the backpack, letting out a muffled, dramatic groan. I tilted my head back and laughed, starting to forget how distraught I was just moments ago. I reached over and patted the middle of Owen's back.

"I might need a drink, but you need a nap," I said.

Owen turned his head to face me again. He didn't say a word—he just stared. We exchanged grins, my hand still resting on his back, and he began to close his eyes. If it weren't for the deafening noise level on that bus, I think he could have fallen asleep just like that. I stared at his face, admiring his features—his boyish cheeks, the gentle slope of his nose, and the softness of his lips. When I realized I was still touching him, I quickly pulled my hand away, not wanting it to linger there any longer than was platonically acceptable.

Across the aisle from us, Jayden Niehaus was fidgeting restlessly and eyeing us closely. "Hey Mr. Gardner," he said, with one knee on his bus seat and his other foot on the floor.

With a mischievous grin, he asked, "Is Ms. Lavely your girlfriend?"

Owen shot up straight and turned to Jayden. "No, Niehaus. Sit down." Jayden and his seat mate giggled uncontrollably, and Owen turned back to me, shaking his head with a deep sigh. I could feel him tensing up beside me.

"I'm sorry," I whispered. I got the impression he was annoyed with me for touching him in front of students like that, so I decided to keep my mouth shut for a while. He looked at his watch about once every minute. And every time he did, I stared at the time, too—why did it seem like the trip back to the school was twice as long as the ride to the museum? We weren't even halfway there, and the kids were getting antsier than the two of us.

A few minutes after Owen's exchange with Jayden, the kid stood up and counted to three. And then, much to our surprise, all of the kids erupted into a secretly coordinated song. But not just any song:

*Mr. Gardner and Ms. Lavely*

*Sittin' in a tree*

*K-I-S-S-I-N-G*

Owen turned to me with a horrified look on his face as the song continued, and I cupped my hand over my mouth, trying not to laugh. "What do we do about this?" Owen asked. His panicked reaction was making the entire situation funnier to me, and I just shrugged in response, desperately holding back a giggle. They'd already reached the "Ms. Lavely pushing a baby carriage" part, which I assumed was the end, but half of them continued with a second verse I hadn't heard since I was in elementary school myself.

Owen looked like he wanted to die, so I grabbed the back of our bus seat and pulled myself up to face the kids. They all stopped singing the second they saw my face pop up. "HEY!" I hollered. They all covered their faces or sank down in their seats, giggling hysterically. Even a couple of the parents looked like they wanted to laugh. "Find a different song," I threatened. And then I sat back down, looking over at Owen, who was now hugging the backpack to his chest. "Well," I said. "At least we know they can collaborate and work as a team on something when they really want to."

He just shook his head, and we sat there in silence as the kids moved on to a different song, per my request—something about a hot dog. I could still sense the tension emanating from Owen's body. I didn't know why he had let this bother him so much—it was just a silly song. They could have just as easily been singing about Mr. Woods and me, had we been sharing a bus seat. It wasn't a big deal.

"You need to relax," I told him. "It's just kids being kids."

He fiddled with the zipper on the backpack for a moment before tilting his upper body closer to mine, saying, "It's not just them." His eyes rose to meet mine. "Cates said something to me about you. Us. Back in November."

My stomach flip flopped as though the bus had just sped over a hill, but we were still on the flat highway. "What?"

"He said…." He stopped to clear his throat. We were sitting shoulder to shoulder, and his face was so close to mine, I could smell the mint on his breath. "I guess there were rumors about us circulating."

"Rumors?"

"He told me to watch the way I interact with you because any rumor of a—you know, of an affair or something—could hinder my chances of getting promoted."

My face and ears turned hot at the mention of the word "affair." I was beginning to understand why he was so uneasy about the K-I-S-S-I-N-G song. I hadn't really thought of its implications until that moment. There weren't just kids on this bus. Some of their parents were sitting there, too, and rumors spread fast in this small town. My skin was crawling with embarrassment, thinking about all the times we'd been a little too friendly. If I had known other people gossiped about us so much it reached Cates' ears, I would've backed off a long time ago. "Why didn't you tell me?"

He kept his eyes locked on mine. "Because we're just friends. If people think there's something going on, that's their problem. And I didn't want to—" Owen abruptly stopped, turning away from me to stare at the backpack as he traced one of its seams with his finger.

"What? Didn't want to what?"

He just shook his head, pressing his lips together. I waited, but he never finished his sentence. And, after sitting there for a moment, I realized he already had. That *was* the full sentence: *I didn't want to*. He never told me about Cates' warning because he knew it would force us to acknowledge our flirty ways and even change the dynamic of our friendship. He wanted things to stay the same.

Of course, that was before—well, everything. The Christmas party. My engagement to Eli. And his relationship with Kendall, which was still going strong, despite the fact he never liked mentioning her to me. Now that he had her, he was suddenly concerned with how others might be perceiving our relationship. The tables had turned.

"Funny," I said.

"What's funny?"

"If they only knew whose classroom you've been sneaking off to during your prep periods, they'd all change their tune. Literally."

# chapter twenty-four

*owen*

I didn't know whose bright idea it was to schedule an all-day field trip the same day as one of my Robotics Club meetings, but I was cursing that person under my breath as I carried my tired body to my car that evening. Just before pulling out of the lot, I shot Sarah a quick text.

**Owen:** Considering getting a sub for tomorrow just to recover from today.

All I could think about was how badly I wanted to collapse onto my bed. I planned to shut off my phone for a while and take a much-needed nap. But when I pulled up to my house, Kendall's car was parked on the street. I glanced at my phone—there were no texts from her, just a sarcastic reply from Sarah. This was a surprise. She knew where my spare key was, and she'd let herself in.

I cautiously entered the front door to find her seated on the floor surrounded by construction paper and school supplies. She looked up with a smile. "Hey! I hope it's okay that I let myself in," she said, cutting a tooth shape from a piece of white paper. "I figured since you showed me where the spare key was, it meant that you'd be okay with that."

I dropped my messenger bag on the chair by the door. It smelled like vanilla in there. I thought for a moment she'd been baking cookies or something, but then I noticed a lit candle on the end table by the couch. That was new. "Yeah, it's fine," I said. "What are you doing?"

She held up a giant paper tooth. "February is Dental Health Month."

"Ah." I put my hands in my pockets and glanced in the kitchen, where there were Wal-mart sacks on the table. It also looked like she'd cleaned up in there a little bit. I'd told her before she never had to clean at my house, but she always insisted on it anyway. "What's with the bags?"

She tossed her scissors on the floor and rose to her feet, grabbing me by the hand and leading me all the way into the kitchen. "I did something. And I'm not sure how you're going to feel about it, so please let me explain everything before you even say a word. Okay?"

I swallowed and took another cautious step toward the table. "Okay."

"Okay," she repeated, clapping her hands together. She pulled two gray plastic baskets from the first sack. "You and I are constantly schlepping our shit back and forth to each other's houses, and I thought it would be a good idea for me to keep a basket of my things here. And vice versa. "And look at this." She reached for another sack and dumped its contents into one of the baskets. "I got you duplicates of all the things you usually bring to my house. The deodorant you use, shaving cream, razors, body wash, a new toothbrush, and all that good stuff. Everything is an exact dupe of what you already have, isn't it?"

She looked at me for confirmation, and I slowly nodded. As far as I could tell, she'd nailed it, right down to the exact brand and type of razor I used—and I was really picky about those. "Wow," I said. I was honestly taken aback. It was forward of her to take a step like this without having a conversation with me about it first, but I was also finding it a little… sweet. She clearly cared enough about me to pay attention to all the little details. I couldn't remember the last time a woman had done anything like this for me. "You nailed it."

She was beaming. "I did?" She bit her lip before saying, "I was a little bit afraid you'd be irritated with me."

Was I? I put my hands on my hips, assessing the situation that was laid out on my kitchen table. I watched her unload her own hair and beauty products in the other basket before putting the one for me back in the sack. She continued rambling on about how she had been taking note of things I regularly brought to her house, making a list on her phone of all the products I used. She'd been scheming for more than a week. But I wasn't irritated by it—not in the least. No, that strange, prickly feeling at the base of my neck was something else.

Guilt.

Because I never intended for things to get this far with Kendall. And all of this attention just felt... wrong. I didn't deserve any of this. I wanted to tell her to load it all back up and return it to the store, but I was afraid it might crush her. This woman was falling in love with me, and I didn't know how to stop it.

She slid her hands around my waist. "Are you sure you're not mad? You look a little mad."

I rubbed my eyes. "No, I'm just exhausted. It's been a long day. I'm not mad, Kendall. I…."

I lifted one hand to her hip, noticing the new dish towel hanging from the stove handle and the addition of a succulent on the windowsill. I was starting to feel like a stranger in my own home. How did we reach this point? How had I let it get this far with her? I turned back to her big, brown eyes, completely unable to say what was really on my mind.

"I appreciate this. All of it." I kissed her on the forehead and yawned as I pulled away from her, turning to the refrigerator. "I think I'm going to grab a snack and then crash."

"Can we talk first?"

Oh God. Hadn't we talked enough already? I could tell there was a shift in her mood, and whatever she wanted to discuss was going to be more serious than baskets of deodorant and body wash. She scooted the new baskets aside to pull herself up onto the kitchen table. I crossed my arms and leaned against the counter, bracing myself. "What's up?"

"I want to tell my family about you," she said, her dangling feet swinging back and forth. "And... someday, I want you to meet them. Maybe soon?"

Fuck. Not wanting her to read the expression on my face, I turned away from her. I grabbed a clean glass from the drying rack and filled it up with water at the sink, but I never took a drink. I just held the glass in my hand, trying to gather my thoughts. I didn't want to meet her family—of that I was certain. But I didn't know how to tell her that.

"Especially my sister," she continued. "She's my favorite person in the entire world, and it's killing me not to be able to talk to her about you—my *other* favorite person."

"I can't risk it," I said. Her mouth slowly closed. I sat my glass down on the counter and folded my arms across my chest again. "I'm going to be interviewing for the principal position soon, and it's against policy to date a teacher. You know that."

"I know, but... I thought we could work around that."

"How?"

She hopped down from the table and stood in front of me, placing both of her hands on my waist again. "There are always openings in other districts. I don't have to stay at Grissom."

I leaned away from her, shaking my head in disbelief. "No. Don't say you would switch districts for me. That's crazy."

"No, it's not," she said, staring into my eyes. She tightened her grip on my waist. "I mean it. There are four other elementary schools in this county alone. I'm sure at least one of them will have an opening in August. And if not, well, I've got retail experience. Kohl's would welcome me back in a heartbeat."

"Jesus Christ," I whispered. I drew one hand up to my face and rubbed my eyes with my thumb and pointer finger. This was all too much—the baskets, the candle, the succulent, and this entire conversation. "I'm too tired to be having this conversation right now."

She pulled away from me with an exasperated sigh. "If not now, then when? You always try to change the subject when I start talking about our relationship, so let's just get this over with." There'd been a shift in her tone. Now she was annoyed with me. "And then you can go take your nap."

"I don't know what you want me to say," I said, dropping my arm back to my side.

"I want to know what you thought was going to happen between us. Were you planning on keeping me your dirty little secret forever? I mean, what even am I to you?"

"Do we have to put a label on it?"

"So you're okay with us having a basket of things at each other's places, but you still can't call me your girlfriend. Got it." She let out a soft chuckle, but I could tell she wasn't amused. "That's not confusing at all."

Dammit. I should have come clean with her about my feelings ages ago, before I let it get this far. The appropriate time to rip off this band-aid had already come and gone, and the longer I waited, the harder she was going to take it. I searched my brain for the right words, but they all escaped me the second I gazed down into her eyes.

I thought about our first night together, and how I'd only kissed her to begin with because I was feeling rejected and hopeless and desperate to feel wanted. Her presence outside that restaurant when I was at my lowest was just a convenient coincidence. If she hadn't been there, would I have just gone home alone that night? Would I still be sitting alone in my house every single night from then on, lamenting about my loneliness while refusing to do anything about it?

Probably.

"Say something," Kendall begged.

I knew I was being unfair. She'd done nothing wrong. She was, by all definitions, the perfect girlfriend. If I made a pro and con list, the pro column would fill up pretty fast. She laughed at my jokes. She was smart and quick-witted. She loved all the same shows as me, and I genuinely enjoyed binging Netflix and vegging out with her. And she obviously cared about me an awful lot, something I could learn to be more appreciative of.

Maybe—if I could somehow force Sarah out of my heart— I could make room for Kendall there.

"Listen," I said, my throat feeling a little scratchy all of a sudden. I took her by the hands and pulled her closer. "I'm sorry if I seem really guarded. It's been a while since I've been in a relationship, and this all feels new to me."

"It's okay." She looked down, squeezing my hands. "You just have to let me know where I stand with you. If I'm wasting my time, just tell me."

The opportunity was right there in front of me—I just needed to say the words. It would have been so easy. But just as I had many times before, I let the moment pass. Suddenly, I found myself saying, "I suppose it's okay if you tell your sister

I'm your boyfriend." A compromise. I was buying myself some time—giving my heart a chance to catch up with my words.

Because I *could* love her. Potentially.

And judging from the smile spreading across her face, I knew this satisfied her enough. For now, at least. Before she could say anything, I quickly added, "But I don't know if I'm ready to meet your family. Let's just… keep taking it slow, okay?"

"Okay. Yes. Absolutely." She slid her hands around my body once more, allowing me to pull her in close for a kiss. And before long, she was fiddling with my belt buckle so she could slip her hand down the front of my pants. Add another pro to the list, I guess—Kendall was always eager to get her hands on my dick. She rubbed me through my boxers, nuzzling against my ear to whisper, "Still want to take that nap?" That ship had already sailed, along with my last remaining shred of dignity.

And as she dropped to her knees in front of me, taking me into her mouth, Sarah's face flashed before my mind. I closed my eyes and could almost hear the sound of her giggling on the bus beside me, her hand ever-so-delicately resting on my back. I tilted my head backwards and opened my eyes to stare up at the ceiling, but I still couldn't shake Sarah from my mind. Fuck, this wasn't going to take very long.

*Con: She's not Sarah.*

And though it was the only bullet point on that side of the list so far, it carried more weight than everything in the pro column combined.

# chapter twenty-five
## *sarah*

The first weekend in March promised clear skies and a high of 68°, making it ideal for our first hands-on workday for the garden project. The garden committee scrambled for a week to gather all the materials needed to at least get the raised garden beds and greenhouse put together. Jerry Hagan had become such a permanent fixture around the school, answering questions and dropping off supplies, that he was given a laminated visitor pass.

In the meantime, we rounded up as many volunteers as we could, inviting anyone involved with GES to come lend a helping hand. I'd hoped for at least a handful of parents or some enthusiastic community members who might have a green thumb and a philanthropic heart.

What I hadn't expected, however, was for there to be so many volunteers I couldn't even find a job for all of them. Mr. Cates was there, willing to get his hands dirty, as well as some teachers who weren't even on the garden committee. Dozens of students had dragged their parents out to help, and of course Jerry Hagan arrived at 8:00 a.m. sharp, raring to get started on the greenhouse assembly.

Many of us were wearing matching kelly green t-shirts featuring the words *Grissom Elementary School – We Grow Together* and a childlike doodle of a garden across the chest. That was a fundraising idea from Vicki, who knew her way around a vinyl cutting machine and spent the entire previous weekend completing orders. The profit from the shirts, combined with the generous check from the Hagans and several parents' donations, would allow us to create the garden of our dreams.

Well, my dreams, at least.

I spent the morning delegating tasks, answering questions, and helping Judy and her husband, Lyle, with the raised garden beds. After layering some cardboard and mulch in one of the raised beds, I paused for a moment to stretch my back and look around. Owen, Heath, and a few other people were working on the greenhouse with Jerry. Cates was impersonating the Hulk every time he tore open a new bag of mulch, which made all the kids laugh to see their principal this way.

Just a few feet away, Kendall, Vicki, and a handful of our volunteers were placing paving stones between the raised beds. Some of the workers were busy putting the trellises up around the border of the garden, and I could already envision the finished project. Our perfect little garden.

I considered snapping a picture of the scene and sending it to Eli, just to show him how wrong he had been, but he'd be able to see for himself in just a little while. He was reluctant to have anything to do with this, claiming he had enough to worry about at the high school, but ultimately decided it might look good if people saw the varsity football coach doing some volunteer work. I brushed aside the fact he was just doing it to boost his image after that losing season. At least he would be there.

I kept waiting for some crazy mishap to occur, but it was all going according to plan. A lump formed in my throat as I watched a sea of people in their green shirts working hard, all of them giving up their Saturday to be here. It almost felt too good to be true.

As I stood there with my hands on my hips, I caught Owen's eye from across the garden as he paused to take a sip from his Gatorade bottle. He swallowed and screwed his cap back on, looking from the left to the right. And when his eyes found mine again, he nodded in this reassuring way like he, too, was impressed by how well this was all going. I smiled in response, my anxiety beginning to fade.

Just as I started to get back to work, listening to Judy explain the purpose of each layer of the raised beds, someone tapped me on the shoulder. I whipped around to see Bentley standing behind me on the walkway.

"Bentley!" I smiled at him and the woman standing behind him, whose hair was the exact shade of blonde as his. His mother, I presumed. Neither of them was wearing the *We Grow Together* shirts, but then again, it wasn't necessary. "I'm so glad you're here."

"I thought he was lying to me when he said he had to come to school on Saturday," his mom said. "Either that or he was in trouble again."

"Nope! I'm so happy he wanted to volunteer." I reached out to shake her hand. "I'm Bentley's homeroom teacher, by the way. Ms. Lavely."

She didn't return the introduction. "I'm sorry you have to deal with this shithead." I did my best not to react to her name-calling the kid who was standing a foot away from her. "If it's not one thing, it's another, isn't it?'"

"He's definitely had a few struggles," I said, bringing my hand up to my eyes to block out the sun. I looked at Bentley, who was watching Jordyn Ellis and some other kids spread mulch nearby. Since the field trip incident, he'd been pretty quiet in the classroom, even in newspaper club. I'd put the manga pen set in my desk drawer, feeling uncertain about the ethics of allowing him to use them after he'd attempted to steal them. He didn't ask about them, either.

I'd been picking up on a little resentment from him, too, which is why I was a little stunned to see him volunteering for the project I'd been obsessively talking about in class for the past week. And from the sound of it, he'd led his mom to believe this was required. I looked at the woman who'd never once volunteered or signed up for a parent-teacher conference, trying to keep my judgmental thoughts at bay.

"I've been so proud of the work he's done with his comic strip for the newspaper," I continued. "He's extremely talented."

His mom rolled her eyes. "Well, if he put half the effort into his homework that he put into those comics, maybe he wouldn't bring home Ds and Fs all the time."

Jesus. *Just let me compliment your kid*, I wanted to say. "Well, I'm going to get back to the job I'm doing, but you can join the volunteers working on weeding the landscaping up by the building, if you want?"

They seemed okay with this assignment, and I returned to work. A few minutes later, I was interrupted again—this time it was Owen, standing behind me with a garden hoe. "The reporter's here to talk to us," he said, nodding in the direction of the double doors that led to the playground, where Meghan was standing.

"Oh, good," I said, wiping my dirty hands on my pants. I had called her earlier in the week to let her know we were getting a jump-start on the garden, but I'd been so busy all morning, I almost forgot about this interview.

She led us around the side of the building where her recorder wouldn't pick up any background noise from all the people. As we stepped into the shade, I got my first good look at Owen since earlier that morning. It was unusual to see him wearing anything besides dress pants and button-up shirts, so the rugged dark jeans that hugged his butt perfectly were a welcome sight. He wiped sweat from his brow, an intoxicatingly musky scent emanating from his body. It only made me want to move closer to him as Meghan began her rapid-fire questioning.

Why is it that men smell so good when they've been working outside? My own arms clung to my side just in case my deodorant wasn't doing its job. If I smelled bad, he either didn't care or didn't notice. His fingers, wrapped around the handle of the garden hoe, grazed against my arm as he spoke to Meghan.

"So tell me," Meghan said, looking mostly at Owen, "what are some of your main goals for the students with this garden? How will this benefit them?"

"Well," Owen started, scratching his cheek. "There's a lot that can be learned from growing your own food. And these children will get to witness the whole process, from seed to table." He glanced over at me as if looking for affirmation, and I nodded. I felt a sense of pride as he continued talking about this project—our project—that stemmed from a random idea of mine. If I wasn't mistaken, it appeared he was now just as passionate about this garden as I was.

"This will provide a hands-on learning experience for all of our students," I added once Meghan turned toward me with her recorder. "My hope is that it becomes more of an outdoor classroom for them."

After talking to Meghan for about ten minutes, she said, "Well, I think I got everything I need. I'll call if I need you to clarify anything." She put her notebook and recorder in her bag. "I'm going to get lots of candid shots of everyone working, but can I get a portrait of the two of you? Maybe right here, in front of the school?"

"This whole thing is really Sarah's brainchild," Owen said. "Should I be in this?"

"Are you kidding me? Come on." I grabbed him by the arm and pulled him over to the area where Meghan was pointing. There were a couple of tall evergreen shrubs to the left of the double yellow doors. Owen started to lay his garden hoe down on the ground, but Meghan insisted he use it as a prop. "We're just like that American Gothic painting," I told him.

"I'm pretty sure that guy was holding a pitchfork."

"Close enough," I said, sliding closer to him as Meghan fiddled with the settings on her camera. She apologized for taking so long, explaining they'd just downsized and let their staff photographers go due to recent budget cuts. Owen and I nodded in unison—we were no stranger to that kind of thing.

He chewed his bottom lip as we waited, trying not to smile, like he'd just thought of something clever to say. He glanced over Meghan before leaning close to me, saying, "There's nothing I love more than standing between two hoes."

My mouth fell open. "Oh my god, stop it," I said, giving his chest a hard shove as I began to laugh. He beamed right back at me, obviously feeling proud of his little joke. There weren't a lot of people who could get away with saying something like that to me, but Owen was one of them. "That wasn't even remotely clever, but nice try."

He stretched his non-hoe-holding arm behind him with a yawn. "There's a hoe lot more where that came from."

It wasn't the words—but his casual delivery—that sent me into another fit of laughter. "Shouldn't you become a dad before you start telling dad jokes?"

I was so distracted by his lame attempt at humor, I hadn't even noticed Meghan was ready to take our portrait. Much to our surprise, however, she'd already snapped a couple of candid shots while we weren't paying attention. "I actually think I got what I need already," she said, staring at the back of her camera with a grin. "Yeah, this is definitely better than any posed picture could be."

I glanced from Owen to Meghan, desperate to ask her if I could see the photo in question. But she was already slinging the camera strap back over her neck, giving us a thumbs-up. She wandered off to grab some more candid shots of all the volunteers. "Damn," Owen muttered. "I really wanted to see that photo."

"Me too," I said with a laugh. "I suppose we'll get to see it in the paper."

We slowly walked around to the other side of the building, with him using the garden hoe as a walking stick. We paused at the corner of the building, taking in the scene before us. Everything was really coming together—the trellises were up, and the greenhouse was halfway finished. Some of the kids were playing a game of tag, chasing each other between the raised beds and beneath the garden arbors. Bentley had found Jordyn, and the two of them were sitting cross-legged in the landscaping up by the building, probably conspiring about something.

My eyes stopped on Kendall, who was taking a break to get a drink from an aluminum water bottle. She was wearing short denim shorts and green Chuck Taylors the exact shade as her t-shirt. With her hair pulled back into two perfect braids, she looked adorably put-together. Meanwhile, I was wearing holey jeans and an old pair of Nikes I'd dug out from the bottom of my shoe bin. I'd forgotten a hair-tie, too, so my tangly, sweaty hair was starting to stick to my neck. I self-consciously ran my fingers through the ends of my hair, feeling like a hot mess compared to her. "Kendall looks really cute today," I said.

Owen sighed. "Yeah, but have you seen Mrs. Nichols? That visor… it's really doing something for me." He let out a low whistle.

I giggled, but I wasn't about to let him change the subject. "How are things going between you and Kendall?"

He stared down at the ground, one hand on the garden hoe handle and the other on his hip. "I don't know. We don't have to talk about that."

I sighed. "Why not?" Kendall was obviously pretty important to him now, and it was the only aspect of his life he wouldn't share with me. "Who else are you going to talk about her with? Your mom?"

"Please," he said with a chuckle. "My mom isn't aware Kendall exists."

"Really?" That came as a surprise. "You've been dating the same woman for three whole months, and you've somehow kept that from your mom?"

"It has not been three months," he corrected, shaking his head. I didn't know why he was on the defensive about this. "Anyway, how about this weather, huh?"

"You really aren't comfortable talking to me about her, are you?"

"What do you want to know? I'm an open book."

That couldn't have been further from the truth. "I don't know. Anything. There's this whole portion of your life that you keep from me completely, and I'm just letting you know it doesn't have to be that way."

Owen ran his fingers through his hair, with one hand still wrapped around the handle of the hoe. He was ever-so-slightly shaking his head, but I could tell I was close to cracking him. He was about to give in. He could just tell me what Kendall liked to eat for breakfast, for all I cared. I would be satisfied with any tiny morsel of information he was willing to share if it meant he could finally get over his discomfort about this topic. "Well," he started, dropping his hand back to his side, "she's been gradually moving some of her stuff into my place."

I blinked. "Really?"

"Yeah. First it was just, like, a little basket in the bathroom, you know?" I nodded in response and let him continue. It seemed like he was on a roll, and I was afraid if I interjected or showed too much emotion in my face, he'd regret opening up. "But now I think half her wardrobe is at my house—and all her hair stuff and whatnot. It's taking over." Though he was venting, he smiled from one corner of his mouth, like it wasn't really bothering him all that much.

"Wow," I said, lifting my hand to my face to shield the sun from my eyes. "So it's getting pretty serious, huh?"

"I don't know," he said with a shrug. He gazed ahead at the garden, where Kendall was carrying two paving stones and laughing with one of the volunteers. "It's just different."

"And you're still going to interview for the principal job?"

Owen nodded, draping his arm over the end of the hoe. "Yeah. But she's got a whole plan for that." I stared up at him, confused, until he continued. "She says she'll switch districts if she has to."

"Holy shit," I blurted. Thankfully, there weren't any kids in the vicinity. This was huge. All of this new information was a lot to process after hearing next to nothing about their relationship up until this point. It was dizzying. Switching school districts so they could stay together? That sounded like commitment. I stared straight ahead, but I could feel Owen's eyes on me, gauging my reaction after this last little tidbit of info. I tried to hide my shock, but it was probably too late for that. "Well, she must really like you if she's willing to do that."

"Yep." He clicked his tongue.

"Is that what you want?" This discussion was taking me back to our conversation over a slice of pumpkin cheesecake at Poppy's long ago, when he'd asked me the very same thing about Eli. And if I recalled that night correctly, I never gave him an answer. I studied his face, trying to read his thoughts, but he was lost in space. "Owen."

He came back to earth, bringing his eyes up to meet mine. "Who wouldn't want that?"

"That's not what I asked you. Do *you* want that? Would you really have her switch school districts for you?"

"I'm not asking her to do that. That was entirely her idea. I…." He glanced over at Kendall, who was watching us now. They waved at each other with a smile before he turned back to me, saying, "Honestly? I don't feel like I'm worth it."

"Are you kidding me?" I couldn't help but laugh. "Of course you are. She's the lucky one, Owen."

He still looked skeptical. "I don't know about that." He flipped his wrist over to look at the time before gripping the handle of the hoe with both hands again. "We should get back to work before they start singing the K-I-S-S-I-N-G song again, right?" And then, after a playful pat on the back of my arm, he walked off toward the garden to start helping Jerry and the other guys with the greenhouse again.

I swallowed, letting the next few months play out in my mind like a movie: Owen's settling into his principal role, and he's publicly dating Kendall, the new love of his life. As for me? I'm the annoying fifth-grade teacher who's constantly bombarding him with insane project ideas. Just a side character in his story, starring in my own tragedy: the one about the girl who was too late.

# chapter twenty-six

owen

"I've seen more butt cracks today than I have in my entire life."

Kendall laughed in response to my observation as she bit into a slice of cheese pizza. Hours into our workday, everyone's stomachs started growling, so Cates ordered enough pizza for all of the volunteers, and then some. I had a feeling all the leftover pizza would end up in the refrigerator in the teacher's lounge after this. At least, I hoped it would.

We were sitting on the lower platform of the playground equipment since all the picnic tables and edges of the raised garden beds were already taken. Other than the kids playing on the monkey bars nearby, there was nobody else around us. For a moment, I worried how this might look, but nobody seemed to notice or care.

Eli was dominating everyone's attention now. He showed up just in time for lunch and helped himself to a hefty serving, despite having not lifted a finger so far. And he was wearing one of the *We Grow Together* shirts like the rest of us. Of course Sarah had bought it for him, but I found it a little irksome. To make matters worse, he only stuck around long enough to talk football with Cates and tear open a couple bags of potting soil for Sarah before dipping out to go play golf.

"Why did he even bother showing up at all?" I asked Kendall. "He's just trying to make himself look good."

"Why do you care?"

"I don't. It just seems a little self-serving, that's all."

"Someone's jealous," Kendall said, taking a drink from her water bottle.

"Jealous?" I laughed. "Of what?"

She just rolled her eyes and smirked before hopping down from the playground equipment, wiping her mouth. "I don't know, Owen." She tugged at the bottom of her shorts to adjust them. "I'm going to get back to work."

She headed back toward the area where she'd been working all morning, leaving me behind. Of course, it wasn't hard to figure out what she was implying with that accusation. She'd already made the false assumption Sarah had feelings for me, but maybe she'd worked out by now that it was actually the other way around. I let out an exasperated sigh as someone behind me hollered, "Mr. Gardner, look at me!"

I looked over my shoulder to see Jayden Niehaus sitting atop the dome over the spiral slide, which was very much against the rules. He knew that, too. But today was Saturday, and this kid was not my responsibility. "Try not to break your neck, Niehaus," I said, wiping my greasy hands on my jeans before returning to work.

Now that the greenhouse was nearly put together, the rest of the day sped by. As the afternoon sun got lower in the sky and the temperature began to drop, the crowd of volunteers started to dwindle. We had completed just about everything we could at that point, anyway. There would be more garden workdays in the future to plant the vegetables and flowers, but we'd have to work around the unpredictable Midwest weather to schedule those days.

By five o'clock, only a few of us remained—Mrs. Nichols, her husband, Kendall, Sarah, and me. The only work left for us to do was to clean everything up. The PE teacher was generous enough to clear out a spacious corner of a nearby storage shed for us to keep everything. We filled the space with all the extra paving stones, leftover bags of mulch and potting soil, and all the gardening tools.

Kendall was the next person to leave. She had a bachelorette party to get ready for, which meant I'd be dealing with Drunk Kendall later that night. When Mrs. Nichols' back was turned, she pulled me down and planted a kiss on my cheek. "I'll be home around one or so." Just after she turned to leave, she spun back around, clamping her eyes shut. "I meant to say, 'your house,'" she said, opening her eyes again. "Not 'home.'"

I sucked my bottom lip in, choosing not to acknowledge her little slip-up. If I acted like it wasn't a big deal, she might do it again—on purpose. And I wasn't ready for that kind of commitment. Trying to hide my unease, I told her, "Just call me if you can't get a ride, okay?"

And then there were four. I could tell Sarah was a little annoyed nobody else stuck around to help with the clean-up. Maybe it would have been better to stagger the volunteers' hours. I didn't point that out to her, though. After we put everything away, I carried all the empty pizza boxes around to the dumpster at the back of the building, disappointed there wasn't a single slice of leftover pizza. I should have known better, with all those hungry kids in attendance.

When I got back to the garden, Mrs. Nichols and her husband were on their way to the parking lot. All that was left to do now was gather my own things and say good-bye to Sarah. She was standing in the landscaping next to the building, coiling the garden hose back into the hose reel. I grabbed my Gatorade and the hooded sweatshirt I'd arrived wearing that morning and joined her by the side of the building. "I'm beat," I said, holding my bottle between my knees as I pulled my hoodie over my head.

"Me too. But just look at all we got done," she said, turning the crank on the hose reel. As I bent over to unkink the hose for her, she let out an exhausted but elated sigh. "What an amazing turnout."

"Wasn't it?" I took a sip of my Gatorade, which was still refreshing despite being completely warm now. I couldn't wait to go home and get a cold drink and a shower, but I wanted to wait for her to finish so we could walk to our cars together. Though I could tell she was tired, she somehow looked even more beautiful than normal. Her cheeks were flushed, and the sweat on her forehead made her wild hair stick to her face in this really sexy way. I looked down and took another drink before I let my mind get too carried away.

All of a sudden, I felt a cold blast of water across my chest and arm. I was so startled by it, my Gatorade bottle slipped from my hands and spilled on the sidewalk between my feet. I looked up at Sarah with my mouth open wide, fully expecting her to apologize for accidentally spraying me, but this was no accident. She was doubled over in laughter. "The look on your face!"

"Wow. Just—wow. Big mistake, Lavely." I bent down to put the lid back on my bottle, leaving it on the ground. I was going to need both hands for what I was about to do to her. She backed away as I approached her, but there was nowhere for her to go. I had her cornered.

"Don't you dare," she said, turning her back to me and folding her body over the hose nozzle in an attempt to make it harder for me to pry it from her hands. As I came up behind her, she twisted around and tried to wriggle away, laughing the entire time. As feisty as she was, I still managed to wrestle the end of the hose away from her. Since she was trapped between me and the building, she cowered and covered her head with her hands. I clamped my hand down on the sprayer and aimed it at her back, completely drenching her. I would have stopped had she shown any sign of displeasure from this counterattack, but she was still laughing hysterically as I swept the nozzle back and forth to make sure every bit of her upper body was soaked.

When I felt like she'd had enough, I finally relented. With an overdramatic flick of the wrist, I let the hose fall to the ground. Sarah straightened her body and turned to face me, water dripping from the ends of her hair. "Oh. My. God," she said, holding her arms out to the side. Water droplets fell from her fingertips. She looked like she'd gotten stuck in a car wash or maybe stood outside during a hurricane. "That water is *so* cold."

I took a step forward. "Don't start a fight you can't finish, Lavely," I teased.

"Lesson learned. I hate you so much right now," she said, but her smile told me otherwise. She shivered before me, hugging herself to keep warm. Or she may have been trying to hide the way her wet t-shirt was now clinging to her breasts. When her teeth started to chatter, I felt a little guilty for taking things too far.

Stepping even closer to her, I tugged on one of my hoodie cuffs with my opposite hand and used my sleeve like a towel to dry her arms. She just stood still, staring up at my face as I patted her skin dry with the sleeve of my sweatshirt. Then, lifting my hand to her face, I used my sleeve to catch the droplets of water rolling down her cheeks. She kept her eyes on mine the entire time. When I put my hand back down, I could see she was still covered in goosebumps. "Here," I said, pulling my hoodie over my head. I gestured for her to take it from me.

"Oh, you don't have to do that," she said, though she shivered again. When I didn't pull the hoodie away, she grinned and let out a defeated sigh, taking it from my hands. "Fine. Turn around." I stood with my back to her, putting my hands on my hips like that would prevent people in passing cars from seeing her partially unclothed body. But we were at least fifty yards from the street, and there was a tall trellis just across the walkway from us. I cleared my throat while she changed, trying not to imagine what was happening behind me.

When Sarah gave me the okay to turn back around, the sight of her wearing my favorite hoodie made my heart feel like it might leap right out of my chest. The sweatshirt practically swallowed her tiny frame, the hem skimming her upper thighs. She held her wet t-shirt by her side, using her other hand to wring out her hair. "I'll wash this and give it back to you on Monday."

"No, keep it," I said. Sarah slowly lowered her hand from her hair, locking her eyes on mine. I took a step forward, reaching up to playfully tug on the ends of the frayed drawstrings that dangled against her chest. "Looks better on you anyway."

I started to withdraw my hand, but she reached for it, enclosing her fingers around mine. I gave her a puzzled look, thinking at first I'd crossed some sort of line and she'd meant to push me away, but her eyes were telling me a different story. They were lustful. Hungry. I looked down at our hands, gliding my thumb over her soft fingers. I smiled in amusement at the way there was a build-up of dirt under every one of her unmanicured nails.

I lifted my eyes to meet Sarah's gaze again, suddenly aware of just how close we were standing. She dropped the wet shirt on the sidewalk at our feet and reached for my forearm, tracing my tattoo with her thumb. Her touch sent this electric prickle across my skin, and I craved more of it. I carefully and hesitantly slipped both of my hands just inside her hoodie pocket, as if it were somehow less of a risk than grabbing her by the waist like I really wanted. I gave the sweatshirt the gentlest tug to bring her body closer to mine. Sarah met my effort, pressing the curves of her body against my chest. She brought her hands to my waist, giving me the courage I needed to slip my arms around her body. My cheek skimmed hers, and the way her breath tickled my neck almost brought me to my knees. My lips hovered just an inch from her mouth, and all either of us needed to do now was turn ever-so-slightly to bring them together.

No.

I inhaled as I jerked away from her. Holy fuck. What were we about to do? Sarah turned her body away at the same time, both of us coming out of our trance. "I'm sorry," I spit out, watching as she bent down to pick up her wet t-shirt. Trembling, I held my hand up to my forehead in total disbelief that I'd let things get so far. "Got a little carried away there."

She wrung out her shirt, refusing to look me in the eye. "It's okay. Nothing happened. We wouldn't have… let it get further than that." I wasn't sure who she was trying to convince more. Herself, or me. She forced out a casual-sounding laugh. "I think we're both just so exhausted, we're not thinking straight."

"Right." I picked up my Gatorade, hoping she couldn't tell I had a massive hard-on. "It's been a long day."

"It sure has."

I walked Sarah to the parking lot like I'd intended, but we both scrambled to get in our cars after hurried good-byes. I was thankful she drove off first, because I needed a moment to collect my thoughts. So many questions were swirling through my mind, like—did she actually want me just as badly as I wanted her? What do we do now?

And how long was it going to take for this erection to go away?

I gripped the steering wheel, my stomach churning with remorse. Although we both resisted the temptation to bring our lips together, the intimacy of the moment crossed every single unspoken line. The fight with the hose was borderline, at best. But it should have stopped there. As much as I loved the way her body felt pressed against mine, I could never be reckless enough to let it happen again.

And Kendall…

She deserved better than this.

# chapter twenty-seven



Monday mornings were bad enough on their own, but spilled coffee and missing keys really amped up the "I hate Mondays" vibe. The coffee mess I could deal with, but I wasn't going to be able to make it to work on time if I didn't find my keys within the next five minutes. I cursed under my breath, remembering how Eli once told me not to leave my spare set of keys in my desk at school. It seemed like the most logical place to keep them, but now, with couch cushions scattered on the living room floor all around me, I was second-guessing that decision.

The last time I'd had my keys in my possession was Saturday evening, when I got home from working in the school garden. It wasn't like me to lose things like this, but I was so out of it when I got home that day, who knew where I could have put them? Normally I would have dropped them in my purse or, at the very least, left them on the counter by the back door. But they were in neither place.

I went outside to check my car, but it was locked. And as far as I could tell, I hadn't left them in the ignition. I pulled out my phone to look at the time. I was usually well on my way to school by now.

What could I do? Eli had an early IEP meeting that morning, so calling him wasn't an option.

I scrolled through my contact list, searching for co-workers who might be available to swing by and pick me up. First, I sent

Vicki a quick text, knowing she was probably dropping her kids off at daycare, anyway. After her, I messaged Judy, explaining my situation, but she quickly replied that she and her husband shared a vehicle and he had driven her to school that morning. Shit.

I knew exactly who I could call for help—the one person who wouldn't hesitate at all to come pick me up—and in fact, he'd probably be glad to do it. No questions asked. My thumb hovered over Owen's name, but I couldn't make myself call him. Not after our interaction in the garden.

For the past 36 hours, I'd been replaying that encounter over and over in my mind like it was a movie—or it was someone else's life I was watching from afar. That couldn't have been *me* tenderly stroking the tattoo on Owen's arm. He didn't pull *me* against his body. We didn't almost kiss.

Yet every time I closed my eyes, I remembered every last detail of that moment—my wet hair dripping, his hard chest pressed against me. How he smelled incredible, even after working outside for nine straight hours. No matter how much I tried to fool myself, that was definitely us—and we'd come dangerously close to crossing the line. Maybe we already had.

I stared at his name, realizing it might be beneficial to talk to him one-on-one before we were surrounded by students. Riding to school with him could be the perfect chance to address the tension between us, once and for all. We couldn't keep delaying the agonizingly awkward conversation that had been on the tip of both of our tongues for months.

*Just do it*, I told myself.

I held my breath as I tapped Owen's name on the screen. He answered on the first ring. "Sorry to bother you," I said, "but I'm kind of in a jam right now. I can't find my keys, and I need a ride to work."

A few seconds of silence followed. At first, I thought I was pushing some unspoken boundary by asking him for a favor after what happened between us, but he cleared his throat and said, "I'm finishing up at the gym right now, but... I can probably swing back that way."

I closed my eyes. "That's completely on the other side of town. You'd have to backtrack."

"I don't mind. It'll be cutting it close, but—"

"No," I said, cutting him off. "I'm not having you do that. I'll figure something out. I can ask one of my neighbors, or...." My voice trailed off because I didn't have another plan. I was either going to have to let Owen drive me to work, or I would need to call Mr. Cates and have someone cover my class until I came up with Plan B. Did Woodvale even have Uber drivers?

"Well, there is another option," Owen said warily.

"What's that?"

There was another pregnant pause before he answered. "Your house is on Kendall's way. I'm not sure how comfortable you'd feel about riding with her, but... I can call her up right now." Kendall. Driving me to work. Owen must have sensed my hesitation because he quickly added, "I know she wouldn't mind."

I took a deep breath, knowing I had no reason to turn down this offer. It was going to be uncomfortable, but at the same time, I was relieved to have a solution. "Okay. That would be really nice of her." We quickly hung up so he could call her. A minute later, he texted me to say she'd be there ASAP.

So Owen's girlfriend was going to drive me to work. Great. I was sure we'd have a lot to talk about, like positive reinforcement strategies, professional development opportunities, and what it felt like to nuzzle against Owen's neck while his erection pressed into the front of your hip.

I sat on the stoop and waited for her, tucking my hands under the skirt of my mauve dress. I was wearing a denim jacket, but the cold breeze still made me shiver. Thankfully, Kendall pulled up to the curb only a few minutes later.

"Hey," she said as I yanked the passenger door open. As I slid into my seat, I was immediately accosted by her citrusy air freshener, and there was a *Lover*-era Taylor Swift song blasting over the speakers. She had a tiny succulent hanging from her rearview mirror in a crochet plant hanger and a tower of colorful scrunchies on her gear-shifter. "You can put your coffee in the cupholder, if it'll fit," she said.

It did. "Thanks."

"And you might have to pull the seat up a little. It's usually Owen sitting there, and you know how long his legs are."

"Oh, it's fine," I said, forcing out a weak chuckle.

I pictured Owen sitting in this very seat. I wondered what kind of places they could possibly go to together if they couldn't be seen anywhere. Could they only drive around in the dark, or what?

As Kendall pulled away from the curb, I could sense her glancing my direction. I felt awkward enough sitting there with my tote-bag perched on my knees, but her eyes on me only added a layer of discomfort. I knew Owen couldn't have divulged anything to her—because he wouldn't have suggested this if he had. Yet I couldn't shake the feeling she was scrutinizing my every move.

"Saturday was pretty wild, huh?" she asked, breaking the silence.

"What?"

"We accomplished so much. I've got blisters on my fingers from hauling those paving stones."

"Oh." Another awkward chuckle. "I'm sorry."

Kendall laughed, reaching up to touch the screen on her dash. "Not your fault," she said, turning her attention to a new text message from Owen. I tried to avert my eyes, not wanting to intrude on their private conversation, but it was right there in front of me.

**Owen:** appreciate it

That was it. I breathed a sigh of relief, finding the tiniest bit of amusement in the fact he didn't use punctuation with her—or capitalization, for that matter. But my smile faded when I turned to Kendall—because hers was stretching from ear to ear. "Owen's such a good friend to you," she said, making my skin crawl with guilt. "I love that."

"Yeah, he's great," I muttered, reaching for my coffee. Thanks to my big spill that morning, there were only a few sips left. Just perfect.

Kendall glanced over her shoulder as she merged into heavy traffic. Once she reached a steady pace in the middle lane, she directed her attention back to me. "He told me you're like a sister to him."

I almost choked on my coffee. I coughed, trying to regain my composure. I couldn't imagine Owen actually saying those words. And if he had, it couldn't have been recent. Certainly not within the last 36 hours. "He said that?"

She didn't answer. "He's such a caring person. And that's why he'll make a great principal. Did he tell you about that?"

"He mentioned it, yeah."

"He's totally going to get the job," she said, pulling a pair of sunglasses from her center console. She slid them onto her eyes and ran her fingers through her silky, blonde hair, grinning. "And I'm switching districts so he and I can finally go public."

I could've simply agreed with her or changed the subject, but the words at the tip of my tongue managed to find their way out. "I wish he'd follow his dreams and work on *STEM for the Win* instead."

She turned toward me again, her dark sunglasses preventing me from reading the expression in her eyes. "His podcast? I know he loves it, but longevity-wise, that's probably not the smartest choice." And then, facing straight ahead, she added, "I just want what's best for him."

I wanted to say more to counter what Kendall was saying—how did she know what was best for Owen? She'd only known the guy for three months. Somehow, I mustered up the strength to bite my tongue. "Right," I said.

What was I trying to do, prove that I knew him better? What purpose would that serve?

Though I was willing to drop the subject, Kendall continued. "I have no doubt in my mind Owen could be really successful with the podcast. I think he could probably excel at literally anything he set out to do, you know?" She paused to glance at me. "But there's no stability there. He's gotta think about buying a house someday, starting a family—and if the podcast loses traction, I don't think we could live off of my teacher income alone."

As she concluded this spiel with a casual laugh, a heavy knot formed in my stomach.

Kendall saw herself in Owen's future.

It sounded like… it sounded like she *loved* him.

And I'd never hated myself more. I'd taken something as innocent as putting on his dry hoodie and turned it into something far less innocuous. I was the one who reached for him, tempting him. All weekend, my guilty thoughts had swirled around my almost-betrayal of my engagement to Eli, like there wasn't another heart out there at risk of breaking.

I was relieved when we reached Grissom. It was merely a five-minute drive, but it felt like an eternity. After Kendall shut off her car, she reached into her backseat and pulled out a leopard-print cowboy hat. "Gotta love Hat Day," she said.

"Shit, I forgot!" I slapped my forehead. I never missed a themed dress-up day—*ever*. Pajama Day, 90s Day, Hawaiian Day—you name it. I always participated in the fun, and my students loved it. Oh well, it was too late now. My day had just begun, but it was already in the lead for the Monday-est Monday this year.

"Girl, I got you," Kendall said. She rummaged through her backseat again before pulling a pink knit hat from the floorboard behind my seat. "I swear it's clean, despite the current state of my backseat. And look, it's almost the same color as your dress." I looked down—she was right.

I thanked her and shoved the hat in my tote bag as we both got out of her car. "I really appreciate you going out of your way to pick me up this morning," I said as we made our way down the wide walkway toward the double doors. I crossed my arms tight against my chest as I walked. "I can't believe I lost my keys."

"You weren't out of my way at all," Kendall said. "Don't ever hesitate to ask for a ride—I live just a few minutes from you. And to be honest, it's nice to have a friend at this school. I don't know if you've noticed, but a lot of the teachers here are so cliquey. When you asked me to join the garden committee, that honestly made my entire year."

I turned to face her when we reached the oversized welcome mat in front of the main entrance. "I'm really glad you joined, Kendall. You've been a tremendous help," I said, hesitating at the threshold. Neither of those statements were a lie. I struggled to swallow the lump in my throat before I continued. "And I just want to say… I wish you and Owen the best."

As soon as I said the words, I was momentarily taken aback by the fleeting look of disbelief on Kendall's face. It was just a flicker of doubt, half-hidden by her sunglasses, but I caught the slight downward pull of her lips. "Thank you," she said, stepping aside as I held the door open for both of us.

Owen might not have told her a thing, but that didn't mean she was completely oblivious.

# chapter twenty-eight

*owen*

I must have thought about texting her twenty times since Saturday.

In fact, I even had the words typed out: *Can we talk?* And every time I almost convinced myself to hit SEND, I backspaced until the words disappeared, second-guessing myself. It was the weekend—she was probably sitting at home with Eli. And I needed her to be far, far away from him for this conversation.

Those same two questions still lingered at the forefront of my mind—did she have feelings for me? And what happens next?

It was time for us to have The Conversation™, but I needed to isolate her first.

On Monday morning, I was a hundred times more nervous to see her than I had been the day we returned after Christmas break. But I wasn't going to let myself be a pussy about it this time. I knew I could face her, even though I was sweating buckets. The fact that she'd just spent the morning riding in Kendall's car only made matters worse.

I could hardly believe the words spilling out of my own mouth when I suggested Kendall pick her up for work. Deep down, I knew I was about to let Kendall go—as soon as I gathered my thoughts well enough to say the words—and Sarah was the primary reason.

But when I heard the panic and frustration in Sarah's voice, my instinct to help her by any means necessary overrode the guilt I felt about putting Kendall in such a position. As long as my name hadn't come up too much during the car ride, it was probably fine.

At 7:50 on the dot, I put my Cubs hat on backwards and headed out to the hallway, coffee in hand. Sarah wasn't there. For a moment, I panicked, assuming she was avoiding me. But at 7:52, she appeared in her doorway looking flushed and wearing a pink beanie. I recognized that hat—it wasn't hers. I swallowed, watching her stare down at the hem of her dress as she attempted to straighten the wrinkles out of it. When she lifted her chin to look at my face, I almost dropped my coffee, all the memories of her body pressed up against me flooding my mind.

"Morning," I somehow managed to say.

"Good morning." She wasn't holding any coffee, which was unusual, but I didn't question it. Instead, I focused on her hat. She must have caught my gaze, because she asked, "Do you like my hat?"

"Yeah. Is that—?"

"Yup." She stood with her hands folded behind her back. Something about the sight of her wearing Kendall's hat made me uneasy. It was all I could do not to ask her to take it off, but how crazy would that sound?

As the students started pouring into the building, we put our awkward attempt at a conversation on pause to greet them. I gave Holden Greer a hard time about his Cardinals hat, teasing that I was going to have to deduct a few points from his final grade. Subsequently, Ava's Cubs hat earned her some imaginary extra credit points. It made her face turn the same shade of red as the C on her cap. I looked across the hallway at Sarah, who was grinning, having just witnessed this whole exchange.

When there was a break in arriving students, I took a couple steps forward to ask, "So… how'd it go this morning?"

"Fine. I'm so glad Kendall was able to come to my rescue."

"Yeah, me too."

"Thanks."

I swallowed. "Welcome."

The silence that followed this exchange was absolutely torturous. I prayed for a student to come around the corner and save me from this awkwardness, but Sarah and I were left standing there with nothing to say to each other. Why weren't there more kids in that hallway? Was everybody out sick, or what? Was strep throat making its way around again? I loosened my tie.

And then we both started speaking at once. "Hey," was all I managed to get out—and the only words I could make out from her were "you know."

"You go first," she said with a laugh.

I took another step closer to her, standing in the middle of the hallway now. "Can we talk after school?"

Sarah tugged on the bottom of her hat, pulling it further down over the tops of her ears. She was momentarily distracted by one of her arriving students, complimenting him on his oversized jester hat as he walked between us. Once he made it into the classroom, she turned to me to say, "We really don't have to talk about it, Owen."

I blinked. "We don't?"

After taking a breath, she said, "I mean, it's okay if we just… let it go. It was literally nothing." Literally. She despised that word, only pulling it from her vernacular when she really meant it. And what happened between us—it was *something*, wasn't it?

I was there. I remembered the way she initially took my hand in hers and ran her fingers along my forearm. And she sure as shit wasn't the one to pull away first.

All of that was "nothing" to her?

"Really?" I asked, lowering my chin with a skeptical stare. Either I was misremembering our encounter, or she was lying to us both.

Just as she opened her mouth to respond, another group of kids came around the corner. One of them was Bentley, wearing a hat that resembled a giant Swiss cheese wedge—and the smile on his face was just as cheesy. When Sarah saw how happy the kid was, I knew I'd lost her attention completely. She watched him every step of the way to her classroom door. "Bentley! That's the best hat I've seen so far today. Where did you get it?"

"My dad got it in Green Bay."

"Let me guess—Packers fan?"

As they carried on, I looked down at my coffee and sighed, conceding that our conversation was over, likely to never be brought up again. It would appear Sarah wanted everything to proceed as normal between us. Her standoffish reaction to my invitation to talk after school made it pretty clear she still had every intention of marrying Eli.

I'd been such a fool.

I made my way back to my own side of the hallway and flipped my Cubs hat around so it faced the front. With my back to Sarah, I engaged in conversation with the kids just inside my classroom door who were doing back handsprings for some reason. For the rest of the morning, I did everything within my power not to even look Sarah's direction again. Eventually, I inched all the way inside the classroom, distancing myself from her even farther.

And when the bell rang, I closed my classroom door without uttering a single word.

# chapter twenty-nine

*sarah*

The backwards Cubs hat almost made me second-guess my decision to let Owen go. The hat only amplified his sexiness level somehow, making it even harder to look at him.

My unwillingness to have a discussion with him undoubtedly pissed him off. It was obvious, the way he backed farther and farther away from me until he wasn't even in the hallway anymore. I was just going to have to let him be mad, if that's what it took to preserve both of our relationships with our significant others.

My lesson on similes couldn't hold the kids' interest that day. I'd thought the analogy about March coming in like a lion and out like a lamb would make it easy for them, but it only made Jordyn roll their eyes, and Noah called the lesson "babyish." I gave in, saying, "fine!" in this defeated way and told them to work independently instead of walking them through their worksheets. I had been willing to give them all the answers, but now they had to do the work themselves.

I couldn't remember the last time I'd abandoned a lesson halfway through like this. I could usually steer things in a different direction when I could tell the material missed the mark, but I didn't have the energy for that today. Not when I hadn't had a full cup of coffee or my daily dose of banter with Owen. I was useless.

During the first recess, I called Eli, knowing he had a prep period at the same time. We normally spent this time texting each other, so he sounded alarmed when he picked up the phone. "What's wrong?"

I sighed. "I'm not having the greatest day. I lost my keys, so I had to get a ride to work."

"What's with you lately? You're forgetting stuff all the time."

"I don't know, I'm just distracted."

"Maybe this garden thing is too much. Can't you let Owen take over? I don't like seeing you like this, babe."

"No, you know how important that is to me," I said, putting my elbow on my desk. I rested my chin on my fist. "I just didn't get enough sleep. Anyway, the reason I'm calling is because I'm going to need you to pick me up this afternoon."

"And deal with the pick-up traffic chaos?" He paused to laugh. The after-school traffic around Grissom put the whole neighborhood in a gridlock every single day, no matter how many times they tried to readjust it. If they'd just give me a map and a pen, I'd have it solved in thirty minutes.

"Well, you'll obviously have to wait until it all clears out," I said. "I can find something to work on here while I wait."

It was his turn to sigh. "I guess I can. But are you sure you can't get a ride with someone else?"

I closed my eyes. "I'd rather not have to ask anyone. I already felt like a burden this morning."

"Can you just ask around?" I could hear the irritation in his voice. "I don't want to deal with this if I don't have to."

I slapped my thigh, my irritation level reaching its peak. "Are you serious?"

"I mean, yeah? You're worried about burdening other people, but you're really not concerned about inconveniencing me, are you?"

"You're my partner, Eli. Partners do things for each other."

"I never do anything for you, is that what you're saying?"

"No, I—"

"I didn't come and help you with that garden thing on my day off?"

A surge of anger flowed through my veins. He had the audacity to call that *helping*? "Yeah, and what a remarkable display of assistance you provided," I spat out. "You nearly pulled a muscle carrying those two bags of potting soil."

Eli gasped, stumbling over his words. "You—that—you should appreciate the fact I was even there at all, goddammit. I don't teach at that school. I didn't have to be there. But I was."

"Barely," I said with a cold laugh. "You know what, I have to go. Don't worry about picking me up."

"Just ask Owen Gardner. I'm sure he'd love that," he muttered.

"What's that supposed to mean?"

"Come on. We've talked about it before. I've already had two different people come up to me and ask me about that photo of the two of you in the paper."

I had completely forgotten about the article in the Woodvale Times. Immediately, I pulled my phone away from my ear and put him on speakerphone. "What photo?" I was already navigating to the newspaper's Facebook page. I almost forgot I had Eli on the phone as I fumbled through their recent posts to find the collage of candid photos from the garden workday.

I had to scroll to the very end of the album before I reached the candid photo Meghan had taken of Owen and me. Dammit, we looked adorable. In that moment frozen in time, we looked like a couple, judging from our closeness and the lustful way Owen was looking at me. And my enormous, goofy smile as I gazed right back at him? When did I *ever* smile like that?

No wonder people were talking about this.

"You really have nothing to say to that?" Eli asked, but I hadn't even been listening.

"What?"

"I said he'd jump your bones in a heartbeat if he had the chance."

"You know what? You're right, I think I *will* ask him for a ride. Thanks for the suggestion." Without giving him a chance to respond, I ended the call. I stared at our photo a little longer, saving it to my phone. If it weren't for Kendall, I'd make it my profile picture just to get under Eli's skin.

A moment later, my classroom phone intercom beeped. "Ms. Lavely?" It was Mrs. Houck, the guidance counselor. "Can you pick up?"

I walked over to the phone, pulling the beanie off my head along the way. I might have hat hair the rest of the day, but it was making me hot and irritable. "I'm here, Mrs. Houck," I said into the receiver. "What's up?"

She breathed a heavy sigh into the phone. "Bentley's been involved in an incident at recess."

A knot formed in my stomach. Bentley had been full of smiles all morning, even socializing with Jordyn and a couple of the other kids he'd been getting to know during newspaper club. "Oh no. What happened now?"

"It's not good," Mrs. Houck said. "He pushed one of the fourth-grade students down to the ground and he sort of, well—he kicked him in the head. The other boy's mother is on her way to take him to the ER to check for a concussion."

I felt a sinking sensation in my chest as I instinctively covered my eyes with my hand. A bitter, acidic taste flooded my mouth. "Oh my God. Have you seen the other boy—is he okay?"

"I believe he'll be fine. It's just an extra precaution."

"Why did he do it?" It didn't make a lot of sense. Bentley had been doing so well keeping his hands to himself lately. It was no secret he had an affinity for violence, but it was rarely unprovoked. He must have felt he'd been wronged somehow.

"He won't talk to me," Mrs. Houck said. "Or Mr. Cates. That's why I'm calling you. Could you come up here on your lunch period? He's going to stay with me the rest of the day, but I think he'd like to talk to you."

"Of course," I said, and we hung up. I swallowed, feeling sick to my stomach all of a sudden.

That was strike three.

# chapter thirty

*owen*

By lunchtime, my annoyance with Sarah had brewed into full-on resentment. I sat alone in my classroom to eat, but the sandwich I packed no longer seemed appetizing. After forcing myself to take a single bite, I chucked the entire thing into the trash can beside my desk.

She wanted things to just carry on like normal? Well, I couldn't do that. We were beyond that point now. We had crossed a line, one that couldn't be erased by mere silence and avoidance this time. Of course, I had always been content just being her friend—it's not like I needed her to give me any more than that. But she was toying with my emotions, and I was no longer interested in letting her get away with it. It was time for the two of us to have a tough conversation, whether she was ready for that or not.

The intercom on the wall buzzed. "Gardner, you in there?" It was Cates' voice. I walked over to the phone and picked it up.

"Yes sir?"

"Did you get an email from Delgado's secretary this morning?" Marc Delgado was the superintendent of the Woodvale School Corporation.

I turned to look at my laptop. "Uh—I actually haven't checked my email yet today. I've had some things to catch up on."

"That's all right. Well, we're wanting to get your interview scheduled. How's next Tuesday, one o'clock sound? You ready for that?"

"Oh." I swallowed. "Yeah, that's fine. I'll need someone to cover—"

"I'll get someone to cover your class. Let me worry about that. And listen, I want you to bring a copy of all the garden plans. One of those green folders I know you all had. The panel would love to see all you've done."

I could have told him it was Sarah who had meticulously gathered all of that information, but for some reason, I didn't. I couldn't even say her name. "Will do."

"Good, good. And now for more pressing matters…." My heart skipped a beat, wondering if he'd somehow learned of my relationship with Kendall, or that someone saw me almost kissing Sarah in the garden and passed the info along to him. Cates cleared his throat, and I braced myself. But his tone was casual when he said, "You joining me for crêpes first thing Sunday morning?"

Oh, right. The IES conference was that weekend. For the past few years, Cates and I had been meeting up for breakfast at this ritzy restaurant connected to our hotel before the second day of workshops. Crêpe Expectations was a little on the pricey side, especially when you considered the fact our hotel offered free continental breakfast, but Cates always insisted on paying for my meal.

This tradition of ours was easily the highlight of the entire weekend for him. Maybe even his entire year, now that I thought about it. The man lived for those crêpes.

I forced a chuckle into the receiver. "You know it. I'm salivating already, just thinking about the dulce de leche crêpes."

"That's what I'm talking about," he said with a laugh. "This will be our last year for this, you know."

"That's right. We better make it count."

"Breakfast bloody marys?" he suggested.

"You betcha."

Cates let out a big hearty laugh in response. Truth be told, I didn't care much for bloody marys, but if my boss wanted me to have one, I wasn't going to put up a fight.

As I started passing out science study guides for my afternoon lessons, I realized I'd accidentally printed the wrong unit. We were learning about types of energy this week, but the papers in my hand were labeled *PROPERTIES OF MATTER*. Damn it. I looked at my watch, thankful to see I had enough time to rectify this, as long as nobody else was using the good copier.

Yes, we had a good copier and a bad copier. The one in the main office, which Sarah had lovingly nicknamed Xena for some reason, could copy, print, collate, staple—you name it. And it could get the job done in seconds flat.

The other one, however, seemed to have a personal vendetta against us. The machine was older than me, and it was constantly jamming or just flashing the word "err" without giving us a reason. Lori was always having to come to the prep room to unplug the thing and get it back on the network while on the phone with IT. None of us wanted to be the unfortunate soul responsible for triggering the machine's meltdown—because that meant facing Lori's wrath.

Sarah called that copier Bertha.

Much to my dismay, there was a line of teachers waiting to use Xena in the office. I hung my head and made my way to the prep room. Bertha would have to suffice.

The room wasn't much bigger than a closet. Along with the copy machine, it also held the paper cutter, laminator, and a long counter for doing prep work. And, if we were feeling really adventurous, we could delve into the cabinets full of the most cringe-worthy bulletin board décor from the 90s.

When I pushed open the door to the prep room, I hesitated when I saw Sarah standing in front of the paper cutter. Her hair was messily pulled back with a clip—she was no longer wearing Kendall's hat, which brought me an unusual sense of relief.

I licked my lips. "Hey," I said, passing her on my way to the copier. We were the only ones in the room, meaning this could be the perfect opportunity to say what I needed to say. That if what she asserted that morning were true—what happened between us in the garden meant *literally nothing* to her—then it would be really helpful if she would adjust the way she interacted with me from here on out.

"Hi," Sarah responded. Without looking up, she aligned her stack of papers on the gridlines before lowering the paper cutter blade. The blade wasn't sharp enough, though—it never was—and she yanked her sloppily cut paper off of the tool and tried again with a smaller amount. And then even fewer, muttering a few curse words under her breath with every try. She was pulling the blade down with more and more force each time, making it rock back and forth on the counter. I was half afraid she'd cut her hand off.

"Easy there," I said, feeding my original copy into the copier. "I mean, I'm first-aid certified, but I didn't want to have to see blood today."

"Funny," she said through gritted teeth. Something was off. I hit the start button on the copier and continued watching her, wondering if her foul mood had anything to do with me. Her shoulders were slumped forward, and when a tendril of hair fell in her face, she didn't even bother to pull it out of her eyes.

No. There was something else eating at her. This wasn't about me. At least, not *only* me.

I leaned against the counter beside her and crossed my arms. "Everything okay there, Lavely?"

"No."

She pulled the blade down again, and by now, the paper cutter had scooted so far toward the front of the counter that one of the legs slipped off the edge. The entire thing nearly fell to her feet. I lunged forward to get between her and the paper cutter, nudging her out of the way as I lifted it back onto the counter. "Okay, that's enough," I said. "I'm pretty sure your students want their teacher to come back to class in one piece, all right?"

She covered her face with her hands, her entire body trembling before me. Although I couldn't see her eyes, I knew she was crying. I put one of my hands on her shoulder, leaning around her to use my other hand to push the door of the prep room shut so we wouldn't be interrupted.

"Hey," I said, lowering my voice. I had a firm grip on both of her upper arms. "Look at me."

When she finally did, all of my resentment and irritation toward her rapidly melted away. My only concern now was to figure out what had her feeling like this, and whether or not I could help her fix it.

"What's going on with you?"

"I'm—" She stopped to take a deep breath, putting her hands on her temples. Her eyes were welling up with tears. "It's just—everything."

"You wanna tell me about it?"

Sarah inhaled. "For starters, Bentley got himself in trouble again and I'm beginning to lose my faith in him." She pulled the loose piece of hair away from her eyes, staring down at the ground. "And it kills me to say that, because I've held out hope for so long."

"What happened?"

"He kicked a kid in the head at recess. A fourth grader." She shook her head, using the cuff of her jean jacket to wipe her eyes. "The kid even went to the ER to get checked for a concussion."

I winced, releasing my grip on her arms and dropping my hands to my sides. "Ouch. Is the other kid okay?"

She nodded. "Cates just updated me on everything. The kid's fine and he even came back to school already."

"That's a relief." I clicked my tongue. "Damn it, Bentley. Why'd he do it? Have you talked to him?"

"I just did. He's so ashamed, he wouldn't say much. But apparently someone threw Jordyn's hat in a puddle, and he was defending their honor."

Though I couldn't blame Bentley for wanting to retaliate, kicking someone in the head was pretty excessive. I put my hands in my pockets and leaned against the counter again. "Okay, so the kid got into a fight. It's happened before. The other kid's okay. It's not such a big deal, is it?"

"It's his third strike," Sarah said, picking at her fingernails. I stared at her hands for a moment, remembering the way she touched me with them just two days ago. And then she began speaking again, snapping me right out of it. "He's out of the newspaper club and there's nothing I can do about it. I can't remove that consequence."

I nodded, finally comprehending why this was weighing so heavily on her mind. Her entire purpose for creating the newspaper club in the first place was to give Bentley a creative outlet in hopes of keeping him out of trouble. I knew Sarah well enough to understand she felt like she'd failed him.

"Look, I get that it's a huge disappointment, but you can't let his behavior get to you or take it personally, Sarah," I said, sliding down the edge of the counter to get closer to her. "You've worked your Sarah Lavely magic on that kid this year, and he's improved by leaps and bounds. I've seen it with my own eyes. He's got friends now, right? And he's going to have a few slip-ups here and there—who doesn't? You're not going to give up on him now."

It was a command, not a question.

I wasn't sure what it was I said to make Sarah break down, but that's exactly what she did. Without warning, she collapsed into my arms, her shoulders shaking up and down as she cried. I just held her, resting my chin atop her head, and let her get it all out. "I'm sorry," she said, trying to catch her breath between sobs. "I just hate—everything—right now."

Though I couldn't be sure if she was still talking about Bentley or not, I gave her a squeeze and said, "You've given that kid a shot in the dark at recognizing he's good at something." I whispered every word, my mouth hovering just over her ear. "That's more than enough." She sank further into me, burrowing her face into my chest. Behind me, the copier began beeping to alert me of god-only-knows-what kind of problem, but I ignored it. I would hold Sarah in my arms for as long as she needed me.

It was when I realized I was fighting the urge to kiss her on the top of her head that I remembered everything I'd wanted to talk to her about. I was going to say all these things about how we probably shouldn't come within close proximity to one another, but look at us now. Fully embraced. Damn it. Why couldn't I keep my hands off this woman?

"You always know exactly what to say," Sarah said. I loosened my hold on her in an attempt to break away, but her grip on me only tightened in return. And then, lowering her voice to a whisper, she said, "Why can't Eli just be a little more like you?"

# chapter thirty-one

## sarah

As soon as the words fell out of my mouth, Owen took me by the shoulders, pushing me away in a movement so abrupt it took my breath away. "Why would you say that to me?" he asked with a scowl.

"I—I'm sorry," I choked out. "It's just that he and I are fighting, and I…." I let my voice trail off, knowing I didn't have much of an excuse for what I'd whispered in his ear seconds ago. *Why did I say that??*

He turned away from me and smacked a button on the copier to stop its incessant beeping. "Yeah, well, what else is new," he muttered.

"Hey!"

"What?" he shot back before I could say anything else. "I'm sorry, but the guy's an asshole, Sarah. Why do you put up with him, huh? It doesn't make any sense—you're so much smarter than this."

"That is really inappropriate for you to say." Waves of humiliation washed over me, and I suddenly felt hot with rage. I'd always known that Owen didn't like Eli, but now he was insulting me right along with him. "I don't need to justify my relationship to you."

"You brought his name up, not me."

"But I didn't ask for your opinion. You're really crossing the line here, Owen."

"Oh, I'm sorry, I couldn't find the line," he retorted, taking a step closer to me, "because it's *constantly moving back and forth!*"

This wasn't the first time I'd heard Owen raise his voice. I'd seen him at his absolute worst—after a confrontation with a parent went south, or the time he was denied a raise because of budget cuts. I'd witnessed him kick his empty trash can across the room after a particularly bad day.

But this? This was different. Because for the very first time, his anger was directed at me.

I watched him return to the copier, yanking out a paper that got jammed. He fed his original copy into the machine again and pushed another button, shaking his head the entire time. "Look, I'm sorry," he started. He ran a hand through his hair, keeping his eyes on the papers that began to spit out of the printer. "All I'm trying to say is that you deserve better."

"You mean someone like *you?*" Why couldn't he just say what he really meant?

Owen clenched his jaw, refusing to look up at me. A wrinkle appeared between his brows, the way it always did when he was upset.

Those last words obviously struck a nerve.

His shoulders rose and fell as he took a breath. "I like being your friend, Sarah." He stared down at the copy machine, leaning onto it with both hands. "You give me something to look forward to every morning as I drag myself out of bed. You are the highlight of my day, every day. Your name comes up in so many of my pro and con lists. I—" He stopped himself mid-sentence, his throat bobbing as he swallowed. He bent over to pick his copies up from the tray and drew in a long, shaky breath. And then, still refusing to look me in the eyes, he said, "I think a break from you will do me some good."

"What—how?" I stared at him, dumbfounded, before finally settling on the most important question: "Why?"

"Because we can't seem to keep our hands off of each other, can we?" Owen ripped his original copy off the machine and turned his body toward mine, giving me the tiniest amount of space between him and the row of storage cabinets behind me. His sudden movement startled me, and if he noticed the way he made me jump, he made no attempt to apologize for it.

I took a small step backwards, but there was nowhere to go. One of the knobs from the cabinets was pressing into my upper back, but if I moved even an inch forward, I'd be touching him. He was still towering over me, his eyes piercing right through me as he put one of his hands on the cabinet next to my head.

"I've wasted a really unhealthy amount of time thinking about you," he continued, his voice tinged with desperation. As much as it troubled him to meet my gaze earlier, he wasn't breaking eye contact now. "And I can't do this little dance with you anymore. I'm done, Sarah. You've got Eli, and I'm happy with Kendall. I think it's best if we put some space between us before we fuck everything up."

Space. He wanted space? Right now, he was suffocating me with his words and the proximity of his body to mine. My legs were trembling, and I was half afraid I'd collapse into him again if he didn't leave the room right that second. The sooner he got out of my face, the better. "So what you're saying is that if you can't fuck me, then you don't even want to be my friend?" I spit out. "Is that it?"

I could see the ache in his eyes as my words started to sink in. Good. I wanted Owen to hurt. I wanted him to feel at least an ounce of the pain I was feeling at that moment. His shoulders slumped forward, and it looked like there might even be tears welling up in his eyes. "Don't," he said, barely opening his mouth.

I was holding back tears myself, but there was no way I would let him see me cry again. Not now. Not over him. "You're a real shitty friend," I said through gritted teeth.

"If that's the picture you want to paint of me, fine. I guess I just imagined all the flirting and the touching and the hundred-dollar birthday gift and how close you came to kissing me in the garden Saturday."

"That was you!"

"That was both of us, and you know it," he shot back, his stare growing more intense. "Don't act like you don't know what I'm talking about. And I guess we can just disregard the fact you've been pretending to be unaware of how I've felt about you this entire time, like you didn't know exactly what you were doing to me." He tore his hand off the wall and pulled away from me. "So who's the shitty friend?"

I did my very best to channel every bit of the hurt I was feeling into anger. "Get away from me. Now."

He yanked the door to the prep room open. "Gladly," he muttered before walking out. I slammed the door behind him, turning around to finally release the sob I'd been holding back. It was all I could do not to crumple to the floor. My best friend, my favorite person in the world, was *done* with me. The only reason our friendship had lasted as long as it had was because the possibility of getting me in bed had given him false hope.

It was a good thing he wanted to distance himself from me, because I didn't think I could stand to even look at him.

# chapter thirty-two

*owen*

The rest of the week went by without so much as a glance from Sarah. She avoided me, just like I'd requested. Every morning, she found something else to occupy her time—decorating the bulletin boards along the fifth-grade wing, having a morning dance party to greet the students, or just sitting at her desk. And every morning, I stared at the empty space in the doorframe where she usually stood, longing for the way things used to be.

Over the past few days, my emotions had cycled from shame to sorrow and back to resentment. Sarah's words to me in the prep room that day stung like a slap across the face. I would have much preferred the latter, actually. Her accusation that I only hung around because I might one day get to "fuck" her made me feel like scum.

If only I had explained myself better instead of letting my emotions take over. If I had just put the tiniest amount of thought into my words, I could have set a boundary without the all-or-nothing approach. We didn't need space—we needed to have a conversation, a real one, preferably outside the walls of that school. I could have just told her how much it killed me every time we almost crossed into romantic territory only to have to pretend like it never happened. For our friendship to survive, we just needed to establish some rules. That would have been the mature way to handle the situation.

But no—I'd told her I was *done* with her and yelled in her face.

I couldn't blame her at all for her reaction.

We spent a week working on garden plans—separately. And somehow, Kendall had become our oblivious go-between. I skipped the next committee meeting, but I asked her to take diligent notes to keep me up to speed on the progress. A couple days later, she delivered a handwritten list of various types of garden edging from local stores along with their pricing. At the bottom, Sarah had written, *"Thinking of going with the brick unless you disagree."*

"Weird that she didn't just give that to you herself, considering she's right across the hall from you every single day," Kendall observed.

"Yeah, weird," I said, trying to sound nonchalant. I laid the list on my desk. "Tell Sarah the brick is fine."

As for Kendall, I'd reached a decision—I would break up with her on Sunday when I returned from the IES conference. I had been rehearsing what to say, trying to choose the words that would cause the least amount of heartbreak. In the meantime, I'd been trying to keep things between her and me as normal as possible.

On Friday morning, we had our monthly staff meeting in the conference room. I sat next to Kendall without giving it a second thought. Sarah took a seat clear at the other end of the table. I couldn't remember the last time I'd endured a staff meeting without her by my side, gossiping in my ear or scribbling inappropriate messages in the margins of my printouts. As Cates rambled on about positive behavior interventions, I caught Sarah glancing my direction a couple of times. The third time, I tried to hold her stare, but she looked down at the table to avoid my gaze.

We were in the same room, but she felt miles away.

I managed not to flinch when Kendall pinched my thigh under the table, which was no easy feat. However, I had to cover my mouth to hide my annoyed grin—and she made no attempt to stifle her giggles. "Stop," I murmured into my hand, trying my best to pay attention to what Cates was saying—something about giving students silent signals to remind them to stay on task—and my eyes wandered back to Sarah. I could tell from her stony stare she had been watching me interact with Kendall. It may not have been obvious to everyone else at the table what was going on beneath it, but we hadn't fooled Sarah, who rolled her eyes in disgust.

The woman hated me.

After the meeting, Heath grabbed me by the arm on my way out of the conference room. He, Vicki, and Sarah were standing in the hallway. "Hey man," he said, "we're trying to figure out plans for riding up to Indy tomorrow."

"We'll save on gas if we carpool," Vicki said.

"That's true," I answered, eyeing Sarah.

"I'm driving up alone," she said. "I have some errands to run in the city in the morning." She turned to Vicki, tucking her hair behind her ears before continuing. "But you and I should talk more about what we want to do Saturday night."

Heath looked over at me, shaking his head. "You hear that? They're making plans for Saturday night without us. The nerve."

"It's just pedicures and wine in the hotel," Vicki said with a laugh. "But I mean, you guys are welcome to join, if that's your kind of thing."

"We just might," Heath said. "Owen and I could bring a twelve-pack. Make it into a whole party."

"Nah, let's let them have their girls' night," I said. I was starting to wish I could skip the conference altogether. A weekend with these people—namely Sarah, who now hated my guts—didn't sound like my idea of a good time.

When we all turned to part ways, Sarah and I started walking the same direction to get back to the fifth-grade wing. I sidestepped out of her way, but she still gave me a wide berth as she walked a semi-circle around me. Like I had some kind of virus she might catch if she got too close. I almost made a comment about it, but I decided to bite my tongue at the last second.

Sarah was just giving me space, like I'd asked, after all.

She just needn't be so melodramatic about it.


After school, Kendall was waiting next to my car in the parking lot wearing sunglasses and blowing an enormous bubble with her gum. Being that it was a sunny and cloudless Friday afternoon, most of the other teachers had already bolted. Only a few cars remained in the lot. "Hey you," Kendall said as I approached. "I have to head to my house to feed my roommate's cat, but do you want me to pick up some chicken lo mein in a little bit?"

I draped my jacket over my arms and stood in front of her. "Yeah, that sounds perfect. Ask for egg rolls, too."

"Okay," she said. "And I have to stop by my mom's first, too, so—"

As she spoke, I spotted Sarah walking to her car out of the corner of my eye. Without giving it much thought, I took Kendall by the waist and planted a kiss on her lips, pushing her against the side of my car.

"Owen!" She giggled into my mouth and playfully pushed against my chest. "You're going to get us seen." When she looked over her shoulder at Sarah as she passed, the giggling came to an abrupt stop. We both watched Sarah climb into her car, slamming the door shut behind her.

Kendall pulled away from me and lifted her sunglasses to the top of her head. "Well. Did you get the reaction you were hoping for?"

"Huh?"

Her icy glare shot right through me. "I'm not stupid, Owen. Do you really think I haven't noticed the way you've been pining for Sarah this whole time?"

My face fell. "Pining for Sarah?" I attempted to muster a dismissive chuckle, but my acting skills weren't quite up to par. There was no point in denying it or delaying what I'd planned to say to her on Sunday. I closed my eyes for a brief moment, gathering the courage to be truthful with her for once. I rubbed my eyebrows with my thumb and forefinger and sighed. "I guess it's obvious, huh."

I lowered my hand so I could see her face. Her jaw clenched, unmoving. She didn't even blink. "I keep hoping you'll get over her. That you'll finally see what's right in front of you and give us a real chance. But it's pretty clear to me now that you never will—not with her around." She paused to let those words sink in. "And I don't know what happened between the two of you recently, but it's really making me feel like I'm just a pawn in this little game you're playing. Especially after that stunt you just pulled."

I looked down at my feet. "Kendall, I am so sorry." I'd been acting like a real jackass lately. All this time, she had known there was something more to my friendship with Sarah than I was letting on, yet she stuck around. Waiting on me to snap the fuck out of it. I cleared my throat, looking at her face again. "I never meant to hurt you. I thought I could get over her, too but I—I don't know if I can."

It was difficult to keep looking her in the eyes, but I wouldn't allow myself to glance away. Giving her my undivided attention in this moment was the least I could do now. She was the one who broke eye contact, sighing with a sense of resignation as she turned her attention to Lori, who was walking toward her car a couple of rows over. She waited for Lori to be out of earshot before she said, "You know, the sooner you realize Sarah's happy with someone else, the sooner you can be, too." She shook her head. "But it's not going to be with me. I can't keep waiting around for you to sort your shit out."

I swallowed, nodding. "I understand. You deserve… so much better."

She pulled her keys out of her purse and hit a button on her key fob to unlock her car, which was parked a few spaces down. Then, she lowered her sunglasses to her eyes and stretched upward to give me a quick peck on the cheek before whispering, "I know."

And that was it. Kendall slipped into her car and drove away, exiting my life just as abruptly as she'd entered it.

I stood frozen in the now vacant parking lot, processing the realization I'd just been dumped—when all this time, I'd thought I'd be the one doing the dumping. And it should have been me. I felt a tremendous amount of shame for stringing her along the way I had. She may have been using me in the beginning, too, but if I had just an ounce of decency, I would have cut this off at the first sign she was falling for me. Before the baskets and succulents started showing up. Long before she accidentally called my house "home."

She was so much better than me.

I was completely and utterly alone, and that's what I deserved.

# chapter thirty-three
## *sarah*

The Walden Hotel & Convention Center was in the heart of downtown Indianapolis, connecting to the shopping mall and other hotels via pedestrian bridges over the streets below. The convention center itself was massive, with multiple exhibit halls and meeting rooms. Every spring, thousands of Hoosier teachers flocked here for the IES conference. We did it for the professional development certificates, but the free meals and a school-funded hotel stay were definitely an added bonus.

Under normal circumstances, I enjoyed the IES conference, but this fight with Owen was making it nearly impossible to focus on anything else. It's difficult to give someone the space they requested when they're standing five feet from you. At the check-in table, he handed me my conference lanyard, and for a split second it was like everything was back to normal between us. In that moment, I thought I caught a glimpse of the old Owen—the one who wasn't repulsed by the mere idea of being close to me. But after I thanked him, he moved to Vicki's other side, putting a literal whole person between us, and shoved his hands in his jean pockets. I guess that interaction was too much.

We made our way through the exhibit hall as a group, taking in all of the vendors offering new curricula, sensory tools, and teacher attire. This year's conference was bigger than ever, with booths spilling into the corridors surrounding the exhibit hall and wall-to-wall people.

And there was one other big change this year—people were recognizing Owen. We'd barely make it twenty feet without someone asking him if he was the host of *STEM for the Win*. You wouldn't think a podcast host would be so identifiable, but he'd been pushing out a lot more video content across social media lately. "I listen every single week," a teacher from Fort Wayne said, posing for a selfie with him. "I bought all your worksheets and workbooks, too." Another teacher asked him if he was speaking at the convention that year, followed by a "why not?"

I could tell all the attention was overwhelming him. He kept looking at Cates as if he'd done something wrong, but Cates was just nodding along. It was all just giving the man another reason to favor Owen. "Looks like we've got a celebrity among us," Cates said, turning to Vicki and me as one of the vendors asked Owen for a selfie.

It didn't help that Owen looked annoyingly sexy that day in a grey henley and those tight, dark jeans. And I didn't know what made him decide to start growing out his stubble, but it made me weak in the knees. His hair was starting to get on the longer side, too—he had to keep pushing it back out of his face. No wonder all these women were approaching him.

I was relieved when it came time for us all to split up and go to separate workshops. We scattered across the convention center, each of us with a different agenda. Just as I stepped into the wide corridor circling the exhibit hall, my phone rang—it was Eli. He knew I was attending this conference, so for him to be calling me at this time was a little alarming.

"The landlord is sending someone to fix the A/C today, and one of us has to be there," he said, his voice in a panic. "I don't know what to do."

Our air conditioning unit was completely busted. We'd been trying to get the landlord to do something about it since the first warm day of the season, so of course he'd finally respond on a day when neither of us would be home. Eli had a golf scramble in Bloomington that afternoon. "I don't know what to tell you," I said. "I'm in Indianapolis."

"And I was about to walk out the door," he said. "Fuck!"

I ducked into a bathroom so people wouldn't overhear the argument I knew was about to occur. "Are they already on their way? Maybe you can just join the guys a little later."

He blew air into the phone with a heavy sigh. "I can't do that, Sarah. If I'm not going to be there on time then I might as well not even go."

I closed my eyes as I said the next words, bracing myself for the aftermath. "Can you skip this one, then?"

"You're kidding, right?" he scoffed. "Why can't you skip your damn conference?"

"I'm already here," I shot back. "I'm not driving all the way back for this. Can you please deal with this today? I'll make it up to you, I promise."

"Look, why don't we just have the landlord let him in?"

"You already know how I feel about that." I hated the thought of anyone nosing around our house without either of us present. Having the landlord there was bad enough, let alone some contractor I'd never met. "Please, Eli. I can't—"

"I'm just going to tell the guy to come next week, then. I'm not missing this."

"So you'd rather have us endure a hot house than miss your golf game. Nice."

Another woman came in to wash her hands, so I stepped into a stall and latched the door behind me. I drew my hand to my forehead in frustration and sighed. This was so typical of him. Was this what our marriage would be like? Would he constantly make selfish decisions such as this one, putting important household needs on the backburner so he could play golf? Is this how it would always be?

Maybe it was time to stop brushing aside all the red flags he was constantly waving in my face. "Eli, this is the last straw," I continued. "I mean I—I've reached my breaking point."

"What's that supposed to mean?"

"It means that you and I need to have a big conversation when I get back," I replied, spitting the words out as quickly as I could so I couldn't change my mind.

"A 'big conversation'?" There was a long pause. I said nothing, allowing him to collect his thoughts. "Whatever you have to say to me, Sarah, just say it now."

"I'm standing in a bathroom stall right now, and I'm supposed to be at my first workshop of the day. Now is not the time. We'll discuss things when I'm back tomorrow. Bye." I hung up before he had a chance to argue with me or tell me I was being irrational. I knew that if I stayed on the phone, he'd end up gaslighting me into believing I'd been the selfish one, and I couldn't allow that to happen. Not this time.

He called twice as I made my way through the now empty corridor to the meeting room where my workshop was being held. I let both calls go to voicemail, taking in slow breaths through my nose and exhaling through my mouth just like I told my students to do when things got overwhelming. My heart was just beginning to return to an almost-normal pace when I reached the door for Room 207. There was a piece of paper taped to it with the words 9 A.M. WORKSHOP CANCELLED – SORRY FOR THE INCONVENIENCE sloppily hand-written on it.

Great. I looked at the time on my phone. It was five minutes past the hour, meaning I had no time to peruse the workshop list and pick a good secondary option. The door for Room 208 was open, though, and I could hear a woman speaking just inside. "Now that we got the icebreaker out of the way, we can move on to the fun stuff." Perfect. I had no idea what this particular workshop was about, but it sounded like I hadn't missed anything important.

I crept into the room, keeping close to the wall so I wouldn't draw much attention to myself, but the speaker noticed me anyway. "Welcome, welcome!" she said. "The more the merrier. Find a seat, if you can." I looked around. There were several rows of tables with an aisle between them and only one empty chair, all the way over on the opposite side of the room.

And sitting right beside it was Owen.

Suddenly, I understood exactly how Bella felt walking into biology class on her first day at Forks High School. And judging from Owen's wide-eyed stare, he was having an Edward moment himself. I scanned the room for another empty seat, but it looked like I had no choice but to take the one beside him.

He kept his head down, staring at his program guide, as I slid into the chair next to him. I opened up my own program guide to see what I was about to learn about for the next hour. *9:00 A.M., Room 208: 10-Minute STEM Projects for Elementary Students.* Of course.

"Didn't know you cared for STEM," Owen murmured to me as the speaker started a slide show presentation at the front of the room.

"My workshop was cancelled," I whispered, "and this was the closest one."

He just nodded, staring straight ahead. I looked down at my phone, noting all the text message notifications from Eli rolling in. I couldn't read them now—not with Owen sitting less than two feet away. I didn't want to look at them, anyway.

I did my best to focus on the presenter at the front of the room. She'd brought plenty of visual aids, showing us all the projects we could do with students using materials we already had lying around in the classroom. Pencil catapults, paper boats, towers made from plastic cups—these were all projects Owen was familiar with. He could be teaching this workshop himself.

"And now you all get to try this next STEM project yourselves," the presenter said in an overly chipper voice, like we were children. "This is the best part! You'll all notice there are straws, tape, and a cup full of pebbles at each table. What I would like for you to do is partner up—there's four of you to a table, so just work with the person beside you—"

Partner up. Great. Out of the corner of my eye, I could see Owen bow his head, his reaction to this predicament mirroring my own.

"—and begin building a bridge that is capable of holding a cup full of pebbles. I'll give you some time to work together, and then we'll have a contest to see which bridge can hold the most weight. And I may have a little prize for the winning duo," the presenter said with a wink, holding up two Starbucks gift cards.

All around us, everyone started chattering and began planning their bridges, tearing tape and getting started. But Owen and I sat still in our seats, neither of us making a move to reach for any of the supplies.

He leaned onto his elbows, folding his hands against his chin with a solemn expression on his face. That is, until "Bridge Over Troubled Water" by Simon & Garfunkel started blaring from the front of the room. When the presenter started humming along to the music as she walked past our table, I saw the corners of Owen's mouth turn slightly upward. Once she'd made her way past us, his grin blossomed into a full-blown smile, which he tried to hide behind his fisted hand.

That smile felt like home. "What's so funny?" I asked.

"It's just—so unnecessarily loud," he answered with wide eyes.

I bit my bottom lip, basking in the relief that he was actually talking to me. "I know."

He shook his head. "If she plays that Fergie song—'London Bridge'—I'm outta here," he muttered.

I tilted my head to the side. "I'm not getting Fergie vibes from this presenter," I said, nodding toward the woman who was now twirling through the aisle past us. Her long hair was graying at the roots, and she was wearing a patchwork skirt, so it was probably safe to assume the only Fergie this woman knew of was the Duchess of York.

"Well," Owen said, adjusting in his seat to sit up a little straighter. He folded his arms. "Ten bucks says she plays 'Under the Bridge' by the Red Hot Chili Peppers next." He was probably right. I watched her dance her way back to the front of the room, silently thanking her for giving us something to talk about. The ice between us was at least beginning to crack. Just a little.

My phone buzzed again, and I flipped it over on the table so I wouldn't have to see all the notifications. "Should we get started on this?" I asked Owen. He looked over at me, making eye contact for the first time since I'd walked into this room.

"Oh, we're going to win," he said in this matter-of-fact way, uncrossing his arms to reach for some straws. I sat back and watched him build a couple of trusses for our bridge, handing him little pieces of tape when he held out his hand. Owen did most of the work since projects like this were completely in his wheelhouse. I was content just being his trusty tape-provider, sometimes doing the taping for him while he held two straws together.

We finished the bridge without communicating much—mostly through hand signals and nods. Since there weren't any specified rules against using an overabundance of tape, I pulled the bridge closer to me and reinforced every joint with more of the thin washi tape. Once I was satisfied, I leaned on my elbows on the table, looking around at everyone else's bridge as Owen reached for the cup full of pebbles. None of the other structures quite compared to Owen's design, which resembled a real suspension bridge. As he carefully dumped the pebbles on the table between us, that Adele song "Water Under the Bridge" started playing.

"Ah, I should've known," Owen muttered, balancing the red solo cup on the center of the bridge.

"At least it's not Fergie?" I offered.

He smiled from one side of his mouth as we both started dropping pebbles into the cup, one at a time. Before long, we'd used up all of our pebbles. The presenter had to give us some extras, and then we even took some from the two people at the other end of our table who were struggling to even get their cup to balance on their flimsy bridge.

"Our cup runneth over," Owen said when the glass pebbles reached the rim.

The presenter clapped her hands together in delight when she saw this. "Oh my, you two have really done a brilliant job!" With a quick glance around the room, she said, "Well, we have a clear winner here. Oh and look, you're from the same school!" She nodded at our lanyards as she handed each of us a $5 Starbucks gift card. I almost wanted to give mine to Owen, considering he'd done most of the work, but I couldn't resist free coffee.

When the workshop was over, I picked up my phone and program guide and walked out to the corridor, with Owen trailing behind. There was a twenty-minute break between workshops to give us time to explore the exhibits. I stood in the center of the hallway and stared down at the vendor map to plot my next move, but I could feel Owen's presence a few feet away. Out of the corner of my eye, I could see that he, too, was looking over his conference guide.

Now that we were no longer forced to work together, it meant we could go back to ignoring each other. Inside that meeting room, he'd acted just like his old self, but when I closed my eyes, I could only think of the way he snapped at me in the prep room just five days ago. How I'd called him a shitty friend, only for him to return the sentiment. I wasn't just going to forget all of that because we won a STEM challenge together.

I continued looking over the vendor map in my hands, but I wasn't retaining a single word I read. I was too focused on the way Owen was inching toward me. I heard him take a deep breath. "Hey, did you know there's a Starbucks attached to this building?"

I lifted my head to look at him. He was casually holding his notebook against his side, fiddling with his lanyard with his other hand. He had this sorrowful look in his eyes as he studied my face. There was that familiar wrinkle between his eyebrows—I'd been seeing a lot of that lately. I folded my program guide and put it in my back pocket. "Where?"

* *

The Starbucks was located in the lobby of one of the three connected hotels, just a few minutes' walk away. We used our gift cards and, since we had some extra time, found a metal bench in the middle of the pedestrian bridge overlooking Meridian Street. Its long, glass windows gave us a perfect view of the city below. As Owen and I settled onto the bench, every part of me just wanted to grab him and hug him. I missed my friend.

As if he could read my mind, he turned to look into my eyes, saying, "So, I wasn't prepared for how hard it would be to… not have you in my life."

I exhaled. "I'm so glad to hear you say that." I looked back at him, watching his features soften. "This past week has been hell."

Owen looked down at his coffee cup. "I want to apologize for how I handled things the other day. My behavior was way out of line."

"Not entirely," I said. "I think, maybe, some of it needed to be said. I mean, the way I've always flirted with you—if it was bad enough that Cates had to warn you about it, then I guess it was happening more frequently than I realized."

"It still doesn't make it okay for me to act the way I did. And listen, I never want you to think that I…." His voice trailed off as he tried to gather his words. A group of people walked behind us, so he leaned in close and spoke lower. "It doesn't have to be all or nothing between us, all right? I'm perfectly content just being your friend. I'm sorry if I gave you the impression I was expecting more from you. Because I don't."

I stared down at his bouncing knee. He was nervous, which I found kind of endearing. This conversation, as awkward as it was, was long overdue. "When you told me you needed a break from me, that just killed me, Owen."

"I know, I know." He winced, running his fingers through his hair. "And I'm sorry. I realize now it wasn't a break from you that I needed; just a shift in our friendship dynamic. We sometimes cross over into this more-than-just-friends territory, and that's where things get messy. Especially when you say it's 'literally nothing.' I think we both know that's not true."

I nodded slowly. We were putting everything out in the open now, yet something stopped me from saying what I really wanted to just then—that what happened between us in the garden was *everything*. How I'd craved his touch ever since, even when we were at odds with each other this past week.

But that was exactly the kind of thing he was talking about, wasn't it? To say those words would fling us right over the wall into romantic territory with no chance of returning. And I couldn't do that to him. Not now. Not when he was finally happy with someone else. I couldn't let myself interfere.

So I pushed every lustful thought aside and suggested we establish some ground rules. "You know, we could set some boundaries."

"That's exactly what I was thinking," he said. "Maybe a hands-off policy?"

"Yeah, that's a good one." I looked down at our knees, just millimeters apart, and slid far enough away from him that we wouldn't risk accidentally bumping into each other. He let out a quiet laugh, shaking his head. Grinning, I said, "There. What else?"

"I don't know. You come up with the next rule."

"Okay." I thought for a minute, remembering everything that had happened between the two of us to cause so many complications over the past couple of months. "No flirting?"

He squinted, pondering this for a moment. "It might be hard to establish what constitutes flirting and what doesn't."

"True," I said. "I guess that's where the line tends to get a little blurred."

"Exactly. Therein lies the problem."

We sat in silence for a minute or two, sipping our coffee and people-watching. Most of the other people walking around were wearing lanyards like ours, all of them with the same idea, carrying Starbucks cups or soft pretzels. I glanced down at the time on my phone. We'd have to head back into the convention center soon if we didn't want to be late for our second workshops.

"How about this," Owen started. "If you wouldn't say it to Vicki, don't say it to me."

I laughed. "I suppose that works."

"Okay. Good. I think those are pretty solid rules, then."

"Right. No touching, no flirting. Easy enough." I reached up to tuck my hair behind my ears, and when I pulled my arm down, some of the strings on my sweater sleeves got snagged on one of my hoop earrings. "Shit," I muttered, struggling to get my earring unstuck. Every attempt I made to free my earring from the loops of fabric only made my sleeve unravel more.

Owen sat his coffee cup atop his notebook by his feet and leaned over to help me, delicately touching my ear. "What the hell did you do?" he asked with a laugh, attempting to pull the strings from my sweater off the earring. "How do these earrings work? I don't—" He scooted closer to get a better look, and I tilted my head to the side. He was still struggling, with both hands now.

"I think if you just open the clasp—"

"The strings are all wrapped around the clasp. I can't—" He let out a frustrated sigh, his knuckles brushing against my neck as he continued to fiddle with the earring.

I realized this would work a lot better if I could get my arm free. I maneuvered around to wriggle out of the sweater, carefully lifting it over my head in a way that wouldn't rip my earring off. I was wearing a white tank top and a padded pink bra, so it's not like I was stripping in front of all of these people on the skybridge. My entire sweater hung from my ear now, inside out. Owen chuckled at my ridiculous appearance, watching me easily remove the earring now that I had both hands free.

"Jeez, Lavely, try to keep your clothes on."

"I just couldn't help myself," I teased, laying the sweater across my lap before turning it inside out. A smile spread across my lips as I pulled the sweater back on over my head. And then, as I ran my fingers through my mussed-up hair, I froze. Owen's knee was pressed into my thigh, and I was leaning back onto his arm, which he had draped on the bench behind me. In the past thirty seconds, we'd broken not just one, but *both* of our newly-established rules.

He must have just come to the same realization because he gave me a horrified look before drawing both hands to his face. "I'm sorry," he said, sliding away from me.

"We're really bad at this."

# chapter thirty-four

*owen*

There are few things teachers love more than a free meal, especially when that free meal involves tacos. At the end of the day, all the convention attendees were welcomed to a catered dinner in one of the banquet halls. We were told it would give us a chance to unwind and let loose, despite the two-drink minimum at the bar.

The room was enormous, all decorated with black, white, and gold balloons and tulle. You would have thought we were crashing a wedding reception if it weren't for the cheesy, framed education-themed quotes on every table. Ours said *REMEMBER YOUR WHY*. Sarah's eyes flashed my direction as we took our seats beside each other, and though she didn't say anything out loud, I knew what she was thinking. This was a phrase we were often told at the end of meetings about budget cuts, active shooter drills, or increasing our class sizes. Sometimes, our "why" didn't always feel worth it.

At least not for me.

Cates motioned toward the sign, making a "psssh" sound with his lips.. "Tonight, our only 'why' is to forget we're teachers for a couple of hours and have a good time. Right, folks?" Everyone in our group vehemently agreed.

"I can't believe this is our last year with him," Vicki said, taking the seat on Sarah's other side. She had been working with Cates for something like fifteen years. Longer than any of us sitting at that table. "It's going to take a mighty special person to fill those shoes."

Sarah shot a quick glance in my direction before shifting her attention to Vicki. "Yes. They're definitely big shoes to fill."

Those words lingered in my mind as we all got in line for the taco buffet. I couldn't imagine any teachers at GES crying over my eventual departure. Sarah, maybe. But that was different. For the first time, I pictured myself at the head of the table during the staff meetings with the goal of motivating a roomful of teachers. They'd probably roll their eyes.

"You look a little lost in thought there," Sarah said, turning around to face me as we inched forward in the line. She was wearing a loose, long-sleeved black dress and black heels that almost brought her eye level up to mine. Something was different about her hair—was it curlier than normal? Part of it was pinned back, and she looked beautiful.

We were encouraged to wear casual-dressy attire for this. Earlier that week, Kendall had picked out my outfit—a dark grey button-up with a black tie and black slacks. It didn't differ much from what I wore at school on a daily basis, though she'd insisted I swap out my usual, everyday shoes for a nicer pair of loafers.

"Just thinking about filling my belly with tacos," I answered Sarah, rubbing my silk tie between my fingers.

She nodded in agreement. "You look really nice, by the way." And then, once she realized what she'd said, she turned to Vicki and grabbed her by the arm. "Vicki, you look really nice tonight."

"Oh, thanks? You do, too."

Sarah turned back to me with a grin. Just as I opened my mouth to return the compliment, a tall, brown-skinned woman wearing a khaki pantsuit approached me. "You're Owen

Gardner, right?" I nodded as she gave me a firm handshake. "Hi, I'm Deb Lacy, the workshop coordinator for IES. Everyone's been telling me the host of *STEM for the Win* was in attendance today, and I couldn't believe it until I looked you up and saw you really are from Indiana."

"Yes. Born and raised."

"I would love to talk to you about hosting a workshop at next year's conference. That would be sure to draw a crowd. Would you be interested in doing something like that?"

"Oh, I hadn't really thought about it," I said, taking a couple steps forward to move up in line. Deb walked with me. Sarah was eyeing us over her shoulder, and even Cates was watching with curiosity. By this time next year, I could be principal of GES, meaning I wouldn't have the time for things like this. The district might even consider it a conflict of interest. I cleared my throat. "I would definitely love to learn more about that, though," I said, giving her a non-committal, but honest, answer.

"Great," she said, holding her palms together. "Your email address on your website—is that the best way for me to contact you?"

"Yes, it is."

"Perfect! You'll be hearing from me within the next couple of weeks, then. And if you don't, please reach out to me. All of my contact info is on the IES site."

"Sounds good. Thank you so much for considering me," I said.

People had been approaching me all day about *STEM for the Win*, which was overwhelming enough, but this took things to a whole new level. I knew I could probably come up with an attention-grabbing workshop topic. Hell, I could probably do it with only five minutes of prep time.

When we got back to our table, Sarah leaned in close. "You're going to do it, right?"

I took a bite of my taco and swallowed before answering, glancing over at Cates. He was deep in conversation with a principal from another school. "I don't know if I can. If this interview next week goes well, then I'm probably going to be putting my side hustle on the back burner."

"You're an idiot," she blurted.

My mouth fell open in feigned offense. "Wow, Lavely. That hurts."

"Do you want to know what I really think?"

"That was you holding back?" I asked with a laugh. "Then maybe I don't want to know what you *really* think. I'm not sure my heart could handle it."

"Don't do this interview," she said with an intense stare, ignoring my joke. "It'll be the worst decision of your life."

"You really think so?"

She nodded. "Come on. You've got the podcast, and pretty soon you're going to have a book. Not to mention all those worksheets and workbooks. And now, you've had a speaking opportunity just handed to you. Most people have to apply for things like that. How many streams of revenue does that make—four?"

I inhaled. "It would actually bring me up to five, if you count all my affiliates…."

"Which is why I think you're an idiot." I wondered why it took her so long to tell me how she really felt. Then again, neither of us were all that great about being honest with one another. Until today, anyway. "You're really going to kiss all of that goodbye to be principal?"

"Well, now I don't know." I stared down at the flecks of gold confetti on the white tablecloth. "Truthfully, the closer it gets to becoming reality, the harder it is for me to picture myself as Cates' successor. To imagine everyone at Grissom looking up to me the way they do with him…?" I glanced over at Cates, who had been so busy fist-bumping or shaking hands with random acquaintances he'd barely taken a bite. "I just can't see it."

"Please don't take offense to what I'm about to say," Sarah said, scrunching her face as she spoke. "But I can't picture it, either. This role isn't right for you, Owen. I should have told you this a long time ago. And you know I support you and want what's best for you, which is why I'm telling you all of this now. You're not going to be happy if you take this job. And I really hope you don't, as much as it kills me to think of losing you as a co-worker."

We ate in silence for a few minutes as I considered all of this. Could I really run *STEM for the Win* full-time? It was a terrifying risk to take. However, after everything Sarah just said, pursuing this principal job was beginning to sound like the bigger risk. "If I don't take the spot, I wonder who will?"

"Who knows. But whoever gets hired, I hope they actually respect and trust teachers the way Cates always has. And I hope they're just as progressive as he is. My biggest fear is that Grissom will—"

"Oh my god," I interrupted, swallowing the bite in my mouth. "*You're* the idiot."

"Um, what?"

I blinked at her. "Why haven't *you* applied?"

"Me? Don't be ridiculous."

I scooted my chair closer so I could speak lower, not wanting to risk any of our colleagues eavesdropping on this conversation. "Out of all the teachers at GES, you're hands-down the most qualified. You might not have been there the longest, but just look at what all you've done. You want to talk about Grissom's progress? Well, how much of that is because of you?"

I watched her rub the condensation from her glass as she processed everything I was telling her.

"You're already a great leader," I continued, thinking about how she'd been handling the garden project so far. "You're an expert communicator. Everyone already respects you. Think of the impact you'll have. Not just on the sixty or so kids we have, but the whole school—and the whole community."

I knew I was saying all the right things to sway her. I could practically see the gears turning in her head as she became silent. The longer I thought about it, the more this felt like the obvious choice. Principal Lavely? That made perfect sense.

"What's stopping you from applying?"

"Well," she said, picking at some of the gold confetti. "I'm too young, for one."

"I've only got two years on you. What else?"

"I—I don't have all the required licensing for an admin role."

I gave her a dismissive shrug. "That'll take you no time. And I know the district would work with you on that. So it sounds like you're out of excuses. I'm withdrawing my application," I stated decisively, not even giving this a second thought. I didn't need to. "And I'll write you a letter of recommendation. If you want me to, of course."

"I don't know," she said, sounding wary. But a smile spread across her face. "Yes? No? Ugh, now I don't know what I want to do."

"Do you need me to make you a pro and con list?" This made her laugh. "I think you should seriously consider it. But you should probably decide soon because they're starting interviews next week."

Suddenly, the ceiling lights dimmed, and the DJ at the other end of the room asked the crowd if we were ready to "get funky" in an attempt to entice everyone to make their way to the dance floor. When the Cha Cha Slide started blaring from the speakers, Cates rose from his seat and adjusted his bowtie, saying, "You don't have to ask me twice." He and one of his principal buddies disappeared into the crowd. Heath mumbled something about wanting to meet women before he took off, too.

I finished eating while half-listening to Sarah and Vicki solidify their evening plans. From what I could gather, they had a night of wine-drinking and self-care ahead of them. As for me, I couldn't wait to get up to my room to start writing Sarah's letter of recommendation. She might not end up using it, but maybe it could help convince her to take this job.

Knowing I was going to withdraw my application gave me an enormous sense of relief. It was like I now had a valid excuse for not going after the job. All I needed was that little push in the right direction. Maybe after writing Sarah's letter, I could get a jump-start on my new business plan.

I felt my phone buzz in my pocket and pulled it out for a quick glance. One of my scheduled posts was going semi-viral, and the notifications were rolling in. I'd have to take a peek at those later to make sure people were behaving themselves in the comments.

"Was that Kendall?" Sarah asked, her attention focused on me again.

I glanced up from my phone at her and reached for my glass. "No," I said, leaning forward to shove my phone back in my pocket. "I don't think I'll be getting any texts from her for a while."

"Uh oh." She fidgeted with her straw wrapper. "Are you guys fighting?" I thought I might have caught a hint of hopefulness in her voice, but I wasn't going to let myself read too much into it.

"Actually, she broke up with me yesterday."

Sarah lifted her eyebrows in surprise. "Wow, really? I thought she was crazy about you—and the two of you seemed so happy both times I saw you together yesterday. What happened?"

"I guess she noticed I've been a little distracted lately." I brought my eyes up to meet hers, wondering if that would be enough to hint at the real reason without having to explicitly state it.

"Oh," Sarah said. She understood. "I'm really sorry."

"It was inevitable." I smiled from one side of my mouth. "She really put me in my place, but I think I needed it." I started to let out a self-deprecating chuckle, but something about the sudden look of concentration on Sarah's face caught my attention.

"So it's—you're—"

Before she could get the words out, Heath collapsed in the chair on my other side, cutting her off. "Hey, let's get out of here and go to a nightclub. Apparently there's one just a block from here, and that's where everyone's heading after this."

"Oh, I don't know…."

"No, listen. I just talked to these girls from Terre Haute I met in one of my workshops today, and it looks like they're both single. Look, they're right over there." Heath nodded toward two women sitting at a nearby table with their heads together, whispering. One of them gave Heath a little wave, and he waved back before turning to me. "You can have the other one."

I couldn't control the laughter that burst from my chest. "I'm sorry, but I didn't come here for that. You're on your own, man."

"Come on. Don't do this to me. I can't just show up alone."

"Sure you can. Besides, I've got to get up early for breakfast with Cates. I'm going to call it a night early." When I was younger, I might have let someone talk me into going clubbing. As a matter of fact, that's exactly what I did the first time I attended this conference, and I spent the second day of workshops nursing an intense hangover.

Now, at thirty, I couldn't think of anything less appealing.

"Right, your breakfast with Cates," Heath said, a hint of annoyance in his voice. For a second, I thought about extending the invitation to him, but it wasn't really my place. So I just pretended not to hear him, turning back to Sarah.

Much to my disappointment, she and Vicki had gathered their things and looked ready to go. As Sarah turned to leave the table, she extended her arm to touch my shoulder—but just before her hand made contact with my body, she recoiled and drew it back to her chest. That was close. "I'll see you in the morning," she said.

"Goodnight, Sarah. See you, Vicki. You ladies have fun."

As soon as they were out of earshot, Heath leaned in close to whisper, "If Sarah were single, I would be all over that. She looks good tonight, doesn't she?" Horny little bastard. He craned his neck to watch her walk away.

Keeping my eyes fixated on my empty plate, I said, "Indeed, she does."

# chapter thirty-five

## sarah

Twenty-two.

That's how many text messages Eli had sent since our argument that morning. As I sat cross-legged on the bed in Vicki's hotel room, I stretched to nudge my phone out of reach so I could attempt to forget about him for a while.

I kept waiting for regret to sink in, half-expecting myself to call him all weepy and apologetic like I often did after our fights, but that never happened. Something was different this time, and it had more to do with my own jumbled emotions than anything Eli had said or done.

When I told him I'd reached my breaking point, I'd meant it.

But even more so, my head was spinning with thoughts of Owen. How differently would our boundary-setting conversation have gone if I had known he and Kendall had split? And, if he knew I was on the verge of leaving my fiancé—what then?

We'd come so close to communicating honestly with each other, laying everything out, yet we still managed to miss the mark.

"You have no idea how much I needed a weekend away like this," Vicki was saying as she pulled a four-pack of mini white zinfandel bottles from the fridge in her hotel room. She handed me one. "I don't even care that I had to sit through some boring workshops, if it means not having a toddler attached to my hip for two whole days."

With a shake of my head, I forced the thoughts of Eli and Owen from my mind so I could focus on the task at hand: unwind with Vicki. I laughed as I twisted open my bottle, watching her unload everything for our spa night from her suitcase. She'd packed face masks, pedicure kits, lavender Epsom salts, and even some plastic basins for soaking our feet. She was anything if not prepared. "You really thought of everything," I told her, rummaging through it all. I pulled an avocado face mask from the pile. "I might not have a toddler at home, but I do have a man-child I'm happy to free myself of for the weekend." Maybe forever.

"They're practically the same thing." She clinked her bottle against mine. "Cheers."

"Cheers."

We sat at the foot of her bed to soak our feet in the lavender foot baths, indulging in trashy reality TV, wine, and a shared bag of peanut M&Ms. As we applied our face masks, I played the role of the listener, letting Vicki vent about her husband's inability to care for their children without pestering her with a million questions. "All day long, it's been 'where's Mila's green sippy?' and 'do they have to take baths?' I'll be lucky if they're all still alive when I get home."

"You're making me never want kids."

She groaned as she took a sip of her wine. "They're stressful, but I promise it's all worth it. Don't let me scare you. You'll be a great mom someday—if you want to be, that is."

I looked down at my feet, wiggling my toes in the water. I tried my best to picture Eli as a father. If this weekend was any indication of how he'd handle household issues, I couldn't imagine bringing children into the mix. With kids, you can't always put yourself first, and that would be a problem for him. "I think I want to focus on my career for a little while," I said, desperate to change the subject. "I might put in my application for the principal position."

Vicki clutched my arm. "Oh, honey, you absolutely have to. I actually assumed you already did."

"Not yet. I hadn't really thought about it, but Owen's encouraging me to give it a shot. He's withdrawing his own application to focus on his business." I popped a peanut M&M into my mouth. I didn't tell her Owen would probably resign at the end of the year, unsure whether he wanted that information out there yet or not. "With him out of the pool of candidates, I might have a chance."

"Of course you do. If they took up votes for it, you'd be my first pick." Just then, her phone went off—she was getting a FaceTime call from her husband. "Ugh, what now?" She wiped her feet on a towel and went into the bathroom to talk to him in private. While she was gone, I reached for my phone, not at all surprised to see yet another text from Eli.

**Eli:** I hope you at least call to say goodnight.

I didn't have the energy this conversation required. Not yet. So I ignored that message, too, choosing instead to take a selfie to document how silly I looked in that avocado sheet mask, holding my little wine bottle up to my face. I tapped Owen's name and sent him the picture along with the caption: *jealous?*

As I chugged the last bit of wine from the bottle, my phone buzzed in my hand.

**Owen:** And here I am building myself a pillow fort, all by my lonesome.

**Sarah**: Pics or it didn't happen.

As soon as I sent that reply, Vicki emerged from the bathroom sans face mask, her eyes all blotchy and red from crying. "What's wrong?" I asked her.

"Mila was having a nightmare and she wanted to talk to me," she said, smiling through her tears. "Gah, now I just want to pack up and go home to her."

"Aw."

Vicki reached for a bottle of lotion infused with tea-tree oil and began rubbing it on her feet. "Okay, I need you to distract me or else I'm going to get really sad and run home to my babies."

I pulled my feet from the water basin and dabbed them with a white hand towel. "Well," I started, sucking in a deep breath. I knew just the thing to divert her attention, but could I really say it? I swallowed, feeling a warmth spread from my face to my neck and collarbones. With an exhale, I finally confessed the words I never thought I'd speak aloud: "I think I'm in love with Owen."

Vicki was a statue before me. She was in the middle of bringing an M&M to her mouth, but her hand froze a few inches from her face. Slowly, a goofy grin began to appear. "Shut the hell up."

I laughed. I could count on one hand the number of times I'd heard that woman swear. "I know, it's crazy."

"Crazy?" She slapped her leg. "Girl, I think that's the sanest thing you've ever said." I could only giggle in response, and suddenly I was fourteen years old again, talking about a schoolgirl crush. "And does Mr. Owen Gardner know this?"

"No," I quickly answered. "And actually, we established some friendship boundaries earlier today, but that was before…." I let my voice trail off, knowing I couldn't mention Kendall—that wasn't my secret to tell. "I think that was a mistake."

I looked down, realizing I was fiddling with my diamond ring, twisting it around my finger. Vicki was watching me, too, with wide eyes. "What are you going to do?"

That was the million-dollar question, wasn't it? As my phone buzzed on my lap, I hesitated to check, fearing it might be another text from Eli. But curiosity won, and when I saw it was a message from Owen, my stomach fluttered.

"Is that him?" Vicki asked.

I didn't answer her, though she probably figured it out herself from the way I grinned the second his message loaded. As requested, Owen sent a photo of himself sitting amidst three pillows arranged in a U-shape, with his laptop on the bed beside him.

I quickly typed a reply.

**Sarah:** You call that a pillow fort? Lame.

Turning to Vicki, I sighed, drawing my hands up to my forehead. "I don't know what to do, Vicki." I brought my hands back to my lap and played with my ring again. "I'm supposed to get married."

"Says who?" she blurted, taking me by surprise. "Who's forcing you to marry Eli?"

"Nobody."

"Exactly." She picked up a zipper pouch full of nail polish and started rummaging through it. "If your heart's not one hundred percent in it, don't do it. I mean—maybe I'm just reading too much into things, but it didn't seem like you were all that eager to say yes in the first place."

I turned to her, furrowing my brows, and she rolled her eyes with a little smile.

"I saw you and Owen together that night, just before the proposal. I don't know what happened, but I was picking up on a little bit of a romantic moment. Am I right?"

I bit my bottom lip, confirming her suspicion with my silence. Just then, Owen replied.

**Owen:** You think you can do better, Lavely?

Vicki pulled a magenta polish from the bag before passing it to me. I began rummaging through it, my mind all tangled up with thoughts of both Owen and Eli. I pulled a bottle of forest green nail polish out of the pouch, but I made no move to start painting my toenails. Instead, I held the bottle in my hand, staring at the floor as I considered Vicki's words. I struggled to come up with a single reason to justify my relationship with Eli. Was I in love with him, or just sticking to what was comfortable and familiar?

I waited to reply to Owen, and Vicki and I began the pedicure segment of our night. I chuckled as she awkwardly made her way to the mini fridge with her wet toes to grab a second bottle of white zinfandel for both of us. "Here," she said. And then she dropped her hand to my shoulder. "Don't hold off on the love you deserve, okay? You owe it to yourself to be happy."

She was right. I didn't want to hold off. Not for a second longer. I just had one thing I needed to take care of first. I grabbed my phone and carefully slid into my flip flops, not wanting to smudge my freshly-painted toes. "I need to make a phone call," I said, taking a long swig from my bottle. I excused myself to step out into the hallway.

Eli answered after the first ring. "Ah, so you're not dead."

I cut right to the chase. "Did the air conditioner get fixed?"

"Yes," he said with a sigh. "You'll be glad to know I skipped my golf scramble and stayed here to take care of it. It took the guy all day, but it's done. So, you're welcome."

I didn't thank him. That would only validate his belief he was doing me a big favor, like I owed him for this. "Good, I'm glad it's done," I said, looking down at the geometric pattern on the carpet beneath my feet. "Can I ask you a question?"

"Yeah?"

"Do you think I could be principal of Grissom?"

"You?" There was a prolonged silence. "I mean, do you want my honest answer?"

"Yes, that's why I asked."

"Okay, then… no. You already get way too emotionally involved with just the kids in your class. Imagine running the whole school. I think you'd do a great job, but you think you're stressed now? If you were principal, you'd be venting and crying every single night. Why are you asking? You're not thinking about applying, are you?"

"No. You're right, I'm too emotional." I clenched my jaw, trying not to let his words sink in. Reminding myself why I'd asked in the first place. As easy as it was for me to picture myself as principal, I couldn't imagine coming home to Eli at the end of a long day. I didn't want to be Principal Meeks. When I envisioned my perfect future, Eli wasn't part of it. "We need to talk when I get home tomorrow evening."

"You're still on that 'we need to talk' bull? I thought we were good now. The A/C is fixed. I skipped my golf scramble, just like you wanted. Are you really telling me you're still upset with me after all that?"

"It's not just the A/C and the golf scramble. It's everything."

"Like what? Can you give me a fucking hint as to what you're talking about?"

"I'm not happy, Eli, and I haven't been for a while," I said, lowering my voice when a couple of people emerged from their room a few doors down. "Have you really not noticed?"

There was a pause on his end, a silence as the weight of my words sunk in. "Evidently not," he said. His stunned response almost made me falter, a lump forming in my throat. I thought about him being alone and having to tell his friends and family I left him, and tears began to form in my eyes.

But I blinked them away. "Let's finish this discussion tomorrow when I get home, okay? I have to go. Don't call me anymore tonight."

"I don't want to talk tomorrow. Let's talk now. Just fucking say the words you're dying to say, Sarah. I can take it."

With a slow, hesitant breath, I muttered, "I'm done," fully aware of the ambiguity of those words. And then I hung up, having said just enough to get the point across. We would finish this conversation face-to-face—and I wouldn't allow him to cuss at me, either.

Unsurprisingly, my phone rang right away, but I switched it to Do Not Disturb mode. He never was that great at following directions.

I held my phone to my side and stared across the hall at the door I'd seen Owen step out of earlier that evening before the dinner in the banquet hall. A little voice tugged inside of me, reminding me of my newfound liberation. In letting go of Eli, I'd made room for something more—a chance at true happiness, maybe? As I gazed at the modern numbers next to Owen's door, I smiled, thinking about his last text *(you think you can do better, Lovely?)* and leaned against Vicki's door, contemplating my next move. The time for subtlety was long gone. I tried to think of a response that would in no way be perceived as innocuous, friendly banter. I wanted to make it crystal clear: *I want you.* What was the point of our rules now, anyway?

Sarah: Maybe I could come show you my skills. We could even turn it into a STEM challenge and build one together. 😉

# chapter thirty-six

*owen*

Sleep often eluded me in hotels. I could never get used to the different sounds. Indianapolis wasn't exactly a huge metropolis, but it was a lot more alive at night than rural Woodvale. And my hotel room seemed to have two temperature settings: Antarctica or the seventh circle of hell. I kept fiddling with the thermostat, but I couldn't get comfortable.

I wasn't tired, anyway. The coffee I had after dinner was only partially to blame for that. My mind was racing. After writing Sarah's letter of recommendation for the principal job, I'd come to realize she was more qualified for it than I could ever dream of being. While I still planned on withdrawing my application, I probably wouldn't even need to. When you put our resumes side-by-side, there was simply no comparison—hers outshone mine in more ways than I could count.

Even Cates, who didn't exactly hide his favoritism for me, couldn't deny that.

I wondered what Cates would think of my resignation announcement. I'd have to tell him sooner rather than later in order to cancel my interview and ensure Sarah got one in my place. It's not like it would affect him personally, but it would certainly be a surprise.

Cates had always been supportive of *STEM for the Win*, but he was unaware of the scope of it. I couldn't just casually disclose how much I was earning from my side hustle with my boss. So for the past couple of years, I never brought up SFTW unless he asked. As far as he knew, it was just a little hobby I had on the side.

However, I spent an hour crunching the numbers in my hotel room that night, and I knew that if I played my cards right, I'd be able to out-earn my teaching salary by this time next year. And if it didn't work out? So what. I could always go back to teaching.

Just after midnight, I was still too energized to even try to sleep. I closed my laptop and threw some jeans on to take a walk around the hotel. I was wearing an old, faded Robotics Club tee, which had long been retired from everyday wear and was now a pajama shirt.

Grabbing my room key and wallet, I stepped out into the hallway. Our group from GES was scattered around the 24th floor of the hotel, and I had to guess the majority of the other guests were also teachers.

As I passed the room I'd seen Sarah entering earlier that day just after check-in, I slowed down, nearly coming to a stop. Thinking about her last, playful message. Wondering if she was still awake, too. Considering there was a keynote event at 8:00 in the morning, she was probably already sound asleep. Then again, it looked like she and Vicki were still hitting the bottle just a couple of hours ago, so they could still be carrying on, for all I knew.

Either way, it didn't matter. Nothing good would come out of talking to her right now. Not this late. Nope.

As tempting as it was to knock on her door and ask if she wanted to join me for a walk, I continued down the hallway without looking back. If I was strong enough to only respond to her suggestive text with an emoji—when I'd really wanted to say something borderline explicit—I was strong enough to walk away from her door now.

As I waited for the elevator, I looked down at my watch. 12:20 a.m. Besides the rumble of the approaching elevator, the hallway was eerily quiet. Not a single crying baby or a blaring television. Above my head, the downward arrow lit up with a *ding!* just before the doors opened.

And there she was.

"Owen, hey!" Sarah said, stepping just outside the doors. I held my hand up to keep them from closing. Her hair was pulled back into a side braid, and she was all bright-eyed and fresh-faced after her spa night with Vicki. If she was tired at all, it didn't show. In fact, she looked more beautiful right then than she had earlier that night with all the make-up and perfectly-styled hair.

And she smelled… delicious.

"Look who's a night owl," I said, lingering in the doorway to the elevator. Half in, half out. "What are you doing up?"

She played with the end of her braid. "I just needed to go on a walk to clear my head."

"I was about to do the same." I put my hands in my back pockets. "Are you, uh, too tired to go on another walk?"

Without answering, she stepped back onto the elevator and leaned against the back wall onto her hands as I hit the L button. The doors closed and I settled into the corner farthest from Sarah, taking in her appearance from the opposite side. I'd never seen her at this level of undress—a low-cut tank top and pink cotton shorts that rode a little high on the thighs. And though I wasn't certain, she didn't appear to be wearing a bra.

"So, uhh," I said, fixing my eyes upon her face. "I finished writing your letter of recommendation."

"You did? Already?" she asked, crossing her legs at the ankles. I answered with a nod. "Can I see it?"

"You just want to proofread it, don't you?" I clicked my tongue. "You've got no faith in me."

"Well, who else is going to proofread it if I don't?" she asked with a smile. "And I'm just curious to see what you have to say about me."

"All good things, I promise."

"Well, I would hope so. Are you going to let me read it or not?"

The elevator doors sprung open—we'd reached the lobby. I slid one hand between the doors to hold them open, my other hand hovering near the numbered buttons. Being alone with her on that elevator was already making it difficult to follow our newly-established rules. With the added privacy of a hotel room and the proximity of a bed, I wasn't sure I'd be able to contain myself. Especially with the way she was looking at me right then, like she wanted to eat me alive. I swallowed. "You want to take a look at it... right now?"

"Is that okay?"

"Yup." I took a deep breath as I pushed the button for the 24th floor. As a boisterous group of seemingly drunk people approached the elevator, I frantically hit the "close door" button over and over. The leader of their pack—a man carrying an open bottle of Guinness in one hand and a slice of pizza in the other—was shouting for us to hold the elevator, but the doors closed in his face just before he reached us. "Thank God."

With a jerk, the elevator began its ascent to our floor. This was now my fourth time on this particular elevator car for the day, and it seemed to go slower every time. I leaned against my hands on the rail, watching Sarah take out her braid on the other side. She ran her fingers through her hair, shaking it out, filling the space around us with a hypnotizing coconut aroma.

I was in complete agony. I brought my hand up to my forehead and stared down at the floor, like hiding her from my view would somehow make this more tolerable. But I could still smell her, could still hear let out a soft giggle. "Are you okay?"

"I should've just let them get on," I mumbled.

"Why?"

I lifted my head to look at her face. "Because the longer I'm alone with you tonight, the harder it's going to be for me not to break either one of the rules."

The words spilled out of my mouth before I realized what I was saying. And though our friendship rules weren't all that fleshed-out, I knew I'd just broken the second one with that confession. Our only stipulation was that we couldn't say anything to each other we wouldn't say to Vicki, too. And while Vicki was a lovely person, I didn't exactly feel tempted by her like I was now, with Sarah, who was staring at me all wide-eyed and biting her bottom lip.

I let out an exasperated sigh. If I could somehow back even farther away from her, I would have. But there was nowhere to go—not until those elevator doors opened. "And yes, I'm aware I broke rule number two just by telling you that," I continued, "but I don't think it's possible for me to *not* flirt with you. Or touch you, for that matter. I'm not strong enough, Sarah. Every time you're near me, I only want you closer. You—"

"Owen."

"—have no idea the effect you have on me." I began to pace on my side of the elevator. "I keep thinking it's going to get easier, but my attraction to you only grows stronger every time we're together. So maybe I need to go back to the original boundary I set, and just distance myself from you. Because—"

"Owen, listen—"

"—if I take you to my hotel room right now, there's no telling what I might—"

"I'm leaving Eli," Sarah interjected, loud enough to cut through my incessant rambling.

My pacing came to an abrupt halt. The intensity in her voice had captured my attention, and I looked at her, searching for answers. Had I heard her correctly? Her frustration was evident as she brought her hands up to the sides of her head to rub her temples. I must have looked like I was having difficulty processing what she'd just said, because she repeated herself, softer this time.

"I'm leaving Eli."

I allowed the weight of her words to sink in, fully realizing their implication. I gazed across the elevator into her eyes, which were like two green lights giving me permission to go. The time for self-doubt and hesitation had passed, and suddenly, the five feet of space separating us that seemed suffocatingly too small just a moment ago was too much.

Three long strides.

Three long strides and six years—that's all it took to get to her.

In one decisive movement, I took Sarah's face in my hands and brought my mouth to hers, pinning her against the wall of the elevator. We kissed soft and slow at first, and then sloppy and hurried, like we were making up for all the kisses that should've happened but didn't. Finally, I knew what Sarah tasted like, what it felt like to have her grip me so tight I forgot how to breathe. My hands embarked on new territory, touching her in places I never had before, only a thin layer of cotton separating my palm from her skin. She emitted a soft moan against my mouth, her tongue circling mine with a tantalizing rhythm.

The elevator dinged and the doors flung open, forcing us apart. I thrust my arm through the doors just before they closed again. Sarah tucked her mussed-up hair behind her ears, her chest rising as she panted. "What was that you were saying about, um, what you might do if I came to your hotel room?"

I grabbed her by the hand and yanked her off the elevator. Instead of telling her, I'd show her.

I peeked around the corner to ensure none of our coworkers were wandering the hall. And we hurried down to my room—why was this hallway so long? Once we got to my door, I fumbled with my room key, tapping it repeatedly against the sensor above the door handle. The light kept flashing red—my hands were too shaky and sweaty for this. "Shit," I muttered just before Sarah ripped the card from my hand to do it herself. It worked on the first try.

Before the door even had a chance to close behind us, she clung to me like a magnet, kissing my chin, my neck. I pressed her body against the mirror outside the bathroom as my fingers found the hem of her tank top. I slid my hands beneath the stretchy fabric, drawing it upward with my wrists. She reached down to help me, pulling it over her head.

I was right—she wasn't wearing a bra. I paused for a moment to take in the sight of her breasts in the dim light from the lamp by the bed. "God, Lavely—you're perfect," I said, cupping her breasts with both hands. She threw her head back, erupting into giggles.

"You're still addressing me by my last name with my boobs in your hands?"

"What do you want me to call you?" I asked, burying my face in her collarbone. I kissed her there, making my way down to her breasts and nuzzling my cheek against one of her erect nipples just before taking it into my mouth.

The giggling stopped and she drew in a deep breath. With a tight grip on the back of my neck, she choked out, "Whatever you want," as I drew circles around her nipple with my tongue. As I sucked on it, I gave her other nipple attention between two fingers. With my free hand, I found the waistband of her pink shorts and yanked them down to her thighs. She pulled them the rest of the way down and kicked them away.

I switched my mouth to her other breast, making sure to give both nipples equal attention. But I was eager to go somewhere else with my hand. Kissing her on the mouth again, I palmed her through her panties first, rubbing the wet fabric against her clit. God, she was ready for me. I slipped my hand into her panties and we moaned in unison when my middle finger found its way to her warm opening. With my thumb rubbing circles around her clit, I thrust another finger inside of her, curling both fingers until I found just the right spot. I knew I'd found it when I felt her lower her body against my hand with a whimper.

My new favorite sound.

I continued, kissing her neck as I worked inside her with my fingers. But I paid the most attention to what my thumb was doing to the most delicate place on her body. She held her breath, digging her nails into my arms as she gasped in more and more air. And with a slow exhale, she whispered, "I don't think I can stand anymore."

I couldn't decipher whether she was talking about the pleasure she was feeling or the act of physically standing up, but there was no time to ask questions. Instead, I grabbed her by the thighs and hoisted her up around my hips. She draped her arms around my neck as I carried her over to the bed, kissing her the entire way.

"Now I know why you go to the gym all the time," she said just before I dropped her onto the mattress. She slid back against the pillows as I undressed myself down to my boxers. As I dropped my jeans to the ground, I paused for a moment to take in the sight before my eyes—Sarah Lavely, in my hotel bed, wearing nothing but black panties. My mind oscillated from wanting to take my time with her, kissing every square inch of her body, and wanting to get inside of her as soon as possible. I was afraid that if I didn't take my time with her, she wasn't going to enjoy this enough.

I crawled across the bed to her, straddling her with a knee on either side of her hips. As I lowered myself onto her, she bit her bottom lip. "I'm still not entirely sure if this is real," I said, brushing the side of my nose against hers. "Because I've had a lot of dreams that go exactly like this."

"You're not dreaming," she whispered, turning my face with her hands so she could kiss me.

"Good."

"Do you have a condom?"

I laughed with my mouth still pressed against her lips. "Slow down—" I stopped myself from saying her last name again. Yet her first name didn't feel right, either—so I found myself blurting, "baby."

I just called Sarah *baby*.

I regretted it for a second—but only a second.

"There you go," Sarah said. My eyes were closed, but I could feel her lips pull upward into a smile. "Good boy."

A guttural. growl-like noise emanated deep from within me, and I gave her bottom lip a gentle bite—kissing her alone would no longer suffice. Reluctantly, I tugged away and pulled myself back up to a kneeling position, trying to remember where I'd put my wallet. "Condom. Wallet. Pants." For some reason, I could only manage to speak in one-word sentences now. Caveman-style. I hopped out of the bed and scrambled for my jeans on the floor, hoping there was enough blood left in the upper part of my body to make my brain function for at least a second. I panicked as I fumbled through my wallet, worrying I hadn't brought anything with me—but the second I saw the Trojan logo peeking out from one of the slots, I mentally thanked God. All of the gods, actually, just for good measure.

I pulled my boxers down and glanced up at Sarah's wide-eyed expression as I stretched the latex over my dick. Apparently, it met her approval. If she gave me another "good boy" right then, we'd likely find ourselves in a really unfortunate situation—but thankfully she just bit her bottom lip as I climbed onto the bed again. Not wanting to waste any time, I yanked her panties all the way down and tossed them out of the way like I was shooting a free-throw. I bent down to kiss her, feeling her legs parting for me. I grabbed her knees, pushing them further out, and used one hand to guide myself inside her.

The sensation was pure ecstasy, to feel someone I cared about this deeply from the inside. Seeing the pleasure on her face. She couldn't stop smiling. With every thrust, she moaned and sighed, getting louder as we went on. Gripping her wrists on either side of her head, I whispered, "Heath's in the next room. Try to be quiet."

"I can't, Owen." Sarah drew out every letter of my name—each vowel, every consonant—turning those four letters into a moan that lasted several seconds. She stuck her mouth against my neck in an attempt to muffle the sounds she couldn't control, and the sensation of her breath on my skin was almost too fucking good.

She wrapped her legs around my waist and dug her heels into my butt, which I took as a signal to thrust harder. Keeping inside of her, I pulled up into a kneeling position, gripping her thighs with both arms and pulling her further onto me. This was even better. "Fuck," she moaned. Behind her, the headboard was clapping wildly against the wall. At first, she reached behind her head to push it and try to fight the noise, but eventually it became too much for her. It was too late to do anything about that now, anyway.

Her legs were hoisted up over my shoulders, her feet dangling over my back. I kissed the inside of her knee as I sank into her again and again.  Her sighs and moans grew louder, but I didn't try to quiet her this time. I couldn't think of any better sound in the world. I looked down at the way her hair was spread out on the pillow around her and leaned forward to kiss her, slowing my pace. "You look so amazing like this," I told her, propping myself up on my elbows on either side of her head. I slowed my pace even more, almost pulling out of her completely.

"You *feel* so amazing like this," she whispered.

And then I slammed all the way into her again, her eyes widening with pleasure as her body scooted backward against the headboard. I followed every silent cue gave me, adjusting the pace and depth of my thrusts accordingly. She clenched her eyes shut, gripping the sheets. I took both of her white-knuckled hands in mine and interlocked our fingers.

"Oh God," she moaned, her hips bucking upward. I felt her muscles tighten around me as her legs convulsed on either side of my body. The look of pure bliss on her face as her eyes rolled backward sent me over the edge. We squeezed each other's hands tight as both of our bodies twitched in sync. I finally released, knowing that she was satisfied. Her hands trembled in mine, but not as much as her legs, still quaking as she relaxed, letting them fall to the side. I lowered my face down to hers and kissed her forehead, her cheek, and then her lips. Beads of sweat rolled down my back as I tried to catch my breath.

"Fucking hell, Owen," she said, her hands on my chest. "Why did we wait so long to do that?"

"You tell me," I said, smiling against her lips.

# chapter thirty-seven

*sarah*

When I awoke on Sunday morning, it took a few seconds to get my bearings. Silvery, early morning light spilled in through the open curtains, and the aroma of coffee filled the air. Along with the sound of the brewing coffeepot, I heard a toothbrush tapping against the edge of a sink. A faucet turning off.

That's right. *I'm in Owen's room.*

Smiling, I twisted my body around to face the other direction and found him standing just outside the bathroom wiping his face with a white hand towel. "I'm sorry, I was trying really hard not to wake you," he said, tossing the towel over his shoulder into the bathroom. "Morning."

His hair was wet, and he was already fully dressed in jeans and a black polo shirt. Owen had somehow managed to not only get himself completely ready for the day, but had also brewed a pot of coffee while I slumbered. I sat up, holding the sheet against my chest. "Morning. What time is it?"

"Early," he answered, feeling his back pockets for a phone that wasn't there. He didn't have his watch on, either—it was charging on the nightstand beside me. "I'm meeting Cates for breakfast in a bit."

"Right. I forgot about that."

He crawled into bed beside me and lifted my chin with his fingers to kiss me. "You know," he said, sliding his hand up to tuck my hair behind my ear. "I think we just might have broken the rules last night."

"I told you we were bad at this."

"I guess I don't want to be good."

I laughed and drew my knees up to my chest. "I don't know, you were pretty good last night." I loved the way those words made him smile. He relaxed into a cross-legged position beside me, grinning down at his lap. "You're adorable," I said.

"Nah."

The man didn't take compliments well, which only made me want to shower him with more of them. I decided to leave him alone for now, though, since his cheeks were already tinged pink. "Hey," I said. "Do you remember when we met?"

His brows furrowed as he struggled to remember. And then he looked up. "You mean the day you were determined to break your neck?"

I laughed. We met just a day or two before the official first day of school six years ago—I was a last-minute hire, and they'd given me an empty classroom to work with. Owen wandered into the room to introduce himself and found me standing on a desk hanging paper lanterns from the ceiling tiles. He was worried I might fall, but he was even more concerned about the possible ramifications of hanging decorations from the ceiling—which apparently violated the fire code. He was afraid the fire marshal might chew me out for it.

But when he saw how distraught I was about all my money and hard work going to waste, he encouraged me to hang them anyway—I could just play dumb until someone made me take them down. "But you didn't hear that from me," he had said, and he spent the next half hour handing me paper lanterns as I tacked them to the ceiling.

"You and those lanterns," he said, with the subtlest of eyerolls. "We were partners in crime from the very beginning."

"And look at us now." I stared down at the hand he placed on my knee, caressing it through the sheet. "It was worth the wait, wasn't it?"

"It was for me, no question." He swallowed, nodding. "But I'd be lying to you if I didn't admit I'm a little afraid you're going to regret what happened, as soon as you have time to think it over."

I shook my head, placing my hand over his. "No. I know what I want."

"Good. So, what do we do now?"

I stretched my legs out in front of me, remembering everything else that happened last night before Owen got on that elevator. Eli and I had never reached a resolution. I knew deep down my "I'm done" comment was too ambiguous, too vague. Looking down at my bare hand, I pictured the diamond ring inside the safe in my hotel room, where I'd stuck it before my walk last night. I could no longer ignore the cloud of guilt floating above my head. "I need to talk to Eli."

"Right."

"He's not going to take this very well."

Owen's eyes shot back up to mine. "What do you think he'll do?"

The thought of having to confirm Eli's suspicions about Owen made me sick to my stomach. As much as it would hurt him, I knew he'd get at least a little bit of satisfaction from being right all along. "It's not going to be pretty," I said, finally answering Owen's question. He was staring at ring finger. "We should probably prepare ourselves for some drama."

Owen had no idea how unhinged Eli could get when things didn't go his way, and I feared he was about to find out. And judging from the crinkle between his brows, he was just as worried as I was. "I'm not trying to be nosey," he said, "but I'm a little curious—where exactly are you and Eli, in terms of your relationship right now? Because last night, I got the impression that it was, you know… coming to an end."

"It is," I assured him. "We had a huge fight, and it was the final straw for me. And I made it pretty clear I'm ready to end things, I just couldn't do it over the phone. It didn't feel right."

Owen nodded like he understood, and he turned to reach for his watch from the nightstand. He slid it over his wrist and gave it a few taps, clearing some notifications. "So, how much are you going to tell him?"

"I don't know. It depends on how the conversation goes. He already suspects there's something going on between the two of us. I—" I stopped to swallow and looked around the floor for my panties. Why on earth had he thrown them so far from the bed? I stood up and walked over to them, feeling Owen's eyes on me as I bent over to pick them up. "I just kept assuring him you're just a friend," I told him as I shimmied the panties up my legs.

"Whoops," he said, smiling as he watched me make my way to the other side of the bed to pick up my shirt. "You going somewhere?"

"It might be a good idea for me to sneak back to my room before everyone else gets up," I said, slipping my tank top over my hair. And then I paused, biting my bottom lip. I knew what I needed to do. I walked over to the bed and slid next to Owen. "Actually, I think—I think I'm going to head home."

"What, now?" He cocked his head to the side. "Why?"

"Because I'm not going to be able to concentrate on a single workshop all day knowing what I have to do when I get home. I don't want to delay the inevitable. I just have to go do it."

I expected him to debate me and beg me to stay so we could spend more time together, but he nodded instead. "Okay. Do what you have to do. But listen to me." He clasped his fingers around my wrist and gazed into my eyes. "Don't let him intimidate you. I've seen him on the football field, I know how angry he gets. If he lays a finger on you—"

"Oh God, he's not going to do that," I insisted. Eli would never hit a woman. However, Owen might want to avoid walking down dark alleys for a while. And I think a part of him knew that, which is why he tensed up in the first place. With my free hand, I reached up to touch his cheek. "It's going to be okay."

His face softened, and his grip on me loosened. He flipped my hair off my shoulder and pulled me into him for an embrace. We kissed and fell back onto the mattress, with me straddling him this time.

"What time do you have to meet Cates?"

"He can wait." Owen clamped his hand around the back of my neck to pull my face down to his like he was going to kiss me, but he stopped just before he let my mouth touch his. The corners of his lips turned up a little bit. And he started to sing. "Mr. Gardner and Ms. Lavely, lying in a bed...."

I threw my head back and laughed. "K-I-S-S-I-N-G."

He squeezed my butt. "Is that all, baby?"

"God, I hope not."

# chapter thirty-eight

*owen*

I met Cates in the lobby by the elevator doors only five minutes past the time we'd arranged. He was facing the wall with his hands in his pockets, observing a black-and-white photograph of the Indianapolis skyline hanging above a console table. "Sorry I'm running behind," I said, running my fingers through my hair. "I had a hard time getting out of bed."

"Not even for crêpes?" What I had up in my room was better than any crêpe, but I didn't tell him that. We made our way over to the restaurant attached to the hotel. His legs were shorter than mine, but I had to take long strides just to keep up. He was probably worried we'd miss our reservation. Crêpe Expectations was an Indy institution, and people fought tooth and nail to get a table there, especially on a Sunday like this.

Thankfully, the host led us right past the crowd of people waiting around on benches—many of them wearing IES lanyards—and took us to a table near the kitchen. The interior of Crêpe Expectations was an Instagram influencer's dream, with exposed brick walls, uncomfortable but aesthetically-pleasing metal stools, and neutral-colored everything. As we took our seats, I remembered that I was, in fact, somewhat of an influencer, so I snapped a quick atmospheric photo to share in my stories later.

I mean, I was going to have to be even more active online now that I was going to be doing it full-time.

The server came for our drink order and left us to look over our menus, but I couldn't concentrate. The menu items all blurred together into one squiggly blob, and no amount of eye-rubbing could fix it. My mind was elsewhere. Across from me, Cates hadn't even picked up his menu because he knew exactly what he wanted. Instead, he folded his hands on the table and stared across at me. "You're a man of few words this morning," he said. "Let me guess—hangover?"

I smiled as the server delivered our drinks to the table before disappearing again. "No," I said, reaching for a sugar packet and pulling my mug closer to me. "I'm just a little tired."

"Maybe a bloody mary will wake you up, huh?"

"Actually," I said, stirring creamer into my coffee, "I don't particularly care for those. I'm just going to stick to coffee this morning."

"Coffee ought to do the trick, then." He opened his straw and stuck it in his soda. The man lived off Diet Coke the way Sarah and I were addicted to coffee. The staff room was always stocked with the stuff, and though the bottles weren't labeled, we all knew not to touch them. I had a habit of snagging one from the fridge and bringing it to his office for him during my afternoon prep.

Goddammit, I really was a brown-noser, wasn't I?

When our food arrived—a crème brûlée crêpe for him, and a caramel apple one for me—I had to force myself to take a few bites. It's not that there was a problem with the food. It was delicious. I just didn't have much of an appetite. Part of it was lovesickness, I think, because I kept imagining Sarah's body quivering beneath mine and how eager I was to get that close to her again. And it may have been nervousness about this situation with Eli. While it would be over between the two of them very soon, I had an inkling he was going to make it as hard as possible for us.

And then there was the other thing.

I sat my fork down and crossed my arms on the table, scooting my plate away with my elbows. Cates could tell something was up because he, too, stopped eating for a moment. With his fork hovering over his crêpe, he asked, "You good, Gardner?"

"I need to withdraw my name from consideration for the principal position."

He blinked. "Uh huh… and why's that?"

"Because," I said, taking a deep breath. "At the end of the year, I'm resigning from teaching."

Needless to say, the man was stunned. He leaned back in his chair and gave me this look like he was waiting for the punchline. But when I said nothing more, he raised his eyebrows and shook his head. "Okay. I've got to admit, I wasn't expecting that."

"I know. And I'm sorry to blindside you with this two days before my interview. But I've just made the decision to make my business a full-time endeavor. I'd been going back and forth on it for a while and finally got a sense of clarity about the whole thing yesterday. This feels like the right move."

"*STEM for the Win* for the win," Cates said, finally taking another bite. "Well, it makes sense. I should have seen this coming, to be honest. I could see that it just kept growing."

"Yeah, it has," I said, my knee shaking up and down. "Faster than I ever imagined."

"And you're sure about this?"

"Definitely. And there's something else I want to discuss with you." I dropped my hands to my lap. "I want to formally recommend Sarah Lavely for the position."

His eyes widened. "Lavely? Does she even want this?"

I nodded with confidence. "Yes. The only reason she hasn't applied already is because it looked like I was pretty much a shoe-in. But if you think about it, she's more qualified than any of the other applicants could possibly be, myself included. The other teachers really look up to her. And the garden—that was all her. The financing, the planning, the organization. I can't in good faith take credit for any of it. And that's just the latest thing on her list of accomplishments. I mean, I don't even have to tell you this, right? You've seen it."

He scratched his chin. "No, no, you're right. I hadn't considered her, but she does have a certain leadership quality."

"Exactly."

"She doesn't have admin training like you do, though," he said, a detail I knew he'd bring up. But I was prepared.

"And she'll breeze right through the program this summer. Also, I've written a letter of recommendation for her already."

Cates inhaled slowly, chewing his crêpe. "Well, you've certainly thought this through. And your opinion as someone who's worked closely with her will mean a lot. Go ahead and email that to me."

I nodded and looked down at my crêpe, which looked slightly more appetizing to me now. I took another bite, glad that weight was finally off my shoulders. I couldn't turn back on that decision now, which was a good thing. Decisive Owen was on a roll.

When we finished, Cates picked up the tab and I left our server an extra cash tip just because I was in an obnoxiously good mood. We had some time to kill before the keynote session in the auditorium, so we wandered around the exhibit hall where I bought an IES sweatshirt for Sarah—a green one, her favorite color. I asked the vendor to put it in a bag to avoid any awkward questions from Cates, who might notice it was a little on the smaller side.

My watch alerted me of a notification from Sarah, so I casually stepped behind a fidget toy display to read the message. She was just telling me she'd skillfully made it back to her room and all the way to the parking garage without being seen by anyone we knew, and she wanted me to tell everyone she was sick.

My lying skills were questionable, but I assured her I'd do my best.

After I hit send, I looked over to see Cates had already moved on and was deep in conversation with the vendor at the next booth. However, Heath was wandering through the crowd in my direction. I gave him a little nod when he sidled up next to me in front of the fidget toy booth. "Hey man, what's up?"

He gave me a sly smile. "Just wondering if you ordered yourself some kind of immersive pay-per-view last night, or…." I was confused until he lifted one eyebrow at me.

"Oh. Sorry about that," I said, looking over my shoulder to make sure Cates was still preoccupied. "I guess the walls are pretty thin."

"Gettin' some strange, were you?" He nudged my arm. "What'd you do, meet someone at the hotel bar last night? It was pretty lively down there."

"Well…." I rubbed the stubble on my chin, trying to come up with a story. I couldn't decide which was better—letting him believe I'd had a one-night stand or admitting I'd slept with Sarah. It was pretty safe to assume she wasn't ready for our co-workers to know about us. So I found myself in a half-lie. "Something like that, yeah."

"You dirty dog. And I didn't even go out last night because you flaked out on me. Hope it was worth it."

It was.

Just then, Vicki approached from his other side. "Hey," she said, draping a cardigan over her arms. "Have either of you seen Sarah this morning? I knocked on her door, but she wasn't there. And she's not answering my texts."

I shoved my hands in my pockets. "I talked to her. She had to duck out early because she's not feeling well."

"She's sick?" Vicki asked with a look of concern. "And she's going home?" I just nodded, hoping there weren't any more follow-up questions. I didn't have an elaborate lie planned, so I'd have to make it up as I went along. And I wasn't very good at that. Her eyes narrowed. "That's so weird. She was fine last night. Wait—when did *you* talk to her?"

"Um," I said, giving Heath an unintentional quick glance. Hopefully he wouldn't pick up on my discomfort. "This morning."

I tried to avoid Heath's gaze, but I caught his head jerking upward in my peripheral vision. I looked down at my feet, bracing myself for what I knew would happen next. "No way. No effing way." He shook his head in bewilderment. "It was her."

Vicki squinted at him. "Am I missing something?"

Heath turned to her, his eyeballs practically bulging out of their sockets. "They had sex last night."

"Who did?"

I tried to shush him, but he ignored me, jutting his pointer finger in my direction. "This guy right here and Sarah Lavely, that's who."

"Wait, WHAT?" Vicki's jaw dropped and she lunged forward to maneuver around Heath. With a hopeful grin, she grabbed me by the arm and asked, "Is that true?"

"No, it's not," I said, forcing myself to laugh like this was the most preposterous thing I'd ever heard. I shrugged her hand off my arm and sidestepped away from her. "I just saw her on the elevator this morning on her way out."

It could have just been my imagination, but Vicki actually appeared disappointed.

Beside her, Heath was chuckling in denial. "Bro. You are so full of shit right now." He turned to Vicki. "I heard them going at it around midnight. And he already admitted he slept with *someone*. I'm telling you, it was Sarah."

Vicki turned away from him to look up at me. I could tell she was trying to confirm whether Heath's accusation was true or not based on my reaction. I made every attempt to signal to her with my eyes that Sarah wouldn't want us to talk about this in front of Heath. After carefully studying my face for a moment, she turned to him and said, "No, Sarah was in my room pretty late. Couldn't have been her."

But she knew. Of course she knew. And as one of Sarah's closest friends, it sort of meant she was one of mine by extension—and she had my back. I gave her the most subtle look of gratitude before turning to Heath. "See? This is how rumors get started. You're letting your imagination run wild."

Heath grunted in frustration. "Whatever. I know what I heard." He accepted I wasn't willing to discuss it, though, and dropped the subject—getting in a quick "bow-chicka-bow-wow" as he walked away to visit some of the exhibits.

Vicki couldn't stop grinning. I shook my head at her, but I couldn't help but smile myself. "Don't worry, I'm sure she'll give you all the details."

"Oh, I'll absolutely insist on it." She crossed her arms. "So where is she, anyway? She's not actually sick, is she?"

"She's fine. She wanted to get home and take care of… a situation with Eli."

"Oh." Her smile faded, and I knew I didn't have to explain it any further. Having spent a few hours with Sarah last night, she probably knew more about this fight with Eli than I did. "I hope things don't get ugly."

My eyes widened. "You and me both." I looked at my watch. We'd need to head into the auditorium to listen to the keynote speaker in a few minutes. The crowd was starting to clear out, and it looked like Cates and Heath were already heading that direction.

"Hey," Vicki said, her fingers grasping my elbow with a sense of urgency just as I turned to follow the other guys. "This is really good."

"It is?" I couldn't help the hopeful tone of my voice, like I was searching for validation.

Her smile radiated warmth. "Of course. You two belong together—everyone sees it. I'm glad the two of you finally figured it out yourselves."

Knowing she was one of Sarah's favorite people, her words were like a comforting embrace. "I figured it out a long time ago, Vicki," I told her, trying—but failing—to suppress the way I was smiling with my entire face. In that instant, I entrusted Vicki with the weight of my feelings, fully aware she would pass my words along to Sarah at the earliest opportunity. "I've always known it. But waiting on her to come to that same realization was undeniably worth it."

# chapter thirty-nine

## sarah

The first thing I noticed when I got home was how empty the house was. I peered out the kitchen window to discover Eli's truck wasn't parked in its usual spot by the alley. However, the TV was on and there was a bottle of water on the coffee table that was still cold. He couldn't be far.

The second thing I noticed was the temperature. While I was glad to hear the air conditioner was doing its job, he had the thermostat set to a chilly 68°. I wrapped my cardigan around myself a little tighter and turned it up a couple of degrees before texting him to find out where he was.

He texted back to say he was in the drive thru line at Taco Bell, but once he learned I was home early and wanted to talk, he texted that he'd be there in five minutes. Restless anticipation filled my every step as I paced around the house, finally going outside to sit on the porch swing. We rented this house together a couple years ago, and our covered porch was my favorite thing about it. I think I spent half my time out there last summer catching up on my reading.

I swallowed, realizing things would be quite different this summer. I didn't even know where I would live. The most likely solution was to move back in with my parents. It would mean my mom would have to convert her exercise room back into a bedroom for me, but she'd probably be happy to take me in, anyway.

Moving in with Owen—that would be too soon.

Would Eli stay here? Neither of us could afford the rent on our own. Not with a teacher's salary, at least. While I waited, I looked all around me at the daffodils popping up in the landscaping, the young willow tree at the edge of our yard, and the neighbor's curious golden retriever, who was watching me through his chain link fence. The thought of leaving this house behind stirred an unexpected ache within me.

I heard the rumble of Eli's truck before I saw it, and my stomach filled with dread. He haphazardly parked by the curb instead of his usual spot. With my hands in my sweater pockets, I inhaled, knowing this wasn't going to be an easy conversation. But the sooner I said what needed to be said, the sooner I could move on.

Eli slammed his truck door and sauntered up to the house. "What's going on?" he asked. I slid over on the porch swing so he could sit beside me, but he chose to lean against one of the porch columns instead. "Aren't you going to get in trouble for leaving early?"

"No. Where's your food?"

"I got out of line to come talk to you." He shrugged like it was obvious. "So go on, tell me whatever it is. Let's hear it."

I frowned down at my lap. "It kind of seems like you already know."

"That you're breaking up with me? Yeah, Sarah, I came to that conclusion all by myself. I'm smart like that." I didn't know what to say. My silence just confirmed his allegation. "You didn't have to drive all the way back here just to say it. Could've saved both of us the trouble."

"I couldn't do that. I—" I spun my engagement ring around my finger, having slipped it back on that morning in the hotel before I left. I wanted to keep it somewhere safe, and that seemed like the most logical place. "That's not something you can just end over a phone call."

"So you're still set on breaking it off, huh? You're just going to throw in the towel after all this time together, like none of it mattered. All because of a stupid fight over the goddamn air conditioner."

"This isn't about the air conditioner. I told you that already."

He crossed his arms. "Right. It was just the straw that broke the camel's back, or whatever. Look, I'm really sorry about it, okay? I shouldn't have been such an asshole about it. But you have to at least appreciate the fact that I missed my golf scramble to deal with it yesterday. I might have put up a fight about it, but the point is, I did it—all so you wouldn't miss your conference. And you know what's really funny, Sarah? You sure didn't seem to have any issue at all skipping it today to come here and do this."

He had me there. I tucked one leg up underneath myself and pushed against the porch with my other foot to make the swing hold still. The breeze started to pick up, and I hugged myself to keep warm. "A lot's changed since then."

"Guess so." He turned around to spit off the porch. "This is really stupid, Sarah. I get that you're mad, but we don't have to throw it all away over some stupid fight. Every couple fights."

"You don't think we fight more than the average couple?"

"No. We don't. Look at my parents. They're at each other's throats all the time, and they've been married thirty years." I wanted to point out that his parents weren't the best representation of a healthy relationship, but he kept talking. "You're wanting perfection from me, and that's just not realistic. I'm going to screw up sometimes. But you have to let me fix it and try to make it right. And that's what I'm trying to do now."

"I'm sorry, Eli," I said, staring down at my diamond. I twisted the ring around and around again like it was one of the fidget toys in my classroom. "But it's too late."

He took a deep breath and fiddled with the zipper on his jacket. If I wasn't mistaken, he was close to tearing up. I'd only seen him cry twice throughout the entirety of our relationship. The first time was at his grandpa's funeral, and the second time was when his team—the high schoolers—made it to the state championships two years ago. If he cried in front of me now, I knew my own tears would be quick to follow. And I hadn't even gotten to the worst part.

"I'm not above groveling, Sarah," he said. "I can't let you go. I won't."

I touched the back of my ring with my opposite thumb.

"Please."

With a trembling hand, I began to pull the ring down to my knuckle.

"Don't do this. Please." He swallowed, and I could see the tears beginning to form. "Come on. Let's work on this. I can do better, I promise. If you take off that ring—"

It was too late. I slipped my finger out of the ring and held it with both hands, knowing the message was loud and clear. But he needed to know the other reason for this. The full truth. Fighting the sob forming at the back of my throat, I spit the words out like they were poison. "I'm in love with someone else."

He stood up a little straighter. "What?"

I licked my lips. "Owen. I love Owen. You were right about him. He's not just a friend."

"*What?*" he asked again, through gritted teeth this time. My eyes shot up to take a good look at his face for the first time in this conversation. His cheeks were flushed red with anger, and his nostrils flared. He pressed his lips together in a straight line as he stared me down, waiting for me to explain.

"I'm sorry." I tried to swallow, but my mouth was too dry. "I've been denying my feelings for him for the longest time, but he—"

"Tell me you didn't sleep with him," he said, pulling himself off the porch column to step closer to me. "Tell me right now you didn't sleep with that motherfucker."

I looked back down at my ring and began to cry.

"I swear to God, Sarah."

"I'm sorry," I choked out. "It just happened last night."

All at once, he let out this animal-like roar and kicked my planter of herbs off the porch so hard it flew into the center of our front yard. The sudden action caused the neighbor's dog to start barking.

"Hey! My rosemary…."

"I don't give a single flying *fuck* about your rosemary. You *cheated* on me? And you let me stand there and beg you not to go like I was the bad guy?"

"Listen, it didn't happen until after I talked to you last night and I knew it was over with you. I didn't—"

"It wasn't over!" He lunged forward until he was standing just before me, putting one hand on the swing's chain above my head. "I spent the entire night tossing and turning, thinking about how I could make things right between us. Meanwhile, you were up there fucking Owen fucking Gardner!"

"Stop cussing in my face. The neighbors are going to hear you."

"I could care less about them!"

"I understand that you're hurt and you're angry with me. I get it. I should've waited until this ended, officially, before moving on," I acknowledged, clutching the engagement ring in my fist. "But for far too long, you've made me feel like an inconvenience in your life—as if I owe you the utmost gratitude for giving me the minimum amount of respect. And I've reached the point where the little respect you give is no longer sufficient. I'm done fooling myself into thinking I don't deserve better."

I held out my hand to give him the ring. When he refused to take it, I placed it on the wicker table next to the porch swing. He gazed at the ring for a few seconds before tearing his eyes away to look at me. I watched him wipe his nose with the back of his hand. "Well," he started, "I hope he knows what he's in for with you." He snatched the ring off the table and yanked open the front door before disappearing into the house. The second the door closed behind him, I buried my head in my hands and cried.

That had gone just about as well as I'd predicted.

# chapter forty

## *owen*

Kendall wasted no time at all in collecting her accumulating possessions from my house.  When I got home from the conference on Sunday evening, I could immediately tell she'd let herself in over the weekend. Her basket of skincare products had been removed from the bathroom, along with her toothbrush and the silk bathrobe she'd been keeping on the back of the door. The laminator that had become a permanent fixture on the coffee table was nowhere to be seen, and she'd even taken the succulent from the windowsill in the kitchen.

I'd been home for around twenty minutes, eagerly awaiting a call from Sarah for an update on the Eli situation, when I noticed a folded piece of notebook paper with my name scrawled on the back of it attached to the fridge with a magnet. I took down the letter and leaned against the kitchen counter to read it.

*Owen,*

*I want you to know how much I still care about you. I'm not going to pretend like you didn't break my heart. I had all these fantasies of building a life with you, but now I know that was never in the cards for us. And as hard as that is to accept, I really just want you to be happy. With Sarah, I hope.*

*The more time I spend thinking about it, the more I think you should just tell her how you feel. This would be a hell of a lot easier for me if I didn't 100% believe she's perfect for you. I might be wrong about this, but*

*I get the impression she's in love with you, too. Please do something about it, now that I'm no longer in your way. Make it worth it.*

*I also wanted to let you know that I plan to remain on the garden committee. That might make things awkward for you, but I'm not going to run away with my tail tucked between my legs like some wounded animal. That's just not me. And while I might need some time to get over you, I would eventually like to be friends with you again, too. Especially if you're going to be my boss next year.*

*You have a good heart; it was just never mine.*

*With love,*

*Kendall*


Well. At least she didn't have to worry about me becoming her boss next year.

I laid the note down on the counter and read it a second time, smiling at the audacity of Kendall's refusal to leave the garden committee. She was bold, I had to give her that. And as much as I knew she was hurting now, it gave me a little bit of solace to know it probably wouldn't be long before she was okay again.

I checked my phone for a message from Sarah. Nothing yet. She was currently cramming some of her belongings into boxes and suitcases and moving them to her parents' house on the other side of town. She'd spent the afternoon trying to get out of her lease early to no avail.

Every part of me wanted to ask her to move in with me right away, but I forced myself to hold off on that conversation. Now that I had her, I didn't want to scare her off by coming on too strong. So I just asked her to stay the night, instead of, you know, forever.

Knowing she'd be seeing my place for the first time in a matter of hours, I spent the evening cleaning up around the house. Fresh sheets, crumb-free counters, a clean bathroom—I even lit the vanilla candle Kendall had left behind. Whatever I could think of to make a good first impression.

It was almost 7:00 when I heard a car pull up at the front of the house—which was strange, since she'd told me she'd call before she left her parents'. I peeked through my open living room window and saw a tan F-150 by the curb. I assumed it was just someone here to visit one of the neighbors—street parking was pretty limited on my block, so it made sense that they'd be parked directly in front of my house. I plopped onto the couch to reply to a couple of emails without giving the truck a second thought.

But a moment later, someone was pounding at my front door. I didn't even have to look to know exactly who it was. Suddenly, I remembered who I'd seen driving that truck before.

Damn it. I really didn't want to deal with this right now.

Couldn't he have just written her a thoughtful letter, like Kendall?

I hesitated on the couch for a moment, wondering if it would be too cowardly of me to pretend I wasn't home. It's not that I was afraid of what Eli would try to do to me—I could handle myself okay in a fight. It just sounded exhausting, and I wasn't particularly interested in hearing whatever it was he had to say.

He pounded at the door again. "Gardner! I know you're home. Let's talk."

Right. Talk.

I swallowed as I got up from the couch and walked over to the door. I yanked it open to find Eli standing a couple feet away from the door with his hands already balled into fists. I stepped down onto my front stoop and let the screen door close behind me. Crossing my arms against my chest and standing with my feet far apart, I said, "All right. Let's talk."

"You fuck my fiancée?"

Okay, so we were going to get right into it. I took a deep breath, trying to make eye contact with him, but his eyes were darting all around like he was nervous. I knew exactly what he was doing—he was assessing my stature. Trying to figure me out. "Listen, I didn't make a move on Sarah until she assured me it was over between the two of you."

"'Over'? Is that the lie she told you?"

"I think Sarah did the respectable thing by driving all the way home to talk to you first thing this morning about it, all right? It was never her intention—or mine—to hurt you."

"Oh, it wasn't, huh?" He took a step closer to me, puffing his chest out. I stood up a little taller, bracing myself for what might happen. The guy was a few inches shorter than me, but what he lacked in height he made up for in utter cockiness. "If it wouldn't risk me losing my job, I'd knock the ever-loving shit out of you right now."

My frozen stance was further exaggerated by the way Eli couldn't keep still. He continued to pace back and forth, shifting his weight from one foot to the other. I kept my gaze locked on his eyes, since they gave the most away. I hadn't had to fight anyone in at least a decade. Jake and I used to throw punches a lot back in the day. And I knew how Jake fought. I could often calculate his next move and be ready with a counterattack.

But Eli was a completely different animal. He was unpredictable. Unstable. Raging.

"I always knew there was something sketchy about you," he said. "You acted like her friend all this time when you were just trying to get into her pants."

"That's not—"

"And now your little scheme came to fruition, didn't it?"

"There was never any 'scheme.' It just happened."

"And it couldn't happen with any of the other hundreds of single girls in Woodvale, huh?" Eli stopped pacing and got in my face again, closer this time. I kept my arms folded across my chest, refusing to let this man intimidate me. "You just had to pick one that was engaged to someone else."

I remained still. I could tell from the way his nostrils flared my refusal to acknowledge his question only angered him more. He lifted his hands to give my shoulders a hard shove, knocking me off balance—but just for a second. I glanced down at his clutched fists. "Come on, man," I said. "I don't want to fight you."

"Yeah, well, actions have consequences, don't they?" He tried to shove me again, but this time I deflected his assault with ease, smacking his hands away.

"I'm not going to fight you, goddamn it," I reiterated. We were standing chest-to-chest now. "We're both adults here, right? If you want to talk—fine. But if you're just here looking for a fight, you need to go. Accept that she doesn't want to be with you anymore and move on. Try to be an adult about it."

The fiery rage in Eli's eyes indicated he was incapable of being an adult about this. He drew back his right arm, but I was ready. I caught him by the forearm, making him swing into dead air. With both hands, I gave him a hard shove away from me. He tumbled backwards off the stoop, but he caught himself before he fell all the way down. After regaining his composure, he lunged at me again, and I ducked out of the way in just enough time for his fist to barely graze my ear.

This was ridiculous. Utterly senseless. After a couple more defensive blocks, I'd had enough. I pulled far enough away from him to rear my arm back and punched him square in the jaw.

The impact caused him to stumble backward a couple of feet. He put his hand up to his mouth before pulling it away to look at his bloody fingers. "You son of a bitch," he muttered.

Suddenly, we were locked in a tackle fight, shoulder-to-shoulder, struggling to knock each other to the ground. Eli was able to break his arm free from my grasp and get in one solid punch just below my left eye. My cheekbone stung, but I couldn't afford a moment's pause to think about it. He readied himself for another strike, but before he could follow through, I threw my body against his, slamming him down onto the ground in front of the stoop. The impact knocked the wind out of his chest, leaving him gasping for air. With all my strength, I pinned his arms to his sides, my teeth clenched. "I said I didn't want to fight you. She wouldn't want us acting like this. You know that."

Just then, I heard a screen door slam followed by the sound of my neighbor, Shirley, screeching at us from her yard. "Hey, hey, hey!" She wasn't just a neighbor—she was my landlady, too, and this entire brawl was taking place on her property. "What in God's name is going on?"

"It's okay, Shirley," I said, pulling up to my feet. I held one hand up to her in an attempt to keep her away. But she was a stubborn woman. Despite the fact she was wearing nothing but a terrycloth bathrobe, she stomped all the way over to us, clutching a cigarette between her fingers.

"Do I need to call the police?"

"No," Eli and I answered at the same time. He sat up in the grass, and I took a couple of steps toward Shirley, trying to catch my breath. "He's leaving now."

"Well, he'd better be," Shirley said, tightening the strings of her bathrobe around her waist. She motioned toward Eli with her cigarette-wielding hand. "I'm not going inside until he's gone."

Eli rose to his feet and wiped his bloody lip, pointing at me with his other hand. "Big mistake, Gardner. Big fucking mistake. Bet Cates doesn't know his prized principal candidate is fucking one of the teachers. Maybe Delgado should hear about it, too."

He turned to walk back to his truck. "Hey, wait!" I called out. "You don't know the whole situation."

"I know enough." He walked around to the driver's side of his truck, muttering "big mistake" one more time before he climbed inside and peeled away.

I turned to Shirley, delicately touching my aching cheekbone. "I'm really sorry you had to witness all of that, Shirley," I said.

She took a drag from her cigarette, a chuckle escaping her lips. "Well, it was better than what I was watching on TV, I'll tell you that. You need to ice that, or you're going to swell up like a balloon."

"I will."

She exhaled a cloud of smoke. "Must be some girl."

I just sighed with a nod, watching Eli's truck disappear around the corner. "Yeah. She is."

# chapter forty-one

*sarah*

Seeing where Owen lived felt illegal. To know this part of him, to get a glimpse of how he spent his time when he wasn't at school with me, was a kind of thrill that was entirely new to me. I dropped my overnight bag on his coffee table and let him take me by the hand for a tour of his cute little house.

"Are you a hot tea drinker?" he asked me as he led me into the kitchen, motioning toward an electric tea kettle. I think this may have been the most shocking detail in his house. I knew it would be tidy, because Owen didn't strike me as a slob. So that wasn't a surprise. Neither was the enormous collection of science fiction novels in his living room.

But the tea kettle? That threw me for a loop.

"No, I'm not, and to be honest, I'm wondering where your coffeemaker is."

He nodded toward the coffeemaker on the other side of his kitchen. "Coffee's a necessity in the mornings, obviously. But at the end of the day, a cup of tea just feels like a warm hug."

I giggled. "I think I need that right now, then." As relieved as I was to be there with him then, I hadn't had the best day. After spending the afternoon trying to negotiate with the landlord to break our lease early, and then fielding questions from my devastated mother, I probably could have gone for a shot of tequila. But Owen seemed really eager to prepare a cup of tea for me, so I accepted the little brown mug he handed me with a smile.

And he was right. It did feel like a warm hug.

My eyes fixated on the purple bruise under his left eye. "Stop looking at it," he said, shaking his head with a grin. He leaned in the doorway between his kitchen and living room. "I'm fine."

"I'm just so sorry. I feel responsible." I stepped forward to carefully trace his bruise with my thumb. It was about two inches wide, and even the corner of his eye by his nose was purpling. "You're going to be getting a lot of questions about this tomorrow."

He wrapped his arms around my waist. "I'm sure Ava Greentree will come up with a very fascinating rumor."

"Maybe she'll write about it?" I smiled, taking a sip from the mug I held with both hands. "I'm more worried about Lori."

"Hey," he said, drawing me closer. "Do you want to come to my room and…." His voice trailed off, and the mischievous glint in his eyes indicated a punchline would soon follow, rather than some suggestive innuendo. Owen reached up to tuck my hair behind my ear, sliding his hand down my jawline to my chin. With his thumb grazing my bottom lip, he continued, saying, "…read that letter of recommendation I wrote?"

A sexy gesture *and* a chance to critique his writing? Goosebumps. Everywhere. "I thought you'd never ask."

He led me through a doorway into his bedroom, where half the room was dedicated to his office space. He had a large L-shaped desk in the corner where his laptop sat. And there was the microphone I'd given him for his birthday, along with some oversized headphones and a ring-light for the videos he'd been making lately.

He sat down in his desk chair and opened his laptop, motioning for me to sit on his lap. I lowered myself onto him, careful not to spill a drop of tea. "So this is where the magic happens for *STEM for the Win*, huh?"

"Yup," he answered, opening a document called *Letter of Recommendation for Sarah Lavely*. So formal. "Unless my neighbor's dog won't shut up, and then I have to record it in my closet."

"You're putting a funny mental picture in my head," I said, taking another sip of my tea. Once the letter loaded on the screen, I sat up a little straighter on his lap and he slid the chair forward so I could get a better look at the screen.

I don't know what I'd expected. I knew before I started reading that I was about to read a list of my qualifications and accomplishments, but knowing Owen was the person behind these words had me emotional from the second sentence.

*"Ms. Lavely makes a lasting impact on every student, parent, and colleague lucky enough to encounter her."*

Without warning, the tears started flowing, making it difficult to read the rest of the letter. The words began to blur together, but I made out phrases like *"fostering positive relationships"* and *"putting students' needs first."*

"Are you crying right now?" Owen asked, pulling my hair away from my eyes with both hands so he could see me better. His face softened into a grin. "Too many typos?"

I giggled. "No, none. It just feels like I'm reading about someone else. You can't have written all of those words about *me.*"

"Oh, did I write 'Sarah Lavely'? Shoot, that was supposed to say... 'Heath Lawson.'"

"Shut up."

He squeezed one of my thighs. "Everything I wrote is true. And it's not just my opinion, it's fact. You're going to make a great principal."

"You say that like it's guaranteed I'm going to get the position," I said, turning to put one arm around the back of his neck. My other hand still clutched the mug. "I'm not you. Cates doesn't worship the ground I walk on."

He squinted at me, and we both started to smile. The bruise beneath his eye looked like it had gotten even darker since I'd arrived. "You're looking at it again."

"I can't help it," I said, as he brought his forehead down to meet mine. I liked this so much—sitting on his lap with his arms around me tight. I closed my eyes, feeling his lips brush against mine. I kissed him back, running my fingers through his hair. "Owen Gardner, hot tea drinker," I murmured against his lips. "What other secrets have you been keeping from me?"

He tugged away and pulled his head back far enough to allow himself to peer into my eyes, and he furrowed his brows like something was bothering him.

"What?"

He swallowed. "I just never want to let you go."

"So don't." I kissed him again, hoping that would do something about the crinkle between his eyebrows, but it remained. I'd never seen him look this serious.

"Sarah, I'm in love with you," he blurted, keeping his eyes locked on mine. "And I'm sorry if that's too much for you to hear right now. I had every intention of taking things slow with you, because I'm so afraid of scaring you away now that I have you. And it's okay if you're not ready to say it back. I just wanted to be honest with you, for once. I've loved you for a long time."

"I'm not going anywhere," I said, putting my hand on his cheek and running my thumb along the bottom of his bruise again. "And I love you, too. I'm just sorry it took me so long to realize it." I pulled his face down to mine and kissed him again. My heart felt like it was ready to dance right out of my chest. Owen's fingers overlapped mine on the mug and he took it from me, placing it on the desk—far away from all of his equipment.

He brought one hand up to the back of my neck and kissed me some more. His other hand found its way between my thighs, swiping along the seam of my jeans.

"Need these off," he whispered. He didn't have to tell me twice. I stood up to unbutton my jeans, but Owen was impatient. He pulled them down before my fingers could even find the zipper. They weren't even past my knees when he reached for the elastic of my underwear to pull them down, too. I gasped when he stood up to lift me up onto his desk.

"Owen!"

He pushed all of his podcast equipment out of the way with very little regard before yanking my pants and underwear all the way off my feet. Then, he lowered himself back onto the computer chair and forced my knees apart with both hands. My mind turned to complete mush, and the only thing I could think about was the fact that this desk was the perfect height for what I knew he was about to do. Like it was made for this.

He pulled my feet up over his shoulders and scooted closer, kissing along the inside of one of my knees. His mouth made its way up to my thigh, where he drew a line on it with his tongue, pulling away just before he reached the very top. Teasing me. He turned his head to do the same to my other thigh, even nibbling it with his teeth. I rolled my hips forward, practically begging his tongue to find its way to the spot where I desperately needed to feel it. And finally, with just the slightest brush of his lips against my most tender area, it felt like every nerve ending was already exploding. "Now," I demanded, hardly aware I was speaking.

And Owen listened, plunging his tongue exactly where I wanted it. I arched my back, pushing my head against the wall and parting my legs even farther for him. His tongue thrashed against me, tracing circles. And just when I thought the sensation couldn't possibly get any better, I felt one of his fingers slide inside me. Then two. He slowly thrust them in and out, working me with his tongue the entire time. He knew exactly what to do. I grabbed his head with both hands, giving his hair just the slightest tug. "Why are you so good at this?"

He let out a guttural noise that was a mixture between a chuckle and a moan, and the vibration from his lips drove me wild. I hoped his walls weren't very thin, because his neighbors were about to get an earful. I couldn't control the sounds coming from me when Owen was sending me to another planet with his tongue. The man was a cunnilingus professional.

I gripped the edges of the desk. "I'm close. Don't stop what you're doing, I love it."

He was such a good listener. He continued lapping me up like I was quenching a deep thirst inside of him, holding the pace he knew was working. An electric, pulsating feeling erupted between my legs and I threw my head back, tightening my core as wave after wave of pleasure washed over my body. I used my feet to pull Owen closer to me, and somehow, the man managed not to suffocate down there. When the desk finished quaking and squeaking beneath me, I let my feet drop to his sides, and he pulled his face away. He gave my thighs one final squeeze before I pushed my knees together.

"I think," he said, wiping his mouth, "I need to tighten the screws in this desk."

"Probably a good idea." I was still fighting to catch my breath.

He leaned back in his computer chair with his hands folded behind his head, looking rather satisfied with himself. As he should. I sat up, putting my feet between his legs on the leather chair. He opened his mouth to say something just as our phones simultaneously chimed.

Owen wheeled his computer chair over to the bed, where his phone was lying face up. And then he gave me a panicked look. "It's Cates."

"What's it say?"

I waited for him to read the email. "He says he wants to talk to us first thing in the morning. Together." He tore his eyes from the screen, looking up at me. "Regarding an email he received from Eli Meeks."

# chapter forty-two

*owen*

"Hold still."

There was only one person in the known universe who could talk me into wearing make-up, and her name was Sarah Lavely. I sat on the toilet lid as she towered over me with a pink make-up sponge, doing her very best to conceal the bruise, which was now an even deeper shade of purple. As gentle as she was, it still stung every time she tapped my cheekbone with the sponge. I sucked air in through my teeth. "Is it at least helping?"

She winced. "Uh… do you want me to lie to you?"

I stood up to look in the mirror. It looked like exactly what it was—a bruise covered with make-up. "Well. It's going to be an interesting day."

"I'm so nervous about this thing with Cates," she said, throwing her make-up back into a little pouch. "I don't like the idea of anyone thinking I've been dishonest."

"Don't fret about it," I said, rubbing the back of her arm. She turned to straighten my tie, looking up at me with a forced smile. I leaned down to kiss her on the forehead before following her out of the bathroom. "At least we'll be together. And hey—do you want to just ride to work together?"

"Should we?" She picked up her purse from the kitchen counter and handed me my messenger bag, which had been hanging on a kitchen chair since Friday afternoon. I grabbed both of our coffees from the counter, and handed hers to her as she asked, "I mean, will that look bad?"

We made our way to my front door. "Would it have looked bad before? We're still just friends, for all they know. Oh, that reminds me." My eyes widened as I held the door open for her. "Vicki and Heath sort of… figured it out. Turns out I'm not a very good liar."

A smile spread across Sarah's lips as she stepped down onto the front stoop. "That explains the random eggplant emoji Vicki sent me!" I raised one eyebrow at her, hoping for some kind of explanation, but she just laughed it off. "Dang it. I wanted to see the look on her face when she found out."

"Well, if it's any consolation, she seemed very pleased with it. We have her blessing."  I held out my hand to take hers, and she slipped her fingers in between mine. I could get used to this. All of it. Waking up with her, getting ready with her. And holding her hand. "Are you ready?"

"As I'll ever be."

* *

Lori was the first person to see me besides Sarah that morning, and she didn't hold back on her reaction to my black eye one bit. "Good Lord, what happened to you?" she asked when Sarah and I stepped into the main office at 7:29. She pulled her glasses off the top of her head and put them on to get a better look at me.  "That looks awful. What on earth did you get yourself into?"

If I shared the truth with Lori, the entire district would know by lunch. So I quickly came up with an elaborate story to tell. Putting on a fake look of concern, I leaned onto her desk and said, "You know those crane robots I have?"

She nodded, fiddling with her necklace as she listened.

321

"It's the weirdest thing. I was working on one of them this weekend, and out of nowhere, it swung around and whacked me right in the face."

"One of your robots did that?"

I nodded. "Mmm-hmm. It's… it's almost like it had a mind of its own."

Lori's worried expression turned into one of annoyance as she peered over her glasses at me. "Oh, your robots are becoming sentient, are they?"

"Owen." Sarah tugged on my elbow. I brought a shaking hand to my face, feigning a horrified expression—like the memory of the crane attack haunted me. Lori decided she was done with me and rolled her eyes before answering the ringing phone. "Come on," Sarah said. "We're going to be late."

I laughed as I trailed behind her toward Cates' office. "Come on. I only have two months left to work with her. I've got to make the best of it."

"You're an idiot," she said just outside of Cates' door.

"But now I'm *your* idiot."

She knocked. "Don't make me change my mind," she said, but I could see the way she was trying to fight a smile as Cates called us in. Good. Maybe my shenanigans helped ease her nerves a little bit.

We took a seat in the leather chairs facing Cates' desk. He told us good morning and jumped right into it, sliding each of us a sheet of paper across his desk. "Thought you'd be interested in reading this," he said. I eyed Sarah as we both reached for one of the printed emails. And I began to read it.

Mr. Cates sighed when he could tell we both finished reading. "Boy, do I feel like a fool," he said, looking from me to Sarah and back to me again. "Is this true?"

"It is, sir," Sarah answered.

Cates was still staring at me. "And does this email have anything to do with that shiner on your face?"

I cleared my throat. "You should see the other guy." The scowl on his face remained. Apparently, this wasn't the time for jokes. I sat up a little straighter. I didn't look at Sarah, but I could see her shaking her head in my peripheral vision. As for Cates, he was completely stone-faced. I felt I'd lost the man's trust. "Sorry. Yes, courtesy of Eli Meeks."

Cates nodded. "I've got to say, I feel as though I've been played. I wasn't aware of your involvement with Ms. Lavely here when we sat down for breakfast the other morning. In fact,

323

when I brought up rumors about the two of you in the past, you assured me there was nothing going on."

"I never lied to you, sir. This is all very fresh. Despite Eli's allegations, this relationship isn't even forty-eight hours old." I motioned toward Sarah, who nodded in agreement. "It was never my intention to hide anything from you."

Cates glanced at her for a second. But he kept his gaze mostly on me. I don't know why Sarah had been so nervous going into this—clearly, I was the one on trial here. "What's really interesting is that it's also been brought to my attention that you've recently been involved with another member of this faculty."

Oh.

Someone must have seen me with Kendall on Friday in the parking lot. I was so dead set on trying to make Sarah jealous, I hadn't stopped to think about anyone else being around to spot me kissing Kendall.

I folded my hands against my stomach and wracked my brain for a way to defend myself, knowing this wasn't looking very good for me. But before I could speak, Sarah exhaled loudly as she put Eli's email back on the desk. "Excuse me for being so forthright, but how is any of this relevant?" Cates and I turned to her in unison, wondering where this was going. She fumbled through her purse for a moment and pulled out a thick, folded packet. "I've got the district policy handbook right here, and unless I'm missing something, there's nothing in here restricting two teachers from dating one another."

She flipped through a few pages of the handbook on her lap.

"There was previously a requirement for both parties to sign a consensual relationship agreement, which I have experience with myself, but that section was removed when the handbook was amended two years ago. So am I correct in asserting neither my relationship with Owen or his former fling with Ms. Devin broke any rules? Especially considering Owen's plan to resign?"

I let out a low whistle and looked down at my lap. I'd never heard anyone challenge Cates like this. Not that he'd ever given us much reason to. But the fact that she said all of that with so much confidence both scared and excited me.

Cates began to chuckle, taking me by surprise. "Okay, touché. You came prepared. Very good, Ms. Lavely. But I think you know that this affair—for lack of a better word, I'm sorry—isn't going to bode well for you as a candidate for the principal position. And I'm sorry, Owen, but your letter of recommendation will no longer carry as much weight once this gets out. And it will."

"I figured," I said, crossing one leg over my knee. "But ask any teacher here—and they'll all tell you the same things. Sarah could get a letter of recommendation from any staff member at Grissom."

Cates folded his hands on his desk in front of him. "Excluding Ms. Devin."

"Er, yeah, probably not her...." I shifted in my chair.

To my surprise, Cates bellowed with laughter. Sarah and I exchanged confused glances as Cates continued to chuckle at a joke neither of us were privy to. He sighed and pushed his glasses up with his pointer finger. "Listen, I didn't bring either of you here to shame you. I mean, look, it was bound to happen sooner or later."

Jeez, had it been that obvious?

"And I like both of ya," Cates continued. "Even if I was left in the dark about some things. I get it." He faced Sarah. "All I'm saying is, if I'm going to back you as my replacement—which I think is a fine idea—I need to be sure this whole thing doesn't blow up. Any more than it already has, that is."

Sarah picked at her fingernails. "Well, Eli is a little unpredictable. But I don't think he'll do anything that will risk his job."

Cates' eyes flitted up to my bruised face. "Uh huh," he said, turning to look at the clock on the wall. It was almost time for students to arrive. "Well, I'm going to let the two of you go out there and start your day. Just try not to rock the boat. Or at least wait until I'm officially retired, please."

And with that, we were finished. "That wasn't so bad," I told Sarah as we walked past Lori's desk in the main office.

"Right? That went way better than I expected."

"Told you not to fret about it," I said. And without thinking, I took her by the hand right in front of Lori and all the teachers waiting in line to use the good copier. She didn't pull her hand away or act like this was crossing the line, even when Lori uttered something that sounded like "oh good heavens" behind us.

The second we stepped foot in the hallway, we came face-to-face with Kendall.

Sarah dropped my hand, but it was too late. Kendall had already seen. "Ouch," she said, staring at my bruise, and I couldn't help but feel like it had a double meaning.

I shoved my hands in my pockets. "Yeah, there was a *Fight Club* workshop at the convention."

"Owen," Sarah grunted.

But Kendall was holding back a smile. "Pretty sure you're not supposed to talk about that."

"Right. I knew I was forgetting something."

Kendall turned to Sarah. "Um—I emailed you this morning about an idea for the garden. Some sensory stuff I think we can add along the walkway."

"Oh, good," Sarah said, tucking her hair behind her ear with one hand. "I haven't seen it yet, but I'll look during my prep."

Kendall's eyes darted back and forth from Sarah to me. "Okay, well… I need to get in there."

"Oh, sorry," I said, stepping out of the way. I held the office door open for her, giving her a polite nod as she slid past. "Have a… have a good day."

"Yep. You too."

As I let the door close behind her, Sarah and I exchanged a wide-eyed glance before we continued down the hallway toward our classrooms. As painfully awkward as that entire encounter was, I was glad to have gotten that part over with. She'd seen that I'd moved on with Sarah, yet she was still cordial. More than cordial. She was making plans with Sarah.

Eli Meeks, take notes.

# chapter forty-three

## sarah

After that meeting with Cates, I had to rush to get my classroom ready for the day. I had an interactive grammar notebook activity I wanted the kids to do as soon as they arrived, but none of my materials were set out. I hurried up and down the rows of desks—first with the printables they'd be cutting out, and then with a pair of scissors for each student.

I'd learned the hard way not to allow my fifth graders to keep scissors in their own desks. They weren't any better than preschoolers sometimes, shoving their scissors in gluesticks or cutting holes in their pants. So alas, the scissors stayed in a canister on my desk until we were ready to use them.

When I got to Bentley's desk, I saw the edge of his sketchbook hanging out of the opening at the front. Normally, I'd leave my students' private things alone, but I saw my name on his latest drawing.

Glancing up at the clock, I pulled out the sketchbook to look at the comic. It was titled 'Ms. Lavely Goes to a WWE Match.' In the comic, I was standing next to a wrestling ring with my hands on my hips, and my eyebrows were slanted inward. The caption read: *"Am I going to have to separate you two?"*

I laughed, sliding the sketchbook back into Bentley's desk. He must have started that one before he learned he could no longer participate in the newspaper club. Or maybe he just drew it for fun, knowing it couldn't be published.

As I finished passing out materials, I thought this over for a little bit. If the drawing was already done, there was no reason I couldn't scan it and include it in the next issue. Right? It wasn't like I'd be completely removing the consequence just by allowing him to participate in one more issue.

I was running so behind that morning, students started arriving before I even made it out to the hallway. After telling the first couple of students good morning, I threw my lanyard over my neck, grabbed my coffee from my desk, and headed out the door.

"…never insult a leprechaun, that's all I'm saying." Across the hall, Owen had his hand up to his bruise, and Ava Greentree was staring at him with her hands on her hips.

"Tell me what really happened," she demanded. "Did you get into a fight?"

"Yes," Owen said, with fake frustration in his voice. "With a leprechaun. I told you."

Ava let out an exasperated sigh and stomped off into the classroom. Owen turned to me and winked before fielding questions from the next kid. Damn it, he made a black eye look so sexy. I half-listened to him make up a story about an altercation with a disgruntled ostrich in the parking lot as I saw Bentley and Jordyn come around the corner together, laughing about something he was showing them in a notebook.

"Good morning," I told them. "Bentley, can I talk to you for just a second?"

His face fell, and Jordyn waved good-bye as they moved past me. "Am I in trouble?"

"No," I said with a laugh. "Actually, I'm the one who did something bad. I kind of snooped in your desk this morning. And I saw your comic about me."

He looked horrified. "Oh. You did?"

"Yes. And I *love* it." His face softened, and he relaxed his shoulders with a sigh of relief. "And while I can't let you back in the newspaper club," I continued, "I wanted to ask you what you thought about publishing that one anyway, since you probably finished it before the recess incident?"

I knew that last part was probably stretching the truth, and so did Bentley. But he nodded anyway. "Yeah, if it's okay…"

"Of course," I said, patting his arm. "And listen, I know you can't make comics for the newspaper anymore, but I encourage you to keep drawing anyway, okay? Even if it's just for your own enjoyment. Never—"

"I already started a web comic," he interrupted.

"You did?"

Bentley nodded. "Yup. Jordyn and I worked on it all weekend. It isn't live yet, but we're going to launch it on Friday. And it's not really for teachers to look at, but… I'll write down the link if you want it."

"Absolutely!" The kid had no idea how much this warmed my heart. And the fact he was embarking on this venture with a friend just sweetened the news even more. "Bentley, I am so, so, so proud of you. And Jordyn, too. The two of you are going to do an amazing job, I just know it."

"Thanks," he said over his shoulder before hurrying into the classroom. I stood there for a moment with my mouth open as it sunk in that my efforts with Bentley had finally amounted to something. The kid was going to be okay.

I caught the end of Owen's latest story. "…a rather unfortunate skateboarding incident," he explained to Holden Greer, who gave him a doubtful look. "My blood is still on the pavement at the Woodvale Skate Park."

"Mr. Gardner, we don't have a skate park."

Owen pretended to be confused. "Then whose empty swimming pool was that?"

I shook my head, sipping my coffee. As Holden laughed and entered the classroom behind him, Owen looked across the hallway at me with a smile so big I thought his poor bruised face might crack open. I grinned back at him over the heads of the students filling the hallway.

"Morning, Ms. Lavely," he finally said, bringing his mug to his lips. "Did you have a good weekend?"

"I did, Mr. Gardner. Did you?"

He tilted his head to the side as he considered his next words, smiling with his eyes. "It had its ups and downs," he said, sliding his fingers down his tie with his free hand. And then his eyes wandered toward something just beyond my left shoulder. "I definitely fared better than Peter Cottontail over here."

I followed his gaze to the Easter bulletin board I'd assembled the week before. The poor rabbit's cotton-ball tail was completely missing, leaving nothing behind but a spot of hardened glue on the aqua paper. Just like with Hilda the witch last fall, Peter had become a target of wandering hands in the hallway. "Oh, poor Peter," I whimpered, shaking my head at the tulips I now noticed were missing, too.

As I returned my gaze to Owen, his intense stare sent my heart into a frenzy, threatening to burst right out of my chest. Because now, he was mine. Our relationship wouldn't exist just within the confines of the school building, Monday through Friday. I'd have him on the weekends, now, and in the summer, too. Mine, mine, mine.

And I could tell from the gleam in his eyes, visible over the tops of our students' heads, he was thinking the very same thing.

# Acknowledgements

First and foremost, thank you to everyone who has taken the time to read this book. I hope you enjoyed reading it as much as I loved writing it.

Most of all, I want to thank my partner, Clint, who motivated me every step of the way and gave *STEM for the Win* its name. Thanks for helping me get inside Owen's head, and for being forced to answer questions like "what's a boner feel like?" on the regular.

I also want to thank my mom, whose reaction to that desk scene I'll never forget. Mom, you are my rock—and I never would have completed this without your unyielding support.

Thank you Mackenzie, Gina, Macy, Lesley, Lori Beth, Haley, Kathi, Carleen, Amy, and Amanda, who read this when it was still in its early, messy stages and loved it anyway.

Thank you to my sister, Mary, who's probably my biggest cheerleader—just behind Mom, that is.

Thank you Hannah Bauman, for helping me make Eli a little bit more human.

I want to thank my illustrator, Eden Lee, who took my "inspired by Jim Halpert" note and ran with it.

Big shout-out to my Instagram street team, who saw potential in this book when it was just a list of tropes and some random quotes—thank you for helping me get *Lesson Learned* in the hands of more people.

Lastly, I want to thank my Dad, who always believed I could do this. I know you would be so proud of me now.

9 798218 230937